Verse to Acclimate

ZEA KAYLEIGH GALAN

To you,
You have not lost it,
It hasn't found you yet.

Playlist

BRELAND, Brittney Spencer – Guilty Pleasure (feat. Brittney Spencer)
Lucky Daye – Over
David J, Frawley – After We Broke Up
Don Louis – Bad Decisions
Ella Mai – DFMU
Robyn Ottolini – Match For My Memory
Tucker Wetmore – Wine Into Whiskey
Rihanna, Mikky Ekko – Stay
Rvshvd – Reverse
Sacha – Confident – Country Version
Payton Smith – Missed the Boat
Sophia Scott – Lipstick on You
Ella Langley – Country Boy's Dream Girl
Giveon – Like I Want You
Tiera Kennedy – I Ain't A Cowgirl
Lennon Stella – Bad
O.N.E The Duo – Stuck In The Middle
Willie Jones, Ben Burgess – Dive Bar
Don Louis – The Ride
Tiera Kennedy, BRELAND – Miles
Faren Rachels – The Rug
Tony Evans Jr. – Yours
Tiera Kennedy – Found It In You
Ari Lennox – Bound
Kane Brown – I Can Feel It
Jimmie Allen – Better Now
Willie Jones – Something To Dance To
Dylan Scott – What He'll Never Have

Content Warnings

Hi Friend!

This is a romantic suspense novel that is suitable for mature audiences only as it includes alcohol and drug use, profanity, sexually explicit scenes, and violence. There are heavier themes in this book that may be sensitive to some readers. For a full list of potentially sensitive content, flip to the end of the book.

Please note that some content warnings may spoil the story and some plot lines.

Happy reading,
Zea Kayleigh

AN ALPENGLOW RIDGE NOVEL

Verse to Acclimate

CHAPTER 1

Tyson Abrams

"PLEASE! HELP ME OUTSIDE Miss! I need to get some air!" He clutches at his chest and I roll my eyes in irritation. Slowing my advance on the woman, an arm's length away from the show he's putting on, just to see what he'll do next.

Is this guy serious?

"Excuse me?" Melody's smile is small and uncomfortable when she looks up from her drink to the mid-height, mid-build guy leaning over the bar top near her.

"You just took my breath away. I thought maybe you could help me get it back." Ceasing his antics, he smiles bigger at her before drinking from his lite beer.

The cringe from this guy has me doing something to interfere on her behalf. "That's the best you've got?" I question, coming up to stand behind Melody.

The douche looks up at me and I ready myself for the confrontation coming my way. Luckily, my near foot of extra height on him makes him think twice about acting on the annoyance written all over his face.

Melody leans around this sorry sack to see me and her surprise is clear with the little squeak that slips from her lips. "Tyson, what are you doing?"

This is my bar tonight. It's my band's name on the moniker out front. The only reason she's here is *because* of me. Ignoring her question for now, I tap the guy to refocus his attention on me. "It's best you get your cheesy pickup line and go, brother," I say with as cool a tone as I can manage at this moment.

He looks me up and down before sliding his beer toward himself, mumbling, "Whatever," before it's only me and her at the bar.

Finally.

I've been bothering my sister, Chloe, for months about getting Melody at one of my shows. When I found out about her divorce, it took everything in me to not go wait at her doorstep like the lost puppy dog I am. I don't think that would have helped me much. Clo says that she is still testy when she tries to talk to her about it.

Though I'm not a resident of Alpenglow Ridge anymore, I have the fortune, and sometimes misfortune, of being related to Chloe Bridges. Even if only through her mom's marriage to my dad. She doesn't miss any details when it comes to her gossip. I love my sister, I do. However, I don't think she has stopped talking since she and her mom moved in with us when I was in eighth grade. It's like I never left with how thoroughly I know about all the town's major events.

As told by Clo, a couple of weeks ago, Melody's ex-husband punched Ellis McNair for talking to her at QB's. The man is unhinged. I get it. He lost big time, losing her.

I know the feeling well.

Bet he wouldn't try that shit with me though. I'd lay him on his ass.

I grew up with the backstabbing piece of shit. There's no time to get into that right now. It'll only piss me off.

"Tyson—" Melody starts, but I sit on the stool ol' boy was in and wave to the bartender. Zack knows me well since this is my fourth show here in as many months.

"Jamison, neat?"

"You know it, man," I nod to him.

"Just making yourself comfortable then," Melody says with a disbelieving huff.

I turn toward her fully. The shade from my hat reaches across her face, but her eyes still sparkle exactly like they used to. Like when she was sad, but had to put on a brave face.

Not with me. Not tonight.

I won't sit for that shit.

My fingers are tipping her chin up before I can control my intentions. "Melody Fletcher, you put those sad eyes on me and I'll have to make it better."

Her eyes widen, "Actually, it's Melody Stewart." She turns her head and I drop my hand. *She still has his last name.* That one stings a bit. After a moment, she meets my eyes. "Don't talk to me like you know anything about me."

She probably meant that to be more callous than it came out. It doesn't seem like she wants me to leave since she's picking lint from my shirt, adjusting my hat before she brushes hair from my face.

We both look at her hand. I snag it between my own. "You're right. It has been a long time since I could say that I knew you. It's a shame, really."

Her head tilts and she considers me.

This.

This is what I miss. It's easy for Melody to tell me everything I need to know from her body alone. Maybe she doesn't realize her body's talking to me. She can't help but express herself with her limbs and grace.

After a few beats of relative silence at the bustling bar, she asks, "A shame?" She tugs her hand gently out of mine and I release it.

"Crying. A crying shame." Wrapping my hand around my fist, I rub my right thumb with my left. "Look, Melody. We've been doing this awkward dance-around bullshit for years. Let's just be friends. Squash it." I hold my right hand out for her to shake.

She looks at my hand for several moments and I begin to feel self-conscious.

She uncrosses and re-crosses her legs. I notice how toned and smooth they look. Her strappy heels are the same light pink color as her frilly dress. Her toes are painted white. The hem of her dress brushes the top of her knees and the little ruffle floats along there, teasing me. I'm staring, admiring for a second too long. I move my gaze from her thighs to her eyes again.

Eyes narrowed, she says, "Squash. It." Each word comes out slow and controlled between her teeth. The change there is staggering. Her eyebrows are pulled together and her eyes are shining with an emotion I can't place. "Do you even remember what happened between us? Or did you blackout for that whole time?"

I sip from my whiskey and use that time to school my expression. "What does that mean?"

"Don't do this where they can see, Ty."

I look over her shoulder and sure enough, my sister, Quincy, Tony and Drea are all watching us. I raise the tumbler of whiskey to them in a cheers before I take a sip of my drink. They cheers back and I smirk.

Melody turns back to face the bar and shakes her head. "Oh, God. I don't know what's worse." She sips her mixed drink and her knee bounces.

"What's that?" I heard what she said.

She leans in close to my ear. I catch a whiff of her hair products, sweet and tropical, as she repeats, "I don't know what's worse."

I lower my tone, sipping from my brown again. "Between what?"

"Having my friends watching me like I'm late-night entertainment or feeling the death glares from these women in this club."

I place my hand on her knee and she stops bouncing it entirely. "Neither. You're safe with me and those women could never have this." I gesture to my chest.

She scoffs. "Right. Like I could? You expect me to believe that sexy crooning Tyson Abrams isn't getting ass by the boatload. I'm not that naive, I'm afraid."

She's not that far off base. There's only one part of that statement that I latch onto. "You think I'm sexy?"

Her eyes meet mine. Those same secret sad eyes pull me in. She opens her mouth to respond, but never gets the chance.

Robert puts a hand on my shoulder. "We're on in ten. It's time to get back there Ty." I see him give Melody an appraising look that I will have to address later.

I clench my jaw. I had almost forgotten what I was here for.

Music.

"Better get out there," I say, standing from the bar and finishing my drink.

She nods and responds, "Good luck," before getting up from the bar too.

We're up to do only covers tonight. It makes no difference to me. Though I hate being a part of a crowd, I love playing for one. Whether it's my lyrics they're singing along to or not, I'm happy to entertain them. It wasn't always that way. Thanks to the petite woman striding over to the table her friends are at, I found my way here.

Melody looks over her shoulder at me once more before meeting every-one at the table again. I tip my hat to her and walk through the door that leads backstage and start preparing for my set.

The lights flicker onto my band and I wave to the crowd as they press a little closer to us. On stage I croon, "These songs go out to a very special person who came to support me tonight." The crowd whoops a couple of times. The stomping of boots clunks and clatters when the first notes come from behind me. Robert plays the chords for the first song in our set and I follow him strumming on my guitar and tapping one boot to catch the beat Zeke plays on the drums.

We all found each other a few years ago, playing the same open mic on campus and we clicked. They are the best friends I have, with the added benefit that they didn't know anyone from my hometown. I wouldn't say we make good music together. We make amazing music together.

Leaning into the mic, I sing with my eyes closed, allowing that first verse to pull me in. Like every other time I step onto a stage, I think back to when Melody and I were younger on stage together.

The moment her eyes lock onto me, I find her in the crowd. There are a couple hundred people in the venue tonight, but I would find her in a crowd of a couple thousand as easily. I play for her all night and the feeling of rightness settles into my muscles as I strum each note.

When I finish the last song, the lights go off on the stage and we all start packing up our instruments. I take that opportunity to find my bandmate and set things straight.

"Aye, Robert?"

"Yea, man?" He says, looking up from his case where he's putting his things away.

"You look at Melody like that again and I'll have to black your eye. Understood?"

"Touchy," he jokes.

"That's me," I reply more sternly, gesturing to myself.

"I didn't know." He holds his hands out in front of him. "We're good." He looks over to Zeke, who is laughing at him.

"The most aggressive 'down boy' I've ever heard from him before. I think he means it."

"Oh, fuck off. Both of you." I'll be damned if I let another man think they have a shot with her. I'll be staking my claim from here on out.

I stomp down the short steps from the stage to find my girl. Deciding to use the back door, I don't have to go through the crowd tonight and miss my chance to talk to her in peace.

After loading my guitar into my truck, I look for my sister's friends. They are all headed to their cars out front since they have a long drive ahead of them back to AR. Believe it or not the traffic is unbearable out of the city back home for them.

It's easy to tell who has been drinking during my set and who hasn't. Quincy basically holds Chloe up with how she's leaning into his side for support. He points to her saying, "I'm gonna get this one home and then take her to bed." He wiggles his eyebrows. "She's already two sheets." His big ass grin makes me smile back at him. One thing I never had to worry about was whether Q had Clo's back. They have been *that* couple since we were in high school. I shake his hand and clap his back before they head for the exit. "Dope show though, man! You sound amazing up there!" Quincy throws out.

"'Preciate it bro!" I yell back to him. It's the four of us now and that feels strange. Tony is a little older than us, but everyone else was at school together once upon a time. Tony and Drea are laughing at something on his phone, heading for the car too. It feels right to be walking with Mel toward the parking spots for the club. She's quiet as we walk together, but she kind of always was in the big group. It's when we were alone that I really got to know her.

My truck is parked right out front since I was one of the first to get here for the show tonight. She spots it, saying, "I cannot believe Old Red is still kicking!" Mel turns to me with the biggest smile on her face. The evening breeze has her hair blowing and she fights with the curls to keep them out of her face.

I step in closer to her and hold a chunk of the soft hair in my hands. So many memories in that truck. "Thankfully, it is." The walnut brown of her eyes holds me. I could blurt out about how much I've missed her. If I did, I'd never stop. I settle for, "I'm glad you came out tonight."

She twists a foot out beside her on the heel. "Me too," she says, taking a step out of my space and smoothing down her hair behind her shoulders. "I, um, parked in the lot around the back."

"I'll drive you over there."

She gives me a questioning look, twisting her fingers. "Are you sure?"

"Positive. I'm going home anyway." The relief on her face is evident and I know I've got her now.

"Hey, Tony," I call up to the big guy, who still laughs at his phone with Drea.

Looking up, he asks, "What's up?"

"I'm gonna take Melody to get her car. You good?"

"Yea..." He looks from me to the woman at my side and she gives him a weak smile.

Drea walks over to Mel, whispering something in her ear. Mel nods and Drea gives me a punch to the arm. "Be good to my girl." She continues to eye me for a while before turning and walking with Tony to his car a little further down the lively street.

We get into my truck and I roll the window down. The lights from the busy street stretch across the dash. With the wind blowing through the cab, it almost creates a sense of calm for me. My need to have Melody alone and with me again hits me so strongly. It's an effort to release the death grip I have on my steering wheel right now.

"It's right here," Melody says. Her voice snaps me out of my wandering thoughts of sliding my hand up her leg and under that little floaty dress.

"Oh yea?" I ask. My voice sounds gruff. I clear my throat before reaching for a water bottle.

Her head follows the street as I pass it. "And you're passing it... why?"

I drink from the bottle and return it to its spot. My knuckles brush along her knee. Her skin is soft as sin. Fuck. She takes a sharp inhale I can hear only because I'm listening for it, but doesn't move her leg away from me.

"Come to my apartment real quick. I'll bring you back to your car." At her silence, I look from the road to her fidgeting with her dress. Making sure to keep my focus on the road enough for us not to crash is difficult. She looks up to me when I look over at her again. "I'll take care of the parking fees, too." I wink.

She nods with a small smile. "Okay, Ty... If you promise to bring me back. I have work tomorrow night."

That's perfect.

I'll have all night with her and I don't plan on letting her leave my sight anytime soon.

"I promise."

CHAPTER 2

Melody Stewart

IF THERE WAS EVER a man that I trusted to take me to an unknown second location... It would be Tyson.

Chloe is constantly telling me about stranger danger every time we go out, without fail—as an adult, no less. She thinks that someone will pick me up and walk off with me. I get it. That is absolutely a very scary and very real possibility. However, I think it might be more about me being short than anything else.

But this is Tyson. Even if he wasn't my best friend's brother, he is still a good guy. *More or less.* Though he and I weren't together long, Chloe is still more like a sister to me than my best friend. I'm an only child, so I can't be positive about all the makings of siblings, but I'm certain she fits the bill. Overprotective and constantly in your business. With love, of course.

When I got ready for this night out, I had no idea how far he had come from when I knew him in high school. On stage, his presence reeled me in. I couldn't stop watching him for a second. The way he effortlessly sang all of my favorites. Like he had my playlist on and sang it only for me. That couldn't possibly be right. Maybe I had actually had too many drinks by that point.

Going to order my second Long Island had caught up to me, surely. Tyson got rid of that guy at the bar like he was at the club for that reason—to ward off cocky guys trying to get lucky. I was already feeling a little bit warm and fuzzy. If he had not been there...

Ty's gaze on me from under that delicious black cowboy hat, ignited something stronger than I had felt in years. Ever since he first touched me, no other touch could compare. A sad but true reality I had resigned myself to.

I could only dream that he would see me and remember what it was like between us. We may have just been too young. I have come to terms with the fact that his life was bigger than AR. That much was made clear in the bright lights of his aura tonight. Gone was the reserved boy and here was the star that I knew he could be. Even when he broke my heart, I still wished that for him.

He holds my hand without a word the whole walk from his parking garage to his front door. I'm in a cloud of nerves and anticipation as I walk into the apartment. It smells like him in here. Warm and alluring. The decor is... clearly Chloe and her amazing skills, but she did it with precision. There is a blend of modern and rustic in here. It suits the man walking from his front door in nothing but socks as his boots sit by the front door next to his guitar case.

The clink of his keys falling into a dish by the front entrance makes me jolt. Recognition that I have been looking nervously around his place from the entryway, lost in my thoughts. All the while, he has been sitting on the couch watching and waiting for me.

I'm feeling all kinds of flustered, standing here with my legs crossed at the ankles. I should take my shoes off and follow him over to the couch. The indecision is killing me. *This was what I had hoped would happen.* I begged my friend Reese for her man-catching perfume with the hopes that I could lure Tyson in a little closer. I told her and my other friends that any man would do tonight. I'd be looking for any guy. There was only *one* on my mind though. They saw right through me.

I should have known that I wouldn't need any of that as Chloe predicted. She knows something I don't. What? I don't know, but she always knows everyone's business. Especially mine, outside of the few things I've managed to keep close to my chest. But everything that happened with Tyson before he left town, she's well-versed. He didn't even acknowledge our past though. Wanted to sweep it under the rug like it never existed.

Squash it.

Those were the memories I had held on to. Even when I shouldn't have... And he wanted to get rid of them with the Monday trash service. It was those moments with him that kept me sane. That I would lie in bed thinking about when things got hard. His voice in my head that finally pushed me to make the choices I needed to.

That allowed me the courage to finally leave my husband.

I'm begging you to fight for someone who at least knows you.

A decision I have paid for in more ways than people realize. The smile that I have shown the world is believable enough. I'm quiet and it all seems fine.

All it took was one look at Tyson for him to see that it was a lie. That I wasn't happy. That I was not okay.

You put those sad eyes on me and I'll have to make it better.

That's all I wanted—needed—was for him to make it better. Letting him have me one more time. To confirm that we aren't meant to be more than friends. We can put it behind us and I can move on.

The one may not have been my ex-husband, but it's not Tyson either.

I can finally let go of that puppy love and get my life back.

Be happy for once.

As long as I don't get attached, it will be fine. I will be able to move on. Does that count as using him?

Reese doesn't think I can have a rebound. Chloe doesn't think I can go through with it either. Drea thinks all men are trash and wants me to *find anyone, pick one, and get it done.*

"Do you want something to drink? Eat?" He asks, coming over to the doorway I'm still standing in front of. I'm such a freak. Why am I still standing in this doorway? I shake my head slowly. I couldn't eat or drink anything right now.

He kneels in front of me and I watch him take a knee. He takes off his hat, placing it on his entry table. Tapping a leg and looking up at me expectantly. I uncross my legs and that persistent throbbing between them only intensifies as Tyson unties the buckle at my ankle with deft fingers. I step out of the shoe and he works on the next one.

"Calm down, baby. I promise to take care of you. You don't have anything to worry about." I gulp. He looks too damn good with his head this close to my center.

Ty has this way of talking. Like he's always keeping this smirk from showing his full smile. Unless he's singing, you can't see how surprisingly perfect his smile is. Never too many teeth showing and the sound comes out between his teeth. It makes you want to lean in closer to make sure you've heard him right when really you want to see more of it. The low timbre needs his teeth to temper it so you can't feel that vibration against your skin. I swear I can feel those vibrations up my calf to the apex of my thighs.

"That is what I'm worried about."

He chuckles. "Maybe you're right. How about I show you around? You can see there are no monsters hiding out here. It's just me. We can talk or watch a movie. Chill. I don't care. It's been a long day and a long night. I'm merely happy you're here."

That organ in my chest flutters at his words. Hopes rising much too high. "You are?"

His smile is blinding, even in the ambient lighting of his cozy home. "Yes." How long has it been since this smile was directed at me?

"But, why?" I press.

He runs a hand over his hair, pushing the twists back for them to flop back over his bandana. "Are you kidding?" I hold his gaze, not kidding at all. When I don't answer, he admits, "I'm the one who has been begging you, through Chloe, to come and see me perform." He does this self-deprecating chuff that ruffles those flutters up again. "Did you enjoy the show?"

"I did. You were amazing up there." He walks towards a hallway to the left, turning on lights as he goes. "I always knew you would be," I confess.

"You were just about the only one to think that when I left."

How do I respond to that? I don't want to talk about how he abandoned me all those years ago. I steer the conversation in a different direction. The room he's showing me has all manner of instruments and a computer with a setup I'm sure he uses to record his music or something at home. The microphone stand that is perfectly positioned in front of the plush stool makes me think of how relaxed he was on stage. How at home he was. "You always had an amazing voice. I guess I'll always be able to say I knew you when."

"You still know me now," he jokes.

"Do I?"

"If you want. I'm an open book. If there's something you want to know, ask me."

A trap. Coming right out with: *Why the hell did you leave me?* Doesn't feel right.

There's so much history between us and even more blank holes where he left me broken and empty.

Still, I want him. God, I don't want to, but I do. I can't help it. I'm attracted to his calm confidence and certainty. Maybe he's changed a lot since we were close. Maybe he's not the same person. I could care less. He looks damn good. I could get lost in the flames licking up my insides from his stare alone right now.

I'm quiet for far too long. We're back in the living room and he purposefully didn't show me down the other hallway. That must be where his bedroom is.

Would I have followed him in there if he'd taken me?

Yes. Without question.

Ruminating on all kinds of excuses and guilt, I can't find it. Any shame over how much I want to do whatever Ty asks of me is missing. Honest truth is, my pussy always listens to this man. Because of him, I discovered my own sexuality.

Owned it.

"No questions. Just observations," I hear myself say.

Too many memories inundate me. I am not this woman. I don't hook up with random guys. I still want to be courted. Dated. Cared for and made promises of forever. Ty is the exact opposite of all those things in my past and probably in my present too.

Yet, here I am, reclining on his couch. Feeling weighed down by warring thoughts of shoulds and should nots.

"Like?" he asks, leaning into my space and sharing his warmth with me.

I'm determined to prove everyone and myself wrong.

I can have a rebound and move on.

I'm not the same girl he knew. I'm older and I've matured.

I've been aching since I saw his tight jeans and partially unbuttoned shirt... Deep voice singing about how his love left him lost and lonely.

"You still want me." I'm close enough to see the glint from his tiny nose ring and the length of his lashes around eager eyes. It's unfair how fucking sexy he is.

The only logical thing for me to do is kiss this man. Right? Though I can't trust him with my heart, I can trust him to show me a good time.

"So badly," he admits, closing the distance between us. When our lips meet, he pulls me onto his lap to straddle him and I let him trail his hands up my dress. He cups my ass as he owns my mouth. The familiar taste of him floods my senses when his tongue explores mine.

I relent to everything he's giving me. I want more of this fire between us. I missed it. I want the freedom to be unbound and carefree again. He squeezes my ass, urging me to move my hips over him. It's been so long since I was this turned on.

I come up for air and we look into each other's eyes. It feels like I never left. Like he never left. He may look a little older, but the boy I knew is still there.

We kiss and kiss more fervently. No time has passed or maybe time is passing too quickly.

I'm caught up in the heady mixture of being held by Tyson and taking exactly what I've wanted for so long.

He surprises me when he gives my ass a smack and says, "Hands and knees, Melody." I waste no time leaning over the back of his couch. The fluffy layers of my dress fall over my ass to gather around my waist. My heart rate picks up and I fight the urge to cover myself back up.

He leans behind me. The anticipation of what he might do next makes my legs quiver. I can feel his breath over my most sensitive parts, keenly aware that he can see all of me. At one point, maybe I could have been shy. At this point, I don't have it in me. "God damn, you know my favorite color is purple. Fuck, my dick is so hard seeing this lace between your lips like this." He traces the fabric so softly I barely feel it.

Note to self, remember to pat yourself on the back for the trip to Lulu Lacey's later.

My lace thong slides down my legs by way of his hands. I rise up for him to completely remove it. "These are mine now," he says before throwing my panties across the room.

This is the point where I can still leave. Where I can still spare my feelings. I don't know how to have sex with no attachments. I don't—

My spiraling is cut short when a different sensation takes over as he slides a finger up my slit. I can hear how wet I am as the soft pressure of his digit spreads me apart. "I'm dying for a taste of you, Melody." My sensitive lips tingle with his slow licks over my opening. He keeps me right on the edges as I feel myself clenching around nothing. I bite my lip to resist the urge to beg even though I really want to. He wants me to. I know it. I squeeze my eyes shut, biting my cheek to keep quiet. *I can't be this easy.*

That doesn't last long. "Oh." I gasp as his tongue circles the tight pucker of my ass. "Tyson," I pant. My back arches and I resist pushing back into his face. It feels too good and too intimate. "Pleeease," I beg. Submitting.

Far too intimate for a hook-up.

Could this ever be only a hook-up?

This is Ty. My first love. My first *everything*. Nothing about this is casual. It could never be.

"Relax, Melody." His other hand smooths down my back while his tongue thrust into me slowly. Each penetration makes me feel a little manic. He goes back to rubbing my clit in the same slow fashion that he's tongue fucking my ass. I grip onto the nearest pillow, biting the corner to quell my moans. They come out in deep groans from my chest anyway.

The orgasm building inside me is overtaking my limbs as the pleasure is winding tighter and tighter. He hasn't even taken my clothes off and I'm already climaxing?

Lord Jesus.

His resonant voice rumbles into the room, "Breathe, baby. You're gonna black out."

It's then that I noticed I haven't been breathing.

How does he know?

Our connection pulls tight and he responds to the question I have not asked aloud, "I'm listening to every sound you make, Melody. I need them in my memories to replay over and over. I won't make you beg for it tonight. But you will soon enough." He smacks my ass again, "Now, let go baby. Let me have it."

With his permission, I split apart. The throbbing is only intensified as two of his strong fingers slide into me with no resistance. He rises from the couch, leaning over my back. "Feel how your pussy is trying to pull my fingers in deeper? Tell me I can slide my dick in this pussy. Tell me that it's everything you need right now."

"It's everything I need right now," I pant out. There is no room for shame. Only need. And he's right. I need him right now.

He tears a wrapper with practiced movements. As I'm turning to watch him, Tyson shoves inside of me all the way to the base. I cry out his name, losing the little bit of breath I was able to catch.

"God damn you feel so good, Melody. Is it deep, baby?"

"So deep. Oh God! I'm gonna come," I whimper into the pillow.

My face is pressed up to the couch. I have the sense to use my hands to push up and adjust his position. He thrust into me again and my legs go weak when the fat head of his dick rubs my spot perfectly, again and again. "Tyson! Please."

"Begging already, Melody?" He smacks my ass again, "Please what? More?"

Matching his efforts, I rock back into him and we both moan. "Harder, baby? Oh, I have more." He quickens the pace and I'm holding on with everything I have. I'm so close to coming. I don't want this to end. Not yet.

He licks his finger, swirling it over my asshole for a moment. I blow out a breath—like I remember doing with him all that time ago. When it was only he and I. Young and dumb.

He spits onto me sliding his pinky in my tight hole to the knuckle.

"Yes. Oh my god. Yes, yes, please yes!"

I tip right over the edge and he never stops thrusting. "I want it all, Melody. Keep gripping my dick and my finger like that baby." He holds my hip with one hand and I'm gone. Floating on a wave of utter euphoria. Like a leap into the air that I don't have to land from. At some point, he pumps into me harder, chasing his own climax while I'm sheathed tightly around him.

If this is a rebound, I'm fucked. Thoroughly so.

He pulls out of me and takes care of the condom.

Tyson returns, kneeling between my legs on the floor with a warm cloth. His gentle movements contrast what we did earlier as he asks, "Do you want to go get your car now?"

"Huh?" I hear myself say.

He laughs, "Your car is still in the lot. Do you want to go get it?"

"I want to sleep..."

"Okay, baby. Let's go." I feel myself float down the hallway he didn't show me before. He quickly unzips my dress and puts me under the sheets. I settle into his embrace with the warm smell of him and his heartbeat lulling me to sleep.

CHAPTER 3

Melody

I DON'T KNOW HOW it's been a week or so that I've been making the trip to Tyson's apartment. I've had time to tell him about my life now. We spend so much time in his apartment that I have clothes and even some body care products here. Our connection is just as effortless as it was when we were younger.

Between my days at Alpenglow Ridge High School and my nights at Quarter Backs, I am exhausted making the drive to Denver. When I get to his place, most nights we talk and he holds me like he used to so I can get some good sleep.

Note to self, bottle whatever it is Ty is doing so I can make millions on this melatonin replacement.

When I fall asleep in his arms, I forget about everything that happened between the last time we were like this and now. Before he left.

I think I'm starting to have feelings too big to explain to him or hide from him. If I stay with him every night, he would have been able to see that I was starting to feel more.

The last thing I want is to end up looking like a fool. Again.

I wake with a start when my phone buzzes on the bed somewhere. I find it, see that it's Reese and answer, "Are you okay?"

"Yea. I'm okay... Are you still in Denver?" I roll out of bed and find the T-shirt Tyson was wearing on the floor to pull on. "It's a little late to still be in bed," she says.

I close the door behind me so that I don't disturb his sleep. I make my way over to the kitchen to pour myself some water. She tells me about what happened when she finally returned her car and it makes me think about Mack.

I wonder briefly why Reese didn't call him to pick her up. They are like brother and sister, with how close they are. I know the situation is a bit complicated there, though.

Mack doesn't come up in my thoughts often because I've worked so hard not to think about how I've hurt him. If I see him, then it's a different story. It's the look on his face when he has sights on me that is my undoing every time. At some point, I expected Reese to defend him or maybe be pissed at me. Thankfully, Reese has firmly sat in neutral ground after a couple of attempts on her part to figure out what happened between us and make it better.

"Do you need a ride?" I ask.

"Please. I will even buy you lunch if you take me back to Alpenglow Ridge."

I laugh because she doesn't need to bribe me, but also because on the stove, I see that it's almost one in the afternoon. Nothing helps you sleep better than being wrapped up in strong arms. I rarely sleep in. My sleep is sub-par at home since I've been sleeping alone. Unless you count my cat, which I don't because he prefers his bed on the floor to my tossing.

I hear Ty call my name and grab him a glass of water as well.

"I don't have work at QB's until five, so I planned on sleeping in..." and maybe letting Tyson help me pass the time. "It's fine. Drop me a pin, and I'll head over in the next five."

"Thank you, Melly!" I end the call and walk back to his bedroom.

Opening the door, I'm met with the mouth-watering sight of Tyson sitting up against his headboard. He's scrolling on his phone with only the blanket over his waist. The trail of music notes tattooed along his chest and down his side leading to the happy trail I've kissed my way down more

19

times than I can count. Those weren't there when we were in high school, but I like the subtle edge it gives him.

"There's a view I'll never tire of having," he says when he takes the glass from my hand.

Looking down at myself, I ask, "What view is that?" He takes the water from me and places it on his nightstand. I place mine down as well. His room is probably my favorite in the house. Not because of what we end up doing in here, but I think his bed is actually made out of clouds. The furniture is this rustic modern blend that I continue to admire. It occurs to me that it would look really good with some of the decor pieces that I have in my room at home. They fit pretty well together.

"You in my shirt. I fucking love it," Tyson says.

I pull the shirt over my head and immediately his gaze heats before he's on me. He trails kisses in between my breasts and down my stomach to the panties I'm wearing.

"Wait, Tyson." I giggle at the warm sensation of his tongue swirling over my hip bones. "I wish I was not saying this, but I need to go."

"Go?" He looks up at me with confusion, face still between my legs. I have to fight to get the next words out because there is nothing better than having him right where he is at the moment.

"Yes. I need to pick Reese up and take her home."

He huffs and flops back onto the bed with a pout, looking both adorable and frustrated at once.

I lean over his body, my small breasts inches from his face. He leans up to kiss one and his hand lands on my waist, pulling me closer. "Are you sure? I can be quick," he mumbles into my chest.

I give him a look and he admits, "You're right. I can't." He sits up against the headboard again, taking me with him. "Do you want me to go with you?"

"That's kinda sweet, Ty. But no. I've got work so I'll need to get ready and head over right after." He swirls a finger around my belly button idly. I coax him to look at my face with a hand on his strong jaw. "Is that fine?"

"Yea...but I'll miss you."

I freeze, my body going stiff at his confession.

He can't say that.

He can not be saying that.

I'm off the bed looking for my top and skirt before I respond or before he can say anything else.

I scoop up the rest of my things and run to the bathroom. Looking in the mirror, my panicked eyes and scrunched brows reflect back at me.

What are you doing Melody?

"You good, Melody?"

No. "Yea. Just gonna borrow some toothpaste and mouthwash." I hurry to make myself look less like I'm doing a walk of shame. I have nothing to be ashamed of. We aren't strangers. We both consented to being together all this time.

So why am I panicking?

I use some water to help the curls that are a little smushed on the side from sleep and try my best to put my smile in place.

Tyson might be able to see through it but I will address what happened later. Maybe...

Walking out of the bathroom, I feel his eyes on me.

I hate confrontation. Tyson doesn't care about confronting anyone, including me.

I'm pulling my phone charger out of the wall when he holds my hand. It's too gentle. I feel his concern in my chest.

"I said, I'll miss you." I continue fiddling with the thin white phone cord and the silence stretches around me as I squeeze my eyes shut. *Do not cry!* This is just a hook-up. We are just casually hooking up.

Why can't I lie? I've done it to everyone else about my feelings for him. Why can't I do that with Ty? Ugh.

"Melody?" He lifts my face and there's no fighting the urge to see his. His hair is sleep-mussed and there are still creases along his cheek from how hard he was sleeping on his pillow. He's vulnerable and I can't lie to him when he's like this with me.

"I'll miss you too," I whisper. My stupid eyes start to water and I quickly rub my arm over my face.

"What's wrong, baby?"

My phone chirps from my purse and I look down at it on my shoulder. "Nothing. I just really need to go pick Reese up. I'll call you. Is that fine?"

Is that fine? Is that fine? Is that fine? I mock myself in my head. It's not fine!

He nods but his brows are pulled together when I turn from him. I practically run from the apartment to my car parked in the visitor spot in his garage.

Oh, Melody. You are in way too deep.

⸻ ◆◆◆ ⸻

REESE PICKS UP A gyoza from the middle of the table with chopsticks before plunking the whole thing into her mouth. I watch in fascination as the resident bad girl eats apps and ramen at a speed I would not have guessed possible for a woman who is all about her image.

"What?" She asks in response to how I watch her with rapt fascination.

"Nothing. I just don't think I've ever seen someone eat extra-spicy ramen so quickly."

"It's a skill. What can I say?" She dabs her mouth with a napkin, prettily. "Do you want these?" She points to the last bao we ordered and I shake my head. I have no appetite right now. I'll have to bring most of this home and hope I can get some of it down before my closing shift at the bar tonight.

"Melly! You have hardly eaten anything. What is going on?"

"I'm not hungry." Another easy lie.

She raises an eyebrow then pointing at me with her chopsticks, she says, "You can't survive on dick alone, honey." I look around to make sure no one overheard her.

"Will you stop? I'm just not hungry. I'll probably eat later."

"If there's anything left... This place is amazing! I'm moving on to your bowl next."

"You're not." I slide my bowl closer to me, protectively.

"Fine. I want to know what's going on with you and Tyson. Also, I want to take this opportunity to say I told you so!"

"We're hanging out."

"Hanging out or sliding in?"

She clicks her chopsticks at me and I regret agreeing to lunch with her in such a public place. "What?"

"Getting horizontal or like a cowgirl?"

I fan my heating face and sip some of my water. "Ugh! Reese, can you not?"

She waggles her eyebrows. "Dirty girl! I knew it! Does Clo know you're still banging her brother?"

"Not exactly." I don't know why I haven't told her either. It's not like she didn't know Ty and I had been together in the past. For some reason, it feels very uncomfortable to try and talk to her about it now. I haven't quite worked out if what I'm doing with Tyson makes me a bad person or one of many women on his roster. There has to be a long roster, right? This man on stage... and what he does with his tongue... That has to mean he's getting around far more than I am.

Reese was honestly the best friend to go to since Chloe wants me to be angry about my divorce and Drea wants me to move on. They don't get it. I stopped trying to make them understand. Not for lack of trying on their part. Maybe I should talk to her about it...

Note to self, tell Clo that I'm hooking up with her brother... eventually.

"Scandalous! Get you some, Melly-Mel!" She clicks her chopsticks in applause this time. "So... what? Is this serious?"

"No. It's not..." *it can't be* "serious. We're... It's a rebound. With Ty, I know I'm safe." Well it was and I was until he said he would miss me with those sensual, dark eyes.

Her face holds pity for me when she says, "Oh, Melly."

"Reese. We're both adults. You see how he lives. He doesn't want what I want from life. He's destined for big things. I'm comfortable in Alpenglow. We aren't right for each other anymore. Maybe once. I don't know. Probably not. This is some fun."

"You've given an awful lot of thought to *some fun*... And you still can't be convincing." She laughs and I smile despite how I should be panicking about her clear revelation regarding my life.

"It is!" I say between giggles.

"It is fun, huh?" I cover my face to hide the big grin. "Oh my God, you are actually fucking his brains out!" Her whistling cat call shreds my ear drums. Now, I really am looking around giving apologies to the people sitting around us.

"Will you calm down? We're just hooking up. It's been a long time."

"Oh, I bet! Ride that dick, girl! You're the only one getting some around here! Love that for you," she says before slurping some noodles into her mouth.

I picked her up from dropping her car off with her not-ex. Her and the landscaper called it quits recently because of whatever she had going on with said not-ex. "I'll probably jump ship with Drea and choose to be celibate." I eye her over the top of my water glass. "Heifer! I can be celibate! Drea is not the only one with resolve."

"Yea..."

"Whatever. What are you gonna do about Ty?"

"I don't know."

"Well, what do you want to do?" I can't answer that question without getting really honest with myself. And unfortunately getting honest with Tyson too.

After how he said he missed me, I have a feeling that he will be asking me the same thing soon enough.

And what did I want? Have my dreams changed since the last time I dreamed about the future with him? Have I changed except for being more sad, more reserved, and more lost than I was when he first saw me on my roof?

"I don't know."

"Fair. That's fair. You know I might be able to help if I knew what exactly didn't work with..." She looks around and I look too. When she turns back around to face me, she whispers, "He who shall not be named."

"It's not like that, Reese. And I still don't know how to explain it, really. I never intended anyone to feel any differently about him. Once it got out that I asked for a divorce and he moved out, Alpenglow set on him like he was vermin. I couldn't stop it."

"He took everything really hard. He won't even tell me what happened." She pouts into her bowl, making a show of swirling her noodles about slowly.

I flash her a self-deprecating smile. "What happened to people's private lives being private? I shouldn't have to air out all my dirty laundry for everyone to leave us alone. Or to let him live his life without their glares."

"Yea, well, AR is AR! They love good gossip and the town's sweetheart divorcing seems like pretty juicy gossip."

"I am not the town's sweetheart."

"Aren't you?"

I grimace and swirl some of my own noodles in my bowl. The town's sweetheart... "I didn't do anything to earn that title."

"Sure. But compared to me and Drea, the harlots in their eyes, you're a saint. Everyone knows that Chloe will refuse service if they piss her off, so the gossip flows through her and not about her." Reese clicks her chopsticks together at me again.

"I guess you're right. How does Drea fall into the harlot category though?"

"She never did recover from that whole teenage pregnancy thing. Couldn't say for sure, but the glares she gets are just as nasty as mine at the grocery store."

I sigh. This time I do eat some of my ramen and we both eat for a while before I ask, "What about you? After everything today, what are you gonna do about Cory?"

She narrows her eyes when she looks back up at me. "Cory who?"

I begin to respond, but the glare she cuts at me makes me reconsider. I change the subject and we finish our meals before I take her back to Mason Ranch.

CHAPTER 4

Tyson

"I KID YOU NOT," I say, unlocking my apartment door. Melody follows me into the apartment, taking her shoes off at the door and hanging her purse on the little hook next to my keys. It's the second week that we've been slowly becoming a part of each other's lives.

Tonight, I had a show in midtown that she sat right offside the stage for. Looking over and seeing her there was the kind of comfort I didn't know I wanted when I performed. As soon as our set was over, I packed up and took my girl with me. The little things like her purse on the hook or her little flats in my shoe rack by the door make me feel like I might be able to keep her with me. She makes an effort to get to know what my life is like now that I don't live in AR anymore. Tries to understand the person I am now. I think tonight will be the night that I ask her to move in with me here. I know she misses her cat when she's here with me. They could both live here.

"Are they really?" she asks after I tell her about my bandmates' girlfriend getting caught cheating on them. She couldn't believe it. I had to warn them off from hitting on her when she came to our show the first time. Christine showed up to the club tonight trying to win them back. There was no way that I was getting involved with that drama. I quickly extracted Melody and me from that mess when I saw her approaching the table we were at.

"Ever since I've known them, they have dated the same woman. It's been like that since they were young. Long before I met them."

"I don't even get how that works. So they basically share her? Together?"

"Together."

"So they're a couple too?"

"I guess. Fuck if I know. Never actually came up." Her phone died while we were out. I see her walking over to the charger she has by the bed and putting her phone on it.

"You're right, I never would have known that. When you said they were looking for a girl, you really meant one girl." She wastes no time taking off her clothes and getting ready for bed. I sit there watching her flit around my apartment like it's hers. She puts her clothes in my dirty clothes basket. The jewelry she wore tonight goes back to its spot atop my dresser before she heads to the bathroom to take her makeup off. The sound of the crinkling bag those little wipes come in echoes loudly from where I'm sitting on the bed.

I lie back, content, on my bed, still fully dressed. "Yea. In all the years I've known them, it's been like that. Robert saw you and I put the brakes on that quick as fuck."

She laughs, rolling her eyes. Melody comes out of the bathroom with her hair tied up on top of her head to lie in bed next to me. "Maybe you should check to see if they're okay. She looked pissed."

I pull out my phone to send a quick text. Melody's goes off with back-to-back notifications now that it's powered up. She grabs it and rolls over toward me. There are several missed calls from my sister and Drea. She looks at me before selecting my sister's contact and calling her back. "Hey? What happened?"

Her eyes grow large as I watch her. I can hear my sister's voice over the phone, even with it pressed tightly to Melody's ear. I can't quite make out the words, but Melody has begun to put her clothes back on. She steps out into the hallway for some privacy while I lie back in the bed. My pillows have started to smell like her tropical hair products making me smirk up at the ceiling feeling satisfied with the direction my life has taken.

We've come to a sort of routine. If she's not working the day shift the next day, then she stays the night at my house. My schedule is pretty sweet since I can do all the work for my accounting clients from home. Because it's the summer, Melody only has the bar to worry about. It's been working out fairly easy for us to make time for each other with the commute from AR between us.

I've started to collect her things in a drawer to make it easier for her to stay here longer. It's not much, but I feel like we are getting back to how we were. It feels good.

She gasps, "Oh, no! That's awful... Online?"

I poke my head out of the bedroom to check on Melody since she sounds pretty distraught now.

There is nothing worse than eavesdropping and hearing something you know that you shouldn't have. I can't stop myself from listening anyway.

"I'm like an hour from AR right now." She leans against the hallway wall with her back facing me. "No, I didn't go to the mall without you." I can see her back visibly tense when Clo responds. "Will you be quiet? I'm not ready for that." More tensing as she makes an effort to relax her shoulders from her ears. She looks down at the phone in her hand before raising it back to her ear. "It doesn't matter... No, it doesn't."

Holding on to the door jamb for support, something in my mind told me to prepare for what was coming next. I hadn't talked to Chloe about how often Melody has been staying at my place. From past experience, I knew my sister couldn't hold water. Telling her about what I had going with Melody felt like jinxing something special that I wanted to keep for myself for a little while at least.

Melody is a private person and a flight risk. She always has been. She avoids oversharing like the plague. Stupid me for wanting to know a little about what she was thinking about us. She had to tell her friends something. What other reason would she be in Denver if not me?

"Because I didn't want to tell you about it, Mrs. I am the Gossip Mill. It's not serious... You wanted me to find a rebound and I have."

I pull my head back inside my room all the way. What did I just hear?

I'm... the rebound?

Quickly, I step backward into my bedroom. My fingers are pulling at the twists on my head when I stare at her drawer which seems more barren than before.

Was she actually moving in?

How could I have been reading the signs all wrong? I thought we were getting back to what we were. I thought I was making my way back to her.

Fuck.

I make a big show of opening my bedroom door this time, so she knows I'm coming. She turns to give me a smile, but I keep walking to the kitchen. I pour some whiskey into a rocks glass and then decide to slug directly from the bottle as well.

Feeling Melody's hand on my lower back, I step to the side and face her. "I think I'm gonna head back to Alpenglow tonight. The girls and I are gonna try to be at Mason Ranch early in the morning. Reese is having a crisis. Is that fine?"

Is that fine? I'm just the rebound, what does it matter?

Spiraling deep in my own mind, I clip, "Yea."

"Are you okay?" She asks with concern on her face.

I work to keep my face neutral when the answer is painstakingly the opposite. "I'm great." Flopping onto my couch, I watch her from over the glass I'm sipping from. She busies herself around my apartment and zips out of my front door.

She's gone.

I grab the closest pillow to me. It smells like her perfume. The lavender assaults my senses like a kick to the head. I throw the offensive cushion at the front door, but it brings me no satisfaction.

Just a rebound.

Am I so gone for this girl that I couldn't tell that we weren't progressing? Am I that deluded?

I hug a different pillow closer to me. It still smells like her. Each inhale feels shittier than the last. It's probably still better than the smell of her hair on my bed pillows. I fall asleep after a while of drinking and stewing in my thoughts.

The next morning I wake from my spot on the couch with the sun blaring in my head like a trombone. I drank way too much. Somewhere in the room, my phone is going off.

It takes me a minute to find it before picking up on speakerphone, I answer, "What?"

"Damn. What's got your panties in a twist?" My friend's gruff voice is too loud in the room.

"Q, I'm not in the mood. What's up?"

"My wife has been calling you for the past few hours to no response. You mind texting her back, or something, so I can stop hearing about it?"

"Shit, man." I look at how late it is and reply, "Sorry."

He keeps talking, but I can't hear what he says as I look at the texts on my screen.

> **Clo: Rebecca posted a bunch of photos of Reese on her Facebook profile.**

> **Clo: Like actual revenge porn.**

> **Clo: Can you report them? We're trying to get them taken down.**

> **Clo: What the fuck? What a bitch right?**

> **Clo: Don't be a creep and look at them though. I know you're hooking up with Melody again.**

Ignoring Chloe's messages, it's the one below them that I open.

> **Mel: Do you wanna stay at my place tonight? (smiling face emoji)**

Do I want to stay at the house she and Mack bought and lived in together when I left? Is that even a question?

She wants me to be a rebound from their failed marriage. She wants me to be okay with the fact that I'm coming second. That I'm not going to be a permanent fixture in her life? That she has no intentions of seeing what we have through.

I've paid my dues. I spent years pining after a woman who was married. Keeping my distance from my home, my family, and my friends. All because I didn't want to make them uncomfortable when it was clear that I was so easy to replace.

That dumb fool couldn't even keep her. Now, she wants me to slot into the place he left like none of this hurts me. Like I don't have a heart. Like I didn't know she moved on when I didn't.

I've allowed her to hurt me again. And this time, instead of the slow ache that these years apart have been, it was a sharp jab that I can't staunch the bleeding from. I can't keep playing second fiddle to the guy we both know is wrong for her. I deserve her whole heart, not what she can bear to give me.

Some fucking rebound.

I loved her with my whole heart, even when she couldn't see it. I tried to move on and I couldn't. No one ever compared. These past weeks with her have been the closest to what should be that I've come across in years. I can't fake that now when she's not willing to see me for who I want to be for her. I wanted to be her person again. Not anymore.

Fuck that.

I close the text, not even caring that my read receipts are on. Let her see that I know what's up.

Going to her drawer, I throw all of her stuff into a box. The dresser and bathroom are my next stops in clearing her stuff out. I do a final sweep through, grabbing any of her other stuff from my place and put the box by the door.

After eating something quick, I sit in the studio, working on tuning my guitar and recording something I think might distract me from the turmoil

I still feel. Deciding that I'm not going to find relief in this apartment, I shower and get dressed. I know there are a few open mics around town tonight.

There's a knock at my door by the time I'm ready to leave.

Fixing my collar, I open the door to Melody whose hand is still raised to knock again.

"Hi," she says, looking a bit unsure. She shifts from foot to foot and I notice the bag by her little sandals. "You didn't text me back, so I grabbed some things..." She trails off when I cross my arms over my chest. "You look good."

"Thanks," I say, slinging my guitar case over a shoulder.

"I'm off tomorrow, so it'll just take me a second to get dressed." Tugging at the hem of her shirt, she leans down to pick up the bag by her feet.

In any other circumstance, I would have grabbed it for her. In this circumstance, I have no intention of letting her into this apartment again. I grab my keys from the hook and box from the console and step out of my apartment.

"Tyson?" her sweet voice almost pierces my resolve. Almost. "What's going on Ty? Can I put my bag in the apartment? It won't take me any time to get ready." I lock the door and turn to face her.

I put the box at her feet. Melody's wide eyes are begging for me to answer her. I want to comfort her and everything in my body is straining to reassure her. Hell, to even answer her, but if I open my mouth, then I know I'll be the fool again.

"Where are we going?" She follows me down the hall to my elevators, leaving her bag and the box by the front door. I can't take it.

I jab my finger into the down button and face her. "We aren't going anywhere. You know that, and I know it now too. Let's just end things here."

"End things? Tyson, I don't—"

"We're done. I'm done."

The elevator dings at the right time, or maybe it's the wrong time, but I step inside anyway. When the doors close, I can still feel her sad eyes begging me, but I refuse to lose her again. This time, it's my choice to let her go.

CHAPTER 5

Melody, Two Years Later

"THEY SAY THAT THE best inspiration for a song is heartbreak," Tyson says with that gleam in his eye. The masochist in me couldn't stay away from the TV as soon as I got off work. I've seen every interview and read every article. No one knows about the fake account I've made to follow him on every platform that shares his music or content. It's both pathetic and illogical. It took me months to finally feel some semblance of normalcy after he left me in that hallway. I never told my friends what really went down because he was *my rebound*. They thought that I was failing at it as they predicted I would.

Regina, the host of the award-winning talk show, Regina Live!, places a hand to her heart when she asks, "And that's what inspired you to get up on stage that night?"

That night will always be one of the worst ones of my life. So many of those involved him or rather involved him leaving me.

Is it ironic that one of the worst days of my life had become the day that changed his life for the better?

I'm not sure.

All the signs of the universe point to one fact. Tyson is better off without me in his life.

"Oh yea. Someone hurt me. Real bad." Ty hangs his head from his shoulders. Each time he talks about this night, it makes something in my chest ache. "I felt that pain for so many years, and then she came back into my life to hurt me all over again." After thinking over the time we spent together it became apparent that he had to have heard me talking with Chloe to get her off my scent. He was right. I had been the one to ruin what we had. I still hated the way he handled everything. "When I saw there was an open mic night, I got up there with my strings and let my heart bleed out in the only way I knew how."

"Through music."

"Yea, through music." He nods his head in that slow way that makes everyone in the studio audience *coo* and *aww* over him. Mostly women, from what I can see when they pan over them.

"They call you Country Music's next star. Do you deny that?"

His smile is self-deprecating when he looks back up at Regina. "I don't deny it, but I've heard it just a little bit differently than that."

"Oh!" Regina looks out into the audience, who join in her playful mood. "Oh, I know what you've heard! I know, I know. It's Country's Sad Boy. Yes, I've heard that one."

"Comes with the territory, I guess." He looks at his boots thoughtfully. "When you sing about what I sing about, there's very little upbeat songs on the lineup."

"So, that's where Jordan Hurst comes in?"

"Hey, no one knows blues like Jordan. I knew his song, *Luck Never Changes*, would speak my pain as clearly as I could right then. He really did say it best. After my video blew up online, he reached out to me."

"*The Jordan Hurst* slid into your DMs?" The exaggerated shock on her face causes the audience to respond accordingly.

He winks and smirks at the camera. The whoops that follow are almost too much for me to take. I grab the remote, prepared to turn the TV off. Maybe I'll watch it later.

I hesitate too long and he starts talking again, "Oh, yea. He hit me up and asked me to work on this new project with him. Started off as a feature and when he saw how special the sound we had together really was—We just kept making music and JT was born. It's been such a blessing." His smile is genuine as he looks over the audience. Rubbing a finger over my lips, I reluctantly sigh at how good he looks.

Note to self, please stop noting how good the man looks. It only makes you seem more pathetic.

"That is amazing!" Regina responds, nodding with the audience as they clap. "Well, we have a surprise for you all!" There is animated chatter as she stands, placing her cards down. "Jordan Hurst is in the building, folks! Come on out, Jordan!"

They pan over to the country superstar as he walks over to where Tyson is now standing in front of the large guest chair. They hug and say something to each other that the mics don't pick up from the rustling of their shirts. Tyson laughs kind of uncomfortably, and then the camera angle is tight on him and his dreamy eyes. Jordan hugs Regina before they all sit in their seats.

"Thank you for coming on Jordan. We are so lucky to have you here tonight!"

"I'm the lucky one. Thank you for having me Regina! My girlfriend is such a huge fan. I'll never hear the end of this one."

"Amazing! I heard a little about that. Look at this picture of you two! Such a beautiful couple." She motions to the screen behind her, where Jordan stands next to a dark haired woman who beams at the camera from Jordan's lap. They both hold large grey cans looking a little flushed. Even Jordan's light brown skin looks a little red like he's had a couple by this point. They look normal, like an all-American couple in a beer commercial. Not a multiplatinum recording artist and his reclusive designer girlfriend.

Tyson is the one who introduced me to Jordan's music and I follow him online. News of his relationship with Lacey went viral because of who her parents are. Her dad is the chairman and CEO at Miles Records, coincidentally the same company Jordan is signed to. Obviously, it was tabloid news for a while.

Lacey Bramble is the mastermind behind Lulu Lacey, a lingerie brand that I stand behind and frequent, though I have no partners to share it with. When I discovered her brand, I knew my friend Reese would lose her mind over it. She might be the only person in town who owns more Lulu Lacey than I do. She creates pieces that are sexy enough to be worn at sex clubs for display and the nicest sleepwear that I am always adding to my cart. If I'm going to toss and turn all night, it might as well be in silk. Am I right?

"Oh, she is going to love that you chose that picture!" He looks right into the camera, pointing at the screen. "See Lacey? I do have good pictures of us!"

Regina and the audience laugh, obviously charmed by Jordan. Something seems very fake about him to me. Too perfect. I've seen the tabloids where he's passed out drunk at public events and the scandal of how he sold his house after a gambling problem caught up to him. That was right before he and Tyson started working together.

Who knows if you can believe everything in magazines though? They run with stories all the time.

The hostess in her designer shift dress attempts to get the interview back on track, asking, "What was it that you said to Tyson earlier? You two seem to have gotten quite close since you found him two years ago."

Jordan chuckles in a self-deprecating manner, "Nothing. Nothing."

The camera pans to Tyson, who wipes a hand down his face, either hiding a grin or a grimace—I can't tell.

Regina says, "It's between us friends. We're all friends here, right?" She nudges Tyson with her elbow looking out to her audience, who whoop and holler. Tyson bobs his head, debating. He looks over to Jordan who nods with a smirk.

"He said I was making him look bad." He says it with a smile, but it doesn't quite reach his eyes.

Regina wears a shocked expression with a hand over her heart. "No way. How could this man, Jordan Hurst, ever look bad?" She stands, walking over to where Jordan is also smiling, but in a fake manner, that I only catch a glimpse of. The frame widens to include Regina standing behind the famous singer, who looks up at her pressing his hands in thanks.

"Talk to us about this new music we can expect from the group."

"I can't share much, but we have been diligently working on the sound, staying consistent with what the fans can expect from us. Giving y'all the same feel but adding a little more life into it."

"Something to dance to rather than cry over?"

"Exactly. We've got a lot to celebrate," he says in Tyson's direction. The camera catches him briefly looking unsettled before catching what Jordan says next. "I know you all are gonna love it." Bright white teeth gleam in the lighting.

"Well, the audience agrees, Jordan, they're going to love it. We have one more treat for you all when we come back from the commercial break. JT will be performing their newest single, *Kisses in the Tall Grass*, for us *liiive!*"

I turn the TV off having seen more than enough. Each time Ty leaves me, he achieves more success. It's my own brand of torture each time I see him doing so well. The sooner I accept that his life is better off without me, the quicker I can finally stop being so morose.

I think...

I hope.

How had I thought Tyson Abrams would ever want anything to do with small-town life? With me, a small-town girl. He's on *Regina Live!* That show reaches audiences overseas. Nothing could compare to that kind of achievement or admiration.

The love I have for him could never compete with the love of millions of adoring fans. Or the thousands of women throwing themselves at him. I see the desperate comments, heart eyes, and things too bold for me to repeat on his socials all the time.

Wesson darts off of the bed where he was sleeping with a hiss when my phone blares Chloe's jaunty ringtone into the room. "Oh, baby. I'm sorry." I call after him though it's pointless. He's probably around under a cabinet somewhere.

I answer the call and Chloe's voice comes onto the line, "Hey, Bon."

Bon, short for Cinnabon. A nickname I earned from her since I usually have my hair slicked into a tight bun on the top of my head for dance. She said it looks like those hot cinnamon rolls that we can only find at the malls in Denver since Alpenglow Ridge only has like two fast-food restaurants.

"Hey," I respond, tone completely dejected, thinking about what I saw on TV.

"You watched, didn't you?"

"As if I could help it. But, I'm fine. Just tired, you know? I had a long day." And I did. A double shift at the bar. It's not like I had anything else to do besides the pile of laundry I folded while watching Tyson gain a couple thousand more fans.

"Mmhmm... And it has nothing to do with the fact that my brother looks dang good on late-night television?" Why did she have to know everything?

"Of course not. I'm good. Like I said, I just want to shower and go to bed. Is that fine?"

There's a pause of silence before my best friend answers. "Yea. It's alright. I'll see you at the party this weekend? Do I need to send over reinforcements?"

This woman knows me far too well. Since it's summer and school is out, I teach a couple of classes at the Senior Center for fitness. They may be older than my high school students by triple, but they get into some trouble all the same. The barre class I teach in the morning is followed by a modified Zumba class that really does feel like a party. Not the kind of party that my friend is throwing though.

I was of the mind that I could say my class ran over and it would be rude to show up late to Reese's engagement party. No one would have bought that ridiculous excuse.

"No, you don't. I'm coming right after my class. I can't believe Reese finally agreed. Can you?"

"I'm still reeling. And, of course, she took her sweet ass time to say yes, and now she's rushing all of us to get this wedding together. And by all of us, I mean me. Call me Jennifer Lopez. Actually... maybe don't." Chloe complains with love. She loves party planning and decorating. Ever since we were young, she has had an eye for it. When I moved here, she helped me to finally decorate my room and eventually the rest of our house. Our walls were completely barren.

My mom's paintings used to cover almost every wall, but there was no way I could withstand that kind of traumatic reminder every day. Her work practically leaped off the canvas to grab you. She would spend hours getting lost creating landscapes or getting the shading on someone's face just right. She *was* the art, leaving a piece of her beautiful soul there for anyone to enjoy. When she was gone, I removed every single one from the walls for our sanity. When we moved from Texas to Alpenglow, we left them in my grandmother's garage. My grandmother moved a few years back and never mentioned the art. Who knows what has happened to them since?

I clear the emotion from my throat and swipe at my eye. Grabbing the basket with all the clothes I folded, I walk over to my closet to put everything away in my chest. "Oh, The Wedding Planner is such a good one. I should put that on tonight."

"You've seen it a million times, Bon. Put on something funny."

"What is more funny than Mary bumping into Steve at the meeting to plan his wedding with another woman?" I snort a laugh. "I mean that scene lives rent-free in my mind, Clo. The shock on both their faces and then trying to contain it! Even then, their chemistry is so obvious. Yep. It is settled. I am watching that tonight."

Clo sighs heavily into the phone. "Girl, okay. If it makes you happy. Call me before you come in?"

"Okay. I love you."

"Love you."

The house is so quiet as I continue putting away my laundry. Working nights at a bar can have its ups and downs. One thing that makes it worth it to me is the buzz. There is always something to do and the sounds of people having a good time to surround me. I hate the silence in my house, so I turn the TV back on and change it to the movie to play in the background of my chores. Running around, refilling beers, and making small talk takes something out of me, this is easier. Thank goodness I got cut early tonight so Drea could finish out the shift.

Wes stalks lithely in and out of my legs as I work my way around the house, straightening everything up. When I finally sink into my bath, he hops onto the fluffy toilet seat cover to keep me company by the bathroom speaker.

It's on low, but Wesson knows when *his* music is playing.

"Wessie, you like the new single?"

He meows something that sounds like agreement as he takes a bath, as well. Licking one paw to swipe over his furry face.

"I like it too," I say. I didn't want to watch Tyson play it live. If it's only Wesson and me listening in the comfort of our house, it can be only for us. I can pretend that he's singing this song just for me. That he wrote it for me and is only sharing it with me. Like he used to.

I sigh, sinking deeper into the bubbles. I could spend way too much time thinking about the what-ifs where Ty is concerned.

We used to do that together.

Dream.

He held all of mine and I held all of his. Kept them safe in my heart.

Not for the first or last time, I wonder, was he being honest with me? Was he really telling me what he wanted from life or did he tell me what he thought I wanted to hear?

It's not like it matters because he has moved on.

Moved up.

His deep voice sings about the girl whose hair twinkled in the night sky and I find myself restarting the song over and over as I get ready for bed. I fall asleep thinking about how his full lips would tell me all those same things.

CHAPTER 6

Melody

CHECKING MY DRESS FOR the last time, I grab my clutch and exit the vehicle.

Walking to QB's, I feel my curls swinging along my back and shoulders as I do my most confident strut to the door. Head held high and hips swaying, I find an ease in pretending this event hasn't worried me.

You finish a thing the way you start a thing. Strong. My mom's words call to me from a memory.

I'm here for my friends, and it will be fine, I say to myself as I near the building.

Two easels flank the main doors as streamers blow softly in the breeze. A collection of Polaroid photos pop out from a bokeh background on the canvas. The top left shows Cory hugging Reese from behind, laughing. She leans forward with a big toothy grin, laughing too. The middle shows Reese holding Cory's chin while she kisses his cheek. The last photo on the bottom right shows them staring into each other's eyes with the kiss print bright on his cheek.

They look absolutely adorable on these candids! They are the cutest couple. It's obvious to anyone with eyes that they are obsessed with each other. I almost can't believe it took Reese two years to finally say yes to his proposal.

I take a deep breath and pull the doors open. It's still pretty quiet since guests don't start arriving for another half hour. I have been in this bar far more times than I can count, but the decorations in the entry have me feeling a little lost.

Making my way into the main bar area, I walk through the employee doors to the small server's station, looking for any of my friends. No one I'm looking for is there or in the office. My stomach grumbles and I give up looking.

Okay, new focus.

Following the delicious aroma of barbecued meat, I find the buffet table on the far left side of the large bar area. A few of the normal tables have been removed from the floor to make space for the new addition. Opposite the food is a microphone stand and a few chairs that are set up like there will be a live band. Reese didn't mention hiring anyone, and I just assumed she'd have a playlist or something.

I don't think about that further because my stomach grumbles again in an obscene way. I look around to see if anyone heard the stomach complaints. A few of the bar's normal servers are helping with the party, but they aren't close enough to me to have heard. I blow out a heavy sigh of relief and take in the bar's new decor for the event.

Bouquets of anemones are arranged in short, clear vases everywhere. A mixture of purple and white anemones are arranged with cobalt blue delphinium and tree fern wisps. *So beautiful!* Must be Cory's doing. There are some along the bartop, on the bar tables, and a few hang from the beams near the walls. Streamers of blue and purple are hung around the doorways and from the posts at each end of the bar. Around the edges of the buffet table are the same streamers and vases. More of the couple's polaroids hang in various places around the low-lit room.

My fingers fidget with my necklace as I look all around me. I'm in awe of the work Chloe has done for the bar outside of the florals. What was once the luxe man space of QB's is now an elegant event space to celebrate Reese and Cory's engagement. Chloe has always had an eye for this sort of thing. My old room at Daddy's always made me think of her.

And *him.*

Heaping potato salad onto a forest green paper plate that is already overflowing with food, I decide to just grab a second plate. Tender brisket, smoked sausage, and two kinds of chicken legs are piled next to the mac and cheese and grilled corn on the cob.

Chandie outdid herself!

Would having the baked sweet potato and potato salad be overdoing it? Eh, better to be safe rather than sorry, so I put the sweet potato half on my second plate, along with some buttered dinner rolls.

Do I regret missing both meals today?

Yes.

But am I happy that I have extra room to taste everything on this table?

Also, yes.

Walking from the buffet table, I spot Chloe arranging name cards near the main couple's table by the performing area. She looks beautiful in her long mermaid dress, which is the color of sapphires. Her sharp nude pumps peek out of a split that runs up the maxi-length dress to her knee. Chloe's long bob flutters in wide curls that swoop away from her face in a side part. A comb with little blue sparkling gems pulls back the hair on her right side behind her ear. "I wanna be you when I grow up, okay?"

Looking up from her task, she does a little jump with her arms tucked in before she wraps an arm around me and squeezes. "Cinnabon, you know there's only one Chloe Bridges." Gesturing to herself from head to toe, she sighs deeply, like the information just pains her to relay to me.

In her mind, it probably does.

The Chloe Bridges is both glam AF and the craftiest chick around. I bet she made all these decorations... with her hands.

I roll my eyes and give her a bump with my hip. I put my plates down on the table, saying, "You know what I mean, Clo."

Each of the cards she's placing has either a picture with Reese and a guest or Cory and a guest. I see the picture of Mack and Reese hugging on the little card Chloe places by his seat. I can feel my eyes starting to water.

I'm happy for Reese. So happy for them! But I don't want to see Mack and have to be okay. To pretend that hurting him doesn't still hurt me. I have always cared for Mack, and I have so much love in my heart for him.

But it wasn't enough.

Nothing was enough.

It's hard living in the same town as him. Our lives are so close to each other. I'd like to celebrate my friend without him though.

Clarity of just how uncomfortable tonight will be runs down my back in a shudder.

"You will find someone, Mel." Chloe starts rubbing my back in soothing circles. She moves a curl back into place before continuing. "Or maybe you will find peace in loving yourself. Reese will appreciate the support tonight but, baby, this…" She motions to the general area of my face with her hand. "The sad eyes need to go. You look stunning and I need you to put the Mel smile on and celebrate!"

The Mel smile.

Right.

I know she means well. She and Mack were friends long before I came into the picture. Hell, they all grew up together. At this moment, I can recognize my selfishness. Tonight is about Cory and Reese.

They shouldn't have to choose which of us gets to hang out with them. What Mack and I had, it's over. It's just awkward now. I'm an expert at figuring out which of the group outings he will be at or not. If Cory is there, Mack likely will be too. Subtle questions about the activities can help too. I don't know how often I've been "sick" or had a class "run long" in order to skip out on the events he is also attending. I don't have the answers Mack wants and I'd hate to have my friends pick up on what actually happened between us. I fiddle with my clutch bag for a beat before I give her a suspecting look.

"Don't give me that look! I'm not picking sides. You both needed to move on. You wanted the divorce. That is all I need to know. I'm not in the middle. Get lost in the ambiance I created for celebrating tonight. Please?" She presses her palms together in front of her face mock-pleading with me. Her bottom lip pokes out a bit, and I know what I have to do.

I reel back and push my hair over my shoulders. Rolling them back, I put my hands on my hips and draw my knees together so that one foot leans to the side. I changed my stance entirely to mimic my very best old Hollywood starlet. "My apologies, darling. Does this suit the ambiance better?"

I'm barely able to hold the pose before we both erupt into laughter.

When I first moved to town, I told Chloe about how my old dance instructor would make us all do this pose before our jazz ballet performances. It was ridiculous then, and it still makes me laugh to think how it did make me feel more confident. It at least helps me get rid of these nerves.

I hug my friend because she really has been there for me in so many ways. She squeezes me back before we both check if we smudged the other's makeup.

"As a matter of fact, I think that will—"

Reese cuts Chloe off by coming over to the two of us, placing her hands on our shoulders. Her face is unsmiling when she looks at my friend saying, "I take it that you haven't told her yet. You said you would tell her, Clo."

Chloe's eyes dart to me quickly before looking back to Reese. They have a silent conversation involving eye bulging and head nodding.

I step out of her hold and face my friends. "Well, can someone tell me? I don't care who." I check my phone and see that the party is only fifteen minutes from starting.

It's Chloe who finally looks at me saying, "Don't panic, okay?"

"You must know that telling someone not to panic, signals them to absolutely panic!" I'm flapping my hands out to the side of my face as if the fanning will cool down how hot it's getting in here.

"Good point. I'm gonna just rip it off like a bandaid!" Reese steps between Clo and me like she's shielding my friend from harm.

Chloe steps from behind Reese. "No. I will. Ty is playing for the event. He and his band will be the entertainment for tonight, and it is not a big deal."

"Oh."

Much worse than I thought.

Much, *much* worse than I thought.

Mack, I can expect. I know him. Tyson... I don't think I can handle. The last time I talked to him ended in... catastrophe.

"Yea, like she said. It's no big deal." Reese gives me an encouraging smile, arranging some curls around my face. "He's gonna play some songs, and that's it. No big deal."

"Oh." I go back to flapping at my face and breathing in and out slowly.

"We didn't want you to freak out. Mel, we know that breakup was hard. But... we are all adults... and we can be civilized. It's not a big deal anymore." Chloe says, but there's a roaring in my ears that's growing the longer I stand here.

Why does everyone keep saying it's no big deal—when it very clearly is!

"You didn't want me to—yeah, okay. I'm gonna just run to the bathroom real quick. Excuse me."

I hear my heels click on the wood floor faster and faster as I go to the bar restroom and push past the door.

How can I still be so upset?

I stare at my reflection. I look flustered under my makeup and my eyes are glassy.

I don't want to deal with any of this tonight.

The drama or the men.

This is for Cory and Reese, who are like family to me.

Shit.

I should have expected Mack would be here. He and Cory have become like best friends,

Of course, he would be there. No big deal at all.

It's been years.

Holding on to that sentiment as tightly as I can, I take ten deep breaths. I blot my face with a cool, damp paper towel, hoping the placebo will take effect. When I feel calm enough, I straighten my shoulders and exit the restroom.

I'm two steps down the hallway when the setting sun nearly blinds me as the side employee doors open.

I stop and hold my hand up to shield my eyes. Continuing to walk toward the main bar entrance again.

With equipment under both arms and the guitar strap I would recognize anywhere crossing his chest, Tyson shuffles into the building.

My feet are glued to the spot because I don't know what to do. The surprise on my face is mirrored in his.

No *big deal.*

CHAPTER 7

Melody

"I NEED TO—I HAVE... I'm gonna go." I say into the hallway before darting into the main bar area.

Ugh. Why?

It absolutely is a big deal! One hundred percent.

This man was on national television, not even three days ago. And now he's here.

"Feeling better?" Drea calls out to me. I'm still far enough away that she can't see how I'm more upset than they likely told her I was when I left. My life has come to the summation of running from one confrontation after the other. The night has not even started yet.

Both Reese and Chloe had that intervention prepared before I ran into Ty. Probably when Chloe had the idea to ask her brother to perform in the first place. They knew I would run or maybe not even show up if I had known both Tyson and Mack would be here. How could I not have picked up on something being off when she triple-checked that I would be here tonight? *Damn it to heck.*

I ran into Ty well before I was ready. Tonight will be very difficult. There is no avoiding that. Shaking my head slightly, I continue hurrying to the seat that has my name in beautiful calligraphy on the embossed card with the picture of Reese and I from high school.

"Hey D. I will, after I eat. I just think my blood sugar is low." I give her a hug and step back, pointing at her dress. "I see you didn't come to play." Drea looks stunning in a slinky grey camisole-style dress that hugs her curves perfectly. This dress, plus her brown waves down and styled, are a special addition since she is normally in yoga pants and a t-shirt, complete with a messy bun tied at the back of her head.

"Not at all! Just because they can't touch—doesn't mean they can't wish on it." She brushes some hair behind an ear with a wink.

I roll my eyes at her, "You are such a tease."

"I know," she smiles with a shrug. "I'm too busy for all that. Plus, they put me on damage control while you were in the bathroom... Freaking out!" She pokes my shoulder playfully, but we both know I will likely need it, the damage control that is. Drea, like Chloe and Reese, saw what Ty and I were in high school and what we are now. Apparently, I was nothing to Ty at either point. Easily disposable.

"I was not freaking out..." Lifting a shoulder, I add, "I wanted to go to the bathroom early. You know? So I didn't miss anything when the party started." Plopping gracelessly in the chair with the energy completely zapped from me all of a sudden.

I slide down the seat until the two plates I prepared are at the same level as my mouth. "Okay. Use the fork there and..." I point to the utensil closest to her and open my mouth wide. Gesturing in a sweeping motion toward my face, I say, "Shovel it in." I'm never one to forget my manners, so I add, "Please and thank you."

My friend chuckles at me. "It can't be that bad, Mel. You knew you would see them again at some point." I look up at her with a tight expression. Drea changes directions by offering, "Why don't I get us some pinot?"

I sit properly on the chair and agree to the wine. Grabbing the aforementioned fork, I stab macaroni from one of the two plates and shove it into my mouth angrily.

How dare he be here? Looking all good like that in his button-down shirt and tight Wranglers. His umber eyes were soft and full of hope and regret. Why should he have any hope when looking at me? Like I could forget how he hurt me and left like I didn't matter. Again! Like what we had meant nothing—again! I would never be able to forget and move past being treated like a used tissue. Even if he did look damn good.

"Here." I look over my shoulder to see Drea extending a very large glass of red wine to me with one hand. I gratefully take the glass and bring it to my lips without hesitation. It helps to have a friend who is also a bartender. She never gets my drink order wrong. I sip it even though I want to gulp it down.

"And here," she says, holding a smaller glass with some unknown clear liquid in her other hand toward me.

I raise an eyebrow at her. "What is that?"

She sits and slides the glass closer to me. "A lil Casa to smooth the edges over." She gives me a pointed look and then looks from me to the glass several times.

"Isn't it a little early in the night to be mixing alcohol? Wine and tequila do not go together"

"Says who?" She flicks her hair over her shoulder and says, "Wait, real quick! I need to get Quincy too. You think I'm gonna let you get lit alone?" I shake my head at my friend and laugh lightly.

She hurriedly returns from the bar with Quincy. "I'm joining this round! But the next one—is only on my tab. I'm not trying to get wild with y'all."

I jump up from my seat and give Q a big hug. Over the years, I saw him go from being a goofy teenager to a successful business owner and partner to Chloe. I'm so happy for them because it gives me hope that a love like that could be out there for me. They are like the big sister and brother I never had. Their happiness touches everyone in the group and I admire their stability so much. There is not a single person who would not want to be loved the way these two love each other.

Putting an arm up and over his shoulder before I ask, "Where's the lady in blue? We can't take this shot without her."

Q scratches the back of his neck and looks to the floor. "She's nagging Ty about something with the music, but she'll be back later."

Ty is Quincy's brother-in-law, I know they talk quite often. His modus operandi in dealing with the two of us has been to keep conversations about the other to a minimum. Well... to me, he barely says anything about Ty.

"What about Reese? This is her party. Sorry, her and Cory."

Quincy shrugs. I narrow my eyes at Q. He looks up from the ground, feeling the way my gaze has zeroed in on him. He is clearly trying to keep his head above water, avoiding talking about Ty but as it turns out, there is nothing I can talk about tonight that doesn't circle back to him.

Reese is the shot queen. If she is not passing them out, she is at the bar collecting a round to pass out. He shakes his head once. And I let it go because I figure she'll be around later to fulfill the duties of her reign as queen. Watching Q grab a shot glass off his tray, he hands one to Drea and then to me.

I wonder briefly where Tony is, but Drea cuts into my thoughts changing the subject again, "Let's do this quick so he can finish setting up behind the bar. People will be getting here soon."

"What should we drink to?" I look between the two of them as we all think about the perfect toast.

Quincy raises his glass and says, "To the family we find and cherish."

"Aww! I'll drink to that, you big softie!" Drea raises her glass. I lightly bump shoulders with the man, smiling, then raise my glass too.

We clink and knock back the first shot. I grimace and reach for a lime wedge on the tray. We sit at our table and Quincy gives us both a hug around the shoulders before he returns to the bar.

Drea chuckles behind her hand at me and I give her a look. "What?"

"Oh, nothing!" She says with her arm outstretched, handing me the other shot glass.

"I never committed to the whole two-shot business." I circle the remaining glasses with a finger, grimacing like the shots are icky. Because they are. "I'll just sip on wine until later."

Drea's lips quirk to the side before she says, "Yea? It does sound like a good time to be sober for the first time you, your ex-boyfriend, and your ex-husband are all at the same event together. You're right." She acts as if she will drink the liquor herself. I reach out to put a hand on her arm, halting the glass a few inches from her mouth.

"Ok, fine," I quip before taking the glass from her.

"Don't forget your lime!" Drea snickers again and I lick the back of my hand and make a point to pour salt onto it. I grab my lime and she shouts, "Wait! We need to drink to something. It's bad luck!"

Several moments pass before I suggest something. "To avoiding Mack and Ty all night?" I ask lifting my glass in the air though she is not raising hers.

She gives me another pointed look. "Girl, you can not avoid both of them all night. Besides, how are you gonna move on if you keep holding on to this guilt forever?"

"I'm not holding on to guilt." She doesn't look convinced in the slightest and I amend quietly between my teeth, "I'm not holding on to guilt over Ty."

"But you definitely are for Mack! Let that shit go, Mel. The relationship is over. You deserve to move on after making the best decision for you. He is not your concern anymore. It's literally been years at this point."

I nod my head because I know that I should. But I don't agree. "And I suppose you have a better toast then?"

"As a matter of fact, I do." She smiles like the Cheshire cat and I prepare myself for whatever crazy words are about to come out of her mouth.

"Oh, come on. Don't start with that, D."

"What? You don't even know what I'm going to say!" She pouts. Her bottom lip juts dramatically before it shifts to a smile and I look over my shoulder to what she's now smiling at.

Chloe walks toward us with Ty. He does a little wave to the table. Leaning to say something in his sister's ear, he gives her a squeeze on the arm before changing directions. Ty throws an arm up at Quincy and strolls over to the bar. She blows her husband a kiss that he pretends to catch before placing it on his cheek. Clo has a big grin on her face when she gets to the immaculately decorated table.

"Like I was saying, my toast is perfect."

Not missing a beat, Chloe asks, "What's the toast?"

Drea clears her throat exaggeratedly before saying, "To getting under someone new!" I had my glass raised not expecting that to come out of her mouth. She clinks the glass to mine and takes her shot. I stare at her with my jaw hanging slack.

"Drea! I'm not drinking to that." Lowering my voice to a hiss, I say, "Sex is not going to 'help me let that shit go.' I just need time."

"Bullshit, Mel! It's been years and you haven't even changed your Facebook status to single. Which you are, by the way! You're single and Facebook doesn't even know yet."

That was true. I've been... busy. "What does Facebook have to do with moving on? Who uses it anyway?" They don't look impressed. "No one on Facebook needs to be in my business," I grumble to them.

Chloe chimes in, "No, D is right. They don't have to know your business, but you leaving your status as 'it's complicated' makes it seem like you're still holding on to your marriage. How is Mack going to perceive that?"

I have had enough of this conversation. I've had enough of their devil's advocate roles. Nothing would change how Mack perceived anything. Kind of like saying nothing to all the people who want to know everything about my divorce has done ziltch to make his life any better. I can't change that or fix his reputation by putting my own neck on the line.

I put my smile in place and hold my glass up again. I'm the only one with a shot left. "To being single and alone." I lick the salt off my hand and throw the shot back, wincing into another lime wedge.

My friends look full of pity when I finally recover from the burn rushing down my throat. I feel the weight of their emotions like they are my own. It's not what tonight is about. I'm not going to let them make it about the sadness they feel for me. I don't want to be coddled. For one thing, I am processing. Three years of marriage is no insignificant amount of time. Moving on feels like I'm hurting myself, too.

They weren't there when I asked him for a divorce. Neither Chloe or Drea were there to witness my own heart torn in half. The pain in Mack's eyes has been my weakness. Always. How can I apologize to someone when I'm doing the right thing now? I couldn't, honestly. But the lies hurt me every time I say them in any form.

"I'm sorry that I'm ending our marriage."

"I apologize for giving up."

"This is what's best for me."

None of them are wholly true. Mack will only see his side. I thought that marrying him would somehow fix me. But maybe there is nothing to fix.

I start deliberately gathering food onto my fork before I look at my friends again. "Seriously, y'all. Being single is the best thing for me. I've never really been single. Maybe I'm better as a solo act? It's what I need." I stuff the food into my mouth, chewing before I add, "What I want." It's a little garbled by the food, but they get what I'm saying.

Drea and Chloe look at each other and I know I haven't convinced them. I'm not going to try anymore. I eat with purpose now because this food is amazing. My stomach might attack me if I keep teasing it with nourishment and then give it more alcohol.

Chloe rises from her seat, adjusting her outfit and hair. "Okay." She drags the word out and backs from the table like it's a crime scene. Throwing a thumb over her shoulder, she says, "I see people are arriving! I'm gonna grab Reese and greet everyone." Chloe's voice brightens and her expression changes to the loving and adoring party host everyone is familiar with.

Before she leaves, she turns back to me. Clo points to the smile on her face and pleads, "You say you're happy, so let's show it."

I give her a quick one and continue piling grilled foods into my body.

A fake smile is as good as it gets.

CHAPTER 8

Tyson, Then

"YOU WON'T BELIEVE HOW lucky I am!" I side-eye my friend and expect something very dumb to come out of his mouth.

"You're right. I probably won't." My tone is dry and my eyebrow lifted.

"Just say what it is, bro. Nobody wants to play twenty questions with you." My other friend, Quincy, has a big smile on his face. For the record, he would play twenty questions if Mack wanted.

It's my last year in this tiny town. It's my last year under William's thumb. He's been pressing me since... well since I was born really. I can't wait to leave AR. My senior year is only a week or so in and already it's dragging. There are parts I'll miss, sure. My boys are staying, so I think they count. I'll miss Clo, but I know she'll still be in my business wherever I end up.

Clo is one of the only reasons I can stand to live in that house with my dad and his new wife, Clo's mom. I guess she's not his new wife anymore. They have been together for almost four years at this point. I'm not trying to be disrespectful toward her. Truly, I'm working on that. I don't dislike Aaliyah. She's nice. Maybe too nice sometimes. She doesn't tell me to call her "mom" or pack me lunches with weird notes or something. I don't know. It's just awkward between us. She tries too hard.

She has so much to say in this open-debate between my dad and me on what I should be doing with my life. Nothing that explicitly sides with me though. But, I get it.

I'm gonna be the one to make that decision. I don't need any well-formed arguments for both sides, but thanks for nothing, Aaliyah. *Let's keep it cordial.* Or better yet, let Tyson make his own choices because he is going to be a legal adult in a couple of months. Music isn't a choice, nor is it an automatic dead end. Plenty of people make a living or make it work while doing what they love!

I'm getting irritated again. As I said, I'm working on it.

I must be silent and thinking for too long when Q asks, "You want to join us back in class? Did you hear him?" He throws his left thumb back toward my other smitten-looking best friend. "Man, Mack is already trying to get with the new girl. She was in Tomlinson's with him!" Quincy's eyebrows are pulling together as he shakes his head in disbelief, but the smile is still as wide as ever in his words. He probably couldn't stop if he was told to.

"So what? Mack is always trying to get with any girl that responds to him. That supposed to be news to me?" I smirk at Mack, who now has his hand pressed to his chest and an aghast look on his face. I side-eye him again, this time with my mouth pulled to one side. We all know that Mack has tried to get with every single girl in this town. Now that year four of high school has come around, there are no more who will even give him the time of day.

Last year, he started to see the effects of his hoein' around come into effect. The worst part about being in a small town is how fast the gossip travels. He's been single and hating it. He's not a bad guy necessarily... just generous with his affection, shall we say. I commend him for the effort, but it's too late now. He might get some play, but nobody claims this fool. It is an ongoing topic of conversation amongst the group. What can Q and I do if he messes his own love life up? That's too big a problem for our resources and experience.

"This girl doesn't know me though, Ty!" Mack tries to keep his excitement contained by whisper-yelling this through clenched teeth. His arms shaking with the intensity of his discovery. I must not respond quickly enough or something because he slams his hands down on the table emphasizing, "It's gonna be different with this one, Ty. Just watch. I'm telling you!"

"Please keep the noise to a minimum, Mr. Stewart! Don't make me regret letting you all choose your own seats." Ms. Clements was our social studies teacher and, now, our Government teacher. She had all three of us two years ago. Another small-town thing that was unfortunate for the dude who was always getting into trouble. And Mack knew trouble well.

"I'm sorry Miss." He smiles innocently at our teacher, who goes back to helping another group with the assignment.

I shake my head and chuckle at him. Keeping my voice low, I question, "Did you even talk to the girl?"

Mack rolls his eyes at me and is about to respond, but Q cuts him off saying, "Yea. She's in Chloe's class right now. He walked her to Richard's over in the Annex. Her name's Melody." He reads from his phone. "She said to protect her from Mack." Her contact is under "Clover" with green hearts and the clover emoji. More messages are popping up on his screen after he locks it so I know Clo is probably pulling together all the town gossip just as quickly as she's sending the information to Quincy.

She doesn't care about double-texting anyone. And she certainly isn't shy about sending Q ten texts in a row to share what she believes is necessary information. Quincy looks back down to his phone and starts softly chuckling. His laugh has very little sound, but you can tell from the way his body collapses into his fist. He puts his phone on my desk before laughing, so I read the last three texts.

> **Clover: This the girl that saw me climbing into the house last night!**

> **Clover: I don't think she'll rat tho**

> **Clover: Her dad works at Brenford with Will.**

Will is my dad. He told me that they finally found someone to replace the last guy on his team which would help out him and the company.

But, wait... She saw Clo last night. The realization comes to me quickly. I suck in a shocked breath that makes me start coughing. I drink some water and Mack pats me on the back to help me clear my throat. I shove him away because this fool always has jokes.

"You alright? What's up?" I can hear the laugh in Q's voice. I nod my head and pretend to work on the assignment in front of me. "Clover's so paranoid about getting caught. I tell her she don't have to do all that sneaking to chill. She could probably walk out y'all's front door with how heavy everyone in your house sleeps."

I say nothing more, choosing to force a weak smile as I nod my head. He knows I know that, but he thinks Chloe's daredevil stunts are cute. I'm scared she's gonna fall off the side of the roof one night, and no one will know until it's too late.

She doesn't know that I know she's been sneaking out. But, I made sure Quincy knew there is someone ready to mess him up if he thought about doggin' her. That someone is me. He won't tell Clo though. I think he worries she might not come if I knew she was going. I'm not a rat, as she put it, but I will make my opinion known about her wildin'. I never had any siblings before her mom and my dad got together.

Once I met Chloe, she stuck herself to me and was constantly in my business. I had no choice but to accept this annoying little sister. Admittedly, I'm not mad about it.

Mack takes my silence as an opportunity to correct Quincy. "She prefers Mel, actually." His smirk is back in place and he goes on telling us about what happened in first period with his new chemistry partner.

Neither of my friends knows that I saw Melody sitting on her roof last night. I was going to tell them about it, but I'm not sharing that information now. Mack looks like he's ready to propose. I know for certain that it was her, though. When I saw her, she looked so lost.

She sat perfectly still, staring up at the sky like there were answers written into those twinkling lights. Her legs were crossed underneath her and I couldn't believe that could be comfortable. But I sat on my couch strumming my guitar while the moonlight danced over her stationary body. I probably should have moved to another place in the living room or closed the blinds, but I was waiting for Chloe to ultimately do her epic dash back to the house. This was the best spot for that.

It was an hour that passed with her sitting there. My fingers had begun to tire before she had even moved an inch. Then I saw her turn abruptly and checked my watch. She was getting the same show that I did almost every night.

I knew I told Quincy to have her home by midnight. Glad to see he was as punctual as ever.

I don't care what they do. She makes her own decisions. That's my sister at the end of the day. I'm gonna look out for her regardless of who she's dating. I'll never tell Q that I actually approve of their relationship.

"So? What do you think?"

I blink a few times, running my hands through the twists on the top of my head. "About what, fool?"

"Mel? Am I lucky or what?"

I shake my head and give him a pointed look. "You just met her, Mack. You don't even know her."

Not that I knew her either, but he swipes a hand in my direction. "She said she would eat lunch with me. It's already serious." He sighs with a dreamy look in his eyes, definitely planning their wedding.

Quincy laughs at his assertion and I side-eye Mack once again.

I can't explain why I feel deeply upset by his comment, but I don't like it. The last thing that girl needs is Mack's bullshit. The general feeling of being upset follows me from class to class until lunch hour.

CHAPTER 9

Melody, Then

MACK LEFT FOR HIS class, so I hurried into mine and found a seat in the corner. I unfold the paper he gave me before he left. It's his chicken scratch again. He wrote his number down along with *See you at lunch*.

So cocky. He knew I'd say yes. And why wouldn't I? He and I could be friends. I didn't know anyone here, and I'm not going to isolate myself anymore. I miss having a normal conversation with someone. He seems nice enough.

Mr. Richard starts the lesson and I try to focus on the packet that he passed out. I'm highlighting and underlining with so much concentration that I barely feel the eyes on me. Just barely. The constant feeling of being watched and hearing the occasional snicker makes me feel like I'm back at Harrison again. I know that word travels fast in small towns. Will they already know about my dad, my mom... my last performance? How could they know? I start to feel self-conscious in a way that has my body stiffening as I spiral into a panic attack.

I make a deliberate effort to breathe in and out slowly. One minute. Two minutes...

After several breaths, I can feel my arms release from my sides as my shoulders start to lower. More oxygen and time always help. It's a miracle that no one can see or sense what just happened to me. Anxiety and depression have plagued me long before I left Harrison High School. A fresh start can be helpful, but not everything can improve with new scenery.

I shake my head and put my smile on. Be calm, Mel. *Relax.* Everything is fine if you say it is. Everything is fine, even though I feel so exposed right now. No one knows. I have been able to keep that from people and it will be the same here.

No one knows.

I wish I had worn my hair down instead of in this bun. At least, I would have had something to hide behind.

Class is almost over, and I'm going to be the first one out of this dusty building. I quietly start packing up my materials and quickly dash from the room and down the hall as soon as the bell rings. Once I get to the main building, I run to the one bathroom that I remember passing earlier and splash some cold water on my face. I stare into the mirror, grabbing a paper towel.

This is familiar, being in the bathroom.

No one is here between classes yet. It's quiet. I practice my breathing again. Shaking out my arms and legs, my backpack swishing with each motion from my body, the tension slowly dissolves. I feel more calm. Pulling my small makeup bag out to touch up, I smile to myself in the mirror until it looks believable. Someone comes in pushing me to leave, now that I feel better. I pull out my schedule and see that finding the rest of my classes will be easy in the main building of Alpenglow Ridge High School.

WALKING INTO THE CAFETERIA, I'm getting in the line for food when I spot Chloe again. Mack introduced me to his friends, who were also in Mr. Richard's class, when he showed me to the annex classroom. It was brief since he still needed to get to his class. That doesn't mean we're BFFs now or anything. I had recognized Chloe from the night before because she lives one house over from me. The newly built neighborhood featured houses that all looked pretty similar to the rest. Our two houses were identical but mirrored with a one-story house between our two-story ones. I saw her climbing into her window last night like a burglar. It was both impressive and bizarre. Not something I ever saw in Houston before.

She's walking into the huge room with Reese next to her. Chloe wears a navy blue fitted polo tucked into bootcut jeans and platform flip-flops. Her bob bounces happily in step as she talks animatedly to her friend. Reese has on a short pleated khaki skirt that stops mid-thigh with a white fitted polo tied to the side. It shows the tiniest sliver of skin as she walks. Her cowboy boots shine a little as she glides through the room of people. I can see all heads turning as they walk through the crowd and the caf starts to fill up. The moment Chloe spots me, I do my best to not appear like I've been gawking in the way that I clearly am. Another great time to have had my hair down. It's much easier to hide behind the mane.

I can't really hide behind anything and I'm next in line to pay for my food. I hear her voice not too far away now as I turn she says, "Hey, Cinnabon!" She has a smile on her face and gives me a little wave. I wave back with my smile from earlier still in place. I'm hoping it says *I'm chill...* Or maybe... *I wasn't watching you last night...It was bad timing.*

Despite my own assurances, I feel my face getting hot under her un-wavering attention as she strolls toward me. This girl does not seem to care that I'm going to melt right here from discomfiture. I enter my lunch number into the register and walk out of the line, following the girls to a table. Neither of them got anything. Chloe sits on the bench seat of the lunch table and Reese is sitting atop the table on her phone. Chloe is typing furiously on hers. I'm reminded how I haven't texted anyone or called anyone in months. I don't know if I even remember how at this point... I stand awkwardly a few feet away from the table. Worse come to worst, I can still walk away if this goes sideways. Sometimes mean girls don't look like mean girls. Chloe and Reese look so much like what mean girls would look like in any movie.

She motions more fervently towards their table at the spot next to her and I... what? Refuse? No way. I carry my things over, setting them down neatly. My movements are precise as I open my water bottle and pretend I'm not starting to think of all the things she could say.

Stop tensing up, Mel.

"I'm not being mean with the Cinnabon thing! Not at all! You look like the sweetest girl I've ever seen, and that bun is everything! Seemed like a good fit. Is it a drawstring or some braiding hair?"

"Umm... Neither. It's all my hair. It's so hot, I just want it off my neck in this heat." I chuff lightly and fan myself, the heat coming from my neck and chest and not from the hot weather outside.

Her mouth hangs open as she leans toward me and inspects my work. "Seriously? Your hair is thick AF, girl!" I run a hand over the hair piled on top of my head, checking that it's still there. It is, obviously.

"I never have time to do mine! Too busy, girl! It's the braids for me at this point!" Reese swings her blonde braids back and forth as she tosses the hair back behind her shoulders, emphasizing how they reach her hip bone.

"That's just because you don't know how to sit down." Chloe rolls her eyes playfully at her friend and turns back to me. "She is my second-best client after all. So, I can't complain." She holds her hands up as if weighing the two options.

"I blow dry mine and put it in a bun. Barely any sitting involved."

"When it works, it works!" Chloe snaps around my head in the shape of what I imagine is a picture frame, like she's getting the best shots. Reese agrees before scrolling on her phone again.

I smile at them both, feeling more comfortable. They are being nice to me and I don't know if it's because Mack introduced me to them or what. I'm grateful either way because this beats sitting at a table alone again.

The energy in the cafeteria changes when the main doors open. In walks Mack, holding two fast food bags, next to two other guys who are also holding bags. I don't know what is in this Colorado water, but all three of them are too damn fine for their own good. Tall and handsome, they look like the actors who would be cast to play the hot senior guys in the movie.

Chloe speaks, breaking my stare. "I didn't know what you'd want, so I told Q to get nuggets and fries. Is that cool?"

"Umm... Yea. That's... umm really cool, actually." I struggle to get the sentence out because I'm too busy taking in the tall guy walking next to Mack. He's smirking and it affects my lower belly in a way that has me blushing immediately. *What's he smirking about?* Is my mouth hanging open? I would not be surprised, but thankfully it's not. For probably not the last time today, I wish my hair was down so I could let it swallow me up.

With nothing to hide behind, I shamefully take in the details as quickly as I can. A few of his long twists flop over his forehead, with the rest of the twists tied back. His sides are shaved to a low fade. He's clean-shaven and... glowing? His skin is crazy smooth looking. I imagine what it would be like to lick that strong jawline. My eyes widen at the thought because... where did that come from?

"Drea's already out there," the other guy, Q, tells Chloe before kissing the side of her head. He trades her the food bags for her backpack and they walk through the rows of tables in the cafeteria toward the side door.

I don't know the last guy's name. He talks with Mack about something that I can't hear. They look over to me and he smirks while still nodding at Mack. Mack waves at me and I wave back. The other guy is not quite as tall as Q, but he has at least an inch or two on Mack. Catching my stare, he seems amused more than mortified that I'm openly ogling him. Strong shoulders are practically ripping through the shoulder seams of his t-shirt as Chloe drags him out the west door of the cafeteria when she catches up to them.

"That's Clo's brother, Tyson, everyone calls him Ty." Reese flips her hair over her shoulder as she climbs down from the table. "You gonna stay here or do you wanna come to the Lawn and eat with us?" I nod because if *he* is going, so am I. She giggles and rolls her eyes before she loops her arm through mine and we walk out to the place they call the Lawn.

CHAPTER 10

Tyson, Then

"Ty! C'mon! I'm starving!" Clo grabs my wrist and starts pulling me outside. "What took y'all so long? It's not like lunch lasts forever." Her complaining continues, but I've heard what I need to. Clo is happy to talk and talk with very little response from me. I haven't heard a word though. I'm thinking about *her* face.

Last night, Melody's long hair was softly blowing around her head and shoulders. It was dark enough that I couldn't see all the details of her delicate face. Round and heart-shaped lips that look pillow-soft catch my attention. High cheekbones and a pointed chin add to the fairy-like appeal of the small girl. With her hair pulled up like this, it's hard to miss the softness in her eyes, the dark lashes that fan around them. Those same eyes widened when I caught her checking me out from head to toe. I could feel each spot her eyes trailed over. When her eyes met mine, I could tell she was shocked to see me. Maybe relieved? The sadness still lingers around the corners like she might break down at any minute.

Her smile gives it all away. I know a genuine smile when I see one and hers is not. She could just be nervous about starting at a new school and being new to town... or that I caught her openly checking me out. After all,

I am a good-looking guy. What do I have to be uncomfortable about? I don't regret the smirk I gave her when she met my eyes.

It's probably because I saw her last night when she didn't know someone was watching. The honesty I had a glimpse of was not something she shares. That much is clear. But why is she trying to look happy when she clearly isn't?

It sucks to be the new kid. Somehow, I know it's not because of that. It's something more. I want to know and I don't even know why I want to know.

Chloe is still talking as we walk quickly to the area we call the Lawn. It's only a grassy knoll that's beside the school's flag poles. The winds are usually rippling through the flags, making it sound like we're a ship on the water. Some days, the ringing of the metal chains banging into the pole makes a subtle appearance and some days it's a constant tolling. I started eating out here last year because I prefer the accidental music of these flags and chains over the loud chattering of the cafeteria. Q and Mack started eating here slowly after that, saying it was weird to text me when I was on campus. And where Q goes, Clo goes... so then Reese and Drea started eating here too. And thus, it became a *we* thing instead of a *me* thing.

I lay out on the grass with my head on my backpack like a pillow next to Drea, who is reading a cookbook with pastel-colored cookies on the front. She barely greets me when I settle down next to her. I catch sight of Reese and Melody walking out of the caf toward us. Mack runs up to them, hugging Melody around the waist and spinning her. She's laughing while playfully smacking him on the shoulders to put her down. Irritation at the closeness she allows him to have, makes me sit up and onto my elbow as I watch them.

Reese makes her way to sit next to me and Clo. Quincy is not far behind her and he plops down next to Clo. He leans closer to the three of us saying, "That's her." He jerks his head in a movement in their direction that I know he thinks is discreet, but isn't. "How long before she figures it out?"

Clo scoffs and rolls her eyes at him. "Quincy, don't you know karma will get you for talking about people behind their backs? I'm a part of the collective you in this instance, so that means it'll come for me too." Q hugs her from behind, pulling her closer in between his legs. She turns her head around to kiss him before she drops her head onto his shoulder. "I mean it," she laughs.

We all watch Mack and Melody walk closer to where we're sitting. "I don't know..." Reese scrunches her nose up and peers out of one eye watching them approach like that makes her view any different. "They're kinda cute together, Q. Don't be a hater!" Chloe must have caught Reese up on what Mack's planning. A short, forced laugh comes out of my mouth, but my eyes are glued to Mack and Melody walking over as he tells her something in her ear that makes her giggle again. Then, Mack's arm drapes casually over Melody's shoulder as they walk.

Clo snatches the bags from my hand. "Let up, will you? Don't smush my burger!" She pulls the paper-wrapped sandwich out of the bag and lightly caresses it while she glares at me. I release my fist and start massaging my hands, trying to figure out why I'm finding it difficult to resist balling them into fists again. I'm not upset that Mack is talking to Melody.

I'm not upset that he's talking to her.

Touching her.

She's not upset. So, I'm not upset.

She is no one to me and I don't even know her.

She doesn't know me.

I need to calm down.

This sweet, but sad girl is not my problem.

It's definitely not my problem that Mack is probably the worst thing to happen to her. She's a person and just because I saw her first last night, doesn't mean that I call dibs on her or something. I can't help but feel like I saw something important and real.

I don't know why I can't let that go.

Melody sits near me and Mack sits by Quincy, digging in the bags for their food. "So you're the creeper from the window last night! Good to meet you." Quincy holds his hand out towards Melody. "I've heard so much about you already," he adds a wink after.

Melody cringes and she shrugs Mack's arm off her shoulder now to stutter out, "That was... I was ... Okay. Yea. Kind of creeping... but not intentionally. I——" Her voice is quiet and soft. Sweet and pleasant even in her panic. High pitched like little songbirds. I'm parched for more of it.

Q is fully laughing now and the other girls join in. I chuckle a bit to myself with everyone else. Clo glares at me. Cat's out of the bag sis, I know about you too. Melody seems too tense and a brittle smile crosses her face. She looks down at her hands, squeezing and releasing them.

"Shut up, Q! Sweetness, don't worry about those jerks." Mack grabs her hand and squeezes. Her eyes trail up her lap to where he's holding her hand. He leans his head down, trying to get her to meet his eyes. She looks up to him and he takes the other hand. That's too much touching for me. "Not a big deal. Q is an asshole! We all know Clo is a ninja. It's a joke." She relaxes a bit. I grind my teeth when Mack scoots closer to her, putting his arm back around her.

"It's actually hilarious!" Drea chimes in, "Chloe thinks she's really in one of those cheesy nineties romcoms. I keep telling her to be real with William so she doesn't have to do that." She lies on her back to continue reading her book.

Clo shoots her a glare before throwing a fry at her that bounces off the front cover as Drea blocks.

"Yea, Drea. I've said it too! Definitely jokes. If anything, I'm laughing at Clover's crazy ass!" Quincy bites the fry that Clo is about to put into her mouth and eats it before she can snatch it back.

"Hey! None of y'all have had to endure the birds and bees talk from Will Abrams." She shudders at the thought and continues, "And thank you Mack, I am a ninja... Maybe more like Simone Biles with how I vault into the window at night. The grace, the skill, the—"

"Accident waiting to happen." I clip out feeling irritated that Mack's hand is still around Melody's.

"Whatever, Tyson. This is talent." She throws a fry toward me and I easily dodge it.

"Gimme my bag," I gruff. Mack finally lets go of Melody to give me my bag and we all start eating.

The conversation flows as they start talking about Mack's party next month. He's the first of us to turn eighteen and he won't let anyone forget it. Chloe and Reese are talking about what they'll wear and who is going to DJ. Mack and Quincy argue about how much booze they can get their hands on.

I remain quiet, watching Melody. I can't help myself. She's eating, but not really saying much. That same fake smile from when Quincy put her on the spot or even earlier when we met eyes still sits there. Just as fake as it looked to begin with.

"Are you going, Melody?" Did I ask that out loud? I cough and try to act casual when Q cuts me a look, nudging me with his foot. It's questioning but I don't acknowledge it, instead looking back to Melody.

Clo makes a noise of annoyance, "Bro, I was in the middle of my sentence! But since you interrupted, are you going to take us?" Everyone looks toward me. Including Melody.

"Take you where?" I was not listening. At all.

"Denver! I wanna go to Cherry Creek and find something cute!" Chloe says.

"For what? Quincy ain't that special."

"Tyson, please act like you know me. I was cute before Quincy. And now I'm cute because of him." She squishes Q's face by the cheeks with one of her hands, making kissy faces at him and using her gross "couple" baby talk voice. "Besides, he and Mack are working! I can't drive and I want something new!" She looks back at me. "Wednesday?"

I roll my eyes at her. "Sure." Reese and Chloe high-five in the air then do some dance.

"You coming with, Mel?" Chloe looks at her and adds, "I promise my brother won't be too aggravating! We should all match! Yaaas! We should right, Drea?"

Drea gives a thumbs up from her book.

"You read my mind, Clo! I was gonna—" Reese starts to say more when the bell cuts her off.

Quincy holds up his hands mouthing *Sorry*.

"C'mon Sweetness, I can show you to your next class." It takes Melody a moment to agree but she does, allowing Mack to pull her to standing. He's already talking a mile a minute to her.

I clench my jaw at the sight of them walking away. Before the door closes, I catch her looking back at me.

I see you too, my Melody.

CHAPTER 11

Tyson

"It was no easy task getting this one to agree. So you know I had to announce to the world that she did!" Cory shares a self-deprecating laugh with us, raising a champagne glass. "Thank you all for being here. It really does mean the world to us." Cory leans his face closer to his fiancé. Reese leans into him, whispering into his ear. His face breaks into a grin before she leans away from him again. "We have one more announcement to add to this event. It only seemed right to let everyone know at once."

Reese takes the mic and winks at someone over to the right of me. Looking over to where she was looking, I see the familiar face. I knew that I would have to see him eventually. I hate that it's tonight. When I didn't see him after everyone sat to eat, I thought I was in the clear and he left for the night. *Nope.* Here he lopes over to the stage.

"My brother, my friend and soon to take on another role—Maxwell! Get up here!" He looks out of breath like he ran from his house to this bar when he must have only been gone a moment or two to get whatever it is in his hand from his truck. "Mack has something very important he was going to grab while all of you were enjoying Chandie's delicious catering." A murmur breaks out among the guests. "Thanks again, mom."

I look over to Melody, who sits with our friends. It's so strange to say that they are *our friends* when neither Melody nor I cross paths anymore. I chose to sit at another table to make things more comfortable for them. A role I've been taking on since I left Alpenglow Ridge. Melody sat there all tense shoveling food into her mouth while Mack talked with everyone else at the table. It feels so reminiscent of when we were in high school. I've left indents in my palm from the restraint I've shown in not going over there. She was always making herself smaller to accommodate him. From the beginning, I saw how they were and it seems like that never changed.

The table I'm at has place settings for Zeke and Rob, who are both out smoking in the back, and a couple of the Ranch hands and their partners. Like the leftovers table. I would be irritated if I gave a shit about being made a spectacle. Besides a few instances of talking about my guest role on *Regina Live!* this week, everyone in this town treats me the same as they did before the fame. Something I appreciate more and more these days. It is a strange thing to be thought of as a celebrity, but it is something I am grateful for and deeply annoyed by.

"Aye, you gonna ease up on the beer or what? Gonna cut your hand right open when it breaks," a familiar voice cuts into my thoughts. I turn from the stage and face the table. Taylor sits next to their girlfriend, Ash.

"Oh fuck off," I say, annoyed at the observation, but putting my beer down next to my empty plate.

"Still pining, I see."

"Still a cocky know it all, I see."

Taylor chuckles and pats Ash's hand before moving to the empty seat next to me. "It's not just cocky if it's the truth. How come you aren't at the table with Chloe?"

At their raised eyebrow, I know that Taylor already knows the answer to the question so I say nothing and swipe up my beer again.

"Oof. I guess I do know it all then."

"You know what? All you hands do is gossip. Only half of it is true," I say.

"Well, this must be the true half. You should be over there."

I grind my teeth, because they aren't wrong. I knew that but was ignoring that voice in my head because I made a choice and I stood behind it... For the most part.

"Do you want to say it or should I?" Reese asks Cory on the mic up front. He answers her, but I don't know what he says off the mic. "Okay, me then," Reese beams. "Cory and I... are expecting! We're fifteen weeks along, today!"

My eyes shoot to Melody. Her back is ramrod straight, with her large wine glass paused against her lips. Drea and Chloe don't notice as they stand and clap with the other party guests. The cheering and excitement ramp up when Cory rubs her belly with the biggest grin on his face.

I want to go to Melody. She is noticeably not celebrating with her friends right now. *Why?*

When Drea turns back to her, she finally stands and pastes on a smile, golf clapping against the stem of her wine glass. As soon as her friends turn back to the stage, she empties the wine glass in one long gulp.

"I know! Thank you everyone! We have had such a hard time keeping this a secret. We are going to be finding out the sex today with you all! Seems like a fair trade." She laughs and leans over to Cory. They look like such a happy couple and I can confirm that it is sickeningly sweet to be around the two of them. Cory is a good man. Not the man I ever thought Reese would end up with, but they're good together.

Chandie, Reese's mom, helps Danny, her dad, over to the front table now. Sammie and Jan, Cory's aunts, are not far behind them. Cory hugs them and returns to his fiancé's side as they all stand up at the front.

Mack takes the mic and Reese settles under Cory's arm as they wait for the news.

I wince when his voice comes over the speaker. He says a few things I don't catch as I watch Melody continue to pretend she's happy right now. I look back to the stage, he says, "Congratulations, sis. You and Cory are having..." he rips the envelope open and his eyes bug out before he throws his head back in raucous laughter.

"What is it? Mack!" Reese scrambles over to him and snatches the paper from his hands. I see her curse and she turns to Cory, "Oh my God!" Shoving the paper into his hands, he quickly reads the words.

"Twins! We're having two baby girls!" Cory yells out, not needing the mic at all. His three sons rush from their table and jump on their dad before they go hug Reese, talking to her stomach. It's all very sweet as camera flashes go off, capturing this moment for them forever.

It's an uproar as more friends and family join them on stage.

I turn back to see the spot where Melody once was, is empty. She's not by the couple.

She's gone.

CHAPTER 12

Tyson

"Occupied." Melody's high-pitched voice states from behind the bathroom door. It's even higher than I remember. Something is wrong.

I lean my forehead on the door. "I know." Holding my hat from tipping off my head, I wait for her response.

She curses and I hear some shuffling before she huffs, "Go away, Tyson." Like that's going to happen. "I'm coming in."

"No—" she starts, but I've already pushed through the door. She crosses her arms over her chest. "This is the women's room."

"I know and I don't care." I turn and lock the door behind me. Her eyes are red as she wipes under them. Her red nose, sniffling. Melody tries to walk away from me, but there is no way I'm letting her do that. I don't know what possessed me to come looking for her. I know even less about what I'm going to do to soothe this woman I have hurt more than once over the years.

"Please go." She whispers, turning away from me to get more tissue from the stall behind her.

"I can't." My boots carry me closer. I step in front of the stall she is walking toward, wiping a tear from her eyes, and she buckles. Falling into me like she knows I'll catch her.

And of course, I do.

I wrap my arms around her, letting her cry into my shirt until I feel the tears against my chest. Each prick of moisture claws at my heart underneath. Pressing my cheek to the top of her head, she relaxes into my hold. Me, the big bad wolf, who has conned his way into the little piggie's straw house. There is something very wrong with this scenario. It should not be me in here comforting her.

Nothing has changed. I'm still the only one who can see the sadness Melody hides. As before, it's me who is trying to make it even a little better for her.

I don't know why she's crying. Only thing I know for sure is that we aren't leaving this bathroom until I do.

Rubbing her back and humming to the music coming from the small bathroom speakers are all I can offer her in these moments. They're the only tools I have in my arsenal. They'll have to be enough for now.

When she finally speaks after a few minutes of this, I listen to her patiently. "How can he have joy, feel so light laughing about them having not one, but two babies? How can he still be so happy for them?"

"Why shouldn't he be? Don't you want him to be happy?" I don't want him to be. Anyone who has hurt Melody does not deserve happiness. *Especially me.* I don't get why him being happy now is upsetting to her.

"Yea... No. Yes."

Don't want to defend that jerk off, but I also don't want to keep talking in generalizations. It's been years since their divorce. I have no clue why they split. It seems that no one really does. I need some answers and I figure she's not likely to share them with me now. Gentling my voice as best I can, I ask her anyway. "Melody. What really happened?"

She shakes her head. "I don't want to talk about it."

"That's not an option anymore. I'm wiping away your tears in a bathroom at your best friend's engagement party turned gender reveal. Whatever it is has gotten too big to hide now, Melody. Let me see some of it."

She looks into my eyes. I try my best not to break my determination under her gaze. Her eyes are my weakness. They always have been. Expressive and deep, I could get lost for hours trying to see them change from sad to content to happy or any emotion in between. Being here for her now can't change the past. I know that. I can't stop the need to try and fix whatever is making her so upset right now anyway.

She's quiet for a moment. Squeezing her eyes closed, she rushes out two words that I never expected to hear from her. "We miscarried." Softer, she says, "I miscarried."

My body goes completely still and my thoughts blank. I could not have been prepared for that blow. How could I have guessed? How could I have known? I didn't know. "Fuck. Melody. I'm so fucking sorry." To hear that she had a baby with another man hurts so badly. Especially with a man who never deserved to have a family with her. Fuck, to know that she lost the baby is even more painful. "When?" Is all I can manage to croak out.

"The day I ended our marriage," she murmurs. Her gaze doesn't meet mine again. She fiddles with the buttons on my shirt, seeming lost in thought.

I gulp. Tears coming to my own eyes. She went through too much all at once. It's a lot for anyone to handle divorce or a miscarriage. But both? I didn't want to hear any of this conversation if it was going to be about Mack. I can't escape that piece of shit if I tried. I already defended him and now I'm in far too deep to leave her in this bathroom alone.

Not that I would. Not that I could. She needs someone and maybe now it can finally be me.

I grab some more tissues and hand them to her. "Did he know?" I ask.

She looks numb as she cleans up her face in the mirror where she stands in front of me. Whatever makeup she was wearing before is all but gone now. Melody is on autopilot, I've seen it before. She nods slowly. She wipes her nose, turning from my reflection in the mirror to face me head on. "How can I be a mother when I still feel her loss every day?"

"You would be an amazing mother. I know it."

Her delicate little heels clip along the tiles as she aggressively tosses her tissues into the trash can. "I miss Cressida. She would know what to do."

Cressida, her mom. I never knew her. She passed before Melody moved to AR. I wonder if I'm still the only person she has talked to about her. "Maybe she would." I chance a few steps toward her. She doesn't retreat, though she pulls out of her reverie to lock eyes with me again. Her posture softens when I touch her arm.

I don't deserve this vulnerability from her. I don't deserve it, but I'm going to soak it all up while I can. Despite the choices I've made, this woman in front of me will always be the missing piece of my soul. The one that's only made up of chords and lyrics. What's a song without melody?

"I don't know if I can do it. Any of it," she whispers.

"She would want you to live your life. To recover and heal."

"For what? To keep breaking? I don't have any more pieces to give. What if I never want that again?" She holds her face in her hands. "To go through that kind of loss again."

"Then you never want that again and you never have to go through that kind of loss again."

She fidgets with her fingers, whimpering, "You say that like it's just so easy, Tyson."

A small chuckle puffs from my lips when I hold her chin and meet her sad eyes. My undoing. "It is that easy, Melody. If you don't want to ever have children, that's your choice. If you never want to be married again, that's also your choice. Fuck anyone who says differently."

"Reese said the same thing. She never wanted kids and now she's helping raise three boys and is about to have two more babies. Andrea has Mireya. It's only a matter of time before Chloe has one. Then it'll just be me. The honorary godmother."

"And what's wrong with that? If it's what you want."

Melody looks at me and I feel the strings between us starting to pull taught. I may have thought I severed them, but they are still there. And with her next words, I know they are because they sound like the chord of the very first song written about her in my head. "Is that what you want?"

I hesitate because I could easily say I want whatever you want, which would be wholly inappropriate. I can't sit here in silence forever, I have to say something. Her glassy eyes search my face and I open my mouth to tell her the truth. "When I left for CU, I never thought I would have anyone if it wasn't you. Not seriously. I have never had plans to start a family of any kind if it was not with you, Melody."

She gasps, stepping away from me. "You can't say that to me, Tyson."

"Why not?"

She points a finger at me, straining to keep her voice down. "Because you left, twice, and you have never come back for me!"

There's a knot in my stomach. "You didn't want me to come back."

"I didn't want you to leave in the first place. Don't you remember?" She admits in a voice so small I almost miss it.

"Remember what?"

"That night." It could be any of the many nights we spent together. Any of the times that bound us tighter and tighter or the nights I fucked everything up. I know exactly what night she's talking about either way.

I grab my hat off my head to push the hair under it again, agitated by my own idiocy. Placing it back in the right spot, I question, "What about it?"

"When everything went down with Reese and Alex, I came to your apartment."

I cross my arms as I recognize how I've crossed from comfort to carper. "I remember," I say in the same softer voice I used before, trying my best not to escalate this conversation.

"That night, I wanted to come clean with you. I had been feeling... strongly about us. That whole week. They all were on my ass about how I couldn't do casual. So many questions about where I was spending all my time. I lied to them every time they asked! Chloe, Drea, and Reese. They saw through me anyway and I was scared because I felt—"

"You felt what, Melody?"

"It doesn't matter," she says voice monotone, dabbing some makeup onto her face in the mirror. "That night, I went to your house to confess my feelings like an idiot and you left me standing in the hallway with a box of my stuff."

I wince. *Fuck. She was going to confess her feelings for me and I was a goddamn idiot. God damn!*

Two knocks on the bathroom door make us both jump and turn to face it. "Ty, you in there?"

I sigh, recognizing Zeke's voice. "Yea, man. Give me a minute."

He sounds unsure, laughing. "Alright finish up. We need to start setting up, man."

He likely thinks I snuck off to fuck some girl in here. The truth is so far from that. "This is not over, Melody. We are going to talk about us."

"Don't bother." She spends a few moments in the mirror finishing whatever she was doing to touch up her makeup. Squeezing eyedrops in each eye, she leaves the bathroom and me behind.

God, I fucked up so big. I'm determined to make this right for us again.

CHAPTER 13

Melody

"WHERE HAVE YOU BEEN?" Chloe questions as I walk back to our table. Using the same bathroom excuse from earlier won't do since I've been gone for quite some time.

"I was just taking a call real quick. What did I miss?" I say as I sit in front of my sentimental little name card. I don't know exactly how long I was in the bathroom, but everyone has calmed down since I retreated. Guests have returned to their tables to have their own smaller conversations while the band sets up.

Reese, Drea, and Chloe are sitting close to each other, staring at Chloe's phone. It's been a long time, but I feel like the new girl in town all over again, somehow out of the loop and on the edge.

How could I be so dumb? Falling into his arms and telling him all those things I haven't even told my friends. These three women have always been there for me. I have no reason to keep secrets from them, but letting them in feels so much scarier than letting Tyson in. The weight of how many secrets I'm keeping could crush me if I let it. I have to get my shit together.

"Nothing much. I think the band is about to start playing," Drea says, looking up from Chloe's phone.

My eyes find Tyson adjusting the mic stand. His biceps bulge against the tight short sleeves of his shirt and I feel flushed all over.

Was I actually breaking down in those same arms only moments ago? You're an idiot, Melody. This man does not care about you. He left you more than once!

Learn this lesson already.

But... he listened and talked me down from the spiraling I would likely still be swirling in if he had not come in the bathroom. How did he even know to come looking for me?

Stop it, Mel.

I'm lost in warring thoughts until his eyes connect with mine and hold. He tips his hat down the slightest bit and I turn from him back to the table. Ignoring him would be much easier if he weren't here. Next time, I'm asking for a comprehensive list of exactly who is invited to these events.

"... think we have that day off," Drea is saying.

"So... you're free then?" Chloe asks.

It's quiet at the table as everyone looks at me. What are they talking about? "Huh?" I ask.

"Bon, are you free Thursday?" Chloe says slowly while typing something into her phone.

"Oh, um yea. For what?"

Chloe raises an eyebrow, putting her phone back into her little purse. "Dress shopping... I made the reservation. Their website is so easy."

Reese rubs my arm, "Mel, I'd love your opinion. Your gown was so beautiful and you're always wearing these cute little dresses." She makes a point of holding out the hem of my skirt and letting it flutter back down to my thighs. "This really should be a team effort."

Chloe bumps my shoulder, adding, "It's ok if you're not comfortable with..."

"No, no it's fine. I can come." I don't know why they treat me like this. It's not like I was heartbroken about my marriage. I am sad, but not because of the reasons they think. "A trip to look at wedding dresses with my girls will be fun." I top it with a sugary sweet smile.

Reese does a little clap in her white bandage dress that already could be an amazing wedding dress. "Great! It's settled. Let's meet at Mason, then we'll all go in the Expedition."

My focus strays back to the performance area, where the band is beginning to make some noise. Ty chats idly with Zeke and Robert, who I recognize from the nights I've seen him play live. His dark shirt shows no sign of my tears, but I secretly hope they stain his soul as the pain I carry does for me. The pick he holds between his teeth bobs as he plucks a few strings and people mill about in the bar. He looks so at home and... right up there. This is nothing like the large stages he is probably used to, but that doesn't change the fact. He was made for this. Even more reason why I should be more embarrassed by crying on him. Ugh.

I break my focus from the band, knowing that I've missed the most important detail that had to have been shared. "When did you set a date?"

The bride-to-be looks around the table and I feel self-conscious. I knew I missed this part of the conversation. "As soon as we found out we're having a baby. Whoops, babies! I need to get this done before all that baby weight catches up to me!"

"So..."

"September 12!" She exclaims. Drawing the date with her finger in the air like she's signing on paper. Her eyes go all dreamy.

A pang of jealousy hits me before I realize how soon that date is. "September? That's in three months!"

"I know! September is the perfect Colorado weather." I don't get a chance to respond before Reese hops from her chair to go hug someone walking over to the table. "Ahh! Tony! You're here!"

"I know. Sorry, I'm late." He hands her a bouquet of flowers that she buries her face in. The woman is never without them now that she and Cory are together. If someone were to paint a portrait of her, it would be a still of her mid-sniff into an arrangement of them.

I could see my mother loving Reese. Being inspired by her and spending hours creating this image. I feel the sting and moisture in my eyes while everyone is still paying attention to the exchange happening between

Reese and Tony. Taking a deep breath, I mold my face into something more pleasant as I sip from my second extra-large glass of wine. "Congratulations you two! Or should I say you four?" He says while rubbing her belly.

"How did you know?" Reese beams, allowing him to hold his hand to her middle. There isn't a bump or anything noticeable about the life growing inside her. I remember my small bump and how hurt I was when it was gone. I hope I can make it through this night without running to the bathroom to break down again.

"Chandie already shared on Facebook. Look at this picture," Tony shows his phone to the table of Reese with her mouth wide open. Everyone laughs and makes their comments on the picture and I feel like I'm slowly falling into a pit I can't get out of.

Reese swats at Tony's arm playfully, laughing with everyone else. "Ooo! Click on that one! We look so good there. Cory, come look." Cory says something to Zeke and Ty before coming over to the table to join his wife-to-be.

He joins in on the laughter, talking animatedly with the group. I'm experiencing this scene from outside my body. Desperately trying not to ruin this special moment. Desperately trying to hold the tears back and keep a believable smile on my face.

I'm fighting between finishing this glass or finding an excuse to leave when my ex-husband approaches the table and Tony claps his back. "Mack, man, take me to the food. I'm fucking starving." I let out a breath of relief that Tony has saved me unknowingly.

"When aren't you?" Drea calls out after them. He gives her a narrowed look and she huffs. "Don't touch the cake. It's for the couple first." He doesn't give her a second look as he walks over to the buffet table to get some food. Drea and Chloe talk with Reese and Cory about the dress shopping plans and I don't know what else. For another moment, I can imagine that I'm not even there. There is the buzz of conversation as people come and go from the table to congratulate the couple and make small talk. It's all so pleasant and happy. But I have no way to move from my seat or join them.

My Mel smile has never failed me before. It never has. Tonight, I can't pull it together. I can't stop thinking about how much time I've lost with the choices I had to make. And I can't stop seeing my mother's happy face fading into the sallow, hollow form before I lost her forever. I'm triggered even now by the smallest things. I can't even be happy for my friends. Everything in my mind is telling me that I should be smiling because I am happy for them. *Nothing is working.*

I can only see and feel what I'm missing. The mess that I caused... and I'm here trying my best not to cry over it.

Maybe I shouldn't have drank at all. That can't be helping me right now, I think as I take another shallow sip from my glass.

Ty's voice filters into the room. "Let's get this night started. I know you all are starting to get sleepy with all the good food Chandie made for us. How about one of my favorites to kick us off?" A few people hoot in the crowd when the starting chords of *Wagon Wheel* float from the speakers. Cory dances my friend over to the cleared area and it's not long before more people join them. I do love this song, but I'm not going on that dance floor. I take my phone out of my purse instead, choosing to look through old emails.

"Hey, mama, rock me..." Tyson's deep voice flows around me from the speakers. I meet his eyes and there's a charge I feel in my chest from his gaze. I scroll some more on my phone, pointedly breaking our eye contact. If I leave now, no one would notice. If I—

There's a hand on my shoulder and I look up to see my ex-husband tentatively smiling down at me. Mack looks good tonight. His baby blue button-down and mid-wash jeans complement the permanent tan he has from working out on the Ranch all week.

"Wanna dance?"

I should say no, but I don't have a reason to. Mack was always good like that. He never let me feel left out. Always tried to include me. Even now when he shouldn't care at all. What's one dance?

We dance to the song in silence. For a moment I can forget about what was bogging me down before. The music changes to something slower and

I allow Mack to put his hands on my waist. I'm startled at first, but there is nothing to be alarmed by. He has seen me at my best and my worst. It's a dance. It's not like I'm going home with him. I wrap my arms around his shoulders and we sway to the music for a while before Mack opens his mouth.

"So what did y'all talk about?" How did I not see this coming?

"Who?" I ask, playing coy.

His sparkling blue eyes look down at me. He holds my waist firmly, knowing I'm a flight risk with his line of questioning. Maybe I *could* still slink off. "You know who. I saw him follow you into the bathroom."

I don't owe him any explanations. I certainly don't like that he intends to have this conversation here, where everyone can see us. I feel the not-so-subtle glances, we're getting. "Who said we were talking at all?"

"I know you, Melody."

I flinch. "Maybe once, you did. I could have been doing anything in that bathroom."

His lips press into a thin line. We dance around a little more. His jaw ticks a few times as he thinks about what I've said. I don't know why I am antagonizing him. He doesn't need an excuse to get worked up. "Is that what you were doing?"

"God, no, Mack. We were just talking." I look around us and try to maneuver us closer to the bar.

He shocks me again with his next question. "But, you have right?"

"Where is this coming from? Don't do this here." He knows Tyson and I were together before I married him. He wants to know what happened after our divorce. With how he's acting, I'm reminded of all the reasons I shouldn't be dancing with him.

"Should I not have a right to know?" When Chloe and Drea talked about giving him the wrong idea about things, I should absolutely have counted agreeing to this dance as doing exactly that.

"No."

"Fine." He says, but I see his jaw ticking again. We dance a little longer because I love this song and dancing of any sort is infinitely better than sulking at the table alone. At least, if I'm dancing, no one will know what my brain is fighting through right now. The words I live by.

"Just tell me one thing." Deliberating for a moment while he bites his bottom lip, "What's the real reason you left me?"

I purse my lips, trying to find the best way to respond without hurting him further or allowing this scene to escalate. "We wanted different things." Generic, but honest.

"No, we didn't. I wanted whatever you wanted."

I shake my head. "No."

His head tilts and he holds onto me a little tighter as we sway. "No?"

"You settled for whatever I wanted. There's a difference, Mack."

His cheeks redden and his brows pinch. "There is no difference. I would have given you anything. I tried to give you everything."

I sigh under the weight he has renewed on my shoulders. "And it was killing you. Killing us."

"That's not true, Melody." We stop moving and I regret agreeing to this dance in the first place.

Note to self, avoiding Mack is always the better of two options.

"I don't want to argue about this anymore. Mack, it's very simple. We're divorced. You signed the papers. You could be happy if you acknowledge that this is over. You can love someone else, someone new."

"But I love you." I can feel the energy around us shift and pull him to the bar top. No one is over here because all our friends and family members are enjoying the night with each other. Here I am, trying to be someone I'm not to make him feel better.

Again.

I don't know if I can apologize again. I won't. "You love the shell of me."

He points a thumb over his shoulder toward the band, saying, "And what? Fucking Tyson gets to love the inside."

Yes. No.

"Tyson is not relevant." I lower my tone, hoping that Mack will follow my lead and keep his down as well.

"Isn't he though? I knew it was him all along. I can't compete with Country's favorite sad boy." He crosses his arms. My back is pressed against the bar top. I can't see around his tall frame to the man in question. Something I'm certain Mack is doing on purpose. It confuses and frustrates me that I feel like I'm missing one of my lifelines because of this.

I cross my own arms, rolling my shoulders back. "Mack, it's not a competition."

"You're right. It's not. He won before I even knew the rules of the game." Turning from me, he makes a point to give Tyson the bird and walks away. Moving through the crowd, I see his head duck out of the bar room doors.

I stand there while everyone else is with their partners enjoying Tyson's song or seeing Mack embarrass me by leaving in a huff.

This time when I grab my purse from the table, I don't hesitate by the front door when I walk to my car and drive home.

CHAPTER 14

Melody, Then

I'M WAITING WITH REESE, Drea, and Chloe by Ty's old red truck in the student lot. I look at my new friends as they lean on the bumper, chatting about what outfit we should get. I've been added to the group text between them and learned far more about everyone's business than I probably wanted to. Besides that, we had spent the last couple of weeks going back and forth on the party ensemble. The trip to the mall got pushed back as a consequence.

"I think we should do neon, but sexy, not raver." Chloe says.

Reese pushes off of the bumper, waving me over to where she stands by the back passenger door. "There's nothing *sexy* about looking like a highlighter in a dark barn, Clo." She drags out the word sexy while she shimmies a bodycon T-shirt dress on under her uniform.

I hold the back passenger door while she changes, so no one can see her as other students meandered to their cars. "A barn?" My eyes wide as saucers. "Mack's party's gonna be in a barn?"

"Well, where did you think it was going to be at?" Chloe asks. "Reese's parents are gonna be out of town with the horses and it's way better to have the party there instead of at any of our houses."

I stare at her. I did not put those thoughts together. I don't know why I thought it would be some party hall or something. She types something quickly into her phone. "Q and Mack are off at eight. Do you think we'll be done by seven so I can be back in time?"

We agree because it's only three, that leaves us plenty of time to look around.

Ty strolls over to the truck with his backpack slung over one shoulder and his guitar over the other. The backpack looks pretty empty in comparison to mine, hanging there limply. I wonder where all his books are.

He steps from the shadow of the school building and the sun catches him in a way that makes it look like he's glowing. Not just the mesmerizing hydration of his skin, but his everything. His eyes glint in a way that makes them shimmer in the light. His hair seems to glow as well. I've never even liked guys with long hair, but imagining Ty without his hair is upsetting. I know he would still be beautiful in a way that is unfair to all women who can't have him, like myself. I wonder how his hair would feel if I ran my fingers through it.

The small silver hoop in his right ear catches my attention as he turns his head to wave at someone across the parking lot. I get the full view of the strong column of his neck and my knees feel a bit wobbly. How easy it would be to place a kiss right where his neck meets his shoulder and up the jawline I've been fantasizing about. *A fantasy is all it can be.*

I feel the moment he notices me. My heart begins to race and my cheeks heat as he walks over. Long legs moving steadily towards me. His smirk is slow but as amused as usual. I grip onto the door for support and he tracks the movement with his eyes. The knees I mentioned before are still very unsteady. My face gets even hotter. We meet eyes and there is a heat there for... Me? His focus is definitely on me. I need to look away before I actually combust under his attention.

Are you going Melody?

His words weren't romantic or even significant. They slip and slide through my mind like silk either way. Smoothing over the jagged edges of my thoughts. Why would he care if I went? I haven't known him long. I get the feeling that he doesn't usually care about Chloe's friends at all.

"Oh good! I thought we were gonna have to send a search party." Chloe opens the door, throwing her backpack to the floor of the passenger seat. "Y'all get in!" She leans across the cabin calling to Reese. "You too! You could have changed at the mall." I finally break eye contact with Ty and shake my head as he loads up the guitar into his truck. He gets in, turning it on, tossing his backpack carelessly in the backseat.

"I didn't want to be in that uniform any longer than I had to. What if someone saw me?" Reese shudders like a spider had crawled down her back and sticks her tongue out at Clo. She shoves Ty's backpack to the floor with the back of her hand like it's dirty. "I have a reputation to uphold, you know?"

"Yea, we know," Drea says with an eye roll, cookbook already open.

With that, Ty peels out of the parking lot toward the highway.

After two stores in the mall, we can tell that we do not all have the same style making this matching situation more daunting than we thought it would be. Reese wants something way too revealing for what I'm comfortable with. Chloe's style is bold, but not quite right for me. Drea wants something that, the other two agree, is too casual for a birthday party of this caliber.

"Mack is going to invite the entire football team and apparently Josh and Allen are both going to be there." Reese explains when we leave the food court. "It's our first senior party and as four of the only juniors present, it's important that we all look good-good!"

We settle on going to a big department store and looking for what we all want and abandon this matching outfit idea altogether.

"Okay. Everyone happy?" Chloe asks the three of us. Drea starts to open her mouth. "Drea excluded because you're getting this fit!" We all agree with her about the slinky crop top and skirt Drea tried on. She adds, "Good, I'm ready to go see my man!"

We change into our own clothes and check out before heading to the other side of the mall where Ty parked. The whole time we were looking around the mall, Ty was missing in action and we didn't really see him again.

I didn't expect him to tag along, but I wanted to see him. Even if I probably shouldn't.

I've been sneaking glances at him during lunch or burning hot whenever he would include me in the conversation or take my side in our lunchtime banter. If he caught me looking at him when he looked at me, I tried my best not to get all flustered and weird, but I could not help it. His gaze was unnerving and the way he says my full name like it's precious to him is very distracting. He's just being nice and there's only us on the Lawn at lunch. To me, it mattered.

Mack wants to pick me up for the party this weekend, but I don't want to give him the wrong idea. I only want to be friends. Buddies. Homies. Pals. Does it matter that I don't want to date him because of my silly little crush on Ty?

No?

No.

It has nothing to do with that.

Don't give me that look! Ty is beautiful. Every time I've seen him, it makes my mouth go dry and my cheeks burn. That smirk. I'm happy to stay quiet instead of saying something weird and utterly embarrassing. I've been nodding at lunch and oftentimes laughing at the silliness that both Mack and Quincy get into.

It's been so long since I had someone who didn't wince when they saw me or get that sad look in their eyes. Chloe is not like any friend I've had before. She tells me exactly what's on her mind. I feel close to her. Close to Reese and Drea too. There is no fakeness. The honesty is refreshing and I'm feeling happy. So happy to have them. It's almost like my luck has really turned around. They are all so close. It's hard not to feel like I'm a part of this small group. They're like family. The last thing I want is to ruin that by making my feelings known about her hot as fuck brother.

"Look at Casanova over there. I swear I don't get why he won't go for me!" Reese plays with the end of her ponytail, blonde braids now piled up high on her head. I follow her gaze to a man leaning over a guitar on the back of

Ty's truck. I will have to come back to her comment another time. I squint at the figure that's still too far to make out.

That's not just a man. It's Ty.

Ty is playing the guitar while perched on the bed of his F150 with one foot resting on the bumper. The closer we get, the louder the song comes to me. He plays some sweet tune that draws me closer in a way that I can't explain. His forearms are flexing with the effort his fingers take to produce the music that lures me closer. His eyebrows pull together in concentration and his twists hang loose around his face. His tank top barely covers the strong shoulders that have me biting my lip.

Note to self, do not objectify this man!

I swipe away the sweat that's about to drip down my forehead. It's six-thirty and the heat has not let up even a little bit. Or it could be because Chloe's brother is so hot. I can't help it. I don't want to be that girl who goes for her friend's brother. I need companionship more. But he's playing the guitar and it's good. Really good. If circumstances were different, I might work up the courage to tell him as much right now.

There is simply no comparison between the heat I feel for Tyson Abrams with anything else I've felt before. This is something wholly different. *New.* I wipe my forehead again and behind my neck as casually as I can manage.

I don't want to start any drama. I don't want to be alone again. I can't risk it.

Despite knowing that, I'm still moving toward him. I'm moving much more quickly than the girls are as they talk to each other about the weekend. Once I walk from between the last row of cars into the lane, he looks up from his ministrations. Our eyes lock as he continues to play slower and somehow more sweetly.

"That a talent of yours?" Ty smirks at me with a playful glint in his eyes. The corners crinkle the smallest bit.

Can we say swoon? All together, now... *Swoon!*

"Umm... Talent?" The words come out breathy and too soft.

"Appearing when I play your song." He watches me closely as I wipe my forehead again.

"M-My song?" I chuckle nervously with my eyes going wide. Placing my hand on my chest, I whisper, "I've never heard this song before."

He changes the key slightly, "Funny because I can't stop playing it."

Little flutters gather in my middle at his response. "Is this Country?"

He drops his eyes and stops playing altogether. "What's wrong with Country?" I did not expect the defensiveness, but it is very present in the line of his shoulders and the way he holds his jaw.

"Nothing! I love it. I grew up listening to it. It was my mom's favorite, so she would have it playing whenever she was working on something new. From Texas, remember? Kinda couldn't escape it because it's everywhere... Plays in the restaurants, elevators, and lobbies of most places." I rush out. "You like it too, I guess..." *Mel, please, for the love of God, stop talking.*

His smirk is back as he nods, "Everyone around here gives me shit for it."

"Aren't your best friends like actual cowboys?"

He considers me. "Yea... but I don't look like the guys playing on the radio."

"Who cares about that? You sound good and I don't actually think this is you trying."

"Like I said, this is a song I can't get out of my head."

"It's beautiful, what's—"

"I was calling your name, Mel! You didn't hear me?" Chloe catches up to us, fully sweating as she balances all her bags and the food she got for Q. "I forgot his stupid gyros, so I had to walk all the way back to get them."

The moment is broken. And thank goodness I'm not the only one sweating out here. Drea and Reese both look sweaty from the walk with all their purchases gripped between their arms and dangling from their hands too.

She throws some of the bags into the bed. "Ty can you roll the cover down? No way all this stuff is gonna fit into the cab with us!" She looks to Reese who nods her head in agreement. "Mel, how did you come out of the mall with just two bags?" She looks at me like I cracked some code.

My first bag held the dress I decided on and the other held cowboy boots. Chloe had helped me pick them before we tried anything on. Handing a pair to me from the display outside the second store we passed, Chloe said, "You're in AR now. We do way too much out in the fields for you to be ankle-deep in the mud with those flats on." I bought the brown boots with pink top stitching traveling all around the toe and calf. They were pretty cute.

Though I shouldn't, I hoped that Tyson would like the outfit I picked for the party.

CHAPTER 15

Melody, Then

AFTER THE BAGS WERE loaded up into the bed, Ty drove us home. It was dark enough that I could only make out the crude outlines of Chloe and Ty's faces from the dashboard lights. They were real family. I don't have any siblings, but I would not believe they were step-siblings with how they acted around each other. Ty may always have something smart to say, but I see he cares for Clo like they were blood relatives.

"—lucky you're my best client. I won't hear it! I'll be fine and you're gonna be okay too." Her best client?

"When I have to drag you into the house because you're paralyzed, then you'll regret not listening to *your best client.*" His voice was low and matter-of-fact.

"Your best client?" I asked because I was still stuck there. I look to Reese, but her face is plastered to her phone as she texted back and forth with someone.

"You think these twists were done by this man's hands? Look at these parts. The moisture alone should have tipped you off. Look at the fade!" She flips his hair over to expose the side of his head, running her hand roughly over the cut. "That's my work." She pokes herself in the chest with pride and enthusiasm. Ty tries to duck his head out of her way as she continues her dramatics.

"His hair is immaculate." I am grateful for the darkness in the car as my face burns. Did I just say that out loud? Why me? Body, you're supposed to work with me. Why don't you ever work with me? "I–I mean, your work is immaculate, Chloe. I agree... With the parts and stuff. Yep. Very good work." I try to recover, but my stammering is making my embarrassment so obvious.

Okay. New Plan.

Open the car door and let me just roll out onto the highway.

Anything to not be here right now.

I look to Reese, who has stopped texting and is trying to stifle a giggle. I give her a pleading look like, *HELP ME!* She shakes her head, putting her hands up in front of her towards me before going back to her text.

Chloe looks at me and then at Tyson. The car is quiet except for the low music on the radio. Tyson looks at me in the rearview mirror. God, I hope he can't see how flustered I am. It's irrational because his hair is definitely the best hair I've ever seen on a guy in real life. Objectively speaking, he has great hair. Why am I so hot under his gaze in the rearview mirror? I chose to sit behind him because I wanted an easy way to look at him. But I hadn't thought about how close we were in the cab of his truck. If I wanted I could touch it and find out for myself about the moisture.

Of his hair! Of. Course.

Brain... and little lady downstairs, please leave me alone now.

"Got the booze!" Reese yells out waving her phone in the air as she dances in her seat. She leans over to bump my shoulder and I could swear that was a wink. *Thank you, Reese!* She does the little jig and then leans through the front seat to turn up whatever was playing before Chloe turns the music down and twists around the seat to look at us.

"I wanna hear how thankful Mack's gonna be that you saved his ass for this party." Chloe looks smug like she knew the guys weren't gonna be able to come through for them. Reese goes back to tapping on her phone before dialing.

"It's your favorite birthday boy speaking." Mack's voice fills the cab from Reese's speakerphone. Her face is lit up as she holds the phone close to her mouth.

"You're not my favorite, but I'm about to be yours." She singsongs into the phone like she's his fairy godmother.

"Say you convinced Mel to get one of those black things too?" Mack's grin is easy to hear over the phone.

A choked sound comes from Ty and Chloe looks to her brother, who is now studiously looking over the GPS on his truck's dashboard, like it isn't a straight drive down the highway at this point to Alpenglow Ridge.

Chloe gives his shoulder a shove anyway. "Pig! Don't follow my friends on Snapchat! It's weird." Ty looks back to the road like he hasn't heard her. Wanting support in her claims no doubt, Clo turns to the backseat. She's waiting for my response with one eyebrow raised. I sit there trying to think through what that response from Ty was about.

"What?" Mack continues. "I have Snapchat too. Josh told me to check that video of Reese twerking in the fitting room before we finished mucking." Mucking the stalls, he means. I learned that means exactly what it sounds like. Both, Mack and Quincy work as ranch hands on Mason Ranch to earn some money.

"Don't act like you didn't enjoy, Maxwell." Reese laughs the words.

"Definitely not. Don't change the subject! You're playing with my heart now. Did she get one too, Riesling?" The last word held the plea of a desperate teenage boy. I almost felt bad for him. Almost.

Reese had come out of the dressing room earlier saying, "Tadow!" She bent at the waist, grabbing her ankles and twerking in the full mirror on the back wall with her tongue hanging out. She held her phone facing the mirror between her legs. We weren't in the frame with how she held the camera in the three-panel mirror. Running her hands up her legs to her waist and then chest, still dancing. Her full-length body suit was solid black with cutouts all along the side of her body. Each connecting piece has a small black bow like it was holding the sides of her one piece together. The neckline dips dangerously low in the front and back. She is much curvier than me and that outfit highlights the fact extremely well. She could have any guy or girl she wanted, and she knows it. Her confidence radiates from her like an aura.

"Umm... Reese? How are you gonna wear any undies with that?" I asked, poking one of the openings on her side.

She shrugged a shoulder and said, "Who says I plan on wearing any?" Apparently not her. My cheeks got hot. I imagine what it would be like to go pantyless anywhere. I'm not that sexy. I think that's some skillset you earn, like a medal or something. I have not passed whatever test is required for it.

"Who is Riesling?" I say to Drea, sitting on the other side of me.

"Mel? You're still with them!" He chuckles low and then a muffled curse. "I was just playing about the..." I can hear laughter from the background before Mack coughs and comes back onto the line. "How was the mall, Sweetness? Text me back." Another raised eyebrow from Chloe. I don't know if it can go any higher at this point.

"I'm Riesling. It's my government name... though everyone knows I go by Reese. *Maxwell*, you're getting off-topic. I called for a reason." She flicks her hair over her shoulder, nearly whacking me in the face with it. This girl takes up so much space between her personality and hair choreography.

"Yeah, what's up?"

"Your favorite person, *Reese*..." she enunciates her name slowly, "...has the booze for your party." She sticks her tongue out and continues dancing in her seat to music that isn't playing.

"No way! A godsend! My savior! Thank you! Okay, text me we're gonna finish up here so these boys can go home."

"Clover! Baby! Did you get me some gyros?" That was Q chiming in before Mack could hang up.

"She got your lamb. Call her on your own phone, Q." Reese hangs up and Chloe gives her a look that says *Are you crazy?!* with her lips twisted to the side and her eyebrows pulled together. "What? Your phone is charged, right?"

Chloe rolls her eyes and turns back around in her seat. "That's not the point, Reese! You know it. Let me put this music back on before you piss me off. I'll text him."

With that, we listened to the radio for the remaining drive back to our neighborhood. When we pulled up to Ty and Chloe's house, Reese's new boy toy is parked in front of the house. She squeals and hurriedly grabs her bags from the bed before throwing a "Bye!" over her shoulder as she gets into the sleek car. Ty took Drea to her car, still on campus, leaving Chloe and I at her house.

"I guess it's just us until Q gets cleaned up. Wanna watch *Bring It On?*" she asks.

CHAPTER 16

Melody, Then

I FOUND OUT QUICKLY that Chloe is obsessed with *Bring It On*. It's a point of contention between her and Reese. Apparently, she always puts it on when she does Reese's hair. Guess I'm going to find out why.

We grab our bags and walk up to her room. Her house has the same layout as mine. The bedroom is just in the opposite position in the house. I sit on her fuzzy black rug instead of the fuzzy moon chair she has in the corner. This room is overall soft. Every piece of furniture has something fuzzy, fluffy, or plush. On her desk are crochet stuffed animals and a shelf that holds all kinds of yarn and tools and baskets with half-finished projects. There are shelves with more of the animals on the walls between large posters of iconic nineties and two-thousands stars like Lauryn Hill, TLC, Nia Long, and Iman. Her stand hair dryer is behind a three-tier rolling cart stuffed with all kinds of hair products, brushes and combs. A mannequin head, with curls pinned into place, is fixed on a tripod, which stands beside the cart. It smells like a hair salon in here and it's oddly comforting. I have not been in one for months now and I'm hyper-aware of that as I start absently rubbing a hand up the back of my head where I've slicked my bun into place.

Chloe throws her shopping bags onto her bed and plops down next to them. She grabs her remote from the nightstand and turns her TV on. I watch as she casually rewinds the movie that is already playing on the screen. "Were you watching this movie before school this morning?"

She chuckles and gives me a look. "No. I watched it last night to fall asleep." Chloe looks at me and now it feels like she's really studying me. "You've never done that?" The surprise on her face is genuine, but she shrugs and starts the movie.

I have not done that before. I don't even have a TV in my room. There is still nothing on my walls. It probably would have been a good idea to look for something at the mall, but I don't think about being alone in my room when I don't have to. I was just happy spending time with the girls. I didn't want to think about my bare walls and quiet house. It's so silent in there all the time. So quiet in comparison to the noise that used to continually bounce around our home.

Loud Country music starts playing and the muffled sound drowns out the movie playing. He must have gotten home recently from dropping Drea off. I had been watching the movie without really seeing anything until this point. Lost to my own thoughts about my empty house. Chloe shoots from her bed and out her bedroom door. Following to see where she's going, I recognize that she must be going to Ty's room. I poke my head out of her doorway.

Chloe bangs on the door a few times before Ty opens it. Both his hands are braced on the top of the jamb. "Can I help you, sis?" He leans forward towards Chloe until she backs up a few steps, rolling her eyes and scoffs. It's exaggerated and insincere. I can tell that she's not really mad as she squints her eyes at her step-brother.

"We're trying to watch a movie! Do you think that maybe you could keep it down?" I don't think Ty knew I was here before now. He turns his head to me and I nod my head in agreement with Chloe though my face is surely starting to sweat. Ty must have taken a shower while we were watching the movie. He's shirtless and in a pair of basketball shorts. His boxer's waistband peeks over the top a little bit. So much of his brown skin is available for my eyes to devour.

Note to self, I have got to stop checking him out...That time is just not today.

My gaze follows the line down his long legs to his feet that aren't bare, as I expected. He's wearing pink pig slippers that look to be crocheted. I'm so shocked by the footwear that a small giggle comes out of my mouth before I can cover it.

A smirk lifts the side of his mouth. "Something funny, Melody?"

"Mel." I correct him. He always calls me by my full name. Have I even corrected him before now? It does sound better than my full name has ever sounded coming from anyone's lips, but it feels too intimate coming from his mouth. Maybe it's the way his full soft lips form the word. Or the way he takes his time to say it. I'm staring at his mouth as it curves into a full smile now. His teeth are straight and white and I... really need to stop staring! I shake my head and add, "The slippers. Where did you find those in your size?"

Chloe uncrosses her arms and leans towards me, bumping into my shoulder softly. "Aren't they so cute? Bro said he would wear anything I made him. I found this kid's pattern for the piggie slippers and modified it for his big ass feet. I'm very proud that they actually fit and he wears them." She's beaming at Ty with a big smile and then her eyebrows pinch and she says, "That is not why I'm here." She snaps her fingers in his face and he turns back to her. "Will you quit staring at my friend? I came here to—" she takes a deep breath seeming to calm down her voice as it was getting louder with each word she said "—ask you to keep your music down. Please."

He gives her an exasperated look. "How many nights do you expect me to listen to Gabrielle Union cheering, Clo? I'm tired of these clovers in the atmosphere." How many nights has Chloe watched this movie? Now I am starting to see the truth in the warning Reese was trying to give me.

"It's my favorite! I don't say anything about the sad love songs you've been playing on repeat!" Ty's eyes flash and flick to me quickly before he looks back to Chloe. Releasing the door frame, he grabs his door like he's about to close it in our faces. Chloe's face, actually, but I definitely am lumped into that gesture if he slams it. "Don't even think about it! I'm not going away. I have a guest, I'd like for us to hear my TV. Turn it down, please."

He sighs deeply before reaching over into his room to grab something. He holds up a pair of headphones and slips them around his neck. "Happy?" He closes the door and Chloe raises an eyebrow at me before looping her arm into mine.

"Teenagers these days. You can't teach them anything!" Chloe says and we laugh. After going to the kitchen, we return to her room with some chips to snack on.

"I haven't seen your parents at all. Are they home?" It's not as quiet here as my house, but I think I would notice two other people in this building. I can't help but notice when someone's parents are in their house with mine so void of life.

Chloe looks up from texting on her phone. "Oh yea, no. They're also at the wedding extravaganza that Reese's parents are at. Won't be back until Sunday night. Which brings me to my next point…" She taps on her screen a few more times. "Quincy's headed over here in like ten minutes."

"Oh." I say uselessly. It's time for me to get out of here is what she means.

Chloe clocks the look I'm making. "Uh-uh." She holds up a reprimanding finger. "Don't give me that look. You know this is kind of a rare opportunity." She holds her hands palms facing up like she's weighing the two options.

"Trust me. I get it. You two are cute together. I don't think I could survive being in the room alone with you though." They can hardly keep their hands to themselves with an audience. My walk home will be short seeing as though I'm only one house over. I start grabbing my bags and Chloe hands me my phone off her floor after looking at the lock screen.

> **Mack: What's up?**

> **Mack: What time are you gonna be done shopping? Maybe we could study for chem after…**

> **Mack: Q's headed your way. I could drive you home (winking face emoji)**

"You gonna text him back?" She gives me a pointed look and I shrug. "Do you wanna talk about him? You've been...Is everything okay between you two?"

I laugh nervously and say, "He's a good friend. We're getting to know each other, you know?"

"Does he know that?"

"Um, yeah. I think so." I actually didn't think so. It's very obvious that he has different intentions. Chloe knows it too.

"Bon, you can be honest with me about anything. Mack is my buddy, but so are you." What about your brother? Can I be honest with you about the feelings I'm having about him?

"I know. It's nothing. I'll text him back." She doesn't look convinced. I type out a quick response and show her my phone.

> **Mel: I'm gonna walk home. Raincheck?**

As I'm showing Chloe my phone screen, he replies to the text. She chuffs and I quickly turn the phone back to me.

> **Mack: Ok, Sweetness. Need a ride to school tomorrow?**

I know he will keep asking. It would be better than riding the bus...

> **Mel: Ok. Sounds good (smiling face emoji)**

Chloe laughs and I give my friend one final hug at the door and start my walk down the street.

CHAPTER 17

Melody, Then

I'M A FEW FEET from Chloe's driveway when I feel someone put their hand on my shoulder. My first instinct is to panic, the surprised little squeak coming out desperate when I turn on my heel to face my attacker. From the warmth and size, I should have known it was just him.

Not *just* him.

My body registers who it was long before my brain. My heart has picked up the speed of its beating and the uncomfortable heat of desire roils through my middle. There is something secretive, but deliberate about him being here now. I look up at his partially illuminated face. In the street lights, his eyes seem deeper and more glinting as he smirks down at me.

Oh.

Our secret, for sure.

I sidestep out of his hold and wrap my arms around my body instead.

"Were you really going to walk home this late at night by yourself, Melody?" he asks. I think about how our houses are not even a full block apart from each other. The rational part of my brain realizes this, but the irrational part can't help but feel a little special that he would try to pull this stunt. Silly, silly girl.

I haven't talked to Chloe about Ty. In fact, I've been brushing off my attraction to him all the while. Is it possible that they talked about me? I'll think about that possibility later.

My silence has dragged on for an awkward amount of time before I finally ask, "Would you walk me two minutes down the street, Tyson Abrams?" I made my voice as sweet as possible, clasping my hands together under my chin. I was only joking but looking up into his face with no one else around has a tunneling effect. His long lashes cast shadows over his face as he slowly blinks. He's looking into mine in the same uninhibited fashion.

It occurs to me that we had never been alone together before this moment. I like his face in daylight and in sunset, but the street lighting offers a different perspective I had not had before.

The magic of cool nights here provided me with comfort alone on my roof. That pales in comparison to how alive I feel under his gaze. If I had a dream guy, it would be this hunky slice of guitar-strumming man in front of me. I could be happy to dream of Ty's face like it is now, half cast in shadows and amusement in the lines around his smirking lips.

I grab ahold of the light post and lean off of it, feeling the need to move. I am beginning to get too hot in my own skin. The slight chill of night wafting around me makes me feel less like I'll self-destruct.

He watches me swaying back and forth before he responds, "And how could I live with myself if I missed this small chance for your attention alone?" My cheeks are now fully inflamed with his admission hanging between the two of us. *So much for cooling down.*

Did he feel this too?

The pull I've been avoiding

And that I was avoiding it.

Avoiding him.

I smile a little at the thought. Though, everything in my mind tells me that I need to get home.

If I never got to know him, then I couldn't like him. I couldn't fall for him. It's so precarious talking to him with no one else around. Now I know how silky his deep voice truly is as it travels from his mouth to my ears and straight to my core. I roll my lips between my teeth and say nothing, choosing to sway instead.

Every thought in my mind keeps saying to walk home and stop lingering. Every feeling in my heart tells me to stay and learn more of what makes him beautiful. To add more detail to the picture in my head. The one where the new girl gets the guy. I'm listening to my heart as I sway here and he leans against the post. We could have been under the light for a few seconds or maybe a couple of minutes being in each other's space. My knuckles graze his side each time I move back and forth. It feels explicit even though it's not.

Ty tilts his head to one side like he is trying to figure something important out. A twist falls from the band that was holding all of them at the back of his head. My hand reaches out to brush the hair back before I can stop myself. A strong desire to prevent anything from obstructing the perfect view of his sharp cheekbones taking over for me. He grabs my wrist gently to keep my hand in place and I rest my palm against his face. His scruff scratches against me and I use my thumb to slowly rub over it. I want more that rough feeling against me.

His eyes close briefly before he meets mine again. "Melody," he says. The emotion in his eyes raises the heat on my desire that was already at a simmer. Under his gaze, I feel as if I'm melting like pure gold. Burning bright and red with potential, my flush rushes up my body to my neck and cheeks. The uncertainty of what shape I will take next excites me more than it should.

He holds my hand with a gentleness that makes me feel less embarrassed by how natural it feels to touch him. To feel him. My hand looks so small in his, even though it fits perfectly. I don't think I ever cared about how any one person's hands looked before. But Tyson's hands are skilled. I've seen him play his guitar and pluck those strings and make music that touched the very organ beating so furiously in my chest right now. I felt the chords like they were spells written to command my body. I can only imagine what other things his skilled hands could create in me.

The questions continue to lurk beneath those long lashes. His brows are starting to furrow. I don't have any answers for him. I don't even know what I would say. Maybe I could say that I want Tyson. I wish I could tell him that I'm interested in what this heat means for us. I wish I could tell him I want to explore why I feel like I'm at home and at peace in his presence. I touched him like I had the right to do so.

And he let me.

Wanted me to.

Out here in the dark of the night with no one to see us, I could be that girl. Just the new girl who likes a boy who lives one house over from her. A really, really cute boy. No one would have to know that I want to walk the two steps it would take to get those soft lips on mine.

Would he let me do that too? I've seen him swipe Carmex on between classes, wishing I could be the one who feels the tingle of mint on my lips from his. The memory is nearly enough to make me take those remaining steps.

Thankfully, self-preservation kicks in and I pull my hand gently from his grasp.

I'm not that girl. Ty is the boy who happens to be my new best friend's *favorite* brother. Clearing my throat, I begin to make progress toward my house again. Ty hesitates but follows close after.

"Melody." We're near my driveway now when Ty speaks up. "I don't think I could ever wish something bad to happen to you. Even if it's something small."

"What?"

"Look, I know Mack is trying to get at you. As his boy, I'm not trying to disrespect him, but I want to get to know you, Melody."

I look up at him, trying to decide how I should feel about his admission. "Y-you talked to Mack? About me?" I stutter as I try not to be irritated that Mack has laid claim to me.

"It's not like that. He told me and Q about how he wanted to talk to you. I'd be a dick if I ignored it. Even if I want to." Ty readjusts his hairband to fit the fallen twist back into place. I watch his shirt rise to reveal those Calvin Kleins again.

Did he say he wanted to?

Ty continues, "You and me can just be cool. I walked you home because it's late and I had to make sure you made it."

I can't decide what to say. I have so many questions. Twice now, he's shown me that he wants whatever this is between us. But he also said that he won't take me. I shake my head once and put a smile on while I walk up to my door. I pull my keys out of my bag and unlock it. "You want a water or tea? Made the tea before school this morning." Ty looks confused and hesitates in the middle of my driveway still. "It's the least I can do, right? You did see me home safely." Slightly laughing at the end. I huff out the last words as if this moment is light or easy when it isn't.

He narrows his eyes, "If you made it, I'm having the tea."

CHAPTER 18

Melody

"WHAT ARE YOU DOING here?" I stand in my open doorway, taking in the man just on the other side of the threshold.

"I couldn't stop thinking about..." Tyson pauses in the middle of his sentence. He scratches at the small bit of stubble along his jaw. I watch him in his discomfort, saying nothing. I'll never know how he would have finished that thought because he starts a new one. "Can I come in?"

"I don't know." After I left the party, I came home and showered to change into a silk camisole set, another treat I bought from Lulu Lacey. It's not like I was expecting company, but I also half expected it to be someone who had ended up at the house by accident. Pointing them in the right direction was as far as the conversation would have gone and all of it could have happened with me hidden mostly behind the door.

Instead, it's *him*. The him who was the catalyst of this night that would have been bad for me either way. It was not helped by being accompanied by a soundtrack literally sung by the source of my reoccurring heartbreak. So, here I am, standing in front of said heartbreaker in my lingerie. A flush of discomfiture crawls up my chest and neck as I regret not grabbing the matching silk robe.

Wesson meows from behind me and before I know it, he's winding his body through Tyson's legs. He picks up my cat and cradles him like a football in one arm. I can hear the purring from where I'm standing and roll my eyes. "Fine."

I step back to let him into the house. He toes off his boots and the sight of them next to my flats by the door gives me pause. *Deja vu.*

He walks around the space, making no effort to downplay how he is inspecting my house. I know he expects to see photos of Mack and me or something he doesn't want to see. My house is small but cute. I'm proud to still own it. It's one of the only things I fought for in the divorce because Mack hated the house. He thought it was too far away from everything and he wanted something more modern. When he moved out, I got rid of everything that reminded me of him. It was too painful to see and I didn't need any reminders of what being the biggest waste of someone's life is like.

Tyson reclines on my couch after doing that jean tug thing men do to adjust his pants. I don't know why it fascinates me. I hurry to the kitchen. "Do you want some tea or water?" Why am I so flustered? I need to keep my hands busy doing anything besides thinking of Ty's thighs.

"Tea is good." He calls back to me. "You still add the lemon at the bottom?"

"You remember that?"

Do you remember us?

"How could I not? I've never been able to replicate it."

Have you been able to replicate me? Stop, Mel.

"Is this hers?" He looks at the little painting of a cottage above my dining table.

"Umm, no." The pink watering can that holds some fresh flowers and the smaller pottery surrounding the frame are reminiscent of something I may have seen my mother create and showcase in our house in Houston. I wonder if Ty remembers the few images I could find of her work online or if he's just making small talk. This piece is close to her style, but not too close to where I get triggered and lost in thoughts of her.

I pull a candied lemon slice from my fridge and add it to the bottom of the glass before pouring the tea from the pitcher over the top. I hold the pitcher to my chest for a moment, hoping it will cool the flush to something more manageable before I see him again.

When I return to the living room, Wesson has made himself at home on Tyson's lap. I give him a look that he returns with a lazy wink before he goes back to kneading Ty's leg. *Traitor.*

I'm still standing by the couch with the teas in my hands, staring at Tyson's lap. "I'm surprised he remembered me," he says.

My eyes flick from his lap to his face. "Cats have an incredible memory. I imagine he would never forget the boy who saved his life."

"Is that what it is Wessie?" He scratches the cat's head and I feel so jealous that he's getting to be as close to this man as I want to be. He starts to sing, "I will be your hero, baby..." Wesson boops his little nose on Ty's when he leans close to my cat's face.

Have I died? Surely, I've died.

I clear the dryness in my throat, holding the tea out toward Tyson. "This feels a little surreal."

He chuckles. "Why?" Sipping from the glass, the way his throat bobs has me licking my own lips.

My brows pinch, "Maybe because you're on like thousands of girls' walls...? Do you remember singing on national television like seventy-two hours ago? Tyson, you're like... a celebrity."

He scoffs. "That's not a thing."

I roll my eyes. "It totally is. In any city, you'd have to wear a disguise or something to leave your house."

He shrugs, rubbing the cat again. "So what?"

"So what? Are you serious?"

"Yea. I'm not in any other city. I'm in Alpenglow and I'm on your couch."

I sip my tea, remembering that I was holding something.

Note to self, please do not embarrass yourself by spilling your drink like a toddler.

Sitting is probably the safer option, so I take a seat on the far side of the couch from him.

I have a celebrity in my house. I dated this man. I cried in his arms earlier tonight. "Why are you here?"

He takes a long pull from his tea and moans a sound that makes me press my thighs together in response. His eyes are shut. I have to assume he's doing this on purpose. Goading me into jumping him right now. *Why is he doing this?* I cross my arms over my stiffening nipples. Tyson's chest is only slightly exposed in his button down, with the soft bit of chest hair peeking from the few buttons undone since I last saw him. He is too much to handle without objectifying. It's not just because he's a celebrity. It's because he was written for me. Everything he does elicits a response from my body that I can't control.

He looks into my eyes and I know that this is the moment I won't be able to take back. Having him alone in my house is a bad idea. He knows me too well. Years later and he still feels like my person. I should not be as comfortable as I am with this man in my house... In my pajamas, which we covered is actually lingerie. "It's the only place I want to be right now," his voice rumbling from his lips and straight through my chest.

"Why is that?" I ask breathless.

His features soften though his gaze never wavers, "What happened tonight?"

Nope. Absolutely not. I am not willing to discuss the source of my erratic mood swings with him. I may feel like he's still my person, but that is not true. *It's not.* He does not get to see those parts of me, even if there is no one who could stand where he stood.

I rise from the couch. "You should leave."

Tyson stands with the cat in one arm and the tea in the other. "I'm not, Melody."

Placing my tea on the coffee table, I take the cat from his arms with a bit of resistance on Wesson's end and place him on the ground. "You are. Take the glass with you, I don't care. But you need to go."

His composure cracks and I manage not to wince when I see the dejection on it. "I was young and stupid and I fucked everything up, Melody. I want to do something about that."

My eyes are already watering though. "I get that, but we're not young anymore. I won't do this again."

His tone is determined when he says, "I'm not leaving." He walks over to where he saw the cat going, passing me in the process.

For a moment, I'm struck speechless and I can't move. It's when I hear him turn on the TV that I'm rounding the corner after him.

Tyson steps out of his pants as I'm entering the room. By the time he wiggles them off, I'm still standing in the doorway. His tight grey briefs are leaving nothing to the imagination. My mouth is dry all over again, taking in his form.

I don't have long to ogle him because he gets under my sheets and fluffs the pillows behind him. He scrolls a streaming app to pick something to watch. Tyson doesn't even look toward me when he asks, "Are you getting into the bed or are you going to stand in the doorway all night?"

I shake my head, confused. Wesson is curled up in his bed on the top of his cat tree, none the wiser. Thanks for the help, feline companion.

"I... You—I can't get into the bed with you in it."

"*Sleepless in Seattle* or *Love and Basketball*?"

"Tyson..."

"I'm tired and it's been a long night. If you make me pick, I'm going for *Love and Basketball* but I know you like old-school Tom Hanks."

I shrug. "As far as single dads go, Sam Baldwin is the blueprint."

He puts the movie on and I am somehow watching a movie in bed with *the heartbreaker* after one of the roughest nights I've had in a very long time. There is a closeness that we were never able to shake. I should be more upset by his presence here. Logic tells me that I should kick him out. I can't though. I'm tired and having him in bed with me, smelling the warm and alluring mahogany and amber of his cologne, is more comforting than upsetting. It makes no sense, but I want him to stay.

116

When the movie is over, I tie my curls up with my scarf in a big pineapple on the top of my head. It's only moments before I feel his warmth on my back while we lie in the dark.

He tentatively slides his arm over my waist. I don't flinch. I still fit into his body like I used to. With a few moments of his slowed breathing, I wish we didn't have the history we have. That I could forget what it felt like to not have him and how him being here is a mindfuck. I wish that I could voice aloud that I want him to stay here with me.

How is he cuddling me like the last two years were nothing? Like we aren't different people from then and even from before he left the second time. I have no clue, but all I do know is that it feels good to have him here. I relax in his arms, so much so that I barely register how I'm falling asleep in them.

Into the silence of my room, he says, "I think you should tell them."

"Tell them what?" I ask around a yawn.

He ignores my question, arms tightening around me. His breath brushes along my neck as we lie here in the dark. "What was their name?"

I close my eyes. "His name was Callan."

"That's a good name." Tyson's voice comes out thick with emotion. I don't know why, but it's clear that he feels the gravity of the information I've shared.

"For an angel." I exhale, squeezing my eyes shut tighter.

"For an angel," he whispers. He holds me against him, heart beating against my back. I don't crumple with the sadness I usually feel when I think about the baby I never had. The weight of that fact feels lighter having shared it with one person.

Even if it was the last person I would expect to share it with.

CHAPTER 19

Tyson

COCONUT AND MANGO.

I feel like I'm waking up at home, when I know it's not my house. It's been two years since I woke on a pillow that smelled like this. After a moment of blinking and yawning, I remember all that happened last night.

In front of me, Melody is still sleeping soundly. I stop moving because the last thing I want is to wake her. I would have no way of knowing for sure, but I don't suspect she gets good sleep. When we were younger she never did. Only on the nights I would sneak over to sleep with her at her dad's house.

When she tried to kick me out last night, I knew I had to take charge of the situation. Melody was never going to invite me to sleep in this bed with her. Even if I knew she needed it. In that bar bathroom, she collapsed into my arms like the weight of the world had been pressing into her for far too long. That much had been made clear to me.

Looking at her, I could tell she was close to buckling. It kills me to know that she had no one to help her through this. If I had not been there, what would have happened? I consider myself lucky that even with everything between us, she still thinks of me as her safe space. Her body does anyway. I'll work on everything else in time.

Watching her dance with Mack at the party was its own brand of torture. I wish I could have come off the stage and gotten between them before he said whatever it was to upset her and make her leave early. I could not understand why she married him in the first place. I couldn't understand how she was married to him for so long. There is so much that I don't understand about this woman.

What kind of masochist wonders about their person being with another man? *Me.*

I was the one who forced her hand. If I hadn't left...

I told her that I fucked up last night. That's the truth. I did fuck everything up. I know that Melody is closed off. She was when I met her. She probably is more so after me. I should have tried to talk to her. It felt impossible when I had no allies except Chloe in Alpenglow Ridge. My hometown no longer felt like home. All because I made some poor decisions as a kid. This town always served as the moral compass with or without adequate information to support how it admonished its residents. A persistent chill toward me when I'd come see my dad or sister. Now that I have some clout, people are friendlier and it turns my stomach.

Though I'm not "back", so to speak, I'm here. Nothing and no one is going to get between us. The time we lost only showed me that she was, in fact, my someone. *I missed her.* It colored my music. It always came up in my dreams. Hell, I only hooked up with women who were her opposite because I couldn't stand to search for those similarities that were not there. She couldn't be replaced. She was the one. We can still work. I will do whatever I must to ensure that's the case.

I felt, more than saw, that something triggered Melody last night. I felt it building like a current in the air. Being in the right place at the right time to catch her wasn't luck. It was fate because we were destined to be together. Our paths will continue to intersect until they are the same.

No one understands this woman like I do. No one understands the kind of grief Melody has had to deal with better than me. Two kids who lost their mom's way too young.

The biggest blow is how she had yet another life stolen from her. I can't begin to say that I understand that. Only a careless fool would assume to in this situation. But I do see how it has taken a toll on her though. Her friends don't know. I know they don't. With how everything went down, I know she is still keeping her pain from them. She always felt like her sadness was a burden to everyone around her. *I should have come back sooner.*

Melody wakes with a start and I pull her even closer to me.

"Tyson?" I'm not able to respond before the cat I rescued all those years ago climbs onto the bed. He stops by her face, meowing loudly. She smooths the fur down his head and back with a palm. "I need to feed him." She taps my arm which I realize is still holding her in place.

"Oh. Right." I release her, reluctantly. The moment she leaves, I feel the absence and follow her to the kitchen where she pours some powder over a mixture of dry and wet food in a bowl for the cat. Wesson practically sings as he dances around her legs while she busies herself preparing his breakfast. When she's done, I watch the cat for a moment more. He is the closest being to her though she is surrounded by individuals who call themselves her friends and family. This little animal I saved for her. I scratch his little head, thanking him silently for holding down the fort.

Melody begins making coffee and it's not lost on me that she's still in her little sleep set. The silk top barely covers her tits and ass. The hardness of her nipples is visible and begging for my mouth. I clear my throat and try to distract myself because I have more important things to talk to her about than the rigidity of her pert little nipples.

She hands me a cup of coffee over the bar that is made exactly how I like it, the perfect color and sweetness. She turns to the refrigerator and hands me water too. There is something domestic and familiar about the whole thing. I try to stop myself from diving into that thought further.

"Melody, have you talked to anyone about..." She squeezes her eyes shut before she opens them, putting her smile in place. She starts moving around the kitchen to make, what I assume, will be breakfast. I almost backtrack. This is not the time to be a chicken shit. Someone has to fight for this woman. At the moment, it seems like I am the only person who even knows how to do that. "Melody. I don't mean the girls but like a therapist."

"Tyson. Please don't start. I'm fine. I was just tired yesterday. It was all too much."

I raise an eyebrow at her blowing me off. I was there. What happened in that bathroom was not *fine*. "How often are you tired like that?"

"Do you want sausage or bacon? I have both."

"Mel—"

"Sausage or bacon?" Her voice squeaks as it rises in pitch. I put my coffee down, joining her in the kitchen.

Placing a hand on both of hers, I ease the pan down onto the counter. She looks up at me with wide, watery eyes. "This is not healthy. You've had so much happening in your life. If you won't talk to them, then talk to me at least."

"I don't want to talk. I'm fine." Her eyes tell me that's a lie but her lips are set in a hard line, unmoving.

I hold her face. "You're not." In another circumstance, it would be inappropriate to say that to someone. In this one, I'm not sure Melody understands that I can see her. I feel the pain in her eyes like it's coming from my own heart. She doesn't think that I, or anyone, will stick around if they see the truth. "I see it and I want to hold it. I'm not looking away."

She steps out of my hold to resume cooking. "You just caught me on a bad day is all," she reaffirms, nodding to herself while she grabs spices from the cabinet above her stovetop. I know she's lying and I hear the crack in my chest. "Sausage or bacon?"

I'm not going to be able to reach her this way. "Sausage," I sigh. Now isn't the time. Soon. So soon, I'm going to revisit this.

I watch her making breakfast. Everything she does has the kind of coordinated beauty that mesmerizes me. It's not long before I'm sitting across from the table with her over food she made for me.

"I have work at eleven." She takes a bite of her food, chewing and then adding, "Are you staying at Will's? Maybe Chloe's free until the salon opens later." I have zero intentions of going to Chloe's and I'm definitely not going to my dad's. I shake my head and continue eating. She eyes me suspiciously. "Well, then what are you doing today? Going back to Denver?"

"No. I'm going to QB's."

She looks confused, fork pausing between her plate and her mouth. "For what?"

"To keep an eye on you." Her shock is apparent. I keep eating my food, taking time to cut my sausage patty into the eggs. After what I saw firsthand last night, I'm not gonna let her out of my sight until I have to.

"For what?!" She gets up from the table to put her plate into the sink.

She doesn't want my help. Maybe some honesty will help her instead. "I missed you."

She turns, letting her plate clatter into the sink she's filled with soapy water. When she picks it back up, scrubbing at it furiously, I come up behind her taking the plate from her hands. She freezes when she feels me at her back. I'm a big man, my dick is just as big. I know she feels me because we're both in our underwear. It's not my intention, but being close to her is a lot for him to process.

"You didn't," she whispers.

I spin her to face me. With her shock, soapy hands press to my chest. I feel the tepid water and soap suds slide down my nipples to the waistband of my boxer briefs. I hiss at the feeling and we both watch the trail to my hardening length.

"I did," I say. Pressing my dick against her body causing a shocked gasp to escape her. "I did my best to stay out of his way and your life because you chose him when I left. It seems like losing you meant that I lost my home too. But he fucked up. I don't know what he's been doing, but it's not enough. He was never right for you. It's been me all along. A couple years back, I wasn't ready. I admit that I made a mistake, but you weren't ready either. I'm sorry for how I hurt you. How I hurt us." I pull her closer to my body, the silk of her little top slides along my stomach and chest as she looks up at me. "I'm really fucking sorry, but it's me now. I'm not going anywhere. Go get ready for work and I'll take you."

Her lips are pursed, but she does what I said without resistance. She'd rather go along with what I've asked than start a confrontation. I go out to my truck to get my overnight bag. She wiggles into a pair of skin-tight jeans in her closet as I walk back into the room. I watch her for a moment before I take a shower and get dressed too.

"You don't have to do this." She fidgets with her keys in front of my truck. She looks so fucking good, I want to kiss her. I can't though. Not yet. When I take her lips, it will be because she wants it too.

I admire how considerate she's trying to be, but I know this is not coming from that considerate part of her. She is no burden to me. Anything I have to do today can be done from a booth at Quincy's bar. "Do what?" I play the fool she takes me for.

"Take me to work... My car works just fine. I'm fine."

I cross my arms over my chest, leaning back onto my door. "Get in the truck, Melody." She huffs and grabs her little apron from her passenger seat and gets in.

Quincy is unlocking the back door when we pull up. He gives me a wave and then frowns when he sees Melody in my passenger seat. I get out of the car and open Melody's door. She looked frustrated to realize I had the child lock on, prepared for her to bolt out of Old Red when I got here. I hold out a hand that she ignores. She chooses to jump down and walks with purpose to the back door of the bar.

"Something wrong with your car?" he asks as she walks up to the employee entrance.

"No," she replies, brushing past him.

Quincy stands in front of the door when I try to enter after her, blocking my entrance. "What are you doing?"

My jaw tenses in aggravation. Would I have to argue my way into this place? With a man who I used to consider my best friend? "What does it look like?"

He crosses his arms over his chest and raises an eyebrow. With the way he leans onto the door, I question if it will make more sense to come back when the bar is open and he's in the back already. "It looks like you're about to start a bunch of shit."

I shrug. "If that's what it takes."

Shaking his head, he replies, "No fucking way, man. Not in my bar."

"C'mon, Q. I'm gonna just sit in the back booth." I hold up my tablet and show him that I'm gonna be working.

"Nah, man. Why?"

"What does it matter?" I'm not gonna out Melody's business to him. It's us working on our relationship right now. The less he knows the better. I honestly didn't expect this much pushback to get into the bar. I cross my arms over my chest in frustration. We both stare each other down with our arms crossed like a couple of jerkoffs. Quincy is no fool. He has been here the whole time. Of all the people who wanted me to stay in Alpenglow Ridge way back when, he was the loudest. He took it somewhat personally when he found out about my acceptance of the offer to Colorado University.

To be fair, no one knew that I had applied besides William and my guidance counselor at ARHS.

We stare at each other for a few moments longer before he throws his arms up and walks into his place. We make it down the employee hallway and I'm almost through the swinging doors before he calls out, "Only paying customers get to be in here so you better order something when we open." I tip my hat and walk over to the back booth.

It looks completely different from last night with all the decor from the engagement party gone. It's hard to believe that so much happened and everything changed in one moment for our friends, but for me and Melody, too.

CHAPTER 20

Melody

"SOOO... ARE WE NOT going to talk about how the ex-boyfriend you were panicking about seeing last night brought you into work today?" Drea asks as we grab trays of beer mugs from the drying rack. She shuffles awkwardly to maintain eye contact with me while I follow her with my tray.

"I would rather that we didn't," I respond, stacking my tray on top of hers. She looks over to the booth he's sitting at and back at me. "We're not," I say more sternly.

"Oh come on, Mel. He is in new clothes and everything. Did he stay at your place? Did you two... you know?" She wiggles her eyebrows.

"Drea, I don't want to do this."

"Too bad." She taps my nose with her index finger. "You look guilty as hell right now. I am kinda loving this. Is that a thing again?"

"I thought you weren't interested in sex." I huff, pushing through the swinging doors to grab another tray of mugs.

"I am not interested in spreading my legs for someone. That doesn't mean I can't get all the details. You're lucky Chloe wasn't here. You would have already gotten the third degree."

"Don't remind me. I'm trying my best to keep this quiet."

"So, you are doing it?"

"No. We slept together." She opens her mouth, but I cut her off. "Not like that. He just slept in my bed."

"You cuddled this man?" I look away from her and start unscrewing salt shakers to refill them. "You did! That is so... intimate."

"Is it?" It kind of was. He held me and I slept more soundly than I have in months. Years. Better than I ever did with Mack. And rarely without a very strict regime to get to bed. One that involved listening to him sing me to sleep...

"Yes! Being that close without sexual action. Ugh. It's like a deeper connection. Not everyone can do that. Even married couples sleep on opposite sides of the bed."

Deeper connection. "What's your point?"

"Years later and you cuddled him... that's it? Something just seems like it's more."

"More than what?"

"Strictly friendly. I wouldn't cuddle a friend."

"Tony has slept over at your house plenty."

"Not in my bed!" She taps on the ordering system a few more times while I let the silence hang there. "I don't know, friend. There is definitely something going on there!"

I did not want something to be going on there. I didn't want him to be here now. Maybe that is a little untrue. A lot untrue. I did feel more settled knowing that he was within walking distance of me. Even in the back now, I can sense him near and it's comforting.

That doesn't make any sense.

The last thing I want is for people, especially my friends, to see that I'm even considering what Tyson is asking. Only a fool would let someone burn them three times. And a fool, I am not.

So what, he caught me when I crumpled yesterday?

So what, he helped me sleep last night when I probably wouldn't have been able to?

So what, he is here now to make sure that I'm not triggered again?

"I can tell you for a fact that nothing is going on. He is just here to work on music or something. Look, he's actually got a pencil out." We both look at him sitting in the booth again and he looks up from his notebook. He nods to us in acknowledgment and I turn back to Drea. "See, just working."

"If you say so." She ties her apron and leans over the bartop waiting for the lunch crowd to come in. Probably looking at recipes or something. She was right. I doubt Chloe would let the conversation drop like this. I'm going to have to avoid her for as long as I can.

One thing I know is that I need to figure out exactly what Tyson is planning. I can't keep dodging these questions. How do I explain to his sister that he stayed at my house instead of hers or their parents' when he was in town for the night?

Was I tempted by this man? Yes. Even if I want to resist him, I don't know how strong I can be if he keeps this up.

AFTER THE LUNCH RUSH hit, I was able to clear my thoughts somewhat of the man sitting in the back booth. It was unusually busy, which is good for tips, so I can't complain. I kept my smile in place, bringing people burgers and fries with very few hiccups in between. Overall, a very good first shift.

Still my focus lands on Tyson because he's still here. I thought maybe he would get bored and leave at some point. No such luck. He studiously scribbles on the paper in front of him. I feel a little twinge of pride in him for making it this far. We both had dreams before he left. Now, he's back and that dream of his has taken shape in the form of a career that continues to soar.

Drea took water to him not too long ago. I'm going to try my best to not acknowledge him more than I have to. Whatever it is that he is doing here—it's not a lasting thing. A big fish like him with his potential needs the whole ocean, not the little bowl of Alpenglow Ridge.

The biggest concern I have for him here is my ex-husband. Though he has never been violent with me, he cannot help himself when he sees anyone else around me. Once upon a time, I thought that was attractive. I liked that he was so possessive of me. Back when it felt like Tyson had thrown me away, it felt good to have someone adore me and put me on this pedestal that I could never fall from. In the present, it's more than problematic. Case in point, him fighting Ellis, a man he has known and worked with for years, all because he was flirting with me. I have given up on dating in this town altogether. It's not worth the hassle or gossip. I want to be as far from the attention as I can. It's no small task with someone like Mack, always trying to cause a scene.

I have had to tiptoe around him ever since we got together. Though Mack and Tyson have never truly had a confrontation, for that I'm grateful, I don't know what I would do. Defending either of them would not end well for me. If I defend Mack, then he will undoubtedly get the wrong impression and begin pursuing me again. If I defend Tyson, then I look like the idiot holding on to something that clearly never was.

What would I do if that kind of altercation made news? Even the small blogs picking it up could make Tyson look bad. I don't think I could stand to be under that kind of inspection either.

I tie my own apron and start refilling sugar baskets to pass the time. If I think too much about this, it will give me a headache. Or, I'll end up crying in the bathroom again. Like a wave overcoming me, I fall into my activity as my thoughts swirl about.

Drea's voice pulls me out of my head. "Hello! Mel, table seven. Go greet them! Once you get their order in, I'm clocking out."

I startle, "Right. On my way." Big smiles.

Drea has long since clocked out when Reese comes in after work. She and Drea sit at a table while I keep working the floor. Only chancing a glance at Tyson's table when Sarah Jane is being a little too friendly topping his water off. I have no right to be jealous, but I don't like how she leers at him, practically shoving her big boobs into his face. He returns her smiles with the smart-ass retorts that I hope will make her give up. No such luck, yet.

I hurry over to the table my two friends are sitting at with their drinks. "Four Shots of Casa Amigos and four limes," I say placing all of them on the table. "Now what makes it a double-shot night?"

"No double shots for us tonight! One is for Drea. And the other is for—"

"Me!" Chloe sings as she plops into her seat next to Drea. "I told them to get this round ready."

Reese continues like she hasn't been interrupted, "And the last two are for you."

"And can I ask why exactly you ordered two shots for me while I am still on the clock?"

"Drea here has informed me that my brother is in the building and has been for the entirety of your shift." She waves a hand lazily behind her head in the direction of where her brother now sits at the bar. Was he watching this whole exchange?

"Oh."

"Yea. 'Oh' is right. What happened to you last night? You missed out on the cake." Reese pouts and I try not to fidget.

"Yea, Mel. What happened to you?" Drea raises an eyebrow and I tell her to knock it off with my face alone. Two reasons.

One, I don't want Clo to know that her brother stayed at my place last night. I hate adding yet another secret to the growing list of secrets I'm keeping. I also don't want to think more about what him staying at my house actually meant. To him or to me.

Two, I don't know if Reese will expeditiously present this information to Mack. Either by choice or by accident. I know she wants to help him. The last thing I need is for her to unknowingly add to the fire that sparked up at the party last night. He is not in the best place to hear that Tyson was at my house.

"I was tired. I went home and slept. Nothing serious."

For whatever reason, Drea is like a dog with a bone. "Hmm... Didn't—"

"Bottoms up," I say getting the first shot down, effectively cutting Drea off. She laughs and my girls join in on the laughter, forgetting about Drea's earlier comments.

"Yes, Melly! Okay, everyone together now! I'm living through you, ladies!"

I grab the second lime and throw the remaining shot back. It burns all the way down. Outside of the few times where I've had a drink for a little confidence boost, I don't really drink. Mostly because of my dad. A little bit because of Mack still. There have been many times when alcohol has changed the trajectory of my life. Two shots aren't enough to get me drunk, but I will be feeling this for the rest of my shift.

"Our lovely wedding planner, Chloe, will be handling all wedding preparations from this point forward. Our first big event will be wedding dress shopping this week. You're still in right?"

"Yep. I'll be there."

"Yay and then—"

The last thing I need is to get behind or to share some truths that I shouldn't the longer I stand here chatting with them. "I really do need to check on my tables and hope I'm not too far behind on orders. We'll talk later. Is that fine?"

They nod, shooing me from the table. Rushing back to check on my other tables' order, I'm a few steps from the kitchen when I feel it.

If Reese is off work, I should have expected that he would not be far behind.

My mistake was thinking I would have more time.

CHAPTER 21

Melody, Then

"No one?" Tyson asks, looking more shocked than I expected after he saw the small wallet-sized photo of me on the fridge. It was a part of the promotional material from last year's show. I stand in the center of the shot posed with the two other dancers from our company.

We've been talking at my kitchen island for over an hour though it doesn't feel that long. I take the opportunity to grab some veggies from the fridge and put them on the counter. Looking over the carrots and bell pepper, I ponder whether I'll cut these up myself or get out the mandolin to julienne them. My stalling isn't making the words come any easier and I can sense Ty on the edge of his seat. I put the container back into the fridge and decide the mandolin will be safer. I shake my head in emphasis. "Not a soul."

"But, you said you were co-captain. That means you had to be good." I note that it's a statement and not a question.

"I was. I'm just not meant for a stage anymore."

"Melody." My name breaks loose from his lips like a plea. I know what he's asking and I won't make it easy on him because it's not easy on me. The last time I danced in front of an audience, I was in the ER shortly after. Alone.

"Tyson." I return the same pleading tone while I force the carrots through the slicer.

He gives me his best puppy dog eyes and pouting lower lip. I almost agree right then. When I don't say anything, he plays with his phone making ooo's and ahh's as he scrolls. "Melody, I'm looking at The Harrison School of Advanced Arts and Academics. That place is fancy as fuck. I know you have to be amazing to be a co-captain. They don't accept just anyone into that program."

"Had." Satisfied with the snack, I grab a pitcher of tea and a couple of glasses for us. Placing a candied lemon in the bottom of the two glasses, I pour tea over the slices, sliding one over to him.

"What?" he questions, looking every bit as incredulous as his tone implies. Is he ever quite this expressive when all our friends are around? I can't remember ever seeing his eyebrows this high. Usually, he's scowling or in a blasé unaffected mood. I kind of like this sillier side of him.

"Had," I respond, dipping a carrot in Ranch dressing. "I was pretty good and I did land the co-captain spot."

He pauses for a moment to think about my words. I munch on the carrot stick loudly to avoid talking anymore to fill the space. After staring at me for long moments, he asks with a voice so soft, "You haven't danced since?"

My chuckle is hollow, responding as softly, "Not for anyone else. Just me."

Tyson stands from the stool by the island. From where I'm leaning onto the counter from the other side, I straighten at his sudden movement. His slow gait to me is deliberate like he's approaching a wounded animal.

Maybe he is.

My foot healed long ago. My pride in what I was told was my gift from God was broken. I'd taped it up poorly. It had pieces missing and it never shone like it once did. How long had I been dragging it behind me like a ball-and-chain shackled to my ankle?

I'm staring at the lemon floating above the ice in my tea when I feel Tyson rub a hand down my arm. I turn my head and see his concerned face. His brows bunch with the puzzle he's trying to solve. He doesn't know that I've already lost too many pieces. I use my thumb to smooth out the frustration. I move my thumb over the crease between his eyebrows and he lets me. His eyes track back and forth over my face for some sign that I'm sure isn't there. I made my choice on the crinkled medical paper-covered exam bench.

Tyson turns me to face him fully. I hop onto the counter and he steps closer to me. His body nestled between my thighs. I hope that he will kiss me and this conversation can be over. I'm not a dancer anymore. Not really. I hoped that would be the one good thing about being the new girl in AR. I wrap my legs around him to pull him closer. My hands rest on his chest. He is beautiful like this. I can't remember ever being happy to be this close to anyone. With Ty, I feel right. This feels nice.

I'd be a fool to share my past with Ty. To share how much of a disappointment I am now.

I blink and small tears run down my face before he catches them with his thumbs. "Don't, Melody. Don't cry, baby. I'm not gonna force you to do anything, especially if it's upsetting you this much." I shake my head. "Melody," he says again lifting my chin with his hand so that I meet his eyes. I close them even tighter as the tears come.

"I just need a minute." My voice is so small as I try to push off the counter to go to the bathroom. Ty holds me in place still desperate to make eye contact with me, but I can't help it. If I stay, I'll tell him everything. I can't do that right now. "Please, Tyson."

The helpless quality of his expression makes me want to reconsider. If anyone can hold what I'm keeping close to my chest, it's Ty. I know that, feel it somewhere deep inside me.

I won't risk it.

He steps back to give me space and leans against the refrigerator. I quickly hop from the counter to my escape.

My eyes and nose are as red as I thought they were when I take stock of my appearance in the mirror. Reason enough to not talk about this anymore. What does it matter? What's in the past should stay there where it hurt me. In the present, I could be happy. I could be a transfer who is focused on her academic success and that's all. I'm not a dancer anymore. I'm not a co-captain. I'm just Mel.

I think of how Tyson pleaded my name earlier. His playful tone at odds with the turmoil swirling in my mind. What reason would he have to even care besides genuine interest? I need to calm down and go back out there. I clean myself up and breathe slowly trying to gather my strength.

I step from the bathroom, Ty is right across the hallway waiting for me. His hands are in his pockets and he seems relaxed. When he sees me, he holds out a hand. "Let me see you, Melody."

"See what?"

"This. Whatever scar this is. The one you're scared to even let me see. I want to know what happened, please. Even if you think it's ugly. I'm here for you." I shake my head and shake my head some more. It's not his problem. It wouldn't be mine right now if he would just drop it. Tyson is not going to though. He wants to see *this*. He doesn't know what *this* is.

"Melody, I'm not everyone else. I'm here. I'm listening not judging. It's breaking my heart to see you cry. Let me try to fix it." His face is no longer relaxed and his hands are pleading. He makes to grab me or my hands, I'm not sure, but I quickly step to the left away from his advance.

"Fix it? There is nothing to fix! You don't think I would have tried to fix things if I could?" My words come out harsher than I intended and my voice echoes through the small space between us. The emotions I tried to keep under control bubble to the surface. "I messed up! I failed. Not in a small way. I ruined the whole routine. No one else could perform the piece we all worked on for the semester. Months of preparation, blood, sweat, and tears that I ruined for everyone on my team that night." My hands fly to cover my mouth, but I've said too much and I know it. I know it more certainly when he continues his advance toward me. This time I stand there with my hands over my mouth like I can take back the words somehow.

His touch is gentle when he grabs my wrists to pull my hands from my mouth. "C'mon." He tucks me under his arm and walks us to the backyard. My eyes burn. I think I'll cry again, but I snuggle into his embrace and accept the comfort he's giving me.

We sit on the back porch steps like that, him leaning on the banister and me leaning into his side. For several minutes, I take my time to relax before he says my name and I look up at him. "I've never told anyone that. Who would I have told anyway?"

"Not your dad?" He looks expectant like I will say a different answer than I will.

"Not my dad." Shock flashes across his features before he looks contemplative.

"The man you see in Alpenglow is different from the man he was when this happened. The bottle had him rather preoccupied when I was in the ER room trying to answer questions I had no answers for."

CHAPTER 22

Melody, Then

TYSON'S SHOCK IS BACK, this time becoming fury. "You... You were in an emergency room? For what?" He takes a breath to calm down and lower his tone. "Please tell me what happened that night." His hands envelop mine and I think again about how perfect our hands look together.

I think about what it will cost me to bear my shame for this boy. I think about what it will mean for him to truly hold this piece of me. Can I trust that he will still be here holding this piece when he sees? Yes. "Okay."

"Look at me, Melody." I look from our hands to his eyes. He's searching my face again and I allow him. "I am not him. I am not them. I want to know because it is a part of you, that's it. I want to know because I care, for real."

Nodding, I take a big breath of air into my lungs and blow it out slowly. "That day, we did the choreography straight through at least three times before the show began. The younger girls have a piece first and our show is broken up into two parts to accommodate an intermission. Those other girls in the photo you saw, my other co-captains had the center roles with me for the show. When we were walking on stage to take our marks, one of them said something to me that messed with my head." I shake my head now like I can clear the words from my memory, but they will be there forever I suspect.

"What did she say?" I can feel the tension in his body growing the more I tell him.

I chuckle mostly to myself when I tell him, "She said, 'This is a gift,' right before the music started."

He's quiet for a minute. "I don't get it. It wasn't a gift?"

"Oh, it was. There were many big names in the industry watching that night. Being able to perform for them could have meant summer internship programs or just favor and recognition in this world."

"So, what then? I'm confused." I inspect his face. Tyson does truly seem puzzled again.

I looked at our hands. "My mother would say that to me all the time. When she complained about her back or elbows hurting from hours over a canvas, she'd say, 'Your art can feel like a gift or a curse. It's all in your viewpoint.' I was always an anxious kid. Dancing was a gift for me. It calmed my mind. It gave me an outlet and I was pretty good. When I'd be too hard on myself or feel like giving up, she would remind me, "This is a gift.'"

I blink back tears and try to clear the thickness in my throat. Ty grips my hand, but I don't look up at him again before I continue. "There is no way Kerry would know that. She was trying to be uplifting and refocusing us before the performance. It had not even been a month since my mom passed at that time. Dance was the only thing keeping me somewhat okay. I was already feeling upset about this being the first show she would miss. My dad was not going to be there either. Text after text and call after call went unanswered the whole day. This was the first recital where I would perform with no support from my family there. I was alone. Since I was six, I had my mom and daddy in the front row." I blew out a breath, sensing the tears stinging my eyes and willing them to go back where they came from. "They weren't only in the front row. They would have the cowbell going and flowers after I joined them at the end. For the really big recitals, we would go to a dance dinner after and we would pick an extra decadent dessert. Not this time."

Ty rubs circles with his thumb over my knuckles. "Go on," he encourages.

I nod my head once slowly, trying to gain my composure to get the words out. "Kerry's words hit me in the gut. I nearly folded right then before the lights found us on stage. I tried to do the choreo like nothing had happened, but her words became my mother's words and then her voice echoed through my head so loudly that I couldn't hear anything else." Swallowing, I try to push the emotion down. His reassuring squeeze of my hand helps me continue. I look him in the eyes even though it's hard. There is no going back now and I want to let someone in. *No, I want to let Tyson in.* "When I was supposed to be hitting a mark, I missed it. I came out of my reverie too late... and I..."

My words get stuck in my throat as I try to make them come more easily. I swallow several times before I can speak again. Finally, I continued. "I rolled over my foot, fracturing one of the bones." Ty's sharp inhale and wince is to be expected. Talking about it reminds me of the pain and recovery from such a traumatic and public mistake. "Ms. Nicholson stopped the show and moved Kerry and the rest of the team backstage as she informed the audience that our senior dance team's performance would be rescheduled. Sophie Nicholson was the only adult able to take me to the ER since no one could get in contact with my daddy."

Ty's anger is palpable, rolling off of him. I can taste the fury in his words and he bites out, "And your dad never came? At any point?" He's trying not to yell. He's trying to keep his composure but it's failing. He runs his hands over his hair and crosses his arms as he waits for my response.

"You know he didn't. Ms. Nicholson called my grandma and she drove from Dallas to take me to the orthopedic surgeon the next day. I had crutches and a walking boot by the end of the day. By that night, she had forced her son to a detox and recovery facility. Everyone at school already pitied me because I lost my mom. Then it got out that my dad was in rehab... I hated the scrutiny. I hated the whispers. I couldn't do anything about it. I let everyone say what they wanted and think what they wanted. When I wouldn't give them the gossip they wanted, they made it up. It's not like I went back to dance so I had no one."

"Did they say you couldn't dance?" His question was soft again like he didn't want to know the answer or hoped I wouldn't answer the way he thought I would.

"No. They said I should slowly get back into activity after about two months."

"I'm lost again, Melody. Then why don't you dance anymore?"

"I do. I've practiced that routine relentlessly after I received the approval to use my foot as normal again. I had to nail the routine and it's flawless now." My voice is strong with conviction. I had *made* it flawless, even improved on the original choreography. I never faltered again.

Ty holds my face with both his hands as we look into each other's eyes. His are open and hopeful, but I see both the understanding and confusion still roiling there. I don't expect him to say anything more.

He closes his eyes tightly and opens them again to hold my gaze. "I'm so sorry that happened to you, Melody. It's not your fault. None of that is your fault. You didn't ruin anything. You were human and made a mistake while you processed something most other people would not understand if it had not happened to them. Kids are fucked up." I nod my head trying to keep from sobbing all over again. "Is that why you sit on the roof?"

"Oh. You've seen me?"

He scratches the back of his neck. "Yea... a time or two. That first night before I met you. I was waiting up for Clo and you were sitting up there."

"I guess so. It's better than being in my empty house. If I'm outside on the roof, I don't have to hear the silence or wonder where my dad is at." I nod my head. "It's not always super helpful. Some things will bring her memories to the forefront more than others. She would have loved how clearly you can see the stars here at night. We never got that in Houston... That's the worst part of it all. She's a part of me and a part of everything. My thoughts lead to her all the time. I refuse to forget her. She was everything I aspired to be. My dad still hasn't let her go. He might be somewhat sober for work but I know he's still drinking. He doesn't do it in front of me anymore. So I hardly see him these days. I don't forgive him for what happened. How could I? I didn't lose just one parent, but two. I can't recognize him anymore."

"I don't blame you," he clears his throat. "How did you lose your mom? If you don't mind me asking about her..."

"Cancer. They found out and she was already stage four. There wasn't much the oncologist could do. It was spreading too quickly. She was there one day and gone the next. I never had time to say the things I wanted to her, or fully comprehend that she wouldn't be there before she was truly gone."

"Fuck cancer and fuck how it steals those we love without any concern for what kind of mess it leaves behind." Emotionally, he admits. "Mine too. Years ago now. I was eleven."

Leaning my head on his shoulder, I think about how I have not met anyone who could understand what I went through before. Whatever possessed me to open up to Ty was right. "It's horrible. I feel like it never gets better."

"It does... It can but it will never be the same. What your dad was going through is his own shit. He may have lost his wife, but he should have been there for you. You shouldn't have been in that ER with your dance teacher. He should be here now. I hate that you went through that alone." He squeezes his eyes close, cursing under his breath. "I'm here and I want to be here for you. For any of it. For all of it. I get it." Tyson holds his arms open for me and I lean into our hug with my whole body weight. Letting him support the full weight of me and my mangled heart. He hugs me tightly and soothes my senses. I remain in his arms while the wind whips through my hair and his.

I showed him the heaviest parts of my past and he didn't run. He's still here holding all these broken pieces.

Chapter 23

Tyson, Then

THE NEXT NIGHT, I find myself back in Melody's backyard. Maybe I could play it off like I'm just a huge fan of her lemon iced teas, which I am by the way. It has more to do with the fact that I'm a huge fan of her. "How about I make you a deal?" I ask from where I sit on the stairs.

She looks at me with curiosity coloring her features. "What kind of deal?"

"Enter the talent show this winter. Dance for me and I'll play for you. Not a cover. But an original song—one I wrote. We can be two nervous people on stage doing the things that make us nervous... Together."

"You don't even know if I'm any good."

"I think we already figured that part out, Melody. As co-captain at some hoity-toity school in Houston, you had to be amazing."

"Had."

"You're right. Maybe I should see what I'm getting into..." She bites her lip. She doesn't know that I've already caught glimpses of her out in the backyard when she thinks no one can see. She is a true talent. I'm no expert and I certainly couldn't make a real judgment, but Melody can dance. I'm positive that she should be sharing this with more people than just me, knowingly or unknowingly. But maybe, just maybe, if she can see that it's nothing to dance for me, then she might go back to dancing for others again. "One verse. That's hardly anything. An audition is only that long anyway."

"One verse," She repeats standing on the top step above me.

"One verse to acclimate, you know? Get your bearings and then you can stop if you want to." I wink and crack a grin. "I don't think you'll want to though." I stand up on the bottom step and she looks down at me with a small smile on her face. Like this, we're looking at each other eye to eye. The jig is up and I admit, "I just want to see once... Please don't if you think it will upset you. You're strong even if you're not ready right now."

"No. I think I want to show you." She sputters for a moment, adding, "The dance. I want to show you the dance. I've been going over the choreo out here when I'm not on the roof. It's not the same but it—"

"You don't have to do all that, Melody. I'm sure it's going to be amazing."

She gives me a shy grin, walking over to the grass and stretching. I don't say anything as she prepares. I've already seen her do this dance perfectly. My room has the perfect view of her yard. Tonight she wears thin leggings and a tanktop that will be more than comfortable to dance in. Her taut body bends in ways that make my blood heat. Staring would be the polite way to say what I'm doing as she contorts this way and that.

She places her phone next to me, "Okay, start it when I get into position." I give her a thumbs-up and tap the phone when she is in the center of the lawn.

When Melody dances, she loses herself in the movements. Every sway of her hips and rise of her leg is fluid and enthralling. I don't look away. I can't look away. Nothing could have prepared me for what the experience would be like up close. She hits each note and I see the moment when she truly settles into her own skin. The first verse passes and the chorus rises.

She looks incredible.

At the height of the chorus, I see the moves where she used to hesitate. Not a single doubt flashes in her gaze. She falls forward onto the tops of her feet before her body follows the movement. Her smile is blinding as she spins on one knee to continue the routine.

After hearing what she went through, I have so much pride in her showing me how far she has come. So much beauty and grace are a part of this girl in front of me. I was standing when she started this dance, but now I am on my knees when the final note reverberates through the charged space between us.

I go to her, scooping her into my arms. I praise her and she laughs. I feel the sound in my chest and when I put her back onto the ground her eyes are shining. "You absolutely need to share this with more people, Melody. You were perfect. This was incredible! Beyond that. I don't know what else to say."

"Say that you will perform with me."

"You haven't heard me sing..." I scratch my neck. "I want to see more." The goofy grin stretches my cheeks.

She smacks my arm playfully, "I'm serious, Ty."

"So am I. How could I follow that performance? I could be terrible and it completely throws off your whole piece."

"Only one way to find out. I'm sure it's going to be amazing," she repeats back what I said to her before with a smug little smile.

I wouldn't say that I am a shy performer. Playing my guitar is second nature. I taught myself and it feels weird not to have it with me now. When I followed her to her house after school, I didn't think to grab it. I only knew that I wanted to be out of the house with Quincy and Clo going at it like rabbits, at least for a while.

To sing a song that I know I wrote about Melody—for Melody—without my six-string has me feeling barer than if I were to actually strip down right here. I don't sing for anyone. My dad has told me time and time again how dumb it is. *You're no Darius Rucker and Black people don't sing country. You'll never make a living from singing that shit.* I never believed him. The words hurt either way. It's artists like Jordan Hurst and Michael Thomas who are paving the way for men who look like me to have a place in the industry. Times are changing and I think I could be a valuable addition to the genre. To get close to that kind of success would mean more to me than he could ever comprehend behind a desk crunching numbers all day. He doesn't understand what the burden of a dream feels like. I don't dream of fame. I dream of acceptance of what my soul has to share. The music that bubbles right beneath the surface and weighs heavy in my heart when I try to repress it. I know he's wrong.

I never had his support. The only person who supported me was my mom. Even as a young kid, music was in my blood. She recognized that and encouraged me. After she passed, I lost that hope. The one person on my team had been taken from me.

She holds my hand as we walk back to her patio steps. I sit next to her and it takes me a few breaths before I speak again. "I haven't done this for anyone in a long time." She looks at me with a pleading expression. She's so pretty looking at me with all the encouragement in her walnut eyes. I know I'll do it for her.

"A deal is a deal." I take a sip of the tea she made for me. That lemon at the bottom sparks on my tastebuds and I close my eyes.

"I'll close mine too," she whispers.

"Okay." Deep breath in, deep breath out. I open my mouth and let the words pour out that have been bouncing through my head all this time.

While I sing, I let the music take me. After the first line, I open my eyes. I don't want to miss any reaction she might have to the music I made for her. Through my lyrics, I tell her how she smells like paradise and likely tastes of mango. How I see her sad eyes that hold the sorrow that never touches her smiles. The way her angelic face takes me from hell to heaven though I'm stuck in this small town. With each line revealing more and more pieces of what I haven't shared aloud about my feelings for her, my heart beats faster. I'm thankful for her closed eyes so she can't see how my hands shake with the emotion.

Her expression changes from calm, to pensive, to a grin that she tries to hide. She opens her eyes when I finish the song and her little smile makes my stomach flutter with nerves. I don't think she'll say anything, but she stands up in front of me, "I think you are going to be in so much trouble with everyone for keeping your beautiful voice from them."

A chuff escapes my lips when I tell her, "You're really fucking sweet, Melody."

"Like mango?" she questions under her lashes, the picture of innocence as she recalls one of the lyrics from my song.

The last of my nerves leave me at her teasing, "You think that song is about you?"

"Oh, of course not," she giggles. "I just think it's interesting that it sounds like it should be accompanied by that song I always hear you playing on your guitar. You know? The one you said was my song before..." Her smile is shy but somehow smug as hell.

I bound from the step after her and she darts from me, giggling all the while. I wrap her up in my arms when I catch her. "I knew I was right," she tells me as we fall into her plush grass.

I angle my head down to whisper, "Okay, you were right." She shudders with my breath wisping across her neck and ear. "I think I'm ready."

Mack may have let me know that he was trying to date Melody. But I don't think I can respect that. Her and I make more sense. That's my boy. I've known him, and been cool with him for years. They don't fit like her and I do. She may not see the full picture but I will show her that it's me she wants. I can be the better choice for her.

I don't want to be that guy leering after his sister's friend. I don't and still, I'm drawn to her. If it comes to it, then I'll deal with Clo. It's dumb to let something like that keep me from something that feels so right.

As Melody tries to wiggle out of my arms, I know that I'm fucked. Little shockwaves zing in my gut when she finally gets free of my embrace, giggling the whole way back to her porch. *Have I heard her laugh like this before?* There's light in her eyes and in her voice. I miss her in my arms even though it has only been a few seconds. *How can I miss her already?*

I want her. If there is even a small possibility of being with her I am going to take it. For now, I'll be content to have these moments with us alone. I knew my irritation with his attempts to win her was rooted in something serious.

This girl was meant for me.

CHAPTER 24

Tyson

"No FISTS AND NONE of that petty shit tonight, T." Quincy points his finger at me.

Wondered when he would come over and go all big brother on me though he and I are the same age. Over at the booth, I could not get his other bartender out of my face so I could get some work done. Sarah Jane would have likely been an easy lay when I was trying to soothe my ego by smashing any girl who wanted it. Hell, I'm not blind but there is only one girl I'm here to see. Judging by the scowl she was not hiding as well as she thought she was, Melody didn't want to see her either. I've been sitting at the bar top ever since, working on new music, waiting for the end of her last shift.

I point to my own chest, affronted. "Me? Why you telling me that? You need to get on your boy." I swig my pilsner, feeling the crisp bubbles burst as I try to keep from raising my voice at my brother-in-law. If anything, I deserve to make a scene. That's not my style which is lucky for both Quincy and Mack.

"Yeah. You! It takes two to have a conversation and a fight. I know you two have your..." He trails off thinking of the best word to describe the fucked off circumstances of the love triangle that included Mack, Melody, and me for too many years to count.

"Reasons to get into a fistfight?" I supply for him.

That guy has it coming. I may have been in the wrong, to begin with, but how he did me was dirty. There is no debating that.

"No!" Quincy slams his hand onto the bar. Not loud enough to alarm anyone, but the bubbles in my pint glass dance rapidly. Looking around to check that no one saw him, he lowers his voice and leans across the bar closer to me. "No. You and Mack are not going to do anything to ruin my business. He comes in here often enough and if you're still here when he gets off work... Look, I don't care. If you get into it—I'm kicking you both out!"

I let the confusion show on my face. "I still don't understand why you are having this conversation with me. You need to have it with him." I didn't even want to say his name out loud.

The sigh that comes from Quincy sounds age-old and weary. I observe my friend and he looks as weary as that sigh sounded. "Can you give me your word that you aren't going to start something with Mack?"

No. "Yea. I'll do my best." And I would. I would do my very best not to put my foot in his ass. He would deserve every hit. I held my tongue. Quincy is the only person who knows what the past years have been like for me. Just him, Clo and maybe Aaliyah. I've been the good guy. The bigger man.

Funny thing about being the bigger man—t's usually the one who wronged you that wants you to step up and do the "right thing" on their behalf. The bigger the wrong, the bigger the man. And I'm standing ten feet tall at this point. If Mack has something to say, I'll show him how big I am now.

His sigh sounds more like relief this time. He looks to the table his wife is sitting at with Drea and Reese who are talking to Melody. The dopey grin on his face makes me envious... I can't help but look at the table too.

Melody's holding up a shot glass by herself, saying something with that fake-ass smile on. My eyes lock on to her little pink tongue licking her hand and then putting the glass to her lips. She closes her eyes for the smallest moment and I wonder if she's taking that shot because of me. No one else at the table is taking a shot with her.

Maybe it's because of our talk last night or this morning.

She looks good. The same as I remember, but somehow even better. Her long brown legs and that tiny waist all barely covered in silk... I'd wanted to press my head into the soft comfort of her chest like I remembered. If I had her against that sink any longer, I might have acted on that longing. To be close to her and in her embrace. Fuck, I wish.

Her eyes held fire but hurt, as well. The fire, I understand. The hurt? I want to know more about.

I'm no fool, though. Melody clearly does not want anything to do with me. Not in that way. The moment was there and gone as quickly as when I brought up her mental health. She pretends like everything is fine when I know it's not. When I know she's not.

There was a time that I had been privy to Melody's moments. She would share her truth with me. Her broken soul. Her heavy heart. Her gilded dreams. I would give anything to hold them in my hands again. I shake my head because it's shit like this that is going to make me break my promise to Q.

I turn back to the bar and down half the beer. Needing to change the subject, I ask, "Can you set a couple cases of these to the side for me?" I hold my pint in front of his face to break the lovesick laser focus he has on my sister. "Aye, man! Did you hear me?"

He blinks a few times and nods his head toward the back corner of the bar. "I already did. They're stacked up in the corner. Got a couple for your mates too." I give him an amused smirk. "What? The best marketing is through word of mouth."

Quincy had turned QB's from being just a local sports bar to a local brewery as well over the last year. Not doing too bad for himself, to my knowledge. It's gaining traction since he and Chloe started distributing to stores and popping up at festivals. I'm proud of my boy and my sister's business. They created something special together. It was clear that they brought out the best in each other.

I turn back to Melody as she grabs the shot glass and empty plates before she leaves. I should be happy that she and that dude aren't on good terms. I should be happy knowing she filed for divorce from him.

But I'm not.

Through the crowd, I can feel her uneasiness. It rolls across the distance like sonar. I follow her with my eyes until she makes her rounds through the tables and back to the bar. She avoids making eye contact with me and works even harder to not get near my side of the bar. I pull out my pen again, working on writing music because it's more constructive to channel my longing into the music than making a scene here. I'm hurting for her bad but it will not do me any favors to make her more uncomfortable.

I check the time on my phone and that feeling of unease sharpens to a point when Mack, Tony, and Taylor come into the bar.

"Two nights in a row? To what do we owe the pleasure?" Tony says when he claps me on the back at the bartop.

I shake his hand and Taylor's, pointedly avoiding Mack altogether.

He scoffs, "What? No love for me?" The fucking jerk.

Quincy is already on the other side of the bar saying, "Enough. Don't make me kick your ass out again."

Mack shrugs and rolls his eyes at our friend. "That happened one time. It's been years since."

"And I'll still kick your ass out." Quincy points a finger at Mack. I feel vindicated that I wasn't the only one to receive this reprimand from Q.

"I've got no cause to fight. Or do I, Tyson?"

I take a swig of my beer, making the asshole wait for the blow that's coming to him. "Considering I'm staying at Melody's house this weekend, I'd say you do." Taylor and Tony hide their shock by slowly moving down the bar top away from us. It's just me and Mack now having this conversation. I could say that I didn't want to be a part of this pissing contest, but that'd be a lie. He had a chance and he fucking blew it. I'll reap any benefits that I can... and pissing off this guy is absolutely a benefit.

"You're trying to fuck my wife!"

"Your ex-wife. You lost her."

"You're sleeping in my fucking house?" He bites out and I can see he is trying his hardest to restrain himself. His face is already red as he stands in front of where I'm sitting.

"It's not your house. If it was, then you'd know I was there, huh?"

He takes a step closer to me. "Fuck you prick. You left her—like an idiot! I was all she had. Where were you?"

The truth in his words sears like fire through my middle. My best, unaffected smirk covers how much those words burn me. I stand from my stool getting in his face. "And I'm here now and that just tears you up, doesn't it?"

Melody's sweet voice cuts into our conversation "Tyson." I turn to her and she's fidgeting with her little cocktail tray. "Can I talk to you?"

"Hey, Mel," Mack says around me.

I step to the side, effectively blocking him from her view. "Yea, let's go out back."

Mel tells Quincy that she's taking a break and we walk over to my truck. She's faster than I expect and I have to pick up the pace just to keep up with her. She whirls on me when we get to Old Red. "What was that?"

"What was what?" I ask, pretending I have no idea what she could be talking about.

"You and Mack. What were you doing there, telling him that you're staying at my house?"

I shrug. "Was I not?"

She huffs a sigh. "You know that's not what it was."

"Then what was it? I slept at your house. In your bed..." Her brows pinch and I take her hand. I thought maybe she would snatch it away but she let me. "With you also sleeping there, of course. Hell, you made me breakfast and we got ready together. Is that not staying at your place?"

The scowl on her beautiful face looks as out of place as it did with her jealousy over Sarah Jane. "You know that's not what I meant."

"Then explain it to me. You could have asked me to leave at any point and I would have gone." I place her hand over my heart and hold it there with both of my hands. "No fuss or argument."

Melody stubs her little nonslip shoes into the gravel. She looks so good today. Did I say that already? Fuck. Each moment that I'm near her, I feel how dumb and ungrateful I was to leave her behind. This woman is the tune that all other sounds should be compared to.

Even though I am the only one who knows about how she broke down yesterday. It seems that I am the only person who has actually seen that Melody is not the sweet and happy person she pretends to be for Alpenglow Ridge. It makes me wonder how long she has been masking for them. What all has my Melody had to endure in silence, behind closed doors.

It pisses me off that Mack, that fucker, has the audacity to still act like he has any claim over her when he hasn't even cared for her. I doubt she ever let him see what's underneath like I have. Everyone could see how I fucked up losing her, but not the woman in front of them.

Her silence lingers. "Did you want me to leave?"

"No," she says so quietly that I'd miss it if I weren't watching her like a hawk.

I grab her other hand and bring it to my chest. "For as long as I'm still breathing, that my heart is still beating, I'll be here for you. Whatever you need, I'll be whatever you need me to be."

She looks up to her hands on my chest and then to my face. "Then why did you leave in the first place? I never wanted you to go. I just had to deal with it."

"Melody, we can talk about it later. I don't have enough time to explain everything that pulled us in opposite directions on your fifteen-minute break. But I will tell you. Anything you want to know, I'll tell you." It's well past time.

She nods and I pull her into a hug. She lets me hold her for the remaining minutes of her break. That embrace could have been hours for how much trust and faith she pours into me.

Before she needs to go back into the building, my phone rings in my back pocket. *Time to pay the piper.*

CHAPTER 25

Tyson

I ALREADY KNOW WHO'S calling me by the ringtone. It's better to not be surprised by Jordan's calls. I wince at the name on the screen. Melody gives me a questioning look, but I wave her into the building and tell her I'll meet her there later.

"Are you still in podunk?" Jordan sneers into the line.

"It's not podunk." Maybe it is a little, but I don't like the derogatory way he talks about my hometown. "I'll be here for the weekend. What's up?"

"I wanted to tell you in person, but you weren't home." I feel an appropriate amount of unease from him being at my place without me being there. With the way he throws his weight around, he likely got let inside to look through all my shit. I've seen him use his fame to get into just about any establishment. My jaw already aches from how I clench my jaw at the realization that he could have been in my apartment without me..

I hear the gravel crunch behind me and I turn. "Keeta booked us for Harmony Hill Rodeo. The lineup is pretty sick. A solo spot for us for the second Saturday."

"What the hell are you doing here?" I end the call, pocketing my phone.

"Like I said, I wanted to tell you in person." He looks almost unrecognizable in oversized sunglasses and a generic ballcap but his unmistakable neck tattoo is a dead giveaway for true fans. And as a former true fan, I would know who he is from a mile away.

"You serious?" Not quite sure if I mean about the fact that he showed up here or that we booked this show. Harmony Hill is a couple towns over from Alpenglow. Much larger, with the legendary Harmony Hill Rodeo featuring many big names in music—especially country—rodeo games and a massive carnival that goes on for two weekends in a row. It doesn't surprise me that Jordan would be able to make that roster but JT is not nearly as big as his legacy. The remnants of it anyway.

"Like I have time to play around with my money. Of course, I'm serious!" He pops the collar of his jean jacket, stepping back behind my truck where I notice his big black SUV is parked. The muscled-up guy in the driver's seat is not from Uber, I'm sure. He calls my attention back to him, saying, "We're the last act of the event. We need to start going over the set."

I look at the bar and then at my watch to check the time. "When?"

"If we're gonna debut any of the new music you've been working on, I'd say now. How is that coming? T-Mac said you haven't been to the studio in weeks." This guy was checking on me like the repo man. I owed him my start, but he seems to think that means I owed him my life as well.

"I'm working on it, man." Most of the songs we sing are written by me. Some of the music is composed with the help of Zeke and Robert. Everyone in the band contributes, except Jordan. The rumors of him having both a gambling and drug problem were not rumors. He's been rebranding himself off our hard work. This industry flourishes on the recommendation of other stars. Without Jordan, we would still be playing local shows. No one would be singing my songs and asking for guest appearances on their late-night shows. I'm lucky. We're lucky. I know that. At what point will I be able to be out of the control of Jordan Hurst's whims?

"You better be. I'm not going to be playing only old songs when everyone else is going big. It's the biggest outdoor rodeo. We would be the laughing stock to have a dusty set." I don't point out how he can't actually play anything or that most of the songs we're singing are my own. It's a petty point and he wouldn't care either way.

"The fans love our music. Everything we've done together has been a big hit." I say instead.

"Because it's my old stuff."

I sigh and try to regain my composure. He is testing me and I am not in the mood when Melody is in the bar right now likely being harassed by her ex-husband. "*Breaking at the Bar* and *Trails* were written solely by me. They love my music just as much as yours."

He scoffs, "They buy it because my name is on it. Finish up wherever it is you're doing in BFE and get back to Denver and into the studio. I expect you to get new tracks down before the end of the month." He gets into the SUV and drives off. I stare at the vehicle driving away in disbelief. *This motherfucker.*

I don't like that he could find me that easily. I've never brought him here before.

I stride back into the bar, barely paying attention to the scenery around me as I go over too many thoughts in my head. Taylor raises their beer toward me from the table they've relocated to. I walk over and put my hat on the table. They pour me a pint from the pitcher and slide it my way. When I reach for the glass, they don't let go. "Do you promise to behave like a grown-ass man?"

"Why the hell is everyone asking me that? It's that douchebag who doesn't know how to behave." The douchebag scoffs and I ignore it.

"That's exactly what I'm talking about. No name-calling and no hitting. Okay, children?" They look from me to Mack and back again.

We both grumble in agreement. I take my beer from Taylor's hand. Tony laughs with his deep voice and it's like a signal for Drea. She comes over with a basket of fried pickles and a shot of something brown.

"Aye! Drea. Lemme get one of those too." I request on her hurried spin from the table to her next destination.

"Since when do you drink Makers?" She questions, looking over the table and grabbing a few empty glasses.

I sit up a little taller, crossing my arms over my chest. "Am I not a man?"

She smirks with a hand on her hip, "Do you want me to answer that?"

"Can I just get a whiskey please, D?"

"I'll see what I can find," she teases before leaving us at the table again.

"Please nothing bottom shelf" I plead after her, walking away. I don't know if she heard me.

"Back to what I was saying before. What is Country's Sad Boy still doing in AR?" Tony says around a mouthful of fried pickles.

"I only came for the party. Chloe asked us to play and I've known Reese as long as the rest of you. I'm just passing through though."

"Ah." He seems satisfied with my answer. Tony thinks over his next words while I sip on my beer. "Maybe you can lend us some of your expertise then."

"My expertise in what?"

"Breaking hearts," he says simply with a shrug.

I reel back, blinking slowly. My mouth hangs open, shocked at the casual blow. "Wow. That's pretty fucked up, man"

"He's not wrong," Mack says under his breath.

"Aye, shut your damn mouth. You don't know about me and it's none of your business."

"Yea, whatever. I know firsthand how you do what you do." He downs his beer and moves over to the table with Reese and Chloe. Good riddance.

I chose not to respond to his accusation. By all accounts, I could let them make me out to be the villain in this situation. I'm not. It's a fucking shit predicament between the three of us. The best thing is that I'm not having to come to blows with that fucker like Quincy suspected we would.

Tense, Tony tracks Mack's movements from our high-top table to the lower table my sister is sitting at. When we see him sit, we turn back to our table and continue our conversation. "Anyway, now that the drama queen is gone... Taylor needs help," Tony says.

"I don't know that I can give anything good, but I'll try my best," I shrug.

They look to me, "It's about Ashley."

"Damn, she's still putting up with your shit," I say.

They give me a self-deprecating chuckle, "Definitely not. That's the problem. She gave me an ultimatum."

"Okay, I'm listening."

"Propose or let her go." They sip deeply from their mug. Taylor and Ash have been together longer than I can remember actually. I met them both as a couple so it's hard to even imagine the two of them not together.

"Oof. And you don't want to propose?" I question.

"I should want to right?" Taylor drinks deeply from the pint glass, this time finishing it. It's clear they are torn up about this.

Tony sips the whiskey in his glass and returns it to the table. With a slap on Taylor's shoulder, saying "I told them that if it was really the move, it would be a no-brainer. Nothing to think about."

"Yea, coming from this guy who is so deep in the friend-zone, he should get reward points." I chuckle and Taylor slaps me five. I can be smug because for as long as I've known Tony he has held a torch for Drea. She has never let him get anywhere near the boyfriend title. It's sad really, but he still holds onto hope. I guess I'm not too far from what he's going through. I slug back the rest of my drink.

He puffs out his chest and raises a fist at me. "Watch your tone. I'm still your elder."

Taylor guffaws, "Even worse." They laugh all while pouring another beer and pretending to wipe at a tear. "Oh wise one, why don't you just ask then?"

"You know why. Drea is not like Ashley." He rolls his eyes at Taylor's suggestion. "She's still the sponsoring member of the Strong Woman Man-Hater Club. I don't blame her and that's not my biggest problem. Sheriff Deputy dickhead getting promoted has made him even more untouchable. Mireya deserves better." Drea's daughter, Mireya, looks at Tony like he hung the moon. He takes protective to the next level when it comes to those two.

"Hey, man. We get it. If anybody deserves the job, it's you." I say that with all the confidence in the world—Tony is a great guy. Clo has told me as much and in the few times we've talked, he's chill.

He grunts. The last of his Makers thrown back until nothing remains in the glass. "I appreciate that, man. Too bad it doesn't count for shit. Drea will never cross that line with me."

Taylor smacks the table, "Back to me! What the hell am I going to do with Ash? I don't want to break up. I just don't want anything to change."

"What would really change though?" I question. "You live together. Are seen in public together. It's just signing a paper. Done."

"I don't know. It's more than just some paper. I need time."

"Eleven years isn't enough time? Damn. You gonna wait until you're fifty? For what?" Tony's words ring inside my head. All that time that Taylor and Ash have been together is about the same amount of time that Melody and I have been apart. What would our lives look like if we had spent that time in each other's lives?

"Exactly. It's the same shit. Pop the question." I say.

Reaching to grab a pickle, Tony smacks Taylor's hand before they can even get near it. "Now it feels like I'm a piece of shit for doing it because she asked."

"Nah. If you make it special, she'll be grateful. Ashley is obsessed with you. Always has been," Tony affirms.

"You think?"

Q and I exchange a glance. Together, we say, "Yes."

Drea returns to exchange Tony's rocks glass with a glass of iced tea. I'm grateful she brought me a Makers. I need something stronger than beer. "Now, to Tyson," Tony says. Both, he and Taylor, turn to me with grins on their faces.

"Oh nah. I'm not in this. My shit is complicated enough. I don't need more people in it. Actually, I need significantly less people in it." One person in particular.

"Technically, we are already a part of it," Tony says.

"Were you really here for the party, or are you trying to get back with Mel?" Tayor asks.

"I'd have to have actually had her in order to get back with her."

"I don't care if you didn't put a name to it. You can't have a breakup like y'all did if you weren't together. Get me?" Tony says.

Much more smug than they deserve to be, Taylor adds, "What was it that you just said to me? Pop the question."

I huff, "I wish. I'm working on it. Don't you worry."

"I'm very worried. You blew it big time. Twice from what I hear." Apparently everyone heard. I internally roll my eyes.

"That was then and this is now. I've got a plan. I'm not a dumb little boy anymore."

"You sure about that?" Tony asks.

I look over to where Melody talks with another table as they place their orders. She must feel my eyes on her because she looks up and catches my gaze on her. I don't look away, instead taking in each of her mouthwatering form in her tight uniform. She busies herself with writing what the people at the table are ordering. There's no mistaking how flustered she is though.

"Oh, I'm sure," I say.

Chapter 26

Melody

"Was it a good night?" Quincy asks when I walk into his office. The large canvas print of him and Chloe hangs behind his desk. It's almost life sized and it makes me smile. I really do love them together. They balance each other out perfectly. I wonder if that is what being with Ty is like for me. Do we balance each other out? Maybe our relationship was never as black and white as theirs but you never really know what someone's marriage is like behind closed doors. I can attest to that fact a hundred times over.

It's incredibly late by the time my shift is over. Tony and Tyson talk at the bar while I busy myself getting ready to clock out. I know Tony is waiting there for Drea to close. On any other Saturday, I might have been happy to be one of the first cut for the night. Tonight, I'm doing everything I can to prolong going home alone with Tyson. I don't exactly know why.

It's my fault. I could have told him that I wanted to drive myself to work and he would have let me. I could have told him to find somewhere else to sleep last night. Hell, I could have finally grown a backbone and demanded the answers I never got all those years ago. I did none of those things.

When I turn in the last of my checks from the night to Quincy, I've settled in my mind that I will be doing that. I'm going to get the answers that I've been waiting for all these years. I don't think I was ready to hear them before. Whatever it is that kept him from me was going to be either worth it or dumb as shit after all these years had passed. It was his choices that led me to make the decisions I had, that led me to Mack. Even when Tyson wasn't in my life, he still had an effect on me. I was in his grasp though I didn't have the luxury of his hands.

"I can take you home if the thought of him driving you there is causing that much grief," Quincy says while I wait for him to finish checking my receipts. "I can feel you fidgeting from over here."

"It's not that. I'm just nervous, you know?"

He raises an eyebrow, "Didn't he stay there last night?"

"Yes, but that was different..."

He raises his palms out in front of him. "I don't need all the dirty details," he chuckles. "I just want to make sure you're good. Chloe would have my balls if I didn't at least offer."

"It'll be ok, Q. There's no one I trust more." And I meant that. Even after everything, I knew I could trust Tyson. Not with my heart though.

I leave the office and sense the moment Tyson sees me. His eyes never leave me once I enter the bar area again. "Are you good?" The concern in his eyes twisting my heart a little.

"Yea. I'm just tired. Can we go home?" Ugh. Why did that sound like an invitation for more?

Was it?

Tony double-takes and then remembers himself and goes back to snacking on whatever it is that Drea has brought him. Apparently, I'm not the only one who caught that. Taylor and Mack are long gone and it's the two of them left. Of that I am thankful. Having that kind of slip-up would have surely caused more drama than it was worth.

Tyson smirks, swiping his hat and notebook off of the table. He ushers me through the bar with his hand on my lower back. I try to walk a little bit faster than him, but it's no use. His legs are longer than mine and people are seeing it anyway. The way he is subtly possessive of me. I don't hate it. I do hate what it means for me with him doing it so publicly.

I loathe being a part of town gossip. It was the biggest reason that I never talked to anyone about what happened in my marriage. I saw how the town ripped into my friend over speculation about her relationships. I am not nearly as strong as Reese and no one would be too scared to talk about what happened with me like they are with Andrea. I keep my gaze on the floor the whole way out.

The moment we are out of the bar I'm much better. My shoulders loosen and the grip on my purse strap relaxes.

Tyson opens my door. I climb in and buckle myself into the passenger seat, all rote like I've done this a thousand times before. "Feel better?"

Despite my swirling thoughts, I give him a small smile. "Much." He gives me a small smile back and an even smaller nod before getting into his own seat.

We drive home with music I recognize, but can't quite place playing in the car. The drive down backroads isn't long since everything in AR is relatively close together. It's a little bit more complicated getting to my place as it sits right between two separate farmlands. The familiar patch of trees down the long private road greets us and I begin to get nervous again.

He parks and I wait again for him to let me out. I make a point of flicking the child lock off on the door frame. He gives me a guilty look saying, "Safety first." The hat casts a shadow over his eyes making his bright white smile appear even more brilliant. I roll my eyes in annoyance and throw my work apron back into my car. He will not be taking me the next time. Unlocking my front door, Wesson chitters and meows around our legs when we get in the house.

I put my things away as I follow my usual routine after getting off work. Putting away my tips, feeding Wessie, and turning the TV on. "I'm gonna shower, okay?" I call out to the bedroom from my closet. I take my time grabbing a towel and pajamas. He sprawls out over the bed and I don't think he's heard me when he doesn't respond. Maybe he'll just sleep, I think.

It's a long shower kind of day. I take my time washing, detangling, and conditioning my hair. I squeeze out as much of the water as I can before twisting the strands into a bun until I'm ready to style it later.

When I move on to washing my body, I sense his eyes on me. A willful path of perusal over my body like fingertips. The glass of my shower door is textured and the steam makes it almost opaque. I know that isn't stopping him from taking in my silhouette from the bed. I can make out the shape of his strong body through the fogginess of the bathroom when he shifts to sitting and eventually standing.

His tall frame leans against the doorway to watch every move I make as I smooth suds over my arm and neck. The memory of those soapy trails down his body this morning, fueling the heat building in my core. The only thing between us is this shower door and the steam— a flimsy barrier at best—more flimsy than those tight grey boxer briefs. Tyson doesn't move any farther into the bathroom.

I run the soapy loofah down my stomach and thighs. Heat that did not originate from my shower head starts to climb up my middle and settle between my legs. I bend over to wash my calves and feet, taking my time with my ass perched high in the air.

I jump a little when he says, "Turn around, Melody." There is no hesitation when I do what he tells me. I stand, facing the back wall of my shower, letting my loofah fall to the shower floor.

This should not be happening. My ass is on full display to him. Now that he is closer to me, there is no illusion of privacy. When he watched me from afar, I could pretend that maybe he couldn't see. *There are no illusions now.* Tyson can see me. And like before, I am unable to hide from him. At once, I remember that I should not be giving in to him. I should be keeping my wits about me.

"Did you like when I could only get a glimpse of heaven with all this steam in my way?"

Something about not being fooled three times...

My thoughts flutter away with the butterflies in my stomach when I hear the click of my showerhead detaching from its base. He holds it over me

162

and each path of water sluicing down my body sends shivers in its wake as he rinses all the bubbles off me.

"Look at you." I peek over my shoulder to see him biting his lip as I stand here bare to his study. I should be self-conscious. I should put a stop to this. I like his eyes on me too much to say anything. "This body has only gotten better with time."

Tyson turns the water off and I step out of the shower. His shirt and pants are splattered with water and sticking to him, but he doesn't care as he backs me up to the wall.

"All day, I've been trying to come up with reasons why I can't stay at your place tonight." My stomach drops at the thought of him leaving. I gasp at the feeling of my heated skin meeting the cold subway tiles.

"Nothing could keep me from this, from you, now that nothing stands in my way." Goosebumps raise the hairs on my heated skin as he lowers to his knees in front of me.

"Tell me that you don't want me here and I'll go." My heart hammers in my chest, the sight of this beautiful man on his knees for me.

Sweet little Melody.

Never makes a fuss.

Never fights for what she wants.

My eyes widen as I think about how much I do want this. How much I want him to stay. I can't let him leave now. No one has to know that I have him here waiting for my answer. The choice is mine and I ache for his touch like my lungs are aching for air right now.

I take a deep breath in and let it out. "I want you here." Desire coats every one of my words and I know he hears it. His ears are attuned to that sort of thing.

Flames dance in his hungry gaze as he taps my leg and I lift it over his shoulder. "Do you miss my hands on you as much as I do?" I'm shaking, quivering with need as he looks up at me from between my legs. He pauses there. Looking at my center like it will respond to him. Maybe he is talking to her. His eyes meet mine and he says, "Your words, Melody. I need to hear them. Should I make you beg for it?"

The scruff from his jaw scrapes along my thighs and it's taking every ounce of self-control I possess not to buck into his mouth. "Y-yes," I stutter. "I mean, no."

He's so close, but not at all where I want him. Where I need him. He's teasing me.

"You don't want to beg for my hands on you?" He asks slowly.

I have waited so long for this. Longed for his touch, the heat of his body, the closeness of our connection for years.

"Tell me because I need to know. Did you miss my hands on you?" There's a hint of desperation in his voice that I want to consume like the nourishment it is. It feeds my broken ego.

Having to see him give his smiles to fans. Move on with his life and achieve everything he had hoped for. My jealousy that I've had to keep to myself because he was not mine. He's not mine now. But he demands this of me. *Only a fool makes the same mistake three times...*

"I miss your hands on me," I whisper the truth. He nuzzles my thighs, squeezing the one on his shoulder, more of that friction from his scruff eliciting a small moan from my lips. I am wound so tight. Years of nothing ever coming close to what it's like to be with him. His soft twists fall into his face and contrast his jaw so acutely that I can't help it anymore. I don't know what he's waiting for. The hard ridge of his length presses along his pant leg. Long and desperate. I know he wants this. We both do.

"Please, Tyson. I need you to touch me." He looks into my eyes again. "Please I want you to feel me." My movements aren't hurried but urgent as I slide his hand from my thigh to my center, waist, and finally to my chest. "It beats for you. To your rhythm."

"Melody," my name comes from his lips on an anguished exhale. He kisses my stomach. "Not my rhythm." A kiss to each of my hipbones. "My Melody." I hold his hair out of the way in time to see his rough fingers find my clit. "Do you remember how much they are the same? Your heart and mine."

He taps my pearl once with the tip of a finger and the whimper from my chest echoes in the the now quiet bathroom. "I could never forget." He hums his approval and I know I'm lost as his face nears the apex of my thighs. My moan is throaty and obscene when his mouth first makes contact.

He makes a few more taps with his tongue before his fingers are inside me. I gasp at the sudden sensation of how his digits are stroking me deep. The gravity of my body, pressing him farther inside. "Show me, baby. Show me that you never forgot," he says. Two curl into me and his pinky wiggles softly against my ass.

I completely forget the words I'm supposed to say when he covers my hood with his warm mouth and sucks while his tongue goes back to flicking over my sensitive bud. His nimble fingers keep curling and uncurling against my G-spot.

Pressing my fingers to my lips, I don't know why I fight the cries that want to break free. My nerves stand on end at the sensation of him giving me the kind of pleasure I only wished to have again. He works my body as skillfully as he plays his guitar. Note for note, each one building me close to my peak.

My mind spins, my vision blurs and it's too much. I'm so close. So fucking close. "Fucking Christ. Tyson. Please. Oh my... please." My leg shakes with my impending climax. He sees I'm breaking and maneuvers my standing leg over his other shoulder. I'm fully straddling his face.

His fingers keep time with his tongue and I lose my mind. My own moisture rolling down my ass cheeks. He notices and uses my abundant arousal with his pinky to notch inside me. It's only a little at first and I squeeze his cheeks with my thighs when he slides the small digit to the first knuckle.

"Do you want more, Melody?" I nod my head frantically.

Delirious with want. I want. I want. I *want*.

"Tell me you want more and I will give it to you."

"I want more" I grunt, bucking my hips on his face and hands.

He chuckles over my clit and I use my leverage to try and sink deeper on his fingers. "Oh, no, no, no. That's not how you ask for me. Tell me what I need to hear and I'll give it to you."

"Tyson. Please. Please baby, I need more." I'm dripping. So wet, I should be embarrassed by how he's got me so gone.

He switches hands and now his two fingers from my core that are dripping down his hand are prodding my asshole and sliding into the tight ring. He puts two fingers from the other hand back into my pussy and I'm bouncing with abandon on his face and hands in time with how he's sucking and fucking me with both.

This man owns my body. He owns every orgasm that he strums from me with precision. He's earned it.

"Ah, God. Tyson, I'm coming. Please, Tyson."

He continues humming. His deep voice urging me on. He adds one more finger to my pussy and it's over. The lead-up to something bigger was nothing compared to the explosion of the orgasm that climbed into my spirit, shaking my very core. The core that clenches insistently at Tyson's fingers. Each convulsing muscle, grabbing ahold of him and begging him not to let go.

Or maybe that's me... My voice echoes around the bathroom until I discern us moving to my bed.

He makes quick work of undressing himself and I'm still quivering from my orgasm on my cool sheets.

His warm body is on top of me. My legs wrap around him on instinct, but he shakes his head. A look of determination in his eyes and the set of his mouth. "Not like this," he says. I can feel his own hands shaking as he removes the tight lock of my thighs. He goes back to the bathroom for a minute and comes back to bed.

I don't know what I've done to bring this man back into my life — please let me keep him.

My room is damn near spinning with how high I am from what he's done with only his hands.

A week ago, having him here would have seemed impossible. A dream within a dream that I could not recall upon waking. I don't know now if this is truly real. Maybe I fell and hit my head in the shower.

Impossible that this is happening to me.

"Come back to me, Melody. Where did you go?"

I shake my head, not wanting to say what I was thinking. How lame would it be to voice how unbalanced this match is... small town waitress somehow lands the Country legend in the making. I can see the headline now.

Tyson slides his hands down my legs and up to my thighs to pull me closer to him. We both sit on the bed now. My legs around his hips and his hands clasped behind me. I watch his chest rise and fall before his voice is rumbling into the room. "Why do you do that?"

"What?" I swirl a finger around the music notes on his ribs, trying not to look into his eyes until I can find my strength again.

"Make yourself small." He unclasps his hands to raise my chin. I close my eyes. Some water from my still wet hair slides down my back. I shiver and catch his gaze, but he holds it.

"I don't know what you mean."

"Tell me what you were thinking. You can tell me anything." His eyes are sincere. Does he know that's my weakness?

I shake my head again, feeling even more silly now that I'm going to voice my thoughts. "I was thinking about how I watched you on national television in this very spot. And now you're here... doing... you know? This." I gesture around us.

"What does that matter?"

"I don't know. It just does."

"Melody, it doesn't," he scoffs. "Did you not hear me earlier? I said I missed you. Does that mean nothing? Do my words not mean anything at all?"

"That almost makes it worse, Ty. The last time you told me you missed me, you..." I trail off because saying the words right now would destroy any semblance of satisfaction I could hold onto from my earlier orgasm.

His expression pinches. "This again? I thought we moved past this."

"We didn't. I didn't. I need to know." Cursing myself internally because I don't want to break this bubble of happiness we've created, but it's not gonna happen any other way. I can't keep guessing and torturing myself with the dead ends. I take a deep steadying breath. "Why did you leave all those years ago?"

Chapter 27

Tyson

This is the moment.

Why did you leave all those years ago?

I knew the question was coming, and still, I'm not prepared for it. I wish I could spend the rest of the night watching her fall apart on my fingers, but I promised that I would tell her everything she wanted to know. I am the mistake she made. Whether I'm here now or not, I am the villain in her story. I did this to her—us—and I am the only one who can answer this question for her.

"I wanted to talk to you. I tried." I take in as much air as my lungs will allow and blow it back out again. "Will was constantly on my ass about my grades and focusing in school. I just thought, hey, he's a Dad. Dads are always trying to look out for their sons."

She rubs my arm at my visible agitation. I'm not the victim here, but it's her way. Melody has always been supportive of me even when I didn't deserve it, just like now. It's not the easiest thing to recall this memory and even harder to bring it back to the surface when I know this is the moment that everything began to change between Melody and me. "And that wasn't the case?" Her eyebrows pinch in confusion.

"No," I shake my head. "It was much more than that." I stand because I can't sit here. I'm naked as the day I came into this world, but I'm not concerned about my dick swaying between us right now. "After my eighteenth, he sat me down for real. I could tell this was going to be a different kind of lecture. A different talk. Aaliyah wasn't there and she had never missed a conversation before. I didn't know if it was better or worse that she was gone. The house was so silent I knew even Chloe was gone too.

"He handed me a letter. I stopped breathing. I didn't know what to think or do or how to prepare myself for what I was going to find when I read who it was from."

In her softest voice, she asks, "Who?"

"It was her big loopy handwriting. Years since I had seen it. It said 'To Tyson on your eighteenth'. It was from my mom." I choke out the last words.

My mouth is dry and like I've been sucking chalk, even though I had the best sex I've ever had and I didn't even nut. *It's her.* She is the reason. The person I've cared so deeply about for more than a decade.

I have to keep going even if sharing this story is painful for me. "Turns out she wrote this letter to me in the last month of her life. I never knew that she wrote it. I was too young to be a part of her will reading and my Dad had never talked about it before this moment."

I don't deserve the kindness in her eyes. "That is so much to take in, Tyson. I know it had to be hard." And I know she could understand. This was the one person in my life who really knew what it was like to have their mother taken from them by a disease that stole from so many. So many lost birthdays, memories, and family members my mom never got to see. She would have loved Melody. Not for the first time, I think about whether she would have approved of the choices I made concerning Melody if she had still been here. "What did the letter say?" Her expressive eyes track me as I continue to pace. I stop when I hear her words. I don't know how I'm able to because, if anything, my thoughts are swirling even more.

"She declined further treatment and chemo. She made the choice to stop fighting the losing battle. After years of going through the hardship that was her cancer, she didn't want to do it anymore. She wasn't getting any better." I tug at my hair. "Reading those words fucked me up. To see on paper in your own mom's script that she didn't want to keep trying. That she was too tired to find the will to live anymore... Everything I thought I knew was bullshit. At eighteen, I thought I was a man. I thought I knew exactly what I wanted from life. Her words turned my world upside down."

I drop to my knees in front of where Melody sits on her bed. My eyes burn with the recollection of that moment in my life. She rubs my shoulders as I try to catch my breath with my forehead in her lap. "My mom's family had left her money which she was using to supplement whatever minimal funds our insurance provided for her treatment until that point. After she passed, the money was put into investments that were compounded and became something entirely different." I lean back onto my heels and grab Melody's hands, holding them tightly. She looks at her hands and back to my face. "Her final request of me was to get a degree. Go to the school she went to and be able to provide for myself with a stable job that would afford me an easy life. One that would be unburdened by struggle. To give me peace after what she put our family through. She didn't want me to feel the loss of her anywhere but in my heart. She said that she still wanted to be there even when she couldn't be anymore."

I feel the tears on my cheeks before a silent sob comes from me. I break down right there. Melody pulls me up to her in an instant. Her arms surround me in an embrace that envelops my body. For several moments I allow it to happen. Resist all the shame society tells me I should feel. If there is anyone who won't judge me, it's this woman who holds me and rubs my back.

"Why couldn't you tell me? I would have understood," she says.

"Because I was dumb. The more I learned about you, the shittier I felt. I lost my mom and still, I have two parents who care about me fiercely. Who I was constantly harping on and ungrateful for, complaining to you about them all the time. I had everything, even another piece of my mom long after she was gone. I didn't know how that would affect you. I thought I was protecting you, sparing you. Each step I took with my degree and being on that campus made me feel closer to her." I look into her eyes and wait for the weight to be lifted off my shoulders with that truth out in the open now. It isn't. Saying those words aloud did not bring the catharsis I thought it would.

Her lips form a thin line as she leans away from me. "Almost everyone we know has two parents and comes from loving homes. That doesn't mean that I can't be happy for the people I care about because my home was broken. You stole our happiness, all because you felt guilty about something you couldn't control. Ty, that had nothing to do with you. I was prepared to follow you anywhere. You were my home. I waited all summer for you to ask me and you never did!"

"I couldn't do that to you! I could not bring myself to ask that of you. I wasn't even going after the goal. My head was in the books until my third year. Everything we talked about, dreamed about—none of that was happening. When everything was said and done, I left to get a fucking accounting degree and it brought me no closer to her or to you. I could have done that online and stayed here with you."

"Who knows where you would be in your career now if you had not gone to Denver? We could have figured it out. Our problem wasn't you leaving—It was you leaving me behind." She holds my gaze as we lay on the bed together.

"No, Melody. You would have given up everything to follow me and try to make things work. That is not what you needed, I couldn't be selfish and bring you on her final ask. To take you from your family and your friends... your new home." I shake my head. "Fuck, I was eighteen. I made the wrong choice to end things. I figured that out right away and when I missed you too much for my heart to take, Mack had already moved in on you. You were with him. You seemed happy. I couldn't be that asshole to try and get between that."

"So, this whole time you made all these decisions for me? You didn't talk to me about it once." She pushes at my chest with new sadness shining in her brown eyes. "Who says I was happy?"

"Everyone! Melody, everyone said you were happy. Told me to leave you alone. Let you be happy with him. So, I did."

"They should not have done that." She shakes her head, her voice choking up. Her forehead meets my chest as she says what has been weighing on her. "They all believed the lie. The mask. The facade. I was not happy. I was struggling every day without you. Battling my own depression of losing my mom, my career, then losing you, then losing Callan, and then my dad..." Her tears hit my shoulders hot and heavy.

I feel like an idiot. I never knew that she was feeling all these things. Ever since she cried in my arms at the engagement party I knew there was more. I know there is a lot. What did I do? *Fucking hell, what have I done?* I want to be there for her and comfort her when she needs it. And I wasn't. I failed her and she still let me barge into her house, into her life. "Do you want me to go?" I ask.

She reels back, confusion written all over her pretty face. "No. I want you to fix it like you said you would."

"I can't. I fucked this up too much. I don't even know where to start to make this better."

"My heart." She places my hand on her chest like before. "Start with my heart. You and me fit together like puzzle pieces. I don't care how much time has passed. I've been using glue and duck tape and sheer willpower to make it work with anyone else. But they aren't you. Your heart and mine are the same broken little organs."

"We fit," I repeat. I scoop her up in my arms and promise her, "I will fix it. I'm going to make it work." She nuzzles deeper into my chest and everything feels better.

Exhausted from the night and the truths shared, we lay in her bed. Melody and I share breaths until the tension coils too tight to resist her any longer. Our mouths entwined in the desperation we have both felt for each other over the years we lost. I hold the back of her head to keep her close to me. Our passion pulses between us and I grab her strong thigh to drape over my body.

I reach for my pants and the condom I put in my wallet. She puts a hand over mine, "Please. I don't want anything between us ever again. I have an IUD."

I don't need any more reasons than that to fill her. My dick finds her weeping core with ease. She writhes along me and her eyes hold mine for a moment longer until they roll back when I dip inside her. It only takes a few tries of in and out before her softness gives way to my big dick filling her. She bites down on my shoulder as I slowly stroke her, dragging out this orgasm as long as I can manage.

We don't fuck. We make love, slow and sensual.

Her little whimpers against my neck, their own special lyrics of pleasure in my ears. "We fit... Feel how your pussy squeezes me so fucking perfectly."

I sink into her again til our hips are flush. "I missed this. You grip my dick like a vice. You're so perfect."

Melody comes on a gasp that grabs my heart and squeezes because it's just for me. I can't believe that I'm here with her. My luck has changed. Each thrust into her sweet heat brings me closer to the brink. Her honeyed voice calling out my name is my unraveling. "I'm so close, Ty."

"Let go, baby. Come for me." Her back arches, pussy clenching tight as she breaks. I've never seen anything more beautiful than the sight of Melody coming. I keep pumping into her, feeling unhinged. She takes every drop of my nut like the goddess she is. I hold her close and that feels like coming home.

"I missed you," she manages, still gasping for air.

"I missed you too," I say, just as breathless. I kiss her neck and her shoulders until she relaxes and falls asleep with my dick still inside her warm, tight body. I don't pull out because we fit and I'm not ready to separate from her.

I don't think I ever will be again.

CHAPTER 28

Melody

"YOU DIDN'T!" I SQUEAL, way too excited about the signature yellow bag and yellow travel cups in Tyson's hands.

He walks over to my patio set, dwarfing the little metalwork chair. "I had to. It's been a while since I've been. Nothing has changed." The sun hasn't been up for very long so I know he must have waited in that lengthy line just to get this for us. If I had the patience I would be there every morning but since I don't this feels like a treat.

"Walter's is a pillar in Alpenglow Ridge. I hope no big coffee chain comes to boot them out of town." I slide into my fuzzy slippers and meet him at the small table and chairs I found way back when. It was Clo who spotted the set and I haven't been able to part with it since it sat behind my dad's house. I brush aside the sad memory this little set holds and take my first sip of tea. I sigh, "You still know my order." He slides the little brown-wrapped package toward me after he pulls a very large breakfast sandwich out for himself.

He takes a big bite of his breakfast adding, "And a lemon Danish." I reach for the package and he places a hand over mine. "The freshest one they had. I know how picky you are."

"I'm not picky... I just don't like it when the pastry isn't the right flakiness."
He hums, biting into his sandwich so he doesn't have to reply. "Remember
when we went during lunch? Everyone was out with the flu and it was so
empty on the Lawn."

"Yea, I do." He chuckles. "I started playing when we sat on the patio
and people started throwing coins into my empty sandwich container." His
twists flop around his head as he runs a hand over them. "Think that counts
as my first gig?"

I remember that day so clearly. The sun glinted off his soft hair and
his eyes looked golden with how the sun reflected on them. How soft
his mouth looked. Tyson had said something about me blushing and I
remember how stunning he looked when he felt loved. Loved by me. I just
knew that I had enough for him.

I laugh with him. "Definitely. You never forget your first." I freeze, hearing
my own words. Looking to the side to see if he caught it too. His smirk lets
me know that he absolutely did.

"I haven't," he responds, with all the suggestion laced through those two
words.

"You weren't my first everything." I take my first bite of Danish, needing
something to do with my mouth other than putting my foot in it. We may
have reached a turning point yesterday but there's still a lot about our
lives now that we need to work out. The layers of the buttery dough mixed
with the tang of lemon are perfectly balanced with the vanilla icing on top.
Nothing could ruin my morning when I have this kind of perfection in my
hands. I moan into my next bite, forgetting all about my earlier blunder.

He clears his throat, bringing me out of my Danish haze. "Sure, sure,"
he answers, noncommittally. Sipping from his coffee, he looks off into the
trees in front of the house like they are so interesting. Always smug.

One thing I love about my house is the location. Where it sits between
the two farmlands works perfectly for me because it's far from either main
house to have the privacy I want but I get the added benefit of green
pastures on both sides. The tall Douglas Fir trees are one of my favorite
things about the driveway up to the house. They remind me of my favorite

place. They provide a lot of natural shade that keeps my house cool in the summer and snowy in the winter. There isn't much of a yard for me to maintain which is amazing to not have to mow grass all the time.

I could imagine raising a family here. This place has character and when I first saw it go up for sale, I knew it was worth the investment. It doesn't seem that a traditional family will be in this house though. First Mack was here, and that didn't work out for so many reasons. Then it was me for a few years. I contemplated growing old alone here with Wesson. Dying here with the wish and fantasy of being with Tyson to keep me company. I could only love him from a distance, just like I had all these years. With his admissions about what really happened, I'm starting to see things differently. It may still be too soon to truly give him my whole heart.

He already has many people who want a piece of his consideration and confidence. His music showcases that longing that every woman wants to hear from her man. It's not hard to see why he was deemed Country's Sad Boy. Women love a broken man. To think that it was me who broke him is far-fetched at best. It's me that's still putting pieces together with a wish and prayer, while he is realizing his dreams like he wanted to.

We have a lot to talk about.

We don't talk though. We eat our breakfasts until he breaks the silence. "You weren't kidding about being a fan, huh?"

I look down at the JT concert tee I'm wearing. It doesn't have their faces on it. Instead, it has a grassy landscape with the album on the front and cities with dates on the back. When I put it on this morning, I had only been thinking of comfort for my day off. I'd ordered it in an extra large in the hopes that it would feel like I had actually borrowed it from a lover...

Ugh lover? From him, more like. Note to self, please don't call Tyson a *lover* to his face.

"You were the one who introduced me to Jordan's music. Kinda crazy that you tour with him now."

"I've always had good taste. He recognized that," he shrugs finishing his sandwich. Tyson takes several moments to ball up the wrapper and put it back into the bag.

Sipping my tea, I confirm, "Probably in most things related to music."

"In all the things I've picked, you're still the best choice I have ever made. Music is just inherent."

I can't help the heat rolling up my neck. This shirt suddenly feels too hot for the cool morning. God, he's playing with my feelings. I don't know how to handle his attention anymore. If I ever did. Whatever switch he is flipping, it's hard to think right now. The smirk and the hat... This man is sin, wrapped in Wrangler stitch jeans. It's delicious and way too much for a mere mortal, such as myself. I stand from my chair and start making my way back to the house.

"Reminds me... I ran into Reese getting coffee." He shuffles from the little patio chair to his truck. I watch his tight ass the whole walk over. He returns, following me inside with the small black box wrapped with a red bow on top.

I take the box from him, eyeing it curiously, "Why'd she give it to you?" I'll probably see her at the bar tomorrow or when we go dress shopping soon. This has mischief all over it.

"Dunno." he shrugs, scooping up Wesson after he toes his boots off at the door.

Walking to my attached bathroom, I drop the box to my bed. When I finish up, the box still calls my attention so I decide to open it. I quickly rip the paper away. A few small packets slide out from between the wrapping paper and box. I pick up the little folded paper, ignoring the packets for now.

> **No batteries required ;) Thank me later!**
> **-Reese**

What the hell?

Tyson's heavy footsteps in the house make me realize that he's still here. I shove the note and little packets into the wrapping paper as best I can and figure I'll deal with it later.

"Melody?" I hear him flop on the couch and I blow out a breath of relief. I've gotta get this thing out of sight, knowing Reese it's nothing good.

Gathering the gift up, with the intention of shoving it into my night-stand drawer, I stop mid-stride when Tyson's voice comes from the doorway of my room. "You wanna watch something or maybe go to the river later? I'm pretty free all day."

"Yea, umm..." I put the bundle back onto the bed behind me. "That'll be great."

His eyebrow arches as he looks around me. "What will be great? I said two different things." Wesson comes into the room behind Ty. He bends over to pet the cat, but he's already out of reach when he leans over. Seeing this as my opportunity to do something with this box, I start moving around the bed. Wes jumps on the bed immediately swatting at one of the packets until it flies off the bed.

It lands near his feet before I can get to it and he picks it up. "Lube?" Tyson shakes the little thing around. "What do you need travel-sized lube for?"

My cheeks flame and I answer, "I don't need lube. It came with what-ever this is that Reese gave me."

He winks, "I know you don't need it, baby." He tosses the packet to the bed, prowling over to me. "What was in the box?"

"I don't know. I didn't check." With what I know, I regret not finding out before Tyson is involved. It's a small box though. It can't be that crazy.

He reaches around me to grab the box off my bed. "Only one way to find out."

He rips the light brown kraft cardboard box and taps another box out into his palm. I can now see that the outside box was for discretion. A hot pink toy rests in Tyson's hand between us. He reads the box saying, "Heartthrob. Ten whisper-quiet vibration settings... Perfect for beginners and partner play..." He looks up to my face to say, "It features their signature heart-shaped base for easy control and that extra cute factor. Why didn't you want to open your beginners anal probe with me?"

I scoff, trying to hide the arousal in my voice. I did not know that hearing Tyson read the features of a sex toy aloud to me would be much too hot to handle, but it definitely is. Am I sweating? "I didn't even know what it was." I take the box from his hand and throw it into my nightstand.

"So it's not for partner play?" He pouts too convincingly for my tastes.

"I-It did say that on the box..."

"Is it me that you don't want to play with then?" His pout is adorable and much too convincing for my liking.

What kind of strange torture is this? "It's a conversation." And worth a lot of overthinking on my part. I don't know if I could recover when he leaves with another one of my firsts. I have to have some sort of contingency plan. "How about that movie?" I ask, changing the subject entirely.

CHAPTER 29

Melody, Then

"DOWN TODAY?" MACK RUBS a curl between his fingers, lifting the curl to inspect it. After wishing that I could hide in the solace of my mango and coconut Cantu wash-n-go, I skipped the blowdrying. Putting my makeup on this morning was enough of an effort as it is. My sleep is still sporadic at best and fleeting at worst.

I thought all night about what Ty and I shared. I already felt lighter after talking about my mom to someone who could even fathom what it had been like. I wouldn't wish this pain on my worst enemy. It still feels like a part of me is missing even though the wound isn't bleeding anymore. That dull ache echoes through everything in my life. Waking up, doing my hair, grocery shopping, sitting down for a meal, seeing a paintbrush or those big claw clips she'd have in her hair. What hurt the most on my first drive here was the grocery shopping. I've gotten into the habit of ordering online, avoiding that store at all costs ever since. Getting groceries was our thing to do together and now I struggle to even picture her in a grocery store. In Alpenglow Ridge, the store isn't the same and that makes me even more upset. Too many memories are getting hazy and the details are missing more and more every day.

I want to move forward, but the more time that passes, the more time I spend holding on to these few memories that are sharp. My favorite is of her sitting out by that tree she loved. Her focus never left the leaves she stippled when she said, "What's up baby," in her sweet Texas drawl. Her thick curls, just like mine, were pulled back into a large clip that had a floral design winding around the handle. She had painted them on earlier that year. Beautiful. The scene is picturesque with the hot Houston air swirling around us on the patio. Not even the overhead fans could cool the oppressive heat of summer. None of that bothered her though. She sat there, in peace, adding the hundreds of small leaves in shades of green and yellow. There is nothing of significance about this memory besides the knowledge that she was happy and healthy. I want to forever hold this memory in my heart.

I hope I never forget this one.

The only thing Daddy asked me before I left with Mack this morning was, " Do you have a ride home too?" Apparently he's gonna be working late again. I still don't know why I continue to expect anything different. The only benefit has been that I've had two uninterrupted nights with Tyson before he gets home.

I nod in response to Mack's question and put my backpack under my feet. He grins at me and his dimple pops a little. I know I zoned out in that memory, but he doesn't seem to be affected by the silence or my unfocused gaze on his face. He just waited. My small grin couldn't be helped. His cheeriness this early in the morning is kind of infectious. He grabs my backpack and tosses it to the backseat.

"I like it!" His grin is back in place, but he's still waiting.

Right. He's waiting for me to put on a seatbelt. *Duh.* Once he's satisfied with how I'm secured, he turns up the radio to leave.

We ride without talking, but I can feel how close and alone we are in his truck. He leaves his hand on the gear shift for the short duration of the drive. I swear the heat from his arm is perceptible even under my sweatshirt. I sneak a peek at him every time I feel like I can. His light brown hair blows softly in the breeze with his window down. Indie rock music plays from the speaker. He hums softly to it and taps the rhythm with his fingers on the steering wheel.

There is an ease to how he's driving with me in the passenger seat. Like he is exactly where he needs to be and maybe I'm where I should be too. With him picking me up in the mornings and us riding to school together. It could be this easy I think to myself. We could be this easy.

We pull up to the student parking lot and that's when the chaos really begins. It starts with a few guys saying *what's up* as he pulls in. The football team, being the only sports team that meets before school, is already hanging out in the lot. Mack waves to them casually, but I can tell he is pleased to be caught driving me here. The boys lean into his window asking about the party and now my window is down too. None of the guys talk directly to me but I feel their curious glances either way.

"Claire said you got brew! I'm definitely getting tanked!" One guy yells into the car reaching across me to bump fists with Mack. They all laugh animatedly at their underage drinking plans. I do not plan to be a part of that but the more they talk, the more I get the sense that this Barn Party is going to be a much bigger deal than I had been expecting.

He takes the key out of the ignition and tries to open his door. "Everybody get out of the way. I'm trying to get Mel to breakfast before class, alright?" Reluctantly, the guys meander toward campus and I'm able to open my door. Mack comes around to my side of the pickup with my backpack slung over one shoulder and his backpack over the other.

"I can carry my own bag, you know?" I say with a laugh because he's pretending my bag weighs two hundred pounds. He leans close enough to my body that his shoulder is pressed to mine. I lightly push him the other way with both hands.

He stumbles dramatically in the opposite direction, then catches himself on the bumper of his truck. His look of shock that I pushed him over there gets a giggle from me. My laughter intensifies as he pretends to climb up supporting himself by his forearms over the gate.

"It's ok! I got it, Mel! I just need to—" He grunts and swipes his forehead. I throw my head back. He is ridiculous. Mack smiles down at me, satisfied with himself when he walks back to my side. He holds another curl in his fingers again. "I feel like I'm being spoiled." He says looking down at me with soft eyes. The blue sparkles in that way that I have only seen in movies. The depth of his stare reminds me of a pool that's reflecting the sun on a perfect summer's day. Inviting and the perfect answer to this heat.

Heat? No, Mel. No heat! Where is that coming from?

"You're the one carrying the bags, remember?" I tug lightly at a strap that dangles from my backpack. "Seems like I'm the one being spoiled." I still can't understand why he's doing any of it. Befriending me, taking me to school, carrying my bag, staring into my eyes... He's popular and all these people love him. Why me?

"Nah, it's me." He says. He pulls the strand lightly, making it bounce back into place before pulling me under his right arm. That cut grass smell hits my senses and I allow him to embrace me. I feel a brief moment of relief like maybe he's holding me up too. A catcall breaks my daze and I jerk out of Mack's arm, putting distance between us again. He flips off the catcaller with his left arm before looking back at me and smiling. My face burns like I've been caught doing something wrong.

I haven't done anything wrong. I can't betray a relationship that I'm not in. Ty is my friend and so is Mack. So, why do I feel so icky about being caught?

The heavy side door hisses as he opens it for me and steps in close behind me. The chatter in the hallway swells around us as students hang out before the first-period bell rings in the next twenty minutes. Mack walks closer to me and our arms brush in the small hallway. I'm far too aware of the stares from other students as we pass through to the cafeteria. There is something familiar in the feeling I have under their scrutiny. Though I know I should maintain the distance between us, I slow my walk to be closer to Mack. The warmth from his body is comforting though it still sends a shiver down my spine.

My shudder makes him chuckle low into my ear. "You know there are worse things than being my girl." His tone is light, but I don't mistake this for anything other than it is. He's asking me out right now. Right now?!

In front of all these gawking nosies? My cheeks and neck flame as I try breathing deeply to calm down. I hate being the center of all this attention. At his question, I feel the eyes on me like he's announced the question on the intercom and everyone knows. I try to play it cool, but I don't know if it's working.

"Oh really? Like what?" My tease comes out much more breathy than I meant as I struggle for air. My heart is beating so quickly at this point I'm certain he can hear it thud in my chest. The anxiety creeps in.

"Not being my girl." The look on his face is sincere. Those inviting pools begging me to trust him. To dip a toe and hope for the best. Trust him with my heart. Trust. And why can't I trust him? He has been good to me. A bit touchy-feely, but not disrespectful. I had gotten used to his constant need to have an arm around me or to hug me at lunch. I had not been in a situation like today where we're doing this with an audience outside of our small group. It feels dirty.

Though I had grown used to his touches, I had also grown used to Ty's dislike of it as well. His disgust is poorly hidden when Mack and I are together. I expect him to say something, anything. He never does. The holes I should have from how his stare bores through me, burn like a hot poker each time. I know that he doesn't miss a single handhold, hug or brush of our bodies. He clocks every single one.

But like he said, he's *respecting his boy's wishes*. What am I waiting for? For Ty to see that is a stupid reason not to be with me?

Highly unlikely.

Overwhelmed with the desire to be free of these prying eyes while I process any of this is crucial. I can't get to the cafeteria fast enough. I dart to the door and pick up the pace when I can see that Chloe and Reese are in the line already. Mack is somehow still right behind me. I can't keep avoiding his hopes this way. I can at least stall until...well, until I can't anymore. I don't want to be away from Mack. I don't know if dating him is what I want. We're friends and lab partners. I want Ty. Even though I shouldn't, it makes me feel slimy with how closely I'm pressed to Mack. I feel comfortable with Mack in a way that I don't want to jeopardize either.

He sees Quincy and catches up to him after a quick, "Morning," to the girls.

"So you and Mack, huh?" Chloe's eyebrows wiggle up and down when he leaves.

Reese giggles while hip thrusting into the air. "I know where you're gonna be at the barn!" She cups her mouth with a mock whisper, "Rolling in the hay!" Chloe and Reese laugh together.

I sigh in exasperation, "And why do you think that is going to happen?"

Chloe wiggles her phone to the side as if that is an answer. "Alex texted Quincy to ask if he knew who Mack's new girlfriend is. Then Quincy texted me. Then I texted Celeste, who said she saw you under Mack's arm in the lot with your purple backpack on his back. So, I had to tell Q that it was you, but don't be messy." She giggles to herself at the obvious absurdity because they were both being full-call gossip girls already. "But even if he didn't tell anyone else, I'm sure you walking down the hallway whispering to each other had nothing to do with why people are talking."

I peek at them from between my fingers because I don't know how to tell Mack what I want without losing his friendship completely. How can I do that when I'm not sure that it's even true?

Do I want to be just friends with him?

That sparkle in his eye from earlier comes to mind. I wanted to be under that stare for a bit longer before that weirdo couldn't mind his own business whistling at us. Denying that I'm attracted to Mack would be a lie from the moment it left my lips. Because I don't know if I would have moved his hand, had he chosen to touch my thigh on the ride to school this morning. Did I want that? Then I think about the fact that he still has my backpack.

I rip my hands from my face and turn prepared to get through another crowd of his friends to retrieve my bag. I hit a solid form instead and look up to find Ty standing there. His jaw twitches from how his teeth are clenched. I step back immediately, shocked at the irritation written all over his body language.

Chloe coughs and drags Reese closer to her and through the line to grab a tray of food. "We'll just go through the line and catch up with you later."

Chloe gives Ty a pointed look and he glares back at her. His icy response has her saying, "Yikes!" before they leave us to awkwardly stand to the side of other students going through the food line.

Tyson crosses his arms, looking down his nose at me, "So, you're really dating that jerk off?"

CHAPTER 30

Tyson, Then

THE BEST AND WORST thing about living in a small town is how quickly news travels. I had barely parked my truck when someone was asking me about Mack's new girlfriend.

I shooed the dude off because it's not my M.O. to gossip and I'm certainly not going to confirm to anyone that Melody was dating someone else who was not me. It's not even nine yet and I'm already pissed about some shit that Mack has done.

After the past few nights, I thought things had changed between us. Melody and I have something. Something better than whatever she and Mack have. I am not the only one that feels it. There is a connection I can't explain. I know she feels it too. *I know it.*

"It's not like that, Ty. Some people just saw him taking me to school and carrying my backpack." Her eyes are big and pleading and I instantly feel like an asshole for approaching her like this. I run a hand over my hair and take some deep breaths.

This is not me. God, why am I acting like this? Melody has me so twisted up.

Looking around, I find Mack and Quincy talking with some other dudes from the football team by the far caf table. I stomp over there with purpose.

Yanking Melody's bag from the table, I ignore the initial balk from the guy. Mack breaks his yapping to say, "Hey! Wh—Oh. What's up, Ty?"

I grunt and nod, but I don't stick around to chat. Melody still stands where I left her, fidgeting with her sweatshirt hem. "C'mon," I say. She takes her backpack back with minimal resistance from me and we go out to the Lawn. It's markedly more quiet out here than in the caf. I sigh in relief from finally not being overstimulated.

"Tyson, I'm sorry—"

"Look, I get it. The gossip is not your fault." She winces and I catch the small movement. "Is it true then?"

"No, I never said he was my boyfriend or anything. He just picked me up for school today."

I give her a look. How is this not something she told me last night? "So, did you deny that something was going on between you two?"

She looks down at her lap, "Not exactly..."

I huff and tug on my hair. "Am I the asshole then? Do you want that guy? Tell me and I'll back off." I chuck her chin and she puts wary brown eyes on me. "I thought last night... I thought we had something. I thought there was something more between us. Was it?" She closes her eyes. I feel like shit that she's in distress because of me. I know how much she doesn't like conflict or confrontation of any kind and here I am, doing just that. I can't help it. I need to know what's going on.

"I didn't do anything wrong, Ty," she says in a small voice.

Why am I acting like this? I feel like I'm out of my mind because maybe I am losing her. Seeing how we could be last night was a tease. A little glimpse of how good we are for each other. Together. And now I'm blowing it. Being a douchebag, charging her up about some rumors going around school. "You didn't," I confirm and blow out some steam from my insecure rage. "I know you didn't. I'm not saying that." I release her face and flop onto my back. "Fuck. I'm not yelling at you. I just..."

Her brows pinched in confusion, "You just what?"

The bell rings and I'm cut off when Mack comes through the doors, "We better get to Tomlinson's before she goes on her lecture about punctuality again."

I wait to see if she'll say anything more, but she doesn't. She lets him put her under his arm as they walk back into the building.

Mack's party is this weekend. Everyone is getting ready for this shit. I was planning on skipping it all together. Crowds aren't my scene and with as many people as he's expecting, it sounds like a nightmare.

I have to get to her and stop anything from going further with him. If I know this guy, even a little bit as much as I think I do, then he is going to try his luck with her on Saturday. There is nothing that will keep me from attending the barn party now.

Music has been priority number one. I don't have time for dating. If I'm not studying at home to make the grades my dad expects of me, then I'm finding somewhere to play my guitar and teach myself something new. I make time for my friends because I'm not a total recluse. Melody is different. I would sacrifice all the time I put the the side to spend more time with her. Melody is music. I want to study and learn her with just as much enthusiasm. Each time I learn something new about her, it makes me want to learn more.

Unlike Mack, I'm not using her to reassure myself that I'm still a valuable member of the dating pool in town to bolster an already over-inflated ego. I don't doubt that he really is attracted to her, but I don't think she really talks to him about anything. I wonder if he knows about what she went through at her old school. Or if she has shared anything about Cressida, her mom, with him. That means something. She let me in. She showed me what pains her. It's not pretty and it's not something that many people would ever understand. The scrutiny of losing a parent. The loss of hope when the person you love most is taken from you.

It's me. I understand. I know what she is going through because I had to do it too. I can be the support she needs. Not the normalcy she fakes.

I bet Mack has not even bothered to ask. His cocky cowboy, sunshine-y Golden Retriever personality has no room for darkness like the shade inside Melody.

How am I the only person that has asked?

I don't think the girls see it either. It makes me so sad for her. I want to wrap her up in my arms and keep her safe from what makes her so sad. On both nights that I've been at her house late, I've never seen her dad around. I wonder if he's out drinking or if he really is working. From the sounds of it, he was not the one who supported Melody through the initial loss of her mother. Her grandma helped her and now she's hundreds of miles from her.

I'm barely able to pay attention in my economics class. And the other classes I have until I get to see Melody again, are a blur as I think about this girl who makes me feel like I'm losing control.

"You're eating food from the caf, man? Nasty." Quincy makes a face at my lunch.

"Food is food," I say, hoping to brush him off so he doesn't break my focus from the door.

"Yea... but Mack's bringing back tacos. You'd rather have the partially hard mac n cheese from the caf instead of that."

"What?"

"Did you even check your phone? He's probably called you twenty times by now."

I check my phone and there are ten missed calls from him. When I look up from the screen, he and Melody are already striding over with several bags of tacos from the truck that posts up on Main. *Damnit.*

Clo, Drea, and Reese come out of the caf door after them and soon everyone is talking animatedly with each other. I watch Melody scoot a little bit farther away from Mack until he inevitably goes into some theatrics that require him to stand and make a big deal about himself. Reese stands and they two-step in celebration of a job well done getting everything together for the party at her Ranch tomorrow. Soon Quincy is pulling Clo into the two-step too and they have a blast laughing and carrying on.

"You like carne asada, right?" Melody's tinkling voice takes my attention from the dancing in front of me. "I got a couple extra since you weren't answering your phone."

"Thank you," I say, squeezing her hands before I accept the to-go box from her. "So, you still thinking about going to this party tomorrow?" This could be my opportunity to pick her up and maybe convince her to hang out anywhere else besides what I'm sure will be a crazy event.

She nods, "Drea and I are going to go together. I promised to be her DD since I won't drink." She's so good.

I scratch my neck, "Promise me you'll save me a dance then?" I try for a tone that says I'm joking, but it sounds desperate even to my own ears.

She gives me a shy smile anyway. "It's yours."

CHAPTER 31

Melody, Then

DREA AND I BARELY make it up the driveway because of how many cars are parked here. She parks on the grass next to a few other cars that have done the same. I've never seen so many people at once in this town.

Drea squeals, "Colton is here!" She links her arm through mine, pointing at the blue Charger we walk by. Colorado is just a little bit chillier at night with the sun gone down.

That is not the case when we finally make it to the barn. It's pretty warm between all the people hanging around in here. There's music blasting into the space from speakers I can't see. It's hazy with smoke and crowded as we're jostled and sometimes shoved around groups of people dancing or talking. I don't look too closely into the darker corners of the many nooks in here after Drea pulled me away from a couple's makeout session that was getting intense. Finally, we find Mack from the chants of, "Chug! Chug! Chug!" coming from the back corner of the open barn space.

We follow the chants toward the birthday boy guzzling beer from a huge keg pump at a rate that couldn't be good for his health. The smell of sweat, weed, and beer is thick in the air. Nausea hits me as the liquor and beer scents remind me of my past a little too closely. I don't even want to get

Mack's attention at this point. He's having a good time and I'd only dampen his celebrating.

"Let's get some air," I yell into Drea's ear over the crowd's obnoxious noise levels. She nods and we head over to a bonfire that has people gathered around. It looks cozy and inviting, way more my speed than the chaos going on inside. Chloe waves to us from Quincy's lap as they share a blunt between them and another couple.

"Bon, this is Jason and Morgan." She gestures to the couple on their right and then with a puff of smoke to her left, "Taylor and Ash. Jason and Morgan are from here, but Taylor and Ash are from Harmony Hill. Ash is the best and they," pointing to Taylor with the booted foot crossed over her leg, "are only minimally annoying." Ash and Taylor laugh, clearly inebriated, while Taylor rolls their eyes.

"We're gonna head back inside. You can take our seats. See you in there?" Jason says to the couples that were sitting there before us and they nod. "Nice to meet you," He says to us. Morgan turns to wave back at us as Jason is determined to find a way over to the keg area in the barn.

"Hey, I'm Taylor." They extend their hand to me and wink. "Don't listen to Clo. She's had way too much to drink... and smoke already."

I wonder how that's possible when we aren't even that late. The party's officially been going on for about an hour.

Ash leans over Taylor to speak much louder than necessary to Chloe, "You were right! She's so pretty. Here, come sit next to me!" Ash says as she sways a little bit. I turn to ask if Drea wants to stay here with them, but she's disappeared.

"Colton grabbed her. She's fine." Quincy says at the panicked look on my face. "A bunch of people from Harmony Hill High are here. That's why it's already so crazy." He tilts his head over toward the two people sitting on the bench next to me. Taylor and Ash cheers their solo cups to that and I feel a little more comfortable about being at this party even though Drea totally ditched me.

"He's not wrong," Chloe chimes in and Ash giggles when she passes the smoke toward her.

"Not all of us though. I'm on my best behavior." Taylor says, swigging from their beer. "I'm the only person protecting our reputation."

"For now," Chloe slurs and nearly falls from Q's lap when she takes the cup from Taylor's hand. Taylor rolls their eyes again. Turning back to their girlfriend, they kiss for a long time before breaking the kiss and blowing smoke out of their lips.

I don't think I've ever seen someone do that in real life. Chloe's eyes never leave them and I must have also been entranced because I barely notice when Mack stumbles over to us.

He thrusts a cup into my hand and the movement is so brash that some of it sloshes over the edge and into my new cowboy boots. My heart sinks a little. A *lot*. I kinda grew to love the boots as I looked at myself in the mirror before coming here tonight. The surprisingly cool beer is running down my calf and pooling in my sock.

"Oh, fuck! I'm sorry, Sweetness. Here..." he looks around as if a towel or napkins are going to be around for him to clean up my leg.

I fix my face into something that's less disappointed in the prospect of cleaning beer out of my boot. "Don't worry about it." I put the beer on the bench next to me. Ash winks before taking the cup and pulling Taylor with her to the barn to give us more privacy.

"Sorry," He rubs over my arm with a sticky palm and I cringe at the sensation. I don't want to pout about my boot or be upset about his weirdly sticky hand. It's a party... some things are to be expected at a party this size. I breathe deeply for a moment while Mack says something to Quincy and Clo.

Taking a step toward the now empty bench, I shove his shoulder. "Happy Birthday," I say. His bleary eyes focus on me and I wonder again how they could be so blue. Even with nothing but the fire illuminating us out here, I can still see them sparkling. "Are you having a good time?"

He laughs, pointing at himself, "M-me? Oh, I'm having a terrible time." He frowns in jest.

"Really?" I ask, lips tugging at the corner. "Seems like you were having a pretty good time to me..."

"How would you know?" He asks, putting an arm over my shoulder. Mack is burning up. Our proximity to this raging fire makes me feel like he's at risk of catching flame right here.

"I think the words chug and chug come to mind..."I joke.

He leans closer, "Yea... Maybe I am having a good time. There was one thing I was missing though." Mack looks into my eyes expectantly.

"Shoot! I left your gift in the car. I figured it might be safe from the partygoers that way..."

"No. No, Sweetness." He stammers. "Not a gift."

"What else did you want for your birthday? This party is pretty nice—" He cuts me off with a kiss that I was not prepared for.

His lips on mine are warm. Hot. Too hot, if I'm honest. I don't pull away thinking, again, that maybe this is the easy route. I could like kissing Mack. I could.

But, I don't. Something is missing. As we kiss for a little longer, I hope that he isn't finding what he is missing.

He squeezes my arm, and when his lips leave mine he says, "A girlfriend. I was missing a girlfriend."

I stand abruptly.

He found something that was not there. "Mack. I—"

He promptly vomits on the other side of the bench and I hop back from him. I wish I could say that he only does a little and recovers but he goes for a long time. Sitting down on the bench again, I rub his back. When he finally finishes, I make it my priority to find some water for him and maybe something to eat. I try to get up from the bench in a hurry but someone places a hand on my shoulder.

Tyson.

Tyson scowls down at me, talking to the guy next to us. "Damn, Mack. Did a boot just come out of you? Nasty."

Mack stands, wiping his mouth with an arm. "Yea, it did!" He punches both fists in the air in victory. Turning to me, he says, "Hold on, Mel. I gotta do something real quick." I step back from him as he holds his hand around his mouth. "I'm the birthday boy!" Mack yells to no one in particular. Several people milling around outside of the barn cheer him on and he stands up on the bench, "Who brought the birthday boy some green? I'm trying to get high as a motherfucker!"

Josh and Allen G. come over to where we stand and each hand him a lit joint. He puts both into his mouth. They whoop and holler with their arms around his shoulders leading him back to the barn again. Mack turns back around to find me. "You coming, Mel?"

Definitely not. "In just a sec," I lie.

"You're not going in there," Tyson states instead of asks.

I peer at him through one eye. "How'd you know?"

"You don't belong here." He walks off, away from the barn and I follow behind like a little lost puppy. Relief overtakes my senses now that I know Ty is here. Wherever he's going, I'm going.

"And why do you say that?" I say when I catch up to him.

He doesn't answer my question, instead, he lifts an eyebrow. "Are you going in?"

"Well no, but I could have been. You don't know."

"I do know, Melody. I know because I actually pay attention to you. I could have told you before you even thought about coming to this party that you weren't going to enjoy yourself."

"I—are you going to yell at me again?" As I ask him, I know it won't change anything. I'll still follow him where he's going because it has to beat where I was. Ty really hates the crowds.

"I hope not," he leans against the fence outside the pasture we've walked to. It's so much more quiet here and kind of peaceful. Somehow, Tyson can find these little places to be at peace. "I just don't want you to end up dating Mack because you feel like you have to..." He looks down at his hands and I watch him fidget.

It's a weird thing to observe since Tyson is not one to do that sort of thing. When he looks up, the intensity that I see in his eyes brings a heat about my body that is so different from what I felt a few moments earlier by the bonfire. I'm silent for a moment as our gazes lock into something new. He walks me back to the fence and I allow him with no hesitation. His arms bracket me and I feel small with his shadow covering my body from the safety lights. He wore his hat tonight. He looks damn good in a cowboy hat.

"You have options, Melody. You could be with him, but I can't let you do that without saying this first."

I'm lost in his dark eyes and instinctively, I lean closer to him. "Say it," I whisper.

"I don't want to be friends with you. I don't want to be some secret. I don't want to watch you make this mistake. Being with him is a mistake and you know it."

"So what are you asking me?"

He leans forward, stare fixed on my lips, "Be my girl."

CHAPTER 32

Melody, Then

BE MY GIRL.

Be my girl. *Be my girl.* Be my girl. It's playing on a loop at three times the speed in my mind. I hoped he would say something like that, but to hear his deep voice rumble out those words is totally different from thinking them.

"That's not really ask—" He cuts me off with a kiss. It's the second time I've been cut off in this way tonight. This is wholly different from the first time. So, so different.

His full lips are soft yet insistent on mine. I lean into him, desperate for more. It only takes a moment before his hands roam over my sides and settle on my waist. His fingertips brush over the exposed skin at my back where the lace-up portion of my dress is. I shiver and he holds me even closer to him. My body sings with his touch. This can't be mistaken for anything other than want. For anything other than longing.

The kiss breaks and we share breath for a few seconds before we kiss again. I feel the rush of blood traveling on a path from my fingers and toes to my core as he holds me against this fence. His leg between mine, we're tangled before I recognize what I'm doing. My fists clench around the back of his shirt, holding me closer to him. I don't want to let him go. I'm so hot and desperate and I need more of this feeling between us.

My body writhes along his strong thigh without my permission. I freeze, so embarrassed about what I've done.

"Are you ok?" he asks me as I'm gone as still as a statue.

I try to turn from him, but he holds my face, "Don't be shy now." His lips curl on the right side. My eyes track the way it only makes them look more appealing to kiss again. "You want something from me, I'll give it to you. Just me."

"Tyson—" A moan escapes my lips when he leans his thigh into my center with more pressure than I had before.

"Please, Melody. Let it be me. Is this what you want?"

Goodness. Unashamed by how much I want him, I nod my head quickly. I hold onto his shoulders. It feels so good. *He* feels so good.

"Tell me. Tell me how I'm making you feel."

His eyes are flames that spread sparks through my body as he looks me over. "I-It feels so good. Kiss me. Ty, kiss me. Please?"

He doesn't hesitate. I feel my shudder wrack through me when his tongue dances with mine.

"When you ask me, it does something to me. Melody, I need your words. You have to tell me if this is what you want. I only want to give you what you want."

"I want this. All of this. Whatever it is." I gasp out while he kisses along my neck and shoulder. The brim of his hat tickles my cheek and he takes it off to place it on top of the post to our left. It's only a second of distraction before he is back to kiss me and rubbing between my thighs with his own.

Can you die from too much pleasure? Because I am pleased beyond measure. He wants my words? I don't have any. Only mind blowing sensations that I would not come close to being able to explain to him right now.

I tip right over the edge of something I know I'll never come back from. He is the one.

The One.

Tyson holds me in a fierce embrace that I never want to step out of. We remain like that long enough for the lust-blown haze to settle into something less dizzying.

"Do you feel that?" he asks. I look up at him while he puts his hat back on his head. "Our heartbeats are syncing up. They're beating at the same rhythm."

I sigh and bury my head against his chest. His heart is beating against my cheek steadily. It's soothing in a way I can't place right now.

We walk back toward the barn. Tyson finds a spot by some other people hanging back from the raging party still going strong. He and I talked for what could be hours. At some point, Quincy brought us a Gatorade that we sip on but I have no clue where he got it from. On the outside of the barn, it's much more chill. This is the kind of night I could look back on fondly. I know I will.

Our little happy bubble bursts when I hear my name being called by Reese. "Mel! Help me!" I run over to her and she grabs my hand. "I can't find anyone else."

At a party full of people, she couldn't find anyone? She pulls me insistently to the other side of the barn where Mack is barely standing and smoking a joint. He's mumbling to himself incoherently.

"Ugh. Where did you get this? Will you stop already?" She snatches it from his mouth and puts it out on the heel of her boot before throwing it across the way. Turning to me she says, "I couldn't find Clo, Q or Drea. I saw you two kiss..." I panic, thinking for a second that she somehow caught the kiss that I had with Tyson earlier. She continues rambling, "I figured you'd want to help. Mack has already been telling everyone that you're his girl after he's been seen taking you to school and everything. He was asking where you were and I remembered passing you. How silly would that be if his girlfriend wasn't here to help him? He's been mumbling like this and not really focusing on anything. It's freaking me out so bad. I don't know how much he's had of anything tonight. Fuck, he's been going hard! Be right back."

I don't bother correcting her. What good would that do now? It doesn't matter because Reese leaves me out here with my thoughts. I look over to Mack who is slowly sliding down the side of the barn. He lands on his butt with a groan. I don't know how he is comfortably sitting in these wood

200

chips. I sit beside him, forcing him to look up at me. "Mack? Can you hear me?"

He nods in a way that makes me even more nervous that he might have alcohol poisoning. His eyes slide close and I grab his face. "Please Mack you have to stay awake with me okay?" He stares at nothing in particular, maybe he's singing a song. I don't know. Not only has he been drinking and probably mixing alcohol, but he smoked two joints by himself. And that was just what I saw. Who knows what he was doing when I wasn't here and when I was with...

Reese returns from around the corner. "Okay. I found a bucket. We need to get him to throw up. He needs that shit out of him ASAP." She set the bucket down next to him.

"He already threw up by the bonfire earlier. What do we need a bucket for?"

"Do you want to get vomit all over you?" At the look of disgust on my face she responds, "I didn't think so. Let's try to sit him up a little more. We're about to get much closer as friends. Are you ready?"

"For what?" I ask.

"I'm gonna try to get him to throw up... You know? Sticking my fingers in his throat. Unless you wanna—"

"Nope. No. I am totally good on that. I'll hold the bucket."

Reese tries to get her fingers into his mouth. He fights her with his noodle arms and thrashes just enough to be difficult. "Will you stop, you idiot? I'm trying to help you."

"Melmelmelmelmel," he murmurs over and over. Reese and I look at each other and it's clear that I'm gonna have to be the one to do this. I cringe for several moments and sit in his lap, reluctantly. Hopefully, my weight will be enough to restrain him from moving too much.

"I've got the bucket," she says. "You do the fingers and I'll be right there to catch," she shudders and I nod. "One, two, three..."

As quickly as I can manage, I try to trigger his gag reflex and after a few tries, he wretches and Reese thrusts the bucket under his face. I hold his head up so he doesn't fall forward. My heart is racing and not in a good way.

I'm reminded of how often I would see my dad passed out in the bathroom, laying on the toilet. And sometimes just laying there in a puddle of his own vomit that I would have to clean up and clean him up too. It's too much. This is way too much.

As soon as Mack's done, I get off of his lap and search out Drea.

I stomp furiously from the stables and someone grabs my hand. "Get off me," I shriek and turn.

"I'm sorry. Where did you go?" It's Tyson, with a hurt expression as he watches Mack stumble out behind me, leaning onto Reese. She's a much better friend than me because I'm so pissed right now. He ruined what was shaping up to be an amazing night.

He brushes a tear from my cheek and I realize I was crying. "God, I'm a mess."

"You're not." He cups my cheek, rubbing the wetness from my face with his thumb. "Where did you go?"

"I am. I just want to go home." I'm overwhelmed and I need to get out of here.

"Let me drive you."

I shake my head. "I'm gonna look for Drea."

"I wouldn't if I were you." I give him an irritated look and he elaborates, "She and Colton are... indisposed... in his truck... it's fogged up..."

"Oh. Ohhh. Okay then. Well, we came in her car. Are you sure you don't mind taking me home?"

"Of course not." He fishes his keys out of a pocket in his jeans and grabs my hand.

"You don't wanna say goodbye to anyone?" he looks back at Mack and Reese behind us.

"Not really. I mean, I'll send a text so they don't freak out when they can't find you." We walk over to his old red truck that is closer to the road than where Drea and I parked. "You know I never did get that dance..."

"I'm not really in the mood to dance anymore," I say, looking at my boots. One is still a bit sticky from the beer. I desperately need to get them off now that they're starting to pinch since they aren't broken in all the way.

Ty pulls me under his arm, where I feel safe and warm, "Let's get you home, alright?"

I nod, knowing I'll go anywhere Tyson will take me.

CHAPTER 33

Tyson, Then

WE PULL UP TO Melody's house before two in the morning. It's dark and though her dad's car is in the garage, she doesn't seem worried at all about sneaking back into her house. She was silent the whole way home. Before Reese called out for her, we were having a good night. Now she's completely withdrawn, chewing her lip as we ride home. She reaches for the door handle and I blurt, "Are we gonna talk about it?"

She turns back to me, long hair whipping around her head with the motion. I know that Melody hates confrontation. She hesitates, "About what?"

"Tonight... The kiss. What were you doing with Mack when Reese grabbed you?"

She sighs and leans back into the seat. "I think he might have OD'd tonight. If Reese wasn't there... he was messed up. So out of it that I couldn't get him to focus on my face or say coherent words. We had to get him to throw up and hope for the best. I've been there before... Not what I had to do for Mack, but seeing someone be so wrapped up in their own shit that they just can't stop drinking. And why? His life is good. Great, even." I reach out to hold her hand. With all I know about her, she has to be talking about her dad now more than Mack. She looks over at me with her glossy eyes and frowns. "Nothing happened with us. With Mack and me. I just helped Reese. He was so gone, Ty."

"Fuck. Everybody has demons, I guess. We never know what goes on behind closed doors." I cup her face. "We can't make anyone share that kind of thing."

"I don't want to be a part of that. I can be his friend, but I don't want the burden of yet another weight on my shoulders. Does that make me a horrible person?"

God, she is so sweet. She deserves the most and whatever happened behind the barn is sitting on her heart so heavily. I think I just fell for her even harder if that could be possible because I'm already in so deep. "No. It doesn't. We can choose. You have a choice." I'm leaning over the console now. She's turned so that we are as close as possible in my truck. I have never wanted a bench seat up front more earnestly than I do right now. Melody looks at my mouth and then my eyes. I speak again, but it comes out more like a plea. I feel like I'm losing her and I don't know why exactly. "You could choose me."

She crumples into the seat again. I'm still leaning here like a fool with my empty hands shaped for her face. "We can't. I mean this... can't."

I finally have the sense to sit back in my seat and close my eyes, preparing for a blow I don't deserve to take. "Why not?" She never actually agreed to be my girl earlier. It bothered me for only a little bit at the back of my mind before but now I need to know.

"Because..."

A disbelieving scoff huffs out of me. "Because Mack told everyone you were together? And you aren't. So, you feel obligated to stand beside him if he's hurting."

She shrinks away from me toward the passenger door. "How do you know that? Maybe I'm the worst kind of person who is cheating on him with you. Did you think about that?"

"Sure. I've thought about it. But, I've also seen you and him together. I see how you are with him. And I know you don't feel for him, what you feel for me."

"Don't do this." She shakes her head and wipes her eyes. "I can't do this. I need to figure everything out."

If I were a different guy, maybe I would be doing something different. Trying to still make a move or I don't know...

I'm not a different guy. *That guy* gets to make mistakes, gets fucked up at his own party, traumatizes her, and still she's thinking it over. *Figuring it out.* All because he opened his big mouth to tell everyone a lie that she is willing to go along with. That she is too preoccupied with staying afloat to argue about. Floating under the shadow of the ego of Maxwell Stewart is somehow easier.

"You just don't get it. This is better."

"This?" My voice is too loud for the small space. I know that, but I can't calm down. "You would rather fall into a relationship you don't really want with that guy? The one who calls you *Sweetness* and forces you to make him throw up at his own party because he can't control himself. That allowed people to spread rumors about a relationship that does not exist! All so that you don't hurt his feelings? He doesn't even see you, Melody."

My heart is about to beat out of my chest. *I have to calm down.*

It takes a few tries, but after the third set of breaths, I continue in a softer tone. "Everyone loves sunny days and smiles, baby. But you... you're not sunny days. You are not this sweet and happy person that you are clinging onto the husk of. This armor you wear to try and fool everyone that you're okay when you are not. The one he fell for. It doesn't work on me. I see it. I see you. They may not like the storms and the rain, but I love it. Nothing would grow without rain. It's a balance. I'm begging you to fight for someone who at least knows you. To see me too."

"Tyson," her eyes well with tears. "I do see you. I wish they weren't there, but there are other reasons why we shouldn't be together. Not just Mack."

"Fuck all of them. I don't care."

She huffs a laugh. "I care. Can you imagine what people will say about me if we start dating? The homie hopper. The slut. Or better yet, what will Chloe think? That I'm friends with her to get to you. And what about you? What will that say about you? I've been the subject of both pity and nasty rumors. Leaving Harrison was the best thing for me to escape that. I could hardly get out of bed and go to school facing all the lies about me. Here, I am someone new and different. I don't want to be in that place again. I can't be alone like that again." She won't look me in the face anymore and I don't force her.

"You're forgetting something in all this speculation." She finally gives me her eyes. "I am not them. I'm me. Things will never be like they were at your old school. You're not alone and I don't care about the rumors. My sister won't care about any of the stuff you're talking about. Our friends aren't like that. And if for any reason, someone has anything to say about it, you will still have me. Even if you break." The urge to be with her is too strong to ignore with this out in the open. Leaning over the console, I squeeze her close to me and talk into her soft curls. "I'll always be there to catch the pieces. Each one is as important as the last."

"Do you mean that?" She says into my chest. I know she's scared of falling into a dark place. And for everything she has endured up until this point, I don't blame her for trying to protect herself from it as long as possible. Her depression is a part of her. It's one that I will keep close and protect until she tells me not to.

"Cross my heart," I respond into her hair and kiss the top of her head. Since she has not backed away from me or moved from my embrace I hold her until we both get tired.

With her hand in mine, we walk into her house and I stay the night in her bed. Holding her against my chest as long as my body allows it. I don't sleep for a long time in the staunch quiet of her home—it's almost alarming. When she told me before I didn't believe her. It's the yawning void around us. No wonder she has a hard time sleeping. At some point in the night, I opened the window I knew she uses to climb onto the roof. The sounds of the crickets chirping and the breeze blowing through the Ash trees filter in and I feel her settle against me that much more snugly.

The next morning I leave with no incident because her dad never even came out of his room.

Q: We're going to the river. U coming?

It's not lost on me that everyone was still having a great time when so much changed for me and Melody last night.

I walk back over to my house, shower, and eat something before I'm back at her door.

When I knock, she comes to the door with her hair all over her head.

"Sleep well?" I chuckle.

"Like a baby," she yawns, stepping to the side. I walk back into her house and really notice how few photos are on the walls. Actually there is hardly anything on any of them. Another way that this house feels so empty.

"Do you want to go to the river with everybody today? It's probably the last weekend it will be warm enough for us to get into the water. The big chill is coming in tomorrow."

She takes me in with fresh eyes. I have on board shorts and a T-shirt which are very clearly for the river. "Umm, sure. Yea. Lemme just," she gestures to herself and says, "fix this. Gimme like twenty."

Melody gets into my truck wearing a long crocheted dress that doesn't quite hide the light purple bikini she has on underneath.

I park next to the other cars and turn the truck off. She looks over to me and says, "So, this is it."

"Yea. There's a natural step into the water from here where the river doesn't flow too quick—

"No, no, no. I mean... We're going to tell everyone now."

I play dumb, "Tell everyone what?"

She huffs and rolls her eyes. It's adorable and playful and I want to kiss her again right now. "You know what I'm talking about. That we're—"

I cut her off taking that opportunity to kiss her. She relaxes into it as my tongue explores her mouth more deeply. Her little whimper into my mouth spurs me on. I grab her waist, my fingers running over her bare skin under the crochet dress.

"Well, that's one way to do it! Get you some, Melly Mel!" Reese's voice breaks our kiss and Melody pulls back from me.

Hopping out of my truck with a smug smirk on my face, Q claps my back. "Bout time," he says under his breath.

Drea and Reese high-five. "I totally called it first though," Drea says.

Chloe is saying something to Mel that I only catch the end of when I pick her up and throw her over my shoulder.

"Tyson, put me down!" She's trying to say as I jog over toward the river.

"Don't you dare!" She giggles. "Tyson, don't!" But I'm already walking down the river steps. When I'm up to my calves, I let her slide down my body. She hisses when her feet hit the cool water.

"Jerk," she says before pulling her dress over her head and throwing it onto the bank.

My mouth hangs open. The little bikini she's wearing barely covers her petite dancer's build. Her strong stomach and thighs are toned. Her perfect little tits are barely concealed in the top tied around her neck and back. I dip down into the cold water to keep my dick from popping up for all my friends to see.

It's not long before Drea, Clo, Q, and Reese are hissing into the water as well. Melody makes her way over to me bobbing over the smooth rocks at our feet. I hold her close to me with her back to my front as everyone recalls what they got into at the party last night.

Drea gets quite a few ooo's from us as she shares about how she and Colton hooked up last night, a fact that Melody and I knew already.

Clo and Q were apparently sharing the same horse stall as Taylor and Ash to their surprise. Taylor got mad that Ash was calling out Quincy's name when it was Clo all along and they laughed about it together.

Then Reese recounted exactly what happened when she had to get Melody to help her with Mack. Melody's tense throughout the whole story. Everyone else shares a mixture of surprised gasps and panic at the recap.

"Awe, I was about to take all your clothes from the bank until I heard how concerned you were about me," Mack says while hissing into the river himself. His sunglasses are dark, likely to hide his hangover, so I can't see them. What I can see of his expression lets me know that he has seen and acknowledged where Melody stands literally and figuratively. Even though she's made herself as small as possible under my arm.

I give him a nod that he returns before defending himself to Reese who is laughing about the night now that she knows for certain her bro is okay. I expected a much bigger falling out from him, but I guess he isn't that pressed about the whole thing. It was a fair play. She chose me, despite his best efforts.

The day rolls on and we eventually get out of the water to dry off and eat some food Reese has from her mom. Though it's a little lukewarm from being in the cooler this long, we dig in. *This feels right.* Listening to my friends talk as normal with Melody relaxed between my legs. Her unforced laughter mixed with everyone else's. Reese pulls out a box of Smironoffs from her truck bed and some of them drink besides Melody, Mack, and I as the sun sets over the river.

We turn the radio up and our headlights on to dance. It's a heady blend of the peace I feel, finally having Melody in my grasp, and being surrounded by good people that make me feel bold enough to ask her outright.

"Melody, will you be my girlfriend?" It's a little redundant, but I need to know for sure that I have her.

She gives me a confused look, but wraps her arms around me as we sway to the music in the headlights. "Yes," she answers against my lips. "I'll be your girlfriend, Ty."

I've never heard sweeter words.

Chapter 34

Melody

"Oh. That's new..." Reese says from the front seat.

I look down at myself after clicking my seatbelt into place in the backseat of Reese's Expedition. The pale lilac top and cream tapered trousers I'm wearing aren't new. I'm pretty sure she's seen me in this outfit before. I rub a hand over the bun. on my head, still tight and in place how it usually is. "What?" I ask, smoothing the pants down my thighs.

Drea inspects my face, turning it one way and then the other. "Chloe, are you seeing what I'm seeing?"

Chloe looks at me in the rearview mirror. "Oh, I'm seeing it!"

We all arrived at Mason Ranch around the same time to leave for a day of dress shopping in the city. Normally, we would all meet inside for something Chandie has cooked, but she is busy overseeing her own preparations around the Ranch for her daughter's upcoming wedding. I fortunately ate before this gathering, so I don't mind missing her mom's scrumptious food. Tyson made damn sure that he fed me after what we got into this morning.

"What are you talking about?" I swat at Drea's hand.

Reese turns from the passenger seat. "Oh my God, Mel. Who are you fucking? It was my gift, right? That glow is insane!" She bounces and claps in her seat.

"It may come as a surprise to you all, but I am a grown woman. I, occasionally, do things that grown women do." I say with a little tilt upward of my chin. I don't know why I feel so protective over what Tyson and I are building right now.

"Yea, yea. Who is it?" Drea queries, undaunted by my comment. "He better be cute." She buckles her own seatbelt and adds, "And nice. Our sweet Melody deserves the best." She taps the tip of my nose and I swat at her hand again. Drea holds everyone to a high standard. I had no plans on divulging who had been in my bed this past week before I got into this car. I didn't think there was anything different... like maybe I could go at least one day with all this goodness for myself. Too bad my friends never miss anything happening in the other's sex life.

Chloe has chosen to be the DD today and is maneuvering the large vehicle out of the long gravel driveway toward the highway.

"It's probably this new makeup," I hedge. "I grabbed a couple of things online that just came in."

"Makeup, my ass! You got some dick! It was good too from how dazzling you look today." Reese waggles her eyebrows. "Who is it? Just tell me..." She does a little huff and turns to check her own makeup in the visor. Looking at me through the reflection of the small mirror she says, "I'll put Chandie on the case and you know she'll get all the tea."

Though Reese had been gone for years before she came home to help out on her family's Ranch, it feels like she never left. I'm happy she is finally back after all the drama she went through, but that doesn't mean I want her or her mother in my business.

I laugh, "Ugh. You all are the worst."

"Spill!" Drea says.

I huff again. They aren't going to drop it. It wouldn't be so bad to have someone else know what was going on with Tyson. Would it? I want to celebrate even if it is far too early to be doing that. "You cannot tell anyone. I mean it y'all. Not even your men. They gossip, too."

Reese immediately raises three fingers in the air. "Scouts honor." She was a Girl Scout so her promise can be believed, I guess.

Drea crosses her chest saying, "Cross my heart and hope to die. Stick a needle in my eye." She shrugs, "And who am I gonna tell?"

"Tony," we all say in unison with a laugh.

"Ant is not my man! I don't tell him everything anyway." We continue laughing. She's deluded if she thinks we believe that. Rolling her eyes, Drea says, "Whatever! I already crossed my heart damnit!"

Chloe is the first to stop laughing to add, "Like Quincy cares, he's barely listening when I tell him town gossip unless it involves someone he cares about." I wince and she catches the movement in the mirror. She always does. "Cinnabon!" Clo drags out all three syllables of the word. "You didn't!"

I roll my eyes and lean against the door. Maybe if I stop talking everyone will drop it. I watch the open land rush by the window as we drive on the highway to Denver.

My silence makes it way worse it seems. "You didn't!" Now coming from Drea.

Reese gasps and holds a hand to her mouth. "Are you fucking Mack again? Ew. Not ew because I wouldn't judge you if that's what you want but ew because... you know. I just want to think of him as a sexless blob who has never touched my friend..."

She continues to ramble and I look out the window trying not to think about Mack at all. I don't want to feel that guilt all over again. With everything Tyson has told me, I feel even worse. I used Mack. I couldn't be alone again. He wanted me to use him to fill the void Tyson created when he left and I let him—for far too long. I almost started a family with Mack because I was so desperate to make things work... I was desperate for Tyson to not be the reason that I was holding on to Mack even tighter. I can feel everyone's eyes on me and it takes a moment to register that they're waiting for my answer to something Reese has said while I've been in my head.

"What?"

"I know you didn't sleep with Mack. He would have told me already. I'm confident that he may have even called me directly after the fact. So if it wasn't him..." She gasps again. Her eyes lock with mine when she asks, "Did you sleep with Ty?"

My face heats and Reese and Drea catch my expression. The Expedition erupts with their loud reactions as Chloe joins in with their exclamations.

"Will you guys calm down? It's not a big deal remember."

"That was before! I said to be civil with him. Be an adult! Not fuck my brother... again." She's not mad, but utterly flabbergasted. I avoid all her looks to the back seat in the rearview mirror. The car is silent while everyone processes the swift change that has happened between Ty and I.

Drea squeezes my hand and scoots closer to me. In a stage whisper, she asks "Was it good?"

"Of course it was good," Reese says. "She's been putting mileage on my gift to her."

"What'd she give you? Knowing Reese, it could literally be anything," Clo says. "She gave me a vibrating cock ring. Not too bad for a solo act too. Holla!"

"She gave me one that would put Hoover Vac to shame with how amazing the suction is," Drea says with a bump of our shoulders.

"You would know what everyone else got if you actually picked up your phone! Where have you been all week?" Reese asks.

I'm full-on fanning my face at this point. It's all fun and games until I'm expected to share real details. No way I'm going to tell them about how many fingers Tyson had inside me or anything else that happened after that. I'm also not going to admit that we haven't been using the gift Reese gave me. That is a conversation that I haven't had with Tyson and I won't be having it with them right now either. "Please can we stop talking about this?"

"Fine, fine," Reese says and shares details about the expansion her family is working on to Masons' Horsing Around to include classes for adults and potentially a hippotherapy program. The news about Tyson and I has, thankfully, receded by the time we get to Olivia Holt Bridal. I know the selection is amazing here and I love how pleasant the staff is.

Shopping for my wedding dress was my favorite part of my first wedding. I love beautiful gowns and strolling through these isles was a dream. Reese is no stranger to couture and I honestly expected her to have a completely custom-made gown with her taste. When I ask her she says, "How could I do that with my girls? This will be more fun. Plus, all the other brides can eat their hearts out that I'm going to look way better in these dresses than them. What better confidence boost?" She is who she is.

There is something nostalgic about all of us shopping together. This place sells bridesmaid dresses as well so we have the chance to try on our dresses too. Reese tried on three dresses that we all feel kind of meh about. When she steps out of the dressing room in the fourth option we know it's the one.

It is something between lingerie and couture with the corset top bodice that shimmers with various-sized pearls all over. The full skirt starts a little higher than the waist, giving her plenty of space for her baby bump to come in. I have a strong feeling that Reese will be the type of woman who won't show until her third trimester anyway. The pearls glint all over as she spins to show us the corset back. There is a sheer cape that attaches to a pearl choker necklace and flows all around her. She looks stunning!

My phone vibrates with a text and I check it while Chloe and Reese talk with the specialist about what they are looking for. I step into the open area for water and the little treats they have for guests while they're shopping. I grab a mint macaron from the table and open my new messages.

Ty: Hey...

Ty: Are you doing anything this weekend?

Little butterflies flutter in my stomach. I don't want to look too desperate, so I finish my cookie and return my phone to my purse. I do a little jig covertly between the row of fluffy dresses we're walking through now.

I flick through the rows and find one that I like in the pale burgundy color Reese chose.

I'm the last to come out of the dressing room when it comes to our reveal. Reese sits on a tufted ottoman in the middle of the changing suite. Her hands are over her eyes and she whines, "Can I look now? I wanna see!"

I remember why this feels nostalgic. Just like the first time we all went shopping at the mall together for Mack's eighteenth. I fight back the shudder of that memory. Chloe starts counting down and we all take these ridiculous poses before she gets to one. "Okay, open!"

"Oh," Reese wipes at her eyes. "These damn hormones. You all look so pretty." She is full-blown blubbering and we try to console her. Drea goes to her first and she shoos her away. "No! I don't want to ruin them with my preggie tears! They're so perfect. Approved! I love them all." Drea, Chloe and I each give each other looks and go back into our respective changing rooms.

After sliding my divider closed I decided to respond to Tyson.

> **Me: I'm teaching those mornings at the Senior Center. Then I work first shift at QBs Sat and Sun.**

There. Not too eager and not too unavailable. My phone vibrates again before I'm able to put it back into my purse.

> **Ty: That's perfect! Wanna go to Harmony Hill Rodeo with me?**

> **Me: Which day?**

> **Ty: Both?**

Both?

"Oh my god! Bon get out here!"

I hurry to get redressed and fling open my curtain. "What is it? What happened?" I look over my friends as they gather in front of Chloe's phone. "What's going on?"

216

"Look!" Chloe thrusts her phone toward me and it takes a moment to focus on what I'm looking at.

"What?" I questioned before my brain registered that it was JT's social media page. In big bold letters, rescheduled is over the post with JT *now performing on the West Stage.* "Oh my god," I repeat Chloe's earlier outburst.

"I'm sorry, ladies. But could you keep it down in here? We have other clients fitting as well."

Reese rolls her eyes and grabs my hands. "Ignore her. You are actually getting busy with the band! Please tell me we're getting backstage to meet Jordan Hurst! I love him!"

My mouth flaps for a while, but no sound comes out. Mind racing because... what in the what?

Tyson is going to be the main act on this humongous stage. It's not even about the size of the crowd, so much as the reputation of the event. Harmony Hill Rodeo is one of the largest, if not the largest, Rodeo and outdoor Country music events in the country. My friends are talking around Chloe's phone as they look at the rest of the lineup for the event.

My phone buzzes a few times and I finally come out of my own thoughts long enough to look at the messages.

Ty: Please don't freak out.

Too late for that buddy.

Ty: Chloe texted me so I know she is there making this out to be much bigger than it is. Since I haven't responded to her text yet.

Ty: I wanted to be the one to tell you first (eye roll emoji) But she beat me to it.

Ty: Yes, both days. Let me take you to the carnival and have you there VIP on Sunday.

Ty: Tell Chloe they are all invited too.

Ty: I feel like Clo with all these texts. (laughing emoji) Don't tell her I said that (grinning face with sweat emoji)

My heart swells in my chest. I've always been on the outside of his career so far. Always watching him grow from a distance. Something in my gut tells me that this will be a big deal.

I look at my phone, realizing that I still haven't responded to his texts.

Me: What time should I be ready?

CHAPTER 35

Tyson

"GOD DAMN, MELODY! ARE you trying to kill me?" I lean against the doorframe, clutching my chest.

She looks over her clothes and it gives me more of an opportunity to look her over. "Kill you? You don't like my outfit?" The gauzy white cropped shirt she has on, billows in the breeze along with the long white skirt she wears. Her cowboy boots peek through the knee-high split and she looks good enough to eat.

"You misunderstand me. My heart is beating much faster than it should be. I'm gonna have a heart attack right here." *Fuck it.* You miss one hundred percent of the shots you don't take. "You look good enough to eat."

"Hmm, I'll take it," she smiles and I wonder for a bit if she'll actually let me.

I hear the lock of her front door which drags me out of my wayward thoughts. I clear my throat, "You still have those boots, huh?" I remember them from Mack's party however long ago at this point.

"Yea... I don't often wear them, but the rodeo seems like the event to put them on for." She shrugs and sticks her foot out. The movement exposes more of her thigh and I clear my throat again. No amount of coughing could ease my dry mouth. I have plans tonight. Gonna stick to them. She walks past me to my truck and it's a lesson in self-control that I don't lay her over the back seat for a taste.

I'm about to open the passenger door for her, but she isn't reaching for it. Her petite hand is over the back door handle. I raise an eyebrow at her in question.

"Maybe just one... taste in the backseat... for old times sake." She says to my now slack jaw. She moves back onto the bench and her skirt falls open. I'm drawn like a fly to honey, following her into the backseat.

"It feels like deja vu with you waiting for me like this," I say between kissing her powerful thighs. She bites her lip in anticipation. I take a moment to appreciate my good fortune. "Do you remember how many times we almost got caught doing this exact thing all over town?"

"There's no one to catch us now..." She raises the split in the skirt little by little with a finger and my eyes devour each additional inch of her brown legs she's exposing.

My heart stutters when I catch the first glimpse between her legs. "Melody?"

"What?"

"Where are your panties?" She giggles as I push her skirt all the way up her hips.

"In the house," she says coyly. "Should I go get them?"

"Oh, no, no, no. It's too late for that." I say into her hot pussy. She smells how I remember. I take a deep inhale before burying my face between her legs. "No take-backs. This is mine now."

Melody moans and it's the music I could live by when I notch a finger inside her. "Tyson, please." I search for that place inside her that I know drives her crazy. Listening all the while for that reaction that does the same to me. She moves her hips hypnotically in a rhythm that quickens my breathing.

"That's not how you ask, baby," Sliding my finger out of her, she grabs my wrist. I look up into her burning eyes. She's getting close and I'm holding her right on the edge. This is my favorite place to be.

"Can I please come, Tyson?" I flick my tongue into her lips slowly at first. Melody lets out a gasp before her fingers tangle into my hair. My hat is gone somewhere in the backseat now.

"Right now?" I ask. She writhes on my finger, my nose pressed into her soft curls all while I'm licking over her clit in slow strokes. I add another two fingers and work them deeper into her slick pussy.

"Right now. I wanna come right now, please Tyson." She whines and clenches at my fingers. My dick strains against the seat, begging for attention too.

"How badly?" Her delicate hands grab ahold of my jaw to hold me right where she wants me. "Rub this tight pussy all over my nose. Just like that beautiful. Show me you want it." She rocks back and forth over me and I could come from the expression on her face as her head leans back onto the window. She throbs and clenches on my fingers. The come down from her orgasm is almost as gratifying as the journey up.

Fuck yes.

I wanted this.

I kiss her neck, licking around her collarbones, never taking my fingers from her body. She comes to and catches my lips with hers. Her sweet lips mixing with her arousal on my tongue make me nearly shoot my load.

I pull her to the edge of the bench and she reaches for my buckle. I shake my head. "It's gonna be a long drive to Harmony Hill. We should get going." She huffs and falls back onto the seat. "C'mon before I really do take you in this backseat."

"It wouldn't be so bad," she grumbles.

"It would. I have so much catching up to do." She leans up onto an elbow, eyebrows raised. "Yes, catching up on what your plans are for the school year. Doesn't that start next week?"

Her eyes light up like I knew they would. She fixes her skirt, putting herself to rights. I hold the passenger door open for her to get into the front seat. Takes me a moment to clean up my face and hands then we're on our way. The whole ride to the rodeo she tells me about all the routines she has set for her classes and the dance team, what music she's picked, and her goals for her students. I listen intently to the pride in her voice when she talks about her girls and the progress she's made with the program.

It's not long before we're collecting tickets for the carnival and walking into the buzzing rows of Western-themed mini-games, food, and fun.

"I figure that's our problem," I say to her after a bit of aimless meandering around the busy event.

"We have a problem?" she asks in a small voice.

"Oh yea. Big time. We have a very big problem."

She gives me a curious glance that turns more confused as she processes what I'm saying. "Well, what is it?"

I hold her hand over the inside of my elbow as we walk down the row of games. The lights are colorful and glaring at night, but it adds to the ambiance of the carnival. She looks so beautiful and glowing on my arm. I guess an orgasm will do that for you. I try not to get choked up on that thought. I finally have her here with me. Years of time have passed, but I have her now. Mine for the night and who knows how long after. Maybe she'll let me stay forever.

I've been daydreaming while she's clearly panicking about what I've said. "Tyson," Melody stops walking and I turn to face her head on. "What is our problem? You can't just say that and then wander off into la-la land."

"Oh," I laugh and scratch my cheek. "Our problem." Pulling her closer to my body with my arms wrapped around her back, I revel in her looking up at me with clear eyes. Bright and focused. It's these moments where her sadness has receded far enough for the beautiful brown to truly shine through that I live for. "Our problem is that we're always too much, too soon."

Her hands press to my chest. "Too much?"

"Too soon."

"What does that mean?"

I brush some hair from her face and cup her chin. "We never take it from the top. You know? After I left, we'd get back together like nothing had changed when it had. We never really dated each other."

"And who's fault is that?" she asks with a smile on her lips. "I'm not the one who needed to eat before we left the house," relief that there isn't something more daunting plays in her voice. She looks too good not to kiss. So I do. In the middle of this busy crowd who makes their way around us. Each time I kiss her it feels like the next note of a song I'm discovering for the first time. A song I hope never ends.

"Mine. Definitely mine." I answer. "I don't want to feel like there is anything between us, but there is. Now more than ever."

Melody stops walking again, confusion in her brows, "I can't change the past, Tyson." If I could drop-kick her ex-husband right out of the picture, boy would I. Unfortunately, life isn't that sweet. I know there's more that I've missed from then til now. He is one problem of many I'll need to solve in her past.

"And neither can I. I don't want to. Not really. They make up the story of us. The one that we wrote, separately sometimes, but now we can write together."

"How do we do that?"

"We start with the basics..." She looks very skeptical, but I direct us in front of one brightly colored food stand. Bright white bulbs ring the top of it that glare brighter than the other attractions it's parked next to. Hot pink stripes bring a nostalgic fifties look to the vehicle. The sign on this one boasts the biggest carnival food around. Extra large turkey legs, massive funnel cakes, and ice cream cones taller than my head with a hat on, all plaster the side menu in front of us. "What are we going to have?" She looks at the truck and then back to me.

"I can't eat one of those! They're bigger than I am!"

"Exactly, we're gonna share. Seems like a first date type of thing." I shrug.

"I don't know... Maybe the cake." She looks back to the menu. "Definitely the funnel cake with the strawberries on top. Oh! And whip cream." Her eyes go all wide as she bounces on her tiptoes, holding onto my arm.

I smile at her enthusiasm and when it's our turn to order, I make sure to get plenty of napkins. I can barely hold the plate. It's so heavy when the guy in the window hands it over to me.

We find a bench that is out of the way of the people streaming through the aisles. It's marginally darker over here. It's like we are in our very own space.

"So what goes into this first date?" She forks some fruit into her mouth and does a little dance in her seat.

"Is it good?" She nods, breaking some of the winding cake off and popping it into her mouth. A bit of cream gets on her nose and I wipe it away with my thumb. Before I can put my thumb into my mouth, she takes my wrist and leans over to lick it off instead. The lick is slow and sensual. I don't even know if she means it to be, but my eyes are glued to her doing it.

"Okay, that was not first-date approved," I say, adjusting myself just a little. The best and worst thing about these jeans is how tight they are.

"What? That was my cream." She looks up at me through her lashes, the picture of innocence. There was nothing innocent about the way she took my thumb into her mouth.

"Sharing. We're sharing, Melody. You can't just put your mouth on me like that." I take the fork and get some cake for myself. "Especially not a first date. I'll expect things." I raise an eyebrow.

Not waiting for the fork again, she picks up a strawberry piece with her fingers and licks the cream off of it. Giving the fruit as much attention as she gave my thumb earlier. "What kind of things?"

I chuckle, "You know what you're doing, Melody."

She giggles and her sweet voice lights up my heart. "Is it working?"

"Of course it is!" I say, putting an arm around her and pulling her onto my lap. "You feel how it's working?"

I hiss when she rolls her hips over my growing erection. "Good," she says. "I don't want first dates. I don't want to pretend like I don't know you already." I start to protest, but she presses her finger to my lips. "I get it. Life has happened. You're damn near front-page celebrity status and I'm a waitress... and teacher. We can talk about all of that without forgetting our history too. There is hurt and pain there." She focuses on straightening the collar of my shirt and I think that maybe it's the end of her explanation. In a lower tone, she adds, "There was also beauty, love, and light in our history between us too."

I hold her face with both hands and urge her to look at me. "That's true. Some of the happiest times of my life are still the times that I had with you. Being without you—living life without you—it's trash." That was the truth. Nothing was the same for me when I came home. It didn't feel like home anymore with her gone from my life. I know I've won somehow and I won't question it.

She startles a laugh and I take her lips with mine. I am still in disbelief that it is finally my time. There was a time when I was begging her to pick me, a time when I knew that she was not another girl but *the girl* who would change my life. And then the woman I could never have again. I want to have her again. In each press of our lips together I want to convey that. I'm going against all I said before about moving too fast, but I can't be bothered to care.

"I've waited years for you. I'd wait even longer if you needed me to. Just please, Melody. I don't want to lose you again."

She blinks. "I'm not running." I can feel that she means it. Her hands fist my shirt to keep me close. "I'm here."

We share breaths and tongues and lips until there isn't enough oxygen between us and I hold my forehead to hers. "Part two of our date—mini games."

CHAPTER 36

Tyson

MY PLAN'S GOING PERFECTLY. It wouldn't be a carnival date without some carnival games.

Melody is in my lap. I know the night is going well. She smiles and lets me set her on the ground. We decide on one game of ring toss on the way since there is no line for it.

Little ducks all bob in the water on boats in the small pool behind the counter. "All you have to do is get the rings on three or more ducks and you get a prize," the woman, Lindsey, from the name on her tag, says from her stool.

There are seven rings and I figure there is no pressure here, they're literally sitting ducks. "How hard could it be?" I say to Melody and her lips curl up at the side. She steps back from where I'm throwing.

"You ready?" Lindsey says and I nod my head in agreement. She flips the switch and cheery music begins blaring from the speakers. Looking back to the pool, the ducks begin swirling in a sporadic pattern all through the pool as water surges in, making a current.

Melody giggles behind me, "How hard could it be, huh?"

"Hey! I thought!" I laugh and try my best to get at least some of the ducks captured. By some miracle, I land three of them just before the music stops.

I throw a fist into the air and turn back to Melody. My arms wrap around her, bringing her ass back to my body where it should be.

"It's your choice. Anything from the middle row." The woman stands and uses a hook to bring the ducks I got closer to her.

"Okay." I rub my palms together. "Your man has won you anything from the middle row. What's it going to be?" I look over the row and notice that all the stuffed animal prizes are duck-themed. I guess I should have checked the prizes before I started playing the game. Oh well. Melody wiggles around in my arms as she looks over her options. I relish the feel of her body next to mine. She's excited and I wish I could bottle this moment up. "The corndog duck with ketchup stripes, the duck with a cowboy hat, or the frog with a duck hat."

She looks over her choices and then looks back at me. I rub the brim of my hat in suggestion and she whispers to me, "Maybe I should go for the corndog..." She taps her chin and I pick her up, kissing into her neck. She catches the hat falling off my head before telling Lindsey, "I'll have the cowboy hat duck, please." She happily takes the stuffed animal, patting his hat in place.

I pat his oversized hat too, "He's not a bad-looking prize."

Her eyebrows pinch, "How do you know it's a boy? This could be a cowgirl."

"Sure, sure," I laugh. "Let's get over to the Ferris wheel before the line gets too long."

While we wait in line, we go back and forth about what would be an appropriate name for a ranching duck with such a large hat. It's not long before our turn comes to load into the next cabin. Melody sits the duck on her left and we look out at all the twinkling lights get smaller as we rise higher in the ride.

When we get high enough, I point out my side. She leans over me to look at what I'm showing her. "Tomorrow night. Right over there. That's where I'll be. The stage seems so small from up here."

"That is no small stage, Ty." She sits back in her seat, frowning into her hands.

"Maybe not." She looks hesitantly toward me. "What's wrong?"

"Nothing. It's nothing." She shakes her head, mustering up a smile. "Are you excited? What is that even like?"

I don't know how to explain it, but I give it my best shot. "In some ways, I still feel like it's the same as it was when we were on stage for the talent show. In other ways, it's so different. Needing security and having to be mindful of what I say or whatever the publicist wants. That can get in the way. But the music. The passion behind the music. It feels incredible to be able to share that with people who want to hear it."

"You do it so well. I really am proud of what you're doing, Tyson." She looks up at me, eyes twinkling bright enough to rival the ones below us.

I nod slowly, processing her response. "Why does it sound like there's a but in there?"

"But..." she sighs. "It's hard for me not to see it for what it is."

My eyebrows touch my forehead. "And what is it?"

"The thing that kept us apart." She looks down at her hands. "I know that's not exactly true now, but for a long time, I thought that you stayed away from Alpenglow because you were so focused on your dream. I understood why you stayed away."

"I did have better luck doing this music thing in Denver. I can't lie and say that's not true. There was more than just that."

"Do you think you'll stay gone? I mean... Living in Denver makes sense, right?"

"I honestly don't know. My music means everything to me. It kept me going when times were hard. I can't put it to the side for—" I cut my thought short and look over to Melody who's arranging and rearranging the hat on the duck, pointedly not meeting my face. "I don't mean that. What I'm trying to say is—"

"You wouldn't pick me over the music."

"Don't be like that. It's not that cut and dry. There is no choice between you and the music. There is room for both in my life."

"Is there?"

228

"Of course there is. Melody, I'm not the first person to go into this industry with a family or a relationship. It doesn't have to be one or the other. I will make it work."

"Make it work..."

"Yea."

"How?"

"I don't know, but it's not like I'm touring worldwide or something. What is the difference if I'm in Denver or AR at this point? I've got a stable thing going with JT right now. We have our gigs, we record and I'm home otherwise."

"That is a lot, Tyson." I wince a little because saying it out loud does sound like a lot. The Ferris wheel pauses with us at the top. It's so high up that the stage looks even more minuscule.

"Melody, I'm willing to at least try to make it work if you are going to try with me." I squeeze her knee. "Are you willing to try? I know it's a lot to ask on a first date."

She swats my arm, "It's not a first date."

My phone rings in my pocket. My manager's ringtone is the Jaws theme music in the most complimentary way, of course. Keeta Redman is a shark and I love that about her. "It's my manager calling. I gotta take this. Do you mind?" Her lips thin, but she nods her head.

"What's up?"

"I'm gonna cut to the chase. Lacey dumped Jordan. Someone from her team told a source that she ended things and Jordan did not take it well. It's spreading like wildfire. Do not comment or give statements to anyone about this. Okay?"

"Okay. What? Why? What did he do, Keeta?"

"I have no idea. He's not answering my calls. His security team told me they have things under control, but he's already been seen out drinking straight from the bottle. He's tanking his progress with sobriety and the image we have been crafting for him. I can't get on a plane to get out there. I thought you should know with your show tomorrow night."

"Thanks for letting me know. I hope he sleeps it off and we'll be good for tomorrow."

"You and me both. I've got to get back to damage control. Please tell me you'll be there. I can't deal with another member going off the handle."

"No, I'll be there. I'm actually here now."

"What? At the Rodeo? Did we book you a hotel? Do they have those there? I'm not sure how small towns work."

"I'm good. It's fine. I'll be there tomorrow. I'll try to get ahold of Jordan for you."

"Thanks, kid. You're the least problematic of the talent I represent. Don't ever change."

I huff a laugh. "Yea. Okay, Keeta. I'll talk to you later." She hangs up and Melody looks at me expectantly. I am already dialing Jordan and it goes straight to voicemail.

"Fuck." They must have loaded the rest of the cars up so we're spinning in the ride now. It's an accurate depiction of my thoughts at the moment.

"What's going on?" Melody asks.

"Sorry." I shove my phone back into my pocket. "Apparently, Jordan and Lulu are over. She broke up with him and he's already on a bender. Keeta's freaking out." As an afterthought, I add, "You can't tell anyone that though."

"I'm not gonna tell anyone. Why does that matter?"

"Well, he has had problems with that in the past. If this goes the way that Keeta suspects, he will be doing much worse things than just drinking all night. He's been more or less sober since he and I started working together. It could ruin everything we've built."

She thinks quietly for a moment. "Are you upset by this?"

"Right now? No. If he screws the band over somehow.... I don't know. It will be a completely different story." If he does something drastic, it could ruin everything that me and the guys have been building for ourselves. Jordan will be fine. He has a legacy already and no one will let him forget that. My name holds some weight but I don't know if I sever ties with Jordan, that I could stand apart and survive. He's always bitching about me making him look bad, but this is what he's doing now. He could take us all down with him.

My doubts assault me full force as we circle from the highest highs and the lowest lows. The ride is finally over and we exit to the rush of people walking around.

Melody's voice cuts into my thoughts. "It's not really first-date advice, but I think you could do this on your own if it comes to it. I know all of your music with JT. No part that Jordan sings, would be made worse by you taking his place. You have the same range he does. And I'm sure you could sing them and play right along on your guitar too."

I consider her as we walk through the throngs of people rushing about. "You say that like you know he's gonna flake tomorrow."

She meets my gaze, eyes shining with an intensity that's infectious. "I don't... but wouldn't that be kind of amazing to perform up there without him?"

"You're kind of wicked, Melody." She buries her face into my chest, chuckling. "If he doesn't show—it's either canceling the whole gig or going up there without him. I hope it doesn't come to that, but you're right. I could do the whole set without him. It'd be me, Zeke, and Robert. Just like old times."

There's a vulnerability in her eyes when she asks, "Just like old times isn't so bad is it?"

"No, it's not at all."

CHAPTER 37

Melody

"WE... ARE JT'S GROUPIES," Reese says proudly to the security guard standing in front of the performer's gate. The lights are already blinding from where we stand to get into the VIP area before the show.

"Do you have a badge to get back here? If not, I'm going to need you to clear the area." He says, unimpressed by her announcement.

"So rude. We have digital passes. Show 'em, Clo!" My other friend strolls past the burly man to scan her phone on the stand. The small beep confirms that they're real and for the nine of us. He gives Clo a nod and unlatches the chain blocking our path through. Chloe, Quincy, Reese, Cory, Tony, Taylor, and Ash all walk ahead of me and Drea. The two of us are arm in arm. Burly security guard number two stops us before we're able to pass as well.

He leans closer to us saying, "Names James. You staying in town for the after-party?" I start to speak, but he nods over to Drea, "What's your name, beautiful?"

I look to Drea whose cheeks have pinkened under her smile, "I'm An-drea... most people call me Drea." She holds out a hand to him and he lifts it to his lips and kisses her wrist. Like a gentleman? I watch the whole exchange, mouth open because she is getting *Bridgerton* treatment when everyone else is like mud under his very heavy boots.

"Umm... We should probably go," I say, urging her through the line.

"Here take my number," he says, writing it onto a paper at his station before giving it to Drea. "Text me. I'll be there tonight too."

She agrees, looking over the paper as we all follow the signs toward JT's trailer. I tug on her arm to get her attention. "Drea! What was that?"

She flaps the paper in the air before slipping the paper into her bra. "You didn't see that fine ass man? You know what it was! I got his number."

"For what?" I ask, genuinely curious.

"Yea, for what?" Tony asks. He hangs back from our other friends to allow Drea to catch up with him.

"I don't think you want to know why, Ant."

He grimaces, "Why not? Folding already?"

"Foldin—What? It's only been five years. There are lots of activities you can do with a man besides having sex." Drea says, rolling her eyes.

"He was looking at you like a stray dog looks at filet mignon. I don't think he had any other activities in mind."

Throwing her hands into the air, she questions, "What does that matter? I can't talk to any men now?"

"That's not what I said," Tony says, crossing his arms over his broad chest.

"So what are you saying?" Drea asks.

Things between them are heating up as they walk closer and closer to each other. I try to interject their argument, saying, "Hey guys, maybe we should—"

Tony cuts me off, talking literally over my head to tell Drea, "That guy was a dick. Why do you even want his number?"

"Did you miss the fine-ass man comment earlier? I like a big muscled man."

"Not all of them." He says under his breath.

"Hey, can y'all catch up? We found the right one." Reese says, poking her head out of the trailer. Another security guard stands at the door now, but everyone else is inside. We pass by the guards into the luxurious space that is much bigger than it looks from the outside.

I feel his eyes on me before I see his black cowboy hat. This one is different from last night. In fact, his hair is different too. The sides are freshly shaved with crisp lines that are like catnip for me. Navy shirt undone and rolled to his elbows... I need to stop looking before I go into heat right here with all our friends watching.

He's talking with Cory and Reese when I make my way over to him. He doesn't break his conversation when his hands find my waist and pull me closer. "Nobody knows where this dude is. He hasn't answered his phone all day."

"Where who is?" I ask.

Tyson looks down at me, "Jordan. He's still missing in action. Lacey is not answering her phone and his security team stopped picking up hours ago. He's completely off the grid."

"Yikes. So he really did flake... What are you gonna do?"

"Fuck it. We're going on without him. Better it be just us than no act at all right?" He says that last bit to Robert and Zeke who are talking up a woman I don't recognize on the other side of the trailer.

"It's the dream team, baby!" Zeke says with Robert throwing up the "okay" sign with his fingers.

"Damn right! My bro is gonna give them a show. Nobody is gonna miss him." Chloe says from the dressing table. She fiddles with the products and sips from a cup of something clear.

Drea sits on the plush lounge chair also sipping from a cup. I don't think their heated discussion from earlier has cooled down any, looking at the set of Tony's jaw. Taylor and Ash are making themselves drinks at the little cart in the corner. It's gonna be a long night, so I might as well start drinking now.

"I want a drink too," I say.

Cory hands me his, whispering, "Here, you can have this one. Reese is trying to get me drunk, I think."

She hears him, regardless of his low tone. "The concert is like two hours long excluding the after-party. You can have a couple shots, babe. You're drinking for four, remember?"

"Angel, I don't think that's how the saying goes," Cory says to her, kissing her forehead.

"Pretty sure." Reese scoffs, dragging him out of the trailer. "We're gonna go so Cory can get pictures of me in this dress in front of the stage before Tyson photobombs me."

We laugh when Cory says, "I live to serve," as they leave. I finish the tequila he handed me and toss the cup into the trash. That shit never gets easier. It burns and this time I don't have any lime.

A woman leans her head into the trailer. "Don't want to interrupt, but guys—you're on in thirty. They'll come and mic you in twenty."

"We're coming with you now. The pre-show ritual needs to get going if we're gonna finish before curtains," Robert says, following the woman out with Zeke right behind him.

"Well, that sounds like our cue," Quincy says, roping his wife from the collection of styling products.

The murmuring of our friends all dies down to silence as I'm the last one in the trailer with Tyson. "Don't go," he says.

I allow him to pull me into his arms again. "You've got to get ready for your show."

"Nothing left to do. I'll be sitting in here by myself anyway."

"With twenty minutes to kill?" I get an idea and the grin that breaks across my face is just as naughty as the thought.

"More or less..." He eyes me suspiciously.

"Are you sure you're ready to go on?" I flip my head over, gathering my hair into a bun on the top of my head. When I'm done, I lower to my knees, thankful I decided on shorts tonight.

"What are you doing?" he asks, voice thick.

"Giving you something," I say, now blotting my lipstick onto a napkin. I don't want to walk back out to my friends being too obvious about what I hope to do here. Sweet Melody would never try this in their minds.

He blinks down at me several times. "What is it that you're giving me, Melody?"

"I want to be your groupie tonight... Or whatever they call them." I mean it. I have thought about it more than once. I've touched myself thinking about having him in my mouth right before he went on stage. I squeeze his thighs and look up at him from under my lashes. "This can be your good luck charm," I say in the soft tone that I know makes him weak.

"Fuuuck. How am I supposed to say no to that?" Here's my chance and I'm buzzing with nervous energy.

"You aren't." I make quick work of taking his belt off. Dragging my nails down his thighs, with his boxer briefs and jeans. I've got to be fast. I only have so much time before they come back to take him to the stage. Or before I lose my nerve. I've never done something like this before. I'm getting so wet thinking about how my lips will be the last to touch him before almost twenty thousand fans will be screaming for his attention.

"I'm not gonna last." He chuffs.

"That's okay. This is kind of a fantasy of mine." He has no idea. The fire in his eyes burns bright for me. He takes his hat off, throwing it to the counter next to us.

"Oh, yea?" he asks, grabbing onto my bun to force my eyes to him. I grip his heavy sack in one hand and lick up his shaft. The broad head is tight and shiny, dark with arousal and need.

I stroke him once and look into his eyes. "You gave all your smirks to those girls in the crowd before now. I had to pretend it was only for me." The velvety smooth skin of his dick in my palm twitches. I stroke him again.

On an exhale, he asks, "You watched me?" I don't understand his disbelief. The man in front of me is crazy talented and driven. So sexy and passionate. I continue licking and teasing him. I am happy to be able to praise him when I know it wasn't what came between us. If I don't start taking his length right now I will get intimidated.

"I never missed a performance." I take him to the back of my throat. Eyes pricking on the gag, I don't even care. It's me. I'm the one gagging on this beautiful man's massive erection that he has for me. The only one who can. So, I keep pace, timing my breathing in a steady rhythm, licking around the base of him as best I can to make it wet and easy for him to glide in and out of my mouth.

His eyes crinkle at the sides when he looks into mine. "Oh fuck. You're gonna make me come doing that." He grips my chin. "Relax your throat, baby."

Why do I feel so special giving this man head? "God you look so fucking good taking this dick down your throat." I close my eyes around a moan that makes me gag and my eyes water for real now.

"Open your eyes, Melody. I wanna see those pretty eyes when my cum fills you up." I blink them open, not sure if I'll see the degrading way that people have told me I should feel giving a blow job like this. I am more than just a groupie and what Ty and I have is more than just some quick blowie between strangers. With me, he doesn't need that. I can be that woman for him. He looks as gone for me now as he did before. I feel powerful. Beyond powerful.

"Shit, I'm so damn close. Grab my balls, baby. How did you know I needed your mouth like this?" His groan almost sends me over the edge. Now, I wish I was wearing a skirt so I could touch myself more easily. The pressure on my clit is not enough.

"Fuck, I'm gonna—" Each thrust into my mouth, tapping the back of my throat has his balls drawing up tighter in my hand. I'm squeezing my thighs together to the point where I know there will be impressions of the fabric on them. "Drink me down, baby. Fuck that's so good." The praise from his lips—in that voice. I love it. I'll never forget it. I want more of it.

I lick him clean. Every drop belongs to me. He pulls me up to him, kissing me fiercely. Licking into my mouth how I wish he were licking up my center right now. "You're the only one I'm singing for tonight. You're the only one I'm playing for," he pants into my neck as we stand there wrapped in each other's arms, hot from arousal.

We have a few manic minutes to put our clothes back together before the woman from earlier knocks, thankfully, to tell him they're ready for him. He kisses and hugs me tight before he leaves and I spend a little bit longer trying to look less like I just got my face fucked by the star of tonight's show.

It doesn't matter because as soon as I'm reunited with my friends, Reese notices. "Yes, dirty girl! We've got a true groupie on our hands!" She sways her hip into mine "We're with the band" she cries out into the crowd.

Everyone is too wrapped up in who they came with to notice her antics and the show is starting before anyone besides our friends can. It's not very full in the center area sectioned off for VIP. There is a small press tent behind us and security that maintains a four-foot area of clearance around us from general admission tickets. I've never been to a concert of this size or caliber. Another first that Tyson has given me. There's a DJ playing some music while we all wait for JT to come on stage. When the lighting changes to something much brighter to illuminate the areas of the stage that now have the other members of the bands situated for the show, the crowd goes crazy in expectation of what comes next. The energy rolling off of JT's fans here is intoxicating and abundant. My heart swells with pride for Ty. *He deserves all of this.*

Ty's guitar is strapped to his back for now with the signature strap standing in contrast with the silver embroidery and pearl snaps on his shirt. He walks to the front of the stage and the murmurs have already begun to buzz as he waves a hand out to us. "I've got something to tell you all. Jordan couldn't be here and he sends his love to you all who came to see him. So, it's just us tonight." He looks believable as he delivers the news. I wish that it was some other reason besides Jordan being on some sort of bender.

There are a few boos from the crowd, but he speaks again, "I know, I know. It's only me singing up here. But, hey! We've got a band and I've got some new stuff for ya. Who wants to hear it? I promise I'll play some of the old stuff too." The crowd soars into applause as he walks back to the stand and puts the mic on. He picks the first notes to a song I know plays on the radio here. It's an upbeat line dance song with a lot of deep beats that make your feet move. The crowd starts going crazy for it.

How was this man just coming into my mouth a few minutes ago?

My friends and I dance along to the music and drink beer as Tyson plays for us. He is magic up there. Tyson, Zeke, and Robert play like there isn't a member of the band missing. That's how it should be. The bright lights and loud music fill our senses. Chloe, Reese, Drea and I all have our arms around each other singing along to the songs we know. It feels good to be here with my girls watching my man.

My man.

I don't think anyone even cares anymore that Jordan isn't here to sing his parts. And that feels even better. Tyson deserves that stage to himself. He was made for it. The crowd is hanging onto every note.

Kisses in the Tall Grass is the next song the band plays. The moment his eyes lock with mine, the crowd falls away. I think back to how I had fallen asleep listening to this song so many times, imagining it was him actually singing it to me. Now here he is, singing to me in front of a crowd. It feels like that anyway. I'm in a bubble floating in the sky right now.

I thought the night couldn't get any better until the song ended and Ty spoke again. "Are you ready for something new, Harmony Hill?"

"Yea!" we yell back at him.

"Alright, alright! Let's do it!" He sits on his stool strumming solo for a while. I begin to recognize the tune he's playing. A familiar one that tugs on one from my memory. The band trickles in and then it becomes more clear.

"This one is called, *The Melody I Lost*. Tell me how you like it." I blink. *The Melody I Lost*. All my friends look back at me before looking at the stage again to listen more intently to what JT is playing.

And it is... It's my song. The one he would play when we were young. The very first song I ever heard him sing. His first love song was about me before we were even together.

My breath catches and I hold onto it. This can't be. I feel the tears rolling down my chin and neck. I can't help it. I wipe at them frantically, smiling all the while.

This version of the song is more than it was before. There are layers and nuance and the lyrics aren't as clunky. It's fully formed and beautiful. *Just like him.*

He calls me his anchor, his first and last note... His greatest love lost... and I'm a fucking mess over it.

Drea hands me a tissue and I do my best not to blubber. I can't help it. She rubs my back and I recognize how silly I look crying when everyone is having such an amazing time at his show. He sings with his eyes closed and each word comes out with precision. When it comes to a close, he opens his eyes, finding me instantly. I can't breathe. I need air and space.

I need to hold my man close to my chest.

JT plays a few more songs before the concert ends and I make a beeline to the trailer. My friends tell me they'll catch me at the after-party, not bothering to follow me to the trailer.

Tyson has some explaining to do.

CHAPTER 38

Melody, Then

THIS AUDITORIUM SEEMED A lot smaller when I was in the seat facing the stage. There are a lot of people here. Like way more than I was expecting. There have been a variety of talents that have gone up there already. From poetry to someone who can play the tuba and stand-up comedy, they have all been decent.

Tyson has already gone, singing his heart out along with his guitar. The song he performed wasn't the one he wrote for me but I loved it just the same. He was amazing! I knew he would be though. He is a natural in front of everyone. I wish I had been able to see him from the seats up front instead of stage left. I'm sure I will be able to one day. Right now, I don't know why I agreed to perform in front of people again. I wipe my sweaty hand on my tights to no relief.

His voice is quiet in my ear, "Breathe, Melody. Everything is fine." I turn on my heel to see him standing behind me. I quickly rearrange the curtain so that I'm completely hidden from the audience again. "In for four counts and out for another four."

I shake my head. I don't remember having these kinds of jitters before. This talent show is much smaller than the kinds of events my old school would hold. Not a single scout or member of an elite dance company is here to watch me. And yet... I cannot stop the spiral.

What if my mind goes blank and I miss my cues?

What if I crumble again?

Who is going to take me to the ER this time?

"In for four—" he waits for me to follow his lead. I do, dramatically sucking air into my body to expand my chest like he's showing me. He nods, "Out for four." I follow his lead again, forcing every bit of oxygen out. He grabs hold of both my hands and we do this slow breathing until I feel my shoulders soften and my body relaxing.

I stretch my arms behind me and bend to one side and then the other, forcing myself to stay loose. "How did you do that? Go up there. I can't do it. Right now, I can't even remember how to make my body breathe properly—let alone do anything good. It's been too long since I've been in front of an audience."

"It will be good. You will be good." He holds my chin to face him. His earnest face begs me to believe him. He kisses me once, sweetly. It's quick. Too quick before he pulls back. "One verse. That's all it takes. Everything works after that."

"Really?"

"Really. Do you trust me?"

I consider his words. Of, course, I trust him. I've never trusted anyone more than Tyson Abrams. "Yes," I respond with no hesitation. Looking back toward the stage, I sigh and look back at Tyson. He holds his hand out to me when the stage crew member motions for me to get ready.

"Let's go."

I grab his hand firmly and we walk onto the stage. He brings me to the center marker and walks off to the left wing. Pulling the black metal folding chair for the crew onto stage left, he sits just far enough to still be seen by the crowd, but also so I can see him there. Ethan, the tech controlling the curtain rolls his eyes at Tyson taking his seat. He runs the mic Tyson had before back over to him and pulls the curtain back anyway.

His guitar rests on one thigh when he looks over to me. I get ready in my first position and wait for him to begin strumming.

The acoustic version of *His Home and Mine* starts off slow. I wonder if he has been practicing this song or if he's able to work out the music as he hears it. It's probably drilled into his mind with how often I've practiced it.

I decided a while ago that I would do a new routine for this show to minimize the panic I felt going back on stage. He would sit and watch me work out choreography and then align everything with the song from Rayne Bramble. When Tyson first showed me her music, I felt an instant connection to it. For this choreography, I leaned more toward the lyrical and jazz training I've had more than traditional ballet. The blend of the two styles made for a unique look and feel that I felt suited the beautiful lyrics of this song when I heard it.

With him still on stage, I can imagine this is like those nights. It's just Melody and Tyson. Only us.

The crowd quiets quickly and the lights dim as a single spotlight follows me on the stage. The first verse is the hardest. I find my rhythm and soon lose myself to the music and movement of my body. His voice, this boy's voice, takes Rayne's lyrics and transforms them with deeper meaning as he changes it to be a song about *his home* in *our place*. It's made more beautiful by the heartbreaking way he describes building the life we love.

The chorus hits with a swift upturn of movements that swell from my body and grow to higher and higher leaps for the stage lights above me. He sings about the size of his heart and how it grew to hold more than just him, but us too. How it'll get bigger to protect our home and my heart.

By the time we get to the last verse, I'm weeping as his rendition of the song feels like, not only a song for me but, a song about us. It's touching and ethereal. I can't separate reality from the truth as my choreography aligns with the same emotions. It's not a song about how Rayne built this life with her man. It's the song about how *Tyson and I* could build our life together. His words are a promise that resonates through my bones as truth and prophecy. Before I know it the song is over and I'm in my final position.

I run to Tyson when he stands to clap for me with stars in his eyes. Then the roar of applause from the audience soars to new heights. The applause for my dance solo accompanied by his music is even louder than when Ty performed a few acts before. He adjusts his guitar to sit against the chair so that when I leap into his arms he can catch me with a spin. "Where did that come from?" I ask, referring the the way he changed the lyrics around on the spot.

He rubs at the moisture on my cheek. "It's a gift like yours," he says.

Our friends rush to the stage front, calling up their congratulations that fill my heart with acceptance and love. I never had this many people show up for me. I'm grateful to have them all in my life. Tyson finally puts me down to hug them before our principal forces everyone to clear out for the next act to come up. I forgot all about the absence of the cowbell, flowers, or my parents. My friends and this boy standing by my side are everything.

"Can we go?" I whisper into Ty's neck when we make it to the left wing.

He looks down at my face partially in shadow from his hat and raises his eyebrows. Not for the first time, I think about how safe I feel in this shadow. "Right now? What about the performers' dinner?" In truth, I couldn't care less about it. I want to be alone with him.

I shake my head, "No, I want to go home..." Everyone is busily moving around us, getting ready for the next act to go up. He stands there frozen with me in his arms. It looks like his brain has short-circuited.

Ever since Mack's party, it's not uncommon for Tyson to sleep at my house in bed with me. We've not done much besides kissing. Never going too far. His cautioning, not mine. Something still kept him from taking that next step.

Holding his gaze, I grab the fabric of his shirt and pull him toward me. "With you," I add. All the adrenaline from the night still coursing freely through my blood.

The seconds tick by where I think he might decline my offer. He steps out of my arms and squeezes my hand in his. "I'll take you wherever you want to go."

CHAPTER 39

Tyson, Then

"YOU DON'T MIND IF I take a quick shower? I've glitter in the worst places right now." I bite my lip to keep from asking her to elaborate on her glitter comment. My mind can't help but wonder exactly which places that could mean.

I nod my head and focus on keeping my jaw from going slack at the incredible view of Melody in her dance leotard. Her light purple dance outfit sparkled and shimmered in her spotlight like she was the little sugar fairy everyone pictures her as. Her strong legs and arms moved in perfect harmony to the notes I played. I would never have known a full orchestra wasn't accompanying us. She provided the story with each sway of her arms and arch of her back.

After weeks of listening to the song Melody chose from Rayne's new album, I took the time to play around with the lyrics a little bit. At first, it was for fun—something to do while she was busy doing what she so clearly loved doing. Then the words began to shift into place a little too easily.

Changing the line, 'This home I made for he and I' to 'This home we made for summer nights', felt more perfect than the original. From that point on, I'd sing it the way I rewrote it in my mind. The chords of the song were simple and practicing them in the few moments that Melody wasn't with me solidified the sound for me. I intended to play it for her one day. I did not know that the day would come so soon. Had I known it would. have the effect it did on her, I would have shared it with her sooner.

The little flouncy skirt entices me even more now that we're in my house alone. She walks out of my back door to the green belt that runs along the backside of our houses to her own. My parents are on the committee for the banquet and Chloe is going to Quincy's after the performers' banquet is over. The house will be empty for the next few hours. It still weirds me out that my sister is dating my best friend, but what kind of hypocrite would I be to be upset? Melody and Chloe have never been closer. I have zero intention of letting her go now that I have her in my arms. Potentially, in my bed.

Fuck. I hope.

While she showers at her house, I shower too, and pull on grey basketball shorts. It takes a few more minutes to get everything set up on the roof the way I want. It's firmly fall here and probably cool enough to need a long sleeve and jeans in normal circumstances. Standing in front of my dresser, I go back and forth on whether to wear a tank or leave it off with how I'm burning up. My nerves and anticipation are rising higher and higher as the minutes tick by until Melody returns. Maybe I should have taken a cold shower instead.

I'm pulling on a t-shirt when a small squeak comes from the doorway. Melody twists her hands looking guilty in a long knit dress. It hugs onto her hips. My eyes follow the curves of her body and I chuff a laugh. "How long have you been standing there?"

"Umm... long enough to see that you're still doing crunches..." she giggles. The deepening shade of her cheeks and the way she looks at her fingers make my lips quirk up at the side. After the performance she expertly executed in front of the school tonight, you would never guess that she was this shy.

I cross the room and hold her hands in mine. "Let's sit on the roof. I already have the stuff up there."

Her head tilts, "You mean your old comforter?"

"You'll see."

It is my old comforter up there. Not that it is ratty or anything. I just have a new one. Doubled up, this older one works to keep the roofing from digging into my ass uncomfortably. I rarely sat on the roof before I knew her. I don't know how Melody does it with nothing underneath her for long periods of time. That comforter is my lifeline, a fact that she teases me about constantly. The little speaker is already playing a playlist I made that has a few of our favorites. I didn't have that much time to put things together so I grabbed some Gatorades from the fridge and chips... Not exactly romantic, but it will have to do.

She looks at the spread with the biggest stars in her eyes. "Tyson. You didn't have to do all this. It was just a talent show."

Though I don't think it's much I tell her, "I did, Melody. You were incredible tonight. I had every faith that you would nail it. You blew my expectations out of the water. It was exactly like when you practiced down there but made even more magic by your skill. When we collaborated last minute like that... something clicked for me." I kneel in front of where she's sitting. The energy between us is sparking with the more words I confess. "We spend all our free time together. We've slept in the same bed for weeks now. Everything about us is real. Every word I said was the truth. I want a life with you. A home with you." I sigh and brush a curl that's broken free from the bun on top of her head and cup her face. "I just want you."

Her eyes shine, "And I just want to be with you. Everything you sang tonight, I want—"

All of a sudden there is a commotion of barking so loud that I can't hear the next words she says.

I stand from the blanket and carefully walk over to the side of the house where the dogs are loudest. Fuck. What now? I need to know what she was gonna say next.

"Do you see something?" Melody asks from the blanket.

"I think they're barking at something in the tree."

"Is it a squirrel or something?" It's then that I spot the little bundle of fur clinging and mewling from the tree.

"It's a cat I think." The thing looks scared to death. Barking starts up again when the cat hops onto another branch closer to my roof.

"You've got to grab it, Ty! Those dogs are gonna rip it to shreds if they get a hold of it." Melody sits up on her knees trying to see what I'm doing.

I make kissing noises at the little fur ball hoping it will at least come into my yard where the dogs can't get to it. His little face looks from me to my yard and back to my arms again. "C'mon little guy. Come this way." He looks at the roof a final time. It's only moments before he hops onto the roof. The little thing climbs up my leg and over my shoulder to Melody.

"Whoa, he is fast!" I exclaim when I gain my bearings, leaning onto a hand on the shallow slant of the roof. I'd probably be all scratched up if I had chosen not to put a shirt on.

He hesitates at the edge of the comforter, sniffing it for safety I guess. I turn to fully face them and he jerks to the side, ready to bolt. "It's ok little guy." He looks dirty and there's no collar on his neck. Melody holds out a hand to him and he sniffs it. He backs up toward me and I snatch him up.

I expect that he'll scratch me or give me at least a little bit of a hard time, but he doesn't. I hold him close to my chest, getting my shirt all dirty in the process. He's purring almost immediately when I rub his head.

Melody crawls over to me slowly and scratches under his chin. "He is so cute, Tyson! Let's get him inside."

"Of my house?"

She giggles, "Yea. Where else could I mean?" She grabs the kitten from my arms and slides down to the garage, carefully.

We find the rags and buckets we use for washing the car and do our best to wipe him down. I thought cats didn't like water, but this one plays in the soap bubbles, sneezing every so often when the bubbles get too close to his nose.

I do some research on my phone to figure out what we should do next with this little animal. "It's too late to get to a vet or shelter and check for any chips. I don't think this kitten belongs to anyone... Should we name him in the meantime?"

"I'm the worst with names," Melody confesses. "You're much better with words and stuff." She dries him off with a towel that's big enough for him to be wrapped up in.

I scratch my cheek, "Well, he was pretty quick. Like a shot. Maybe Smith?"

She shakes her head, "He doesn't look like a Smith."

"Okay, fair. But he does look like a Wesson."

"You think?"

"A cowboy needs a good cowboy name. Gets my vote." I shrug.

"You're ridiculous. This sweet kitten is no cowboy." The cat walks around the garage, never getting too far from where we sit at Will's work table. He makes his way back to Melody's feet after exploring for a bit. "Wesson..." She scratches under his chin and he leans into the affection. "You like that name, little guy?"

He prances in front of her, showing off his newly cleaned fur, tail wrapping over her arm, before ultimately flopping and meowing.

"I'm no cat expert, but I'd say it gets his vote too." Did I expect to be taking care of some stray cat when Melody asked me to bring her home? No. I had very different plans for where this night was going to go. I have to admit that seeing her face light up over this kitten being a kitten is enough for me. Anything that puts a smile on her face is enough for me. We have all the time in the world to be together, I think as I grab all the stuff from the roof.

When I finish putting everything away, I find the two of them playing. She dangles a fishing lure for him to chase and pounce on. She notices me and says, "We know who won't be naming the kids," Then quickly covers her mouth. Eyes growing wide, she backtracks, "I mean... not our kids but... Please just forget you heard that."

I laugh a bit at her discomfort because it's unnecessary. "If you want to name our kids, then that's completely your choice. But I get to name all the animals. Fair?"

She smiles, discomfort forgotten, scooping the cat up into her arms. "Fair. You coming home with me, Wesson?"

"Best he does go home with you. Clo is terrified of cats." He snuggles deeper into her arms and purrs so loudly I could hear it from where I stood. "How many do you want?"

"I think one cat will be plenty for now. I don't want to gain a reputation too soon for hoarding animals, you know? But I guess the old cat lady has to start with something so I'd give it like ten or so years before the number gets out of control."

"Not cats, Melody."

"Oh... I don't know. Probably still a lot. A busy house full of little ones. That sounds like a life I'd want to have."

"A lot?" I choke, "How many is a lot?"

"However many I'm blessed with. I never had siblings, but it's like having friends for life right?"

"Or you end up with Chloe and you want her to leave you alone for even a second."

"You don't fool me, Ty. I know you love her. I didn't believe y'all didn't actually grow up together."

"I guess you're right. So a full house. It'd have to be big for our ten kids."

"Ten? Don't be ridiculous! That's wild! I'm pretty sure pushing out babies is hard. Let's cap it at five, max."

"Sheesh. Five is still a lot." I rub a hand over my face. "I guess you better start picking out names now."

CHAPTER 40

Melody, Then

"HOW DID YOU HIDE that from me on this whole drive here?" Tyson looks at the bag I hold out in front of me in offering. "You didn't have to get me anything."

"I know... but I wanted to." I push at a small rock with my leather bootie, avoiding his gaze before I lose my nerve to say the next part. "I actually got you two things."

He leans against the tree by our favorite spot on the river. Ever since that last day of summer, I have thought about this place often. When there's not too much going on, we come out here and chill. It's the first place where Tyson made a move for everyone to see. A claiming in its own right. It was the first place where I felt like I was his. It only makes sense that this is where our first time together should be. Nowhere else but here.

"Okay. I'll open it. Let me get this set up first. You're already shivering." My Texas body is not used to this kind of weather. I'd likely still be able to wear shorts in Houston right about now. Even in my turtleneck and fluffy cardigan, I'm struggling to keep warm.

Now that the talent show is over and it's pretty cold, the most action our spot sees from us is from the bed of Tyson's truck. We went to a thrift store together to find a bunch of blankets that we could keep back here and be comfortable. Now they reside in the bed of his truck in a huge plastic bag for us to sit under and watch the river run. Sometimes we listen to new music he's found. Sometimes he'll play new music he's written on the guitar and sing for me. Other times, we allow the rushing water to be a soundtrack. From what he has told me, it will freeze up pretty soon so there won't be much rushing water for the frigid temperatures.

Last weekend, he brought out his knife to carve our initials into the tree that we love to sit by. It was a little cheesy, but I look for it everytime we come out here now. It's a permanent marker for our special place. Year after year, we'll be able to reflect back on where it all began.

I resist the urge to roll my ankles and rehearse the choreography I had been working on earlier today while he sets us up in the bed. It was because of a new song Tyson played for me the other day that I even started working on something different. His deep voice plays on repeat in my head and I woke this morning with the beats aligned with movement I just had to experience outside of my dreams. One day soon I'll show him what I came up with.

When he's done brushing the debris and dirt out of the truck bed, he walks over to where I'm leaning against the side. He turns on a portable heater and we sit in the bed together under blankets. When Ty finally looks into the bag, his face breaks into a grin. I can't help, but smile too when he looks back up at me. The skinny rectangular box appears so small and insignificant in his hands when he pulls it out of the Kraft paper gift bag.

As he opens the box, his smile grows even bigger. He puts a hand over his mouth. The tingles start in my chest and travel lower in my belly. Irritation is likely the only emotion others know he can portray. Tyson is not one to show his emotions too much unless he's singing with skilled fingers plucking the strings of his guitar. Not with me though. I get to see all his many moods. I already feel like I've won when he lays the purple and tan handwoven guitar strap over his chest like a sash.

There's appreciation in his eyes when he looks up at me, "This is incredible, Mel. Thank you!"

"Happy Birthday! I found an artisan on Etsy who made this one special for you. There are no others like it in the world... Like you." I say. He moves closer to me under the heavy blankets, cold fingertips brush up under my sweater before he gives me a sensual kiss that I register in my toes. He's hugging me to his chest before we lie down.

He holds my hand to his heart and I feel it beating like I'm something special. We lie on the comforter beneath the large tree, whose shadows stretch out along our bodies as the sun continues to set in front of us. Each thunk in his chest echoes in my mind, knowing that his and mine are the same.

"I've never had a birthday that meant more to me." He finally says, rolling from his back to his stomach. My hand still pressed to him.

"I thought that eighteen is supposed to be a blowout," I say, rolling onto my side to face him.

He gives my hand a squeeze and I look down to our connected fingers. The simple act of holding hands feels more intimate than anything I've done before.

"I'm not him, Melody." *Him.* Mack.

"I know," I say, quietly. "It's not just him. It's everywhere. On TV and... everywhere. When a guy becomes legal, it's the right of passage to go crazy."

"I don't want that. Becoming legal means one thing and one thing only."

"And that thing is?"

Tyson had been counting down this day for as long as I've known him. I assumed he would throw some big party like Mack did. I assumed getting completely drunk and acting like the birthday boy was invincible came with the territory.

"Making my own choices. Being truly free to be myself." He never fails to surprise me in the best ways. I had no way of guessing that's all this was to him. It's the two of us in the bed of his truck and the setting sun behind the mountain peaks. It's beautiful, but hardly a celebration.

I nod, leaning over to rest my head on his arm. "So, what's the first choice?"

"You know the answer to that."

I softly bite his bicep and he chuckles. "Tell me anyway."

"Music. It's always music."

I right myself. Kneeling in front of this beautiful boy who has the entire world in front of him. "You already had music. What changes now?"

He arranges my long, fuzzy cardigan around my legs so that it's not bunched under my knees, while he seems to think over what he's going to say next. His diligent fingers taking extra time to unfold the fabric against the blanket.

When he speaks, his soulful eyes catch onto mine with renewed intensity. "Would you still pursue dance, even if you knew it would never put a roof over your head or food in your belly?"

I don't hesitate, even for a moment, before responding, "Yes. Not in the same way as before, but yes." We have talked about how I want to be behind the scenes now. Potentially teaching dance to young girls. Being the kind of support that Ms. Nicolson was for me.

He nods, looking between both of my eyes, "And what if no one ever cared about when you were performing? If no one ever came to your show besides me, because you know I will be there."

I giggle and respond, "Of course. Even if no one was there, I would still be there giving my best in this hypothetical situation."

"You understand what this..." he gestures to his heart and I try my best not to dream about truly having his heart. I'm still waiting for him to ask me about his second present. "...is like. Having this passion for your art that burns through everything you know and hold close. I can't choose anything, but my music. I refuse to see it any other way. Before now, before I was legal, I could only consider the options I had. The ones Will presented me with. But now... Now, I can do whatever makes me happy."

"Would it truly be so bad to have a degree to fall back on?"

"I refuse to fall back, Melody. If I'm not pursuing my purpose then I'm not living. I am no longer me. He may not believe in me but my mom did. She wanted me to dream big and never made me feel like I had to settle. Life is short. We never know when it's our turn. When I picked up a guitar, I felt like I gained a limb back. When I go to school without it, I feel lost and unsettled. Everything is a stepping stone to now. From this point forward, it's my main focus. I have to do what makes me happy."

Hearing Ty talk about his passion made me feel things that only urged me closer to him. I never knew someone who loved their craft like I do. He is my kindred spirit.

"You understand," I say. "It's like nothing else matters if it doesn't lead me back to a stage or to the counts before the choreo."

"That's why we go together, Melody. We make sense. Nothing goes together more perfectly than music and dance."

"We do," I agree, "It is perfect," and just as twilight settles, we meet for our second kiss. This time it's me taking his lips. They're soft and tender with his acceptance. Before I know it, I'm leaning over him. We kiss like there is no tomorrow because we both want to live in this moment where our passion is free to intertwine and become a part of the same dream.

I worried that I would lose Tyson when he graduated from ARHS because his dad is constantly pressuring and reminding him to apply to school after school. Long-distance high school relationships never last...

I wanted to be his everything. Our complicated connection prevented me from going after what I wanted. Then I gave in. At this very river, is where our relationship started for real. I came here with him with the intention of giving him something that would solidify us as one, long before this conversation.

I knew he was passionate. I knew his soul was akin to my own. He understood me better than anyone else had before. After my injury, everyone expected me to give up and try something new or go back to the person I was before I realized I had no one.

It was like they asked me to become someone else entirely. Only Tyson knew what it was like. He encouraged me and supported me. I felt safe with him.

Ty's hands find my waist and I allow him to touch me, explore my body like there isn't weeks of denying this next step stacked between us. The many reasons why we couldn't go all the way.

Tonight, I won't let anything get in the way.

When we finally stop kissing long enough to catch our breaths, I prompt, "You never asked what your second gift was."

His eyes sparkle even in the low light of the gloaming. My heart stutters from his beauty with curls fanned out around his bandanna and sharp, strong eyebrows framing the crinkles of the smile reaching his eyes. "What could top this?" He asks, lifting the strap from his chest.

"I thought maybe we could..." Saying it out loud makes my heart race. Practicing in the mirror is nothing like looking into his eyes and saying the words. There is no one I would rather do this with than Tyson.

"I feel safe with you. I trust you. For your birthday, I want to give you something that only I can give you... from me. Tonight, I want to go all the way. I want you to be my first." It comes out clunky anyway. I want to swallow the words and then have the ground open up and swallow me too as Tyson stares at me with his mouth open.

Note to self, practice a hundred more times before you say something so important!

He looks and over and I think I broke him. Again.

I sit up because I clearly misread the situation. I thought he wanted more like I had wanted more.

Finally, Ty comes out of whatever frozen state he was in and grabs my hand again before I run all the way back to my house. Stupid tears are already clouding my vision from my embarrassment, but Tyson kisses my hands telling me, "Melody. I've never done it either. I've never done that with anyone before. I... Damn, this would be the most meaningful birthday I've ever had if we had sex for the first time with each other. In our favorite place. At our favorite time of day... Best birthday ever."

"Really?"

"Really, really"

We fit and now I know just how much. Fitting with Tyson is coming home after a long day. It's fresh air and a breeze through the car window on a hot day. Fitting with Tyson is finding that missing piece of the puzzle that connects all the other pieces so that you can finally see what the picture is of.

When we ride back to our neighborhood, I reminisced about out time together. People say that you lose your innocence when you have sex for the first time. Maybe it's cliché to say that my first time was magical. I don't care. He was so perfect with me.

We fumbled and figured it out together. Our bond had only been strengthened by what we did in the bed of the truck that night. He was my friend but more than that too. He cared for me like no one else could. Saw me better than I saw myself. He held my secrets and mended my heart with that care. Each new sensation I shared with him would live with me forever. I wanted to give him every piece of me that I could, hoping that some of it would be good and worth keeping. The cool air licking over our heated skin. The rushing river, a soundtrack to match our heavy breathing. It was perfection.

We shower at our separate houses before he comes back to my room late that night. Everything is the same, though so different. I fall asleep in his arms thinking that nothing could keep us apart now that we are connected in such a beautiful and meaningful way.

CHAPTER 41

Melody

THE SECURITY GUARD OUTSIDE Tyson's trailer takes in my disheveled appearance with concern as I stand in front of him. I cross my arms to try and look more impatient than incensed though neither is likely helping my case. He knocks on the trailer door with JT's name on it and Ty peers out through a small sliver of it. When he sees it's me, he opens the door to let me in.

I walk into the space and everything is a blur as new tears crop up. "You love me?" I accuse him. Really, I'm yelling into his face. I am not someone who yells at people. I rarely even raise my voice, preferring to let the silence speak for me. His eyebrows raise as he calculates why I'm yelling at him.

"What?" He asks with the proper amount of confusion on his beautiful face. He's still sweaty from performing. His hat is somewhere in the room that I can't find. I'm sweaty from dancing and then from panicking in the crowd. My clothes stick to me and I'm aware of how charged the energy is in this trailer.

He reaches for me, but I step back. "You love me," I say more firmly. This time it's not a question. "You tell all twenty thousand of those people that you love me. All of them know... but me."

"I've told you. I meant it when I said it ten years ago. I've said it more times than I can count in every way that I know how." Tyson's eyes soften,

258

pleading. He reaches for me again. This time I don't move away. "That has never changed. I always have."

"Tell me," I whisper, closing my eyes and leaning my forehead onto his chest. I need to feel grounded in him.

He's not having any of that. I can't hide from him or from this. I asked and I have to accept it. He lifts my chin, making me look at his affective browns. "I love you, Melody. From the first note to the last, whether it's uplifting or the blues. You are my melody. My rhythm. My muse before I knew you would be. Even when I didn't want you to be. My heart and soul have been forever tuned to yours."

Closing the space between us, my kiss is urgent as my lips press to his. Our eyes never close as he takes me into his arms, lifting me until he can't anymore. The scrape of his scruff down my neck is flammable as I wiggle out of my shorts and pull my crop down after it. I stand there completely naked in his trailer in front of him. Vulnerable and bare.

"Please show me that I'm—"

"Mine," he lowers to his knees, kissing my stomach and hips and thighs. This moment between us is not lost on me. I don't respond because we both know it's true. I am *his*.

Walking me over to the dressing table, the extra large lighted mirror illuminates our faces in clear view. We both look flushed and wanton.

He doesn't hesitate to undress himself and grab me. He pushes me against the counter edge so that we are both looking at each other in the mirror. He licks his fingers before rubbing them over my slit. There's no point, I'm always soaked for him. "Look at us. Still perfect together. Made for each other. Is that what you need to hear?" One of his hands holds my breast with the other between my legs. We look damn good together and I want more. I nod and wrap my arm around his neck behind me, pushing my ass into him, his dick jerks against me. "Words, baby. I need your words." He says pressing against me.

"Yes, made for each other. Yes!" I sway my hips over him, wedging his dick deeper between my cheeks.

"Let me have it then, my melody." His hand squeezes my waist as he lines his head up with my entrance. His sensuous eyes never break contact with mine in the mirror. I clench around his long hard dick thrusting into me. The moan that escapes me with the feeling of being so full, after aching practically all day and night for him, is throaty and mewling. We look at each other in the mirror for a few moments just enjoying the connection of our two bodies.

We still fit.

He doesn't take me hard and fast. He slows his stroke to a pace that is both too slow and perfectly calculated. He bites my shoulder and I cry out. Ty stills my hips to control the speed of how he works up my climax. The throbbing in my clit is screaming for attention, but he reaches the perfect spot inside me that makes my toes curl. His head rubs along my G-spot like a massage that relaxes and soothes me.

"God, Tyson. I'm going to come everywhere like this."

It starts as a trickle the longer he keeps his paces up. When he starts thrusting into me in earnest making my thighs bump into the counter edge, I scream his name through the explosive peak of what can only be known as sheer bliss. I'm floating in heaven amongst the clouds as he comes right after me, moaning my name into my neck on repeat.

Several minutes pass with us breathing heavily, bodies pressed against each other. His arms wrapped around me, never letting me go.

This, I think, is what forever with him could be like.

"Ayyye!" Our friends all yell over to us from their booth when we enter the VIP section of Lucky's Trailhead. It's one of the only Country Western bars in Harmony Hill. Each of Tyson's bodyguards is behind us as we head into the packed space. The VIP area is the second story that overlooks the dance floor and bar below. It's pretty spacious and on another night it probably would not be as full as it is tonight.

Our friends are on the side wall so we have quite a few people to get through before we can get to them. Some people from the industry and the other performers from the weekend are all mingling around on the floor. Tyson knows a lot of them. I stand behind Tyson's arm as he greets the people he knows. Trying my best not to feel self-conscious about my sex hair and sex face... I probably have RECENTLY FUCKED stamped on my forehead right now. My hair is still a little wild from sweating and his fingers running through it. I could have put it in a bun but I liked having it down in a crowd like this.

After a few people talk with him I see her. Tugging on his shirt, I whisper-yell into his ear, "Is that Rayne Bramble?" I am bouncing with joy as she walks closer to us. I love her music and she seems so down to earth.

"Yep. That's her," he responds grudgingly, moving me from behind his arm to in front of him. I balk at how he's manhandled me, but I can't get the words out before she reaches us.

"Pretty bold of you to show your face after you stole the stage tonight." *Come again?* She sneers the words in Tyson's face. I'm so taken aback by how foul her tone is. I've seen her on social media and doing interviews. Rayne has always come across as sweet and laidback. This is not that.

"Rayne, I'd like you to meet my girlfriend, Melody. Melody, this is Rayne." *Girlfriend! God, yes!* His tone is unfazed by her accusations. She finally stops staring daggers at Tyson to notice me standing there.

She's so tall that it takes a full head tilt down for her to see me and her demeanor softens a fraction. "Hi, it's nice to meet you. You a singer, too?" One of her eyebrows rises with her question as she looks me over.

"N-no. I'm a waitress. Big, big fan of your mus—"

"She's a dance instructor too. Melody actually choreographed the team's last performance with one of your songs. It was really good. I'll send you the video." *Did he see that? I don't know how I can keep up with this conversation right now.*

Rayne's eyes snap back to Tyson and vehemence from earlier is renewed. "Don't kiss my ass, Tyson. I know what you did. Know that shit is fucked up.

Karma is a bitch in this industry. You're starting on the wrong foot. People talk and I have known Jordan for years. Way longer than I've known you."

My man stands firm under her accusations. The same blasé look he held before is still in place now. If he's affected by her words, there is no evidence of it on his face. "What exactly is it that you think I did?"

"I don't think." Rayne jabs a finger at him. I hear Ty's security rustle behind us and two large men I didn't notice before step from the crowd to be closer to Rayne. "I know you set him up."

Tyson rolls his eyes and scoffs. "Set him up?"

She looks around to see if anyone is eavesdropping, "He's been clean for months. Never misses a meeting. My sister called me not even an hour ago to say he's high as a kite at Blackhawk, still calling her! You are supposed to be his bandmate, his support. A fucking team. Not making him look bad so you can get ahead. That's not how we do it in Country."

"You all need a new script. He missed the show. That's all on him. I've been in Alpenglow for the past few weeks. Who knows where that dude is? I sure don't. If you did, why didn't you say anything? Those people came to see us and I was the only one who showed up. If you and Lacey care about him, then maybe you should be keeping tabs on him because I'm sick of his shit. I'm not his babysitter."

"You owe him that much, Tyson."

"I don't owe him shit." He puts an arm around my shoulder and starts moving us around Rayne. "If he looks bad— That's. On. Him."

He leaves the conversation ushering us over the side booth, moving so quickly that people aren't able to get his attention. I'm thankful when we finally reach our booth and I can take a breath. We greet our friends with hugs and they tease us about how we're late.

Chloe wraps an arm around Tyson saying, "My brother's already big time! Did you see how Tyson is such a star getting stopped so many times on the way over here?" He shoves her off lightly, choosing to cling more firmly to me.

She takes the hint and they go back to their own conversations when Tyson's mood, more broody than usual, remains quiet and withdrawn. I sip from the margarita Reese poured me when we got there. Yuck. It's spicy. "I hate jalapeño margs. Why did they let the pregnant woman choose the drink for the table?" I put the glass down on the short table and push it far away from me.

Reese shrugs, "You weren't here for the vote. Drea and I choose them. Technically not the pregnant vote."

Drea lets out a cackle, patting me on the shoulder, "Some spice won't kill you! Next pitcher, you can pick." She slurs.

I don't think there should be another pitcher with how lit all my friends are at the moment.

Before long, the booth starts to clear out. Reese, Cory, Ash, and Taylor leave to go dance to the song that has just come on. Zeke and Robert follow them to the dance floor on the prowl for someone in Daisy Dukes to take home. Tony slides out of the booth pulling a very drunk Drea behind him saying, "Need to get her home before she tries to drink anymore." Then, it's just us, Chloe and Quincy in the huge booth.

I reach for Tyson's hand. He allows me to thread our fingers together. "I'm sorry," he says looking down at them.

"For what?" I say to the side of his head.

"For being a bad date. We had such a good night and Rayne just shat all over it. I can't get over what she said."

I shake my head. "She didn't. The night is not over. You don't have to do anything about what she said right now."

He finally looks up at me, "You're right. The school year starts next week. You need a little fun."

"I had lots of fun already. Your set was amazing. I can't believe you still sound so good live."

"Thanks? Is that a compliment?"

"Maybe." I giggle and sip my nasty margarita.

He squeezes my waist, speaking low into my neck for just me to hear."Oh is that funny? I seem to remember you breaking apart all over my dick from how I sounded on stage tonight."

"I could show you again..." I look up into his hungry gaze, "How much I loved the way you sound on stage."

"Are you sure you want to poke this bear? What I gave you in the trailer was only a sample of what's waiting for you."

Turning to the side I swing my legs over his. "What? Should I be scared of a little fur?"

He nips my earlobe, dragging his nose down the side of my neck, "Nah. I'm pretty sure it's the claws and teeth you should watch out for."

Our faces are so close that I see the beginnings of his smirk. I lean into him, accepting all the kisses and swirls of his tongue. The room and the music fade out of my perception as Tyson carves this little place for only us. When his teeth graze that perfect spot between my neck and shoulder, I yip in surprise. His chuckle is low in my ear and I squeeze my thighs at the sound. I am a lucky girl to finally have this with him. Public displays of affection like this were never something I liked. With Ty, I might let him lay me out on this low table and do whatever he wants.

"Alright. Alright! Get a room." Quincy teases from across the booth. A flush of embarrassment blooms hot and persistent in my cheeks.

Note to self: Don't get arrested for public indecency because this man is sexy as sin, itself.

Tyson waves him off. He slides out of the booth, pulling me along with him. "You know this song?" He asks me half into the crowd taking their places on the dance floor. It's JT's dance single that plays on the radio all the time here.

"Of course," I giggle, feeling lighter now that he feels better too. The line is infectious as more and more people join us in the two-step with Ty's music all around us. Our boots stomp in time with the beat and my heart soars with the knowledge that I'm getting to share this with him.

My cheeks hurt by the end of the night. I don't remember the drive from Harmony Hill ever being this quick. I guess it's hard to keep track of time when you're wracking up another orgasm with Ty's fingers between your legs.

He carries me to the front door and to bed where he makes good on demonstrating how earlier in the trailer was only a sample of the pleasure awaiting me.

I am a very, *very* lucky girl, indeed.

CHAPTER 42

Melody

"REMIND ME AGAIN WHY the groom is here..."

Chloe looks over Cory as he walks through the aisles with a discerning look at the ready-made arrangements. It would be comical if it weren't for his intensity. The man knows his flowers. I am actually surprised he's even allowing someone else to do the arrangements at all.

"Because I don't want my wife walking down the aisle holding a bouquet that looks like someone grabbed it from the grocery store." Then he looks back at Selina with a smile, "No offense."

Chloe steps in front of him, blocking his view of the florist. "Exactly. Neither of us wants that. I would never let her go out sad like that. The Maid of Honor is on the job. I'd like for you not to piss off the only florist we have in Alpenglow."

"We will see. Don't mind me, keep doing what you were doing. I'll be here just in case." He holds his hands out in front of him.

Selina gives him a glib look and starts her spiel up again about the packages she offers and the pricing for each.

Cory offers an occasional scoff or arm cross over the options Chloe and I look at before we all agree on the one that suits Reese and the decor best. The cascading florals chosen are bold and romantic with Sherry colored roses mixed with blush-toned blooms. I learned that it's the dandelion and gardenia mixed with sage leaves and clove berries that make this bouquet passionate, elegant, and timeless. Cory's words, not Selina's.

I think I'm here to be a mediator between Cory and Chloe because it took a few placating words to either party before they could decide on this one. Is it my favorite way to spend my Saturday off? Not exactly, but somehow I was vital to this process of wedding planning. I did, in fact, get my bouquet from the grocery store. Was I going out sad?

Seeing Cory be in his element makes me feel so much more joy for my friend, even as I begin to tumble downward into my own thoughts. She needed a man like this to keep her in line. He's firm when he needs to be but never overpowering. They just make sense.

I wander among the vases for several moments while Chloe settles everything with Selina in order to coordinate arrangements and schedule the wedding delivery. The silky petals soothe me while I consider my new relationship with Tyson. Well... my newest relationship. Third time's the charm they say. Maybe it will be us to do this wedding thing next. Do I even want to be married again?

My hand comes away from the plant with several of the yellow petals crushed between my fingers. "Are you alright?" Cory's voice breaks into my consciousness. "I thought you might crumple another. I'm not a huge fan of irises either, but I don't think Selina will take too kindly to you crumpling them." I look down at his hand on my arm and stutter out of my daze. The petals float to the ground at my feet in a decrepit dance of despair.

"Oh. Um... Yea. Irises are the worst." To tell you the truth, I never even knew what they were called. I barely paid attention. I need to change the subject because I don't need to dump all the negative thoughts I have about marriage on my friend's fiancé. "So, are you ready for the big show?"

"Show?" he chuckles. "You know my girl well. I forget about that. Yea, yea. I'm ready. The twentieth time I asked did the trick and now I wish time would move faster. You know?"

"Twenty?" Geez. I knew Reese was stubborn, but that is a lot of rejection to still keep trying. I'm seeing this man with whole new eyes.

"Something like that," his self-deprecating laugh is endearing. "Lost count." He shrugs. "I never knew I wanted to be married to anyone again." Cory takes a breath and blows it out, gathering himself. "When I almost lost her, I knew that I couldn't take that chance again. That woman is everything to me. I plan on tying myself to her any way I can."

I've met Cory's ex-wife in passing at the Ranch and she doesn't seem that bad. Their relationship is nothing like my ex-husband and I. Could Mack and I ever be that cordial with each other? We don't have any children together to force our hands. I keep waiting for his hatred. It never comes and that feels almost worse. "How did you know it's worth trying again?"

He gives me a questioning look, "You and Tyson make sense. I'm probably not supposed to say that. I love Mack like the brother he is. But, you're better with Ty. No offense, but Mack deserves more." *Ouch.* It's the truth and it still stabs like inadequacy that I can't check this box for Mack. "I didn't mean anything by that. I've heard his side. He has been going through it. When I met him, his life was falling apart like Jenga blocks. I'm not saying you're that bottom block, but your leaving wasn't a pull from the top. God, I don't know if I'm making that any better... We've been playing a lot of Jenga at the house." He rubs the back of his neck. "I'm sorry."

"No, I get it." And I did. I feel so guilty about the way I ended things with Mack, but I just couldn't keep letting him think our relationship would get better. Or that I would ever get better. "I know he deserves more."

"It's done now though. I think he'd still take you back. I beg of you—please don't."

I crush the fallen petals under my flat. The satisfying smear of color under my shoe on the tile becomes my focal point. In a whisper, I say, "I'm not. I can't go back."

He looks concernedly at his phone and pats my arm awkwardly, "I gotta get back to the Ranch. Will you tell Chloe goodbye for me?"

I nod and say, "Thank you for your honesty." I meant that too. I've been suppressing the topic for so long that my friends don't even touch it out of respect for me. The closest they came was at the engagement party. Even still, that wasn't truly talking about it. Maybe I should be talking about it instead of zoning out in my head all the time.

"No problem," he tosses back over the bell ringing at the door he walks out of.

I plop down onto the waiting bench and read through some emails before Chloe finally comes out of the office to grab me. "Ready to eat some cake?" She puts her phone into her purse and looks down at me sitting in the chair. One look at my face and she knows something is up. "Oh Bon, what happened?"

Ugh. I suck at putting this mask back in place. First, Cory, and now, Chloe. *I'm getting clocked by everyone.* I try to muster up a smile, "Nothing happened. Just hungry, I think."

She looks my face over from eye to eye, trying to see if I'll crack or something, but I'm not. Not yet anyway. "Good, you'll need room for this."

We get to Drea's place about thirty minutes later. She lived with her grandmother since we've known her. This house has always smelled of baked goods for just as long. Stepping into the boldly decorated space, brings back memories that I haven't had since we were in high school.

Reese's voice comes in from Drea's hand after I hug her. "Sorry, ladies. I will not be in attendance for this either. The thought of being around so many scents right now makes me want to upchuck. So, instead, you will have virtual Reese, a close second." She flips her long extensions over a shoulder from the phone screen.

"You're not here and you still manage to bring the drama," Chloe says, dumping her oversized purse onto the bench at the island in Drea's kitchen. "And why couldn't you Facetime me from the florist shop? I thought your fiancé was going to get in an honest-to-God fisticuff altercation with Selina when she brought out yellow roses."

"Ha! I would have loved to see that. Too bad I just relocated from the bathroom. Morning sickness has taken over my whole life. I had to send an SOS to Cory, so the kids wouldn't be here by themselves."

"I'm sure Mireya had no problem bossing the boys around in your absence," Drea chimes in.

"Girl! Your daughter is worse than Chloe trying to tell me how to live my life. She is amazing with Gabe, though. I might have to pay her to babysit."

"Don't overwork my baby, Reese. Oh my goodness remember when she tried to tell—"

I start to collapse into myself and out of the conversation, feeling over-whelmed by the baby talk. *It wasn't this bad before.* That wasn't me. All I can feel at this moment is the loss of Callan. My baby boy, who they don't even know about. I never had these kinds of conversations with my closest friends. My sisters. No one knows but Mack—who I absolutely cannot talk to about Callan—and Tyson. The sting of tears catches me off guard and I quickly wipe one before it rolls. I'm too late. The room is silent. All eyes are on me.

"Oh my God. Bon, what's wrong?" Chloe's voice registers in my ears like I'm underwater or just far, far away.

This is not about me. *This is not about me.* This is Reese's cake tasting. This is her baby's time to be fawned over and loved on. I can't talk about him now.

The longer I sit here saying nothing, the more my eyes burn. I can't think. I can't suppress the thoughts swirling in my mind.

"I'm sorry," I say running from the kitchen to the bathroom. I have nowhere else to go, I carpooled with Clo.

I don't know what to do.

I don't know what to do.

I have no one to talk to about this because I've isolated myself so much in this sadness. I can't bring it up now. I should have told them. I shouldn't still be so hurt by this.

This is not about me. I look into the mirror at my red-rimmed eyes and the flush crawling up my neck and I can't look anymore. *Panic.* So much panic, swallowing me whole.

I pull my phone out of my pocket and slide down the bathroom wall to the floor.

I shouldn't.

I should not.

I don't know what to do.

"Melody," Tyson's voice comes in over the phone. I reach for tissue paper and frantically dab at my eyes. The tears are free-flowing now. I can't stop them. "Melody, baby. What happened? Where are you?"

My watery voice is broken and pathetic. Weak. *Fragile.* "I. Don't. Know. What. To do." Each gasp for air, more painful than the last.

"Where are you?" I hear the click of his seatbelt. "Are you breathing? Keep breathing."

"I," gasp, "Can't." My chest can't expand under this weight in my heart.

"You will. Where are you?" He takes a deep breath in, on the line. It's metallic and loud with my phone pressed to my ear, but it's him. "And out, Melody. I need to hear you trying, baby. Please."

I focus on his breath and try to match it. "Where are you?"

"Drea's. The tasting. I'm ruining it." I whisper between breaths.

"Breathe in, baby." He waits to hear me follow his directions. When I do, he continues, "You're not. Breathe out."

Drea knocks on the door, asking, "Melody... Are you okay in there?" I hold the phone away from my face and wipe my nose.

"Yea," I say in as bright a voice as I can manage. "Give me a sec. Is that okay?"

"Um, sure... Are you sure you're okay?"

No. I'm not sure I'll even be able to get off this floor ever again. "Yea. I'll be out in a minute."

"Okay."

She leaves and I focus more on deep breathing. I hold the phone back to my ear. "You should tell them, Melody."

"I can't do that."

"They're your friends. They'll understand." His voice is calm and measured on the line.

"I don't want that. I just need to clean up and go back out there."

"And do what, Melody? It's not fair to keep everyone at a distance. How can they help you—be there for you—if they don't know what's wrong?"

"I told you about him and now I can't control this feeling. It's too exposed. I don't need to tell anyone else."

"You know it has nothing to do with you telling me. You were already feeling this way when I found you in the bathroom. The same way Drea would have found out today. You are not a burden, Melody. Your feelings are not too much for the people who care about you. I know about Callan and I'm still here. If you tell them, they can be here for you too."

Maybe he's right. I won't take that chance. "Not today, Ty. I can't do it today."

"Okay. I'll be there in twenty. Can you make it that long?"

Can I? "Yea." I breathe out long and slow. "I can make it," I tell myself in the mirror, more than just responding to him.

"I love you." My heart thumps hard and heavy in my chest. Even though he's not here, I feel like maybe it's syncing up with his heart either way.

"I love you, too," I say with new determination before he lets me go.

I put in my eyedrops, quickly touching up my face. It's a long walk back to the island with the girls.

"Bon, seriously. what's up?" Chloe asks when I slide back onto my stool.

"Nothing. Something came up. Tyson is gonna pick me up in a bit."

She crosses her arms. "My brother is coming here to pick you up? For what?"

"Let her be, Clo. Was it something we said?" Drea asks.

"No, no. I'm just not feeling well. I need to get home and just lay down, you know?"

"It's three in the afternoon..." Reese says from Drea's phone. The silence hangs for a little too long as I decide whether I'm going to tell them now. The barrage of reasons and thoughts of why I shouldn't are much louder in my head. I can't even remember what Tyson said before as the silence stretches for longer and longer.

I can't be strong enough to share this truth. I'm not strong enough.

It's too much. My grief is too much.

It's too sad. I'm too sad.

I can't be happy for you. I'm selfish. Everything is about me.

"I've been working a lot. I'm just tired." I manage the lie to finally end the yawning quiet between us.

Chloe won't let it go. "You have been saying that a lot lately..."

"I've been working a lot now that school has started. You know how crazy my schedule is."

"Well let's get the tasting over with before Tyson gets there," Reese interjects. "Drea, where are the samples?"

They return to their normal buzz of conversation, allowing me to fall into my reserved silence. Each cake Drea prepared is delicious, but the chocolate with white mocha frosting is a clear winner. Drea is showing all the design ideas she has when I get the call from Tyson to come meet him.

I barely manage a goodbye to everyone before I hurry out of the house and into Old Red. I sink into the familiar scent of him in the cabin.

"Silence or music?" he asks.

"Never silence," I whisper and he takes me home.

CHAPTER 43

Melody

IT'S STRANGE HOW HISTORY repeats itself. In this dark room with him holding me close in my bed. The window opened. The sounds of night coming in to fill the space. My nightstand clock says it's eight P.M. when he slides out of bed, urging me along with him to eat something. *Heavy. I'm so, so heavy.* He sets us up on the couch while he makes sandwiches and canned soup. If Alpenglow Ridge had any food delivery, I'd probably have chosen that. But food is food... when I probably would have slept through dinner anyway. It's all a blur through my depressing lens.

As I sit on this couch with a huge fuzzy blanket wrapped around me up to my neck, *Sleepless in Seattle* is starting to play softly. I don't remember him putting it on. When he sits on the couch next to me, there is a moment when I begin to feel even more pitiful. What happened today? I can't make my brain think back past being on the floor in Drea's bathroom.

A rich voice that I recognize floats through my thoughts over the TV noise. "You should probably eat this while it's hot. I'm no master chef, so I'm pretty sure it'll taste like the can once it's room temperature." My blurry sight clears to reveal Tyson when I turn to him.

Tyson is here.

It's commonplace for people to joke about anxiety they don't have. I never understood why someone would claim it if they didn't experience it.

People don't often talk about those of us who have anxiety that has actually come true. Those doom spirals are based in truth. All of mine have come true. What if my mom doesn't survive her cancer? What if my dad's alcoholism ends up killing him? What if I can't carry Callan to term? What if I lose Ty? I lived through the anxiety and the tremendous grief of all these things coming true. I had no control. I was the puppet swinging from string to string, trying to stand up straight. Buckled, defeated, and worn to the ground, I don't know if I ever really processed any of those things fully or if I simply kept moving and the Earth kept spinning. Lost in my head, moving on autopilot as the days ticked by. I was not fine, though I told that lie more times than I could count.

My old therapist used to say, "If you're feeling sad, try listening to music. If you're feeling anxious, try moving your body." But for me, depression feels like a mixture of the two. I am too sad and anxious to the point where it overwhelms me. I can't get out of my head enough to pick a song. I busy myself so much with work that I don't have time to rest or dance for fun and just for me. I'm always tired. Tired from the combination of hiding my pain and the number of hours I'm working every week. If I'm at work then I'm not alone at home with the truth of my life.

I'm in my head.

I'm still in my head.

I can't get out of my head.

I look down at the soup in my hands, not remembering when I picked it up. The thick red liquid leans to one side in my bowl and I finally register the warmth in my hands. Ty's hand is over mine, keeping it from spilling. "Sorry," I say.

"Don't be." His smile is small but present. Something flickers in my chest. I nod. "Let's eat and watch this movie, okay?"

Tyson isn't obviously watching me, but I feel his eyes on me every so often. When I finish the soup, I feel a little better. I only manage about half of the sandwich before laying back on the couch. How can I feel so alone, in a room with another person?

My body moves and it's Tyson who is behind me again. This time, I smell the mahogany and amber that I always associate with him. It's alluring and deep, just like him. I watch the movie unseeing as I try my best to stay present and not dissociate into another spiral. There is not a moment with him that I can bear to miss anymore. His arms encircle my body and squeeze me closer to him. The consistent in and out of his breath gives me a guide to follow. A heartbeat strong enough to feel on my back adding to the grounding that I cling to. I'm not alone.

Tyson is here.

"Do you want to go back to bed?" He whispers in my ear.

I nod my head and the moment I feel the loss of his soothing heat, I begin to snuggle deeper into my fuzzy blanket. Water runs in the kitchen as I lie here unmoving. There's the sliding whoosh of my dishwasher opening and the following rattle of the dishes being added to the racks. *He's doing the dishes and I didn't even ask him.* I start to feel guilty, but have no motivation to say anything more about it.

"Let's go," he says, scooping my body from the couch and I'm floating back to the bedroom in his arms. He sets me on the bed and we're back in the same position as before.

"I'm sorry," I whisper. Wesson hops onto the bed, moving around to get comfortable, and eventually settles in the silence of what I've said.

Tyson rubs my back and thighs. It's soothing and satisfying to me in a way I can't explain. "What are you sorry for?" he asks.

"This."

"I'm not."

"You're not?"

"No. I'm glad you called me. Of all the people you could have called, it was me who you reached out to for help."

I consider his words for a moment. Tyson's arms are sure and safe around me. Time has passed, but I still think of them as my safe place. Everything else was a poor substitute. I am not surprised that I called him. I am deeply embarrassed by it now that I feel a little better. Isn't it strange how feeling better somehow feels worse?

"Stop, baby. I can hear your thoughts from here. You didn't force me to be here. I want to be the one that you call, always. I feel whole when I have you in my arms."

Whole? Is that what this is? "It feels like I'm being stitched back together."

"For me too. I know you don't want to start new, but I need that Melody. I want to erase all the doubts you have about me. Every single one that makes you feel like I won't be there for you. I want to earn the right to that phone call. Maybe this was exactly what was written for us."

"It was written for me to have a menty b in my best friend's bathroom and call you to pick me up like a scared little girl?"

He doesn't laugh at my poor attempt at a joke. He rotates me to face him, strong hands gripping my waist and hips even when I'm looking into his eyes. "No. The timing has been too perfect for any of this to be an accident. When you were triggered by the pregnancy announcement, I was there to catch you. When you were triggered again by whatever brought up Callan today, you called me." His eyes burn with an intensity that can not be mistaken. "It's me. I'm the one who should be here for you and I am. There is no changing that. I fucked up before. Maybe it was a little of the both of us. None of that matters now. It's you and me. We fit, remember? And you know that it should be me."

"I can't just erase all that we've been through. When you left me... Each time I felt unworthy, inadequate, and used up. You hurt me, Tyson. I barely survived." He holds my cheek in his big hand. I wish I could lie to him. I wish even more that I could be less pathetic in his presence but I'm not. All the weakness I try to hide from everyone else is desperate for him to fortify. I lean into his touch and he rubs my cheek with his thumb.

"I swear that will never be the case again. Never."

"Promise me."

"I promise with my whole heart, Melody."

He kisses me deeply, sucking my bottom lip into his mouth. My hands roam his back and find their way into his hair, holding him closer to me.

Our mouths move over one another until we're both gasping for air. He shifts my body again until I'm straddling him and the blanket is around us.

"Tell me about that day." The dark cloud comes back to shadow me and I drop my head onto his shoulder.

"Please, Ty. Can we just maybe hump a little instead? I don't want to do this now."

"No, we can't *hump a little*. This keeps coming up because it's desperate to come out. It will keep being the "big bad" if you give it this kind of power over your life."

"I don't know if I can," still talking into his chest.

"You can. I can hold some of this weight. That's why I'm here."

I huff out a long breath and inhale deeply trying to think back to that day. "I had one appointment prior. Everything was healthy with the baby. I was doing okay. Mack was so excited about starting a family and begging me to tell his parents at least. I wasn't unhappy per se. I just had too many feelings. So many memories of Cressida coming to the surface. Then, to my shame at the time, memories of you and how you made me feel better when I was sad about her. How you made me feel better when I was depressed. I was feeling both losses so much more acutely. I tried to talk to Mack about it, but he just wanted to talk about the baby. Refocus all the conversations on our new baby when I was struggling. I couldn't blame him or be upset. I should have been happy too."

"No. He should have respected what you were feeling no matter what it was." He shakes his head and curses under his breath. "That fucker. I'm sorry. Keep going."

The first tear rolls down my cheek onto his smooth shoulder. He wipes it from my face and rubs my back in small circles. If I want to stop here, I know I could. But I don't want to. "I was feeling even more unsettled. Something was just off. I knew before I walked into the OB's office that something was wrong. I said as much to him." The words come out choked as the feeling of losing our baby comes rushing back to me. "There was no heartbeat. There was utter silence as I lay there prone on the table. He looked at me and I knew. He started saying all these things and I just couldn't deal. I was still pregnant, but our baby was no longer alive inside me." I squeeze my stinging eyes closed.

Tyson holds me and flips us so that my back is on the bed and he leans over me. Kissing the path of my tears, he strokes my hair back from my face. "Open your eyes, baby. You don't have to hide from me."

I shake my head, ruffling more hair into my face and he brushes it away. "My body had failed me, again. Failed him. I chose to have the surgery that day and luckily they were able to do it right away. Mack came home frantic and freaking out because I turned my phone off. He took one look at me and I couldn't face the hurt in his eyes. I didn't hear a word he said. I didn't want to be strong or put on a happy face for him. I just wanted to be alone. But that wasn't quite right. He needed someone else, not me. It was probably never me that he needed. But I was only holding him like a crutch and it broke that day. I called a lawyer and asked for a divorce the next morning. I couldn't be the woman he needed. I am just me."

"You're not *just* anything! Melody, you are everything!" There are tears in his eyes too. "I'm fucking pissed that you had to go through this alone. You deserved better. You deserve more. Melody, look at me." I turn to look at his imposing frame over me. Heat radiating off of him into my own heated skin. "You are everything. I need you to hear me right now. You did not fail because of what happened to you. You did not fail because your marriage to that piece of shit did not work out." I flinch at his course words. "I'm sorry, but he is. He cared more about the baby than the woman carrying it. There should be enough love in his heart to care for you both. He's selfish. Always has been, and the fact that you didn't feel comfortable talking to him about Callan says a lot, Melody."

"I have depression. I have mood swings. I am—"

"Melody. You are a human who has been through so much in her life. If he couldn't handle you at your lows, he does not deserve you at your highs."

Using the back of my fist, I wipe the moisture from my face, saying, "It seems that you only get me at my lows."

He shakes his head back and forth, "Anytime I get to spend with you is the best high I could have."

We look into each other's eyes as his last words sink in. His eyes caress over me as they linger like fingertips over my heated skin. There is so much love in his gaze as it brands his name on each part of me he takes in. Sliding down my body, he kisses my stomach with newfound reverence until I can't take it anymore. "Tyson, please."

"That's not how you ask," he grumbles into my hip bone. I squirm under him. His soft hair brushing a path over me adding to the sensation of having him so close, but not where I want him. "Tell me that you want me to do this, Melody. Tell me everything. Always."

"Tyson, I need you to bury yourself inside me so deep that I'll never be without you."

He flicks soft eyes up at me. "Do you mean that?"

"Yes. I swear it on my life."

We make love long into the night and the morning. Losing myself in him is the only place where I truly feel found.

CHAPTER 44

Melody

WHEN I SHOW UP at school the next day, I don't feel tired. I feel energized from all the passionate lovemaking that occurred in my house last night.

My class before lunch is running through several cycles of some choreo I've worked up. "And C group. Ready? Five, six, seven, eight..." All three groups are dancing and I watch everyone closely. "And spin, right kick, good! So good. Finish strong!"

They all end with the same pose and I clap vigorously! "Amazing! This looks so good already." I move laces in the studio to get a different view of the dancers. "Switch places. Everyone, move up one group."

I hear a cough from the doorway, "Mrs. Stewart?" Principal Blair calls.

"Ok. Take a break, everyone. I'll just be a second." Murmurs of approval resonate around the room.

"Principal Blair, what can I do for you?"

She motions for me to come out of the auxiliary room that my dance program operates out of. I close the door behind me and notice the guitar strap before I notice the man. He grins down at me from where he leans against the wall. His soulful brown eyes taking in every inch of me.

My unitard and tights leave nothing to the imagination and it wouldn't matter because with the smirk tugging his lips up at the corner, I know he would be imagining me naked anyway.

"You would not believe how much of a shock I got when this one walked into my office." She points a thumb over at him. "There are some people you just don't forget. How special is it that this superstar, Tyson Abrams, wanted to come visit? He says he'll do a little talk at the assembly today. The kids will love it!"

"That is pretty wonderful," I agree and he finally pushes off the wall.

"I thought so," he says, getting close enough that I see the stud in his nose twinkle in the florescent lighting.

"Anyway, I know you have the extra keys for the stage store room. We need to get a proper mic and mic stand. Make that two for his guitar too." She taps her chin and looks between the two of us. "You know? I still remember when you two performed at the talent show. It was simply magical." She coos.

"That's a performance one would not forget," I say with as much restraint as I can. I fan my face starting to feel quite warm after thinking about that time in our lives.

I'm lost in the reverie and Tyson clears his throat.

"I'm sorry, what?"

"The key, Mrs. Stewart. I'll need it to get things set up."

"Oh, right! Let me just grab it from my bag." I hurry into the room and look through my dance bag for the key ring. Returning to where Principal Blair and Tyson talk, I give her the key ring.

"Thank you, dear. Come and grab these from the office at the end of the day."

I nod to her and she walks off with Ty in tow. He looks over his shoulder and smiles at me.

When afternoon assembly comes about, I watch our Principal introduce Tyson as he walks onto the same stage we had performed together on, many moons ago. He looks so different from the teenager he was, obviously, but there is just something wholly new about him. It's the confidence in his stride, the easy way that he commands the stage or maybe it's how damn well he fills out those Wranglers. I mean, how can I look away from that moose knuckle?

"I was a kid just like you coming onto this stage when I went here. I had a dream. A fool's dream and now I'm doing what people told me I couldn't." His speech isn't fancy or full of words these kids can't comprehend. They tell the story of how hard he's worked to rise up like he has. It's very sexy and I don't know why. I cross and uncross my legs in the seat.

He has fire in his eyes when his gaze lands on me. Ty closes his speech and the audience cheers, something I'm sure he's used to. He walks down off the stage to sit next to the principal a couple of rows ahead of me. I bounce my knee impatiently as the final twenty minutes of announcements pass. I will have to read the email with the notes to figure out what was actually said here today.

Principal Blair dismisses everyone and I hang back, leaning against the wall, allowing the students and faculty to pass me. Tyson makes his way over to me through the aisles. "You looked good up there. I liked your speech."

"Thank you, Mrs. Stewart." He barely contains his smirk, pushing his tongue into his cheek.

I scratch my forehead. "I don't know if I like you calling me that..."

He looks me over, eyes greedily taking in my body with heat that sparks something in my own lower belly. "Why? Do you need to see me after class?"

"Ha ha, very funny." I poke his chest. Looking at him from under my lashes, I say, "Maybe I do..."

He leans down to whisper in my ear, "Good. I want to do to you what I didn't get a chance to way back when."

My mind whirrs with thoughts of what he could mean. I huff out a startled breath and fan my face at the rising blush.

Everyone finally clears out of the auditorium and we wait a few minutes after that, "We have to be quick because I don't know if anyone holds classes in here after assembly," I say.

He picks me up, throwing me over a shoulder, and runs up the stairs to backstage. Dropping me to my feet, he turns me so quickly that I catch myself onto the wall for purchase. Lips meet every bit of exposed skin he can get to as he drops to his knees in front of me. He stretches my leotard to the side exposing my center as I bend over for him. I hear the metallic click of his knife opening and the sharp tearing noise before air hits me. I whip my head around, hands still pressed to the wall. "Did you just cut my tights open?" I hiss.

"Yea," is all he says with a smirk, turning me back around. I hate that I love that sexy tilt of his lips and what it does to me. He stands and I unbutton his jeans, hopping into his arms. He catches me and puts me against the velvet curtain gathered next to me. It's better than the brick but not by much.

The blunt head of him rubs along my slit. I'm so wet for him. "Look at you, baby. So ready for this dick, huh?" I nod, forcing my weight down on him to slide slowly down his long shaft. Each inch is better than the last until my ass is flush with the bunched-up fabric of his jeans. A small moan escapes me at the feeling of him inside me. I'm a little sore from last night. The pleasure of taking him deep the way I wanted to that night we shared this stage is overwhelmingly good. We would never have been able to do this when we were students here, but I like the idea of imagining that it's the two of us on that night. A little gasp puffs outs when he grabs my ass to reposition me briefly.

He kisses me, nipping my lip, "You have to be quiet so we don't get in trouble."

I nod. Kissing behind his ear and down his neck. "You're playing with me," he says as I lick a small circle over and over again right where his neck meets his shoulder. He thrusts up into me, and I clench around him, holding on for dear life. Throwing my head back onto the curtain his thrusts get more intentional when he finds that spot. I cover my mouth with my hand to stifle my whimpers. His hands on my hips are moving me at the pace he likes.

I'm lost to him. I'm lost to this. The keening that starts off low in and only grows higher with his thrusts into me reaches a peak of ecstasy that has us both coming together. I wrap my arms around his neck, not wanting to let go of him.

The clatter of the auditorium door opening breaks our little moment. Ty rushes to redress and I adjust my leotard as best I can. "Are you done for the day?" he holds my hands, leading us out the back exit.

It takes me a minute, but I finally tell him that I am.

"Let's get you home and cleaned up then." I don't care where we're going. As long as it's together.

CHAPTER 45

Tyson

A WEEK PASSES BEFORE I get to have Melody to myself. Well as much to myself as I can, for someone working as a part-time waitress and a part-time dance instructor—at two different places. Early mornings and late nights are mine. What we did backstage at our old high school was fucking sexy but I don't know that I can make it happen again.

I've honestly seen more of Wesson than I have of her. Much to his pleasure, having someone to stalk all day, but to my displeasure because of what I need to talk to her about today. I love that she refuses to let me help her. She is the hardest-working woman I know. I admire that about her. But today... today, it frustrates me.

While she was at work, I got the email to get on the call with the label and my agent. I've been hoping for this call for the better part of my adult life. It was the offer. THE OFFER. Not the one I got to work with Jordan on our band. This is the offer to be my own band. The front of the band with only my name on it and my guys, Zeke and Robert, behind me. They saw my performance at Harmony Hill. Heard my new music and want to lay the tracks to release them as soon as possible to play off the momentum I've gained.

One problem.

One big problem.

Country music lives, breathes, and evolves in Tennessee. The one and only—Nashville, Tennessee.

When she comes into the house sagging, I'm rounding the corner to greet her at the door. For some reason, I am extremely nervous. I have way too much energy in my body in comparison to how drained she is. "Long night?" I ask grabbing her jacket and apron from her and hanging them on the hook by the door. She hums a response and leans against the wall to take her shoes off. I'm there in an instant to untie them and remove them for her.

"Thanks," she mumbles practically dragging herself to the bathroom to shower. While she's washing the day off of her, I'm making dinner that I bought all the ingredients for. Wesson trips me up a few times so I finally drop him a shrimp and he happily carries it to his bowl to eat while I finish our meal.

"That smells amazing!" Melody says in my ear, hugging me from behind. "Thank you for making dinner. I could have helped."

"I wanted to. You've had a long day." She considers me for a few moments, before kissing my cheek and grabbing some glasses from the cabinet to pour some tea. She sits at the dining table while I plate everything up. "Tell me about it," I say sitting down myself.

"You won't believe how busy it gets in there on Monday nights! The football season has just started but with the new quarterback... Oh, what's his name?"

"You mean Donovan Edwards?"

"Yea that's the one!" she pops a shrimp into her mouth and chews before continuing. "It was packed. I wonder if it will be like that all year! Ugh. Every single table and booth was full. I was supposed to get cut early tonight."

"I bet the money was good though," she nods enthusiastically while eating more of her food. "I thought you said you were getting off early, but it gave me more time to get stuff for dinner."

"I'm sorry. Were we supposed to—"

"No, we didn't have plans. I just missed you."

Her eyes shoot to mine and the ferocity is unexpected. "You did?"

"Of course. I've been thinking about you all day."

Her eyes sparkle and she leans across her small table to kiss me on the corner of my mouth. "That's really sweet." She puts her fork down. "Enough about me, I could complain for a lifetime. What did you do today?"

This is the time. I don't take it though. "Not much. Worked on some stuff. Scratched Wesson as much as he wanted."

"I might get jealous of how much attention my cat is getting over me if you're not careful."

I scoop her up in my arms and carry her to the couch. "Am I not taking care of you enough?"

She giggles, "I didn't say that..."

"Didn't you? What am I missing?"

"Maybe not missing... But, I've been thinking about a conversation that I said we would have."

My ears perk up. "What conversation is that?" Please, please, please let it be what I think it is.

On graceful legs, she walks over to the bedroom and I'm close behind her in no time. She opens the nightstand drawer. "I've been thinking about this for a while... Maybe, I'm ready now."

"We don't have to do anything you're not comfortable with."

"You've had three of your fingers in my... in there already. I think I can handle this thing. I'd like a little extra stress relief."

I walk her back onto the bed, "It would be my pleasure to help you relieve some stress."

Her jeans and panties are the first to go. The little gasp from her lips is the response from her when my mouth is on her bare thigh. She hurries to get her top and bra off until she's naked and ready for me on the bed.

Melody's little foot trails over my shoulder and stops, pinning me to her, "Don't tease me. I want you inside me."

I shiver at her demand. I don't know how I'll last if she keeps talking to me like that. "What do you need baby?"

Her taut little body slinks down until her pussy is lined up with my mouth. "I need you to lick me until I'm begging for this toy." She holds the pink plug in her hand. I don't recall her opening it but I'm just as ready as she is to work it inside her.

The little packet of lube is just within reach. I coat the end of the toy and spread it around her tight little hole. She moans, eager and ready for what is coming next. My finger slips in and I'm about ready to blow. She's so tight. I can only imagine what she'll feel like on me... I bite my lip, the taste and smell of her still lingers on my face. Looking up at her face, she watches me with as much concentration. I lick her clit quickly, just because I can and it's fun to tease her when she's so willing.

Pressing the tapered end to ass, she flinches, I stop immediately. "What is it?" I don't want to do anything to hurt her.

"It's a bit cold." I start pulling the plug out but she grabs my wrist holding me in place. "Keep going, baby."

"Damn, you look so sexy right now." There are three areas where the toy gets bigger and bigger about an inch apart from each other. She took the first section so beautifully. I do as she says and push it deeper inside, one more level.

She moans as I suckle her clit into my mouth. I wiggle the toy around without pushing it any deeper. "Oh my god. Don't stop doing that. Tyson, I'm gonna come."

"*I'm* gonna come," I chuckle into her dripping wet pussy. She keeps grinding on my face and I'm lapping up everything she's giving me. "Are you ready for it all baby?"

She nods, working her swollen little bud on my mouth. I grab the lube, making sure everything is ready for this final push. Her ass stretches around the last of the toy and we both groan when the heart base is flush with her body.

My thumb rubs over her clit so that I can put at least one finger inside her pussy. I wanna feel how tight she is now that she has the toy all the way in. "Ty... Oh. Ohh." She looks fucking perfect with the little heart glimmering between her legs. Her pussy is already dripping down my hands. She's so heated.

"Can I turn it on?" I ask while I slide another finger inside her.

Her head bobs. "It already feels so good. I want more." At the first setting, she's clenching my fingers. "Ah, come here."

I crawl up her body and kiss her. Her tongue plunges into my mouth, frantic with her climax. She rides my fingers until her body is spent.

Melody is spread out on the bed like a starfish, still panting from her orgasm. I test a wiggle at the toy and she twitches. Chucking again, I lick up all her release, not sparing a drop.

The shower is our next destination for sure. I turn on the water, finally getting undressed. Returning to the bed to grab her, she climbs into my arms. I sigh when I take a look at her sated in my arms.

"I love you, okay?" she asks me under the spray of the water.

"Only if it's okay that I love you back," I respond. This is exactly how I like to see her. Blissed out from an orgasm that I gave her.

"Never stop."

"I never could."

AFTER A COUPLE OF rounds in the shower and her screaming my name into the pillow, I let her catch her breath. We changed the bed sheets, reclining on the couch to watch a movie. With the sound of the movie playing into the room, we talk for a bit until I cannot contain the news I need to share with her when she asks me about my day again.

"Well... I had a pretty amazing day actually. Got a call from the label. The first one I took by myself. Well, Keeta was on the line but you get what I mean." I say.

"From the label? What's going on there?"

"They offered me a solo contract. I still am a part of JT but I'll be releasing my own music as well."

Melody jumps from her seat to come over and hug me. I stand and hug her back tightly, forgetting about the food I was too nervous to eat anyway. I wish I could pause this moment right here so that I can soak in her being happy for me.

When she lets me go, she hurries to the kitchen with wine glasses in her hand. "Should we not be celebrating? I don't have champagne but I've got some wine. Will that do? Maybe we should go get some from the store. This seems like a big deal. It is, right?"

"Melody, come sit."

She sits but not where she was before. She sits next to me and asks, "Why aren't you more excited?"

I have to tell her. "I'm getting on a plane tomorrow. Five A.M."

"Okay..." her brows pinch. "When will you be back?"

"I don't know."

"You have to have some kind of idea, Tyson. They can't just keep you indefinitely."

"They kind of can... Wherever they want me, is where I have to be." She crosses her arms. "At least at the beginning. I'm ready to lay these tracks and start recording now... it's been leading up to this."

"So what does that mean for us?"

"It can be a long-distance thing. Or we can pick up later when I get back."

"Pick up later?" She stands from the table "Are you breaking up with me? At my house? Again? Who does that, Tyson?" She starts cleaning her plate up putting things away

"I'm not saying that at all Melody. We're not—I'm not breaking up with you. I just don't know how long I'll be gone. It won't be possible for me to come back here all the time. I'll be here for the wedding but... Most artists move to Tennessee for it to be easier. I don't know what my future will look like. I don't want to ask you to do that."

Her voice is small. "Why not?"

"You have a life here. You've built so much here."

"What does that have to do with us? You don't want me to be there with you."

"That's not true. Moving is a big change. Melody, I'm leaving tomorrow. You have no time to think it over and make a decision like that. It would be unfair of me to ask you to do that."

"What happened to you making it work? Why would you even suggest breaking up?"

"I didn't suggest that."

"You did, Tyson. Is what we have not serious to you?"

"It is. You are the only woman I have ever wanted to spend my life with. We still have so much time to make this decision. I don't want to rush anything."

"Rush?!" She stalks off to her room where Wesson follows. I follow too because I'm messing this up so badly. I have to make this right before I get on that plane. There is something cyclical about this argument and I can't stop what I've started here again. How do I come back to this same place with each decision I think will be a step forward?

She's turning on her TV and sitting in bed. "Melody, what are you doing?" She hasn't slept with the TV on since I've been here sleeping with her. She would always have it on so she didn't feel the silence of her house.

"Maybe you should stay at your place tonight. It will be easier for you to leave if you're already gone."

I scoff, "You want me to leave?" I look around her room and see all the little pieces of myself that have filtered in from the short time I've been staying here. It hits me just like it did before. I thought I was building something and she has been ready to let me go either way. "You don't mean that."

"You were right before. Maybe we should just pick up when you get back. Denver's airport is closer to your apartment in the city."

"Melody, I don't get how you can be my biggest cheerleader up until I actually grow. This is good news. I'm achieving *the goal*. I did it."

"And I'm happy for you, Ty. I am so proud of you! Every good thing coming your way is well deserved."

"So why do I feel like you're punishing me for going after it?"

"Punishing you? I'm trying to protect myself. Every time you need more space to grow, you leave me behind. You're doing the same thing now!"

"This isn't the same. You know it's not. We can make this work." I feel like I'm not speaking English or something. How can she not see what I'm up against? I thought I was accommodating her life. What I'm doing is no more important than what she is here in Alpenglow.

"Now, it's we?!" She shakes her head, tears in her eyes. Her sniffing rips at my heart. "No, it's you. You are chasing your dreams and I'm not going to stand in your way. Lock the door on your way out. You've got packing to do before your flight."

"I'll call you when I land."

She doesn't respond and I leave without another word.

CHAPTER 46

Melody, Then

THE WINTER HERE IS nothing like it is in Texas. I would probably die from heat stroke if I wore what I have on now. My fuzzy yellow sweater and tan wool slacks are a new addition to my wardrobe. I can't say that I completely hate winter clothes.

This is my first Friendsgiving. To think that I was on a dance team with people who I sweat and bled with but we never had the kind of camaraderie I've found in Alpenglow Ridge is beyond bizarre. This is my little family. I've never been a part of a friend group as tight as this one. I smile up at the little cutout turkeys strung in the doorframe before stepping into the room. The door to Reese's house is wide open.

Clo and Reese come to hug me when they see me walk in, fussing over my sweater and my hair. I took extra time to straighten it and add a little wave. Very different from my bun or the wash-and-go I'm usually sporting. They talk to me about all the decor. Mostly Clo doing, the decorating and Reese getting pictures of it all to share on their socials.

Drea comes to hug me next, though she looks a little green. "Sorry, all the food smells are kinda making me nauseous." Drea is in her first trimester and it's been brutal for her with the morning sickness since it doesn't seem to be restricted to mornings. She quickly makes her way to the couch to sit after we hug and talk for a bit.

Reese's mom brings out another large dish of something that smells amazing and I look at the spread of food she's lined up. One thing for certain is that the food will always be amazing if the Masons are involved. I've learned that from experience I'm grateful to have obtained.

There are a few other people besides us who have lunch together. I look around to see a familiar head of hair or the bandana he's been wearing lately. When I don't see him, I ask Clo, "Where's your brother?"

She chews a little piece of turkey from the on-theme charcuterie board before telling me, "He's at CU for a tour with William. They left this morning." She turns to the people gathered, "But he's not the only one with musical abilities. I've got his playlist login! Music is still courtesy of Ty's JAMZ playlist." The speaker trills a sound as it connects to her phone and music begins to play in the space.

My mind spins as I aimlessly meander over to the snack table myself. "Colorado University?" It comes out as a whisper, in the middle of piling lemon poppyseed cookies on my napkin.

"Yea. I think it's the only one he applied to..." She touches my arm but double-takes at something on the other side of me. Her boyfriend is talking with some tall dude with a fade I don't recognize. "Quincy get off the photo wall you're gonna mess up the cutouts! I'll be back in a bit."

A tan hand reaches around me for a cookie from the table. I turn to see the pity in his eyes. "Oh, you didn't know?" Mack asks. When I don't immediately respond he raises an eyebrow.

I twist my napkin in my hand, "No... I didn't."

"I just assumed you would have talked about it..." He seems to think over his words and adds, "With how close you've been. He told us the other day since Will has been riding his ass extra hard now that he's legal and all."

The news stuns me enough that I tear the napkin with how I'm gripping it. I can hear the rip in my heart just as clearly as I hear the music of the party. He's thinking about leaving me and he didn't even tell me. The cookies drop to the floor, but I can't register the mess I've made. Everyone is eating and drinking while Mack and I talk by the small buffet table with the desserts. I could be in a bubble for how small my consciousness has just become.

Mack doesn't read my expression correctly and continues to talk. "If you were mine, Mel, I would never keep something like that from you. You know that right?" He leans over to put his face in my line of sight as I'm fighting back tears. "Mel, I'd never even think about leaving you. I'm still here trying my best. I've been dry since that night. I want to be more than your friend. It kills me to see you with him when this is how he treats you."

"Stop, Mack!" My voice carries over the music and everyone is staring at me now. Chloe is by my side when I turn to run to the bathroom. She shoots Mack a killing look and he gives her a confused shrug like he didn't just blow my world up.

The tears fall before I can reach Reese's powder room.

I stare at myself in the mirror. How could he do this? Why didn't he tell me?

Why did he keep this from me?

Drea rushes into the bathroom. Reese is immediately by her side, holding her hair out of the toilet as she empties the contents of her stomach.

Realizing that I'm in here too, Reese winces, "I know you're kinda having a moment, but we had to go for the closest one instead of mine."

"It's fine," I say, still trying to fix the little bit of makeup I'm wearing. "I should probably go anyway."

"Don't go because I'm being all gross. No one tells you how weird and nasty pregnancy is."

"It's not weird, Drea. You're carrying a whole new life. It's beautiful."

Reese and Drea share a look that makes me feel a little self-conscious. They've taken to calling me the fairy of the group because I get caught saying things that make it seem like I'm destined to be a princess in a fairytale. I wish that were true. Does the princess continuously get blindsided by blows she wasn't expecting? I feel like I'm in a Brothers Grimm book instead of one manufactured by Disney.

I leave the bathroom and away from the sink so Drea can clean up. My phone rings and I already know who is calling me.

"What?"

"Melody?" His voice is dejected.

"Where are you Tyson?"

"I'm on my way home. Can I come over and talk to you?"

"No."

"No?"

"What is there to talk about? Your sister and Mack told me everything that I need to know. You didn't think it was important to tell me that you're optioning colleges. Visiting? I never even knew you applied."

I make my way outside so that my conversation can't be easily over-heard by people at the party.

"Melody, it's not like that. I'm not optioning. I've only been to one. Applied to one."

The watery tone is a dead giveaway that I'm not the person I thought I was. I thought I was stronger now. Hardened from this feeling of abandonment. No one could hurt me as badly as my mom or my dad. I was wrong. "Is that supposed to make me feel better?" It absolutely doesn't. "How hard is it to tell me the truth about what's going on in your life? How does everyone know but me?"

I hear him sigh heavily. "I can't say what I want to right now. Can I please just come over tonight? I have so much to tell you."

"You're letting him decide what's best for you. Everything you told me about standing up to him, fighting for your music, wanting to be with me... all of it is a lie."

"It's not—I'm trying to do the best I can right now. This is more complicated than you realize."

"It's not. You could be honest or you could lie. So tell me this. Are you still pursuing music?"

Silence. Utter silence. It hurts so much. The silence always hurts.

"Then where do I fit into these plans?"

More silence. And this time I don't add anything else. I hang up because at some point I allowed Tyson to fool me into thinking he would fill the part of me that has felt so broken since I lost my mom and my dad basically checked out. Ty was there for me. Almost every night and he had every opportunity to say something. Anything. But he didn't.

"Mel?" I wipe under my eyes quickly and turn to face Mack standing just outside of the back door. "I can come back..."

"No. You're fine. I'm fine." I smile weakly.

He nods and sits on the patio steps. I sit next to him because I can't put on a brave face that will withstand my girls right now.

He lights a joint that he pulled out from behind his ear. "You mind if I light this?"

I shake my head and lean onto the banister. The sun is setting and I try my hardest not to think about how special those sunsets had felt. I try to think about what it was like when the only thing I had to look forward to was the cover of night and the illumination of stars. For a moment, I thought maybe I was out of the dark.

"So, you and Ty are fighting?"

"I don't want to talk about it."

"We don't have to talk." He blows out the smoke from his lips, offering me the little rolled thing glowing at one end.

"I'm good. I'm gonna just go say goodbye to everyone and head home."

"Don't leave. I'll put it out." He stubs it on his boot and drops it into his chest pocket. "See. I'm listening."

"I said I don't want to talk about it."

"Okay... We can talk about anything else." I don't say anything and choose to let him carry the conversation again. "Sooo... Do you have a favorite color?"

"A favorite color?"

"Yea. You know mine's yellow. What's yours?

"Yellow?" I look down at my sweater and back at him. "Did you say yellow because of this?" I hold the sweater away from my body at the hem.

298

His lips twist to the side and he narrows his eyes. "Maybe..." He drags out the word and bumps his shoulder into mine. "C'mon. What's your favorite?"

"Umm... purple," I say resolutely.

"Oh, mine too."

"Didn't you just say it was yellow?"

"Did I?" He smiles. "I can't remember. But look at that. We have purple in common. I wonder what else we have in common."

"Lemon cookies," I say, recalling how we were the only ones to grab them inside earlier.

"Love me some lemon cookies. Especially if Chandie is making them. Don't tell anyone, but I wrapped up the rest of them in a napkin. Put 'em in my car earlier." He puts a finger to his lips, looking around.

I gasp exaggeratedly, "You didn't." His solemn nod is accompanied by a slow blink of his eyelids. "What if I wanted more?" I ask, crossing my arms.

"Looks like you'd have to come to my car to get some. It'll cost you five though."

"Five dollars? For cookies that were free?" I chuckle at his antics. "I don't even have cash."

"I take hugs, too."

I eye him suspiciously. "I bet you do."

"I give the best hugs. Even my mom says so." He shrugs and grinds the heel of his boot into the step below us. The leaves he caught under the heel crumble into pieces that float away in the breeze.

Not for the first time, I think about how it could be easy to be with Mack instead of Tyson. Mack wouldn't leave me because Alpenglow Ridge is where he wants to stay. It's where I am. It's just a thought but I feel a bit guilty even letting him have this time alone with me. Because I know that he wants more. Because I know that Tyson wouldn't like it. "I'm sorry I yelled at you earlier."

"Ack," He waves a hand through the air. "Water under the bridge. I meant what I said though."

"I know," I whisper. "We should go back inside. I'm starting to get cold out here."

"Right, right," He stands, brushing his jeans off and offering me a hand. I take it and stand, brushing my own pants off. When we go back into the party everyone is engaged in their own conversations. It seems like more people have arrived and though Reese's house isn't small by any stretch of the imagination, there is way too much noise and commotion for what my nerves can take right now.

It takes me only a few minutes to realize that I will not make it in this party with the chaos of thoughts swirling around about Tyson. I find my way back to the front of the party after hugging my friends on the way out.

"Here, I'll walk you out," Mack says, as I'm opening the front door.

"You don't have to. I'm just gonna go home. You should stay and have fun."

"It's fine, Mel. Let's go." I nod and walk over to my dad's car. It's an old Cherokee, but it can handle the snow better than I could have walking here.

I curse under my breath seeing that I'm blocked in by cars I don't recognize. There is no way I'll be able to get out without trying to figure out who's cars these are and getting them to move them. Ugh.

"I can take you home. I walked here," Mack, who I had forgotten was here because of how much I wanted to not be here, points over to his truck unobstructed in his driveway. Mack and Reese are neighbors and basically siblings; they're so close.

"You don't mind?"

"Of course not. I'll even share some of my cookies." I look at him from my twisting fingers. He looks so sincere and eager to help me. "Free of charge," He put his hands out in front of him. I giggle at him before we walk over to his truck.

CHAPTER 47

Tyson, Then

UNBELIEVABLE.

I don't believe what I'm seeing. Mack's truck is parked in Melody's driveway. His fucking truck! Why the fuck is his truck in her driveway?

Before I even reach the front door, Mack is coming out of it. "Hey man, how was CU?" His casual tone pisses me off. How dare he be casual coming out of my girlfriend's house?

"Why were you in Melody's house?" It's late but not that late. Aaliyah made me stay and answer an annoying amount of questions about the trip and my thoughts and blah, blah, motherfucking blah as soon as Will and I got home. I would have immediately left if my dad hadn't continued his long guilt trip and whatnot. All while I dealt with that, this piece of shit was worming his way back into Melody's life.

"Oh," he looks back at the door and points a thumb over his shoulder. "She was tired so I brought her home. Seems like she had a hell of a night." He winks and I want to black his eye.

I take a deep breath to try and find calm. "Why did you bring her home? I thought she drove there. Where's her dad's car?"

"Right. She did drive." He pats his jacket pocket, "I'm gonna drive it back when everyone goes home. She got boxed in. Reese invited so many people. You included. Why weren't you there again?"

I grind my teeth. The restraint is becoming harder and harder to find the longer he runs his mouth. "That's none of your business. Especially for you to go telling Melody."

He shrugs. "You made it my business when I was the one consoling her tonight. You kept this from her... Why? I mean, I don't really care because you gave me an in. Thanks by the way, friend." He strides over to his truck, getting in and starting the engine. "I'll be there for her every time that you fuck up. Just remember that. I'll always be there for her."

"You won't. I won't," I yell at his truck as he backs out of the driveway. He flips me the bird and drives away. *Fucker.*

I need to calm down before I see her even though I want to rush in and see just how much damage I've done. That is not going to win me any favors. I sit on her steps for a few minutes to gather my thoughts. Mack was right. I did fuck up. Melody found out about all of this in the worst way possible. I have to try and make things right.

I clean off my boots and walk up to her closed bedroom door. I've come up to her room just like this so many times before, but something seems different this time. I knock on it softly, but she doesn't reply. I knock again and nothing. I chance opening it, seeing the window wide open.

"Hey", I say when I climb up onto the roof. She sits on a cushion now, hair whipping around her in a manic spray of black waves. She's devastating in this fluffy sweater the color of sunshine. Those sad eyes lock with mine and it guts me right away. I've seen her sadness so many times before but I had never been the source of it. "Melody, I can explain."

"Do your best," She says, crossing her arms when I sit on the cold roof next to her. "Actually, no. I don't want to hear it. I have questions of my own."

"Okay," I respond, hesitantly.

"Why didn't you just tell me you applied? Why keep this secret from me? It feels like you are trying to leave me, to slip away."

"No, Melody. No, that's not it at all. I don't want this."

"Then why? Why not tell me?"

I bite my lip. I could tell her. I should tell her. I feel like it will only make things worse. Melody's parents all but abandoned her. Mine are so present in my life that I can't escape their hovering. How do I tell her that my mom left me with much more? I have another piece of my mom that I never thought I could. Her life is so different, it's just insulting. I want to keep this little bit of what's left of my mom to myself. I don't want to feel bad about that either. It's already been tainted by Will and exploited to control my life.

I don't know what choice Melody would have in falling into the consequences of my decisions.

I choose my next words carefully. "I feel like I'm giving up by doing what he wants. I didn't want you to think differently of me. After everything I said about my real dreams." True. All of that is true. But not truly why. The lie tastes acrid and perverse in my mouth.

She nods and doesn't resist me when I hug her close to me. This is the last night that I'll feel at least a little bit whole. "You're not giving up. It's not a bad idea to have a degree. It's not for me but Will wouldn't push you if he didn't believe in you."

"That's the thing! He thinks he's won me over because I've agreed. He's using this to point out how silly and childish a career in music is. I don't get how he could be so supportive of this when the job market is trash. You can have a degree and still be without a job when everything is said and done. It's the same."

"I know, Ty. It's just a few years. You don't have to give up performing completely. You can do both."

"It won't be the same. It feels like I'm half-assing my music and it kills me a little inside to recognize that."

She rubs my back, "You'll figure it out. If there's anything you've shown me, it's that circumstances aren't as bleak as they seem."

I kiss her fiercely. Every emotion I can manage pouring into this one action that I can control.

I let her feel how desperate I am right now. Desperate to find a solution. Desperate to love her the way she deserves. Desperate to hold on to the woman who never got to see my full potential because she was taken from me too soon.

I don't know how I can hold on to all these things at once.

As my senior year comes to a close, more is expected of me to prepare for the following year. Each task feels like I am slipping away from Melody. I'm helpless to it. Choosing a major, picking a dorm, and deciding whether I will do summer classes to get ahead. All of it felt a bit like sneaking around on her because I started to genuinely be excited about what was in store for me. How do I tell her that? I kept too much from her that it would be more upsetting for me to say something now.

A wedge between us that drove deeper.

Mack began to be a part of all our group events more than he was when Melody and I had first started dating. He was around more and as conversations of our summer plans came up, it was becoming harder to divert the attention away from me.

We all sit on Reese's back porch eating barbecue after school one day. It's Chloe who brings up the fact that she's going to start working at the salon on Main. "I'm gonna get my diploma because Will might have an aneurysm if I don't but I think the experience will be good for me. I might even be able to get a booth!"

Everyone congratulates her and shares what they're doing this summer. It's April and either they're working here on the Ranch or looking for somewhere to work.

"The senior center is looking for dance instructors," Melody adds. "I think I'm going to apply." I didn't know that. At my look of surprise, Mack gives me a knowing one. This fucker knew.

"You're gonna get it, Mel. They would be dumb not to pick you," Mack responds, rubbing her shoulder. I don't like that at all. I stand from the table to sit between her and Mack. There isn't exactly enough room for me on the bench seat but Melody shuffles down the bench to make room for me. Clo raises a brow, but says nothing. She never misses a thing.

"Wait, what are you doing for the summer," Quincy asks the question directed at me. *Goddamn.*

Finally, I have to admit, "I got into the summer program to take a few prerequisites. You know to get ahead. So, I can be done faster. Plus, I can take electives like Music Theory and improve my sound."

Melody blinks at me several times and I get a couple of shocked looks from my friends around the table. "Oh," she finally says. "You did?" Her dejected tone feels like another hammer to the wedge. "Of course you did. You're so smart and the theory class... That's great."

"Yea," I say, feeling like such a dick. I should just let her go. I shouldn't hold on to her when every time I open my mouth I say something else to keep us apart. "You know CU is not that far from here. Just two and a half hours. I could come home to visit all the time."

"Sure," she says, picking at the hem of her dress. "I don't know if I could take daddy's car for that long. If I get this job at the senior center, maybe I'll be able to get a bus or something up there."

"I can always come home on the weekends to see you. You don't have to take a bus."

"Okay," she whispers, not totally convinced. I wasn't either.

That night, I sat up in the living room. I always come back to my guitar. It's the only thing that can soothe me besides Melody. These days, being close to her makes me feel like an asshole. Looking over the roof that I first saw her on, it's empty. I can't even see the moonlight out right now. It's such a dark night. There isn't a light coming from her window either. I don't know how I can fix the distance. I don't know if I should.

"You doing alright?" The couch depresses to my left and I look at my step-mom sitting back against the oversized pillows.

"If I say, yes, will you go back to bed?"

"Probably not. I have eyes after all."

I sigh and place my guitar in the case by my feet. Fine. "No. I'm not doing alright." She waits for me to continue. Aaliyah is used to me making her pull teeth for conversation. She and Clo are similar in their stubbornness, but I get too irritated to outlast either of their meddling. It'll save us both some time not to do the song and dance when I know she'll just keep asking until I talk anyway. "It's Melody."

"Did something happen with her?"

"Nothing happened with her. I'm just... everything is different now."

She nods, "Because you're going to CU... she didn't take it well."

"I don't know. I think she's trying to but I just don't feel like I can be... honest... with her, you know?"

"About what?"

"How I feel about going to school now. Before, when we talked about college, I never wanted this. I was running. But now, after mom's letter, I feel like this is an opportunity for me to be close to her. To walk the same halls and stay in the same dorm. It's another chance for me to have a piece of her."

Aaliyah rubs my back. "Why wouldn't you want to share that with Mel?"

"Melody... lost her mom too. To cancer, just this past year. It's really fresh for her. Her life has just been hard since her mom... passed. I feel like shit thinking about rubbing it in her face that I still have something I can share with mine. I never thought I would have something like this. And I don't know. I feel like a dick because I have you and dad. I at least have parents who still care about me. She has no one. Her dad is barely around ever."

"I see. Losing a mother is hard. I can't say I even know what it's like because Gamgam is still kicking and causing a fuss. You two were both so young."

"I don't want to hurt her."

"You still have your whole life ahead of you, Tyson. And so does she. I do think you should be honest with her. If you can't be... maybe you should just let her go."

My brows pinch. What the fuck? "Let her go? I'm not doing that. What kind of shit advice is that?"

She chuckles and her smile goes a little pitiful at the corners. "It's not shit advice. You can't see it now but you might have many loves in your life. This one feels big and infinite, but sometimes love is not enough. Sometimes you have to make hard choices for yourself because you can't live for another person. You need to do what's best for you. If she can't be happy with this amazing accomplishment, then you need to see that for what it is."

"And what is it?"

"If it's truly meant to withstand time and distance, then it will."

"That doesn't help me, Aaliyah."

She considers me for a second. "If it was meant to be then it will be. Look at me, I left town—had a whole life even. Got married and had a baby. Got divorced and moved back home. I found your father again after all these years and now we're happy together... Sometimes life looks different from how we expected it to and you can still be happy."

"She makes me happy."

"Then why are you plucking this sad tune in the middle of the night?" She leaves and I know what I have to do.

I really don't want to.

CHAPTER 48

Melody, Then

IT'S BEEN WEEKS SINCE Tyson has come over to stay the night.

Maybe I've gotten too used to having someone by my side.

I stopped waiting for him, choosing to hang out with the girls over at Mason Ranch. At least I can be with someone instead of being at my quiet house. I can't be alone again. Reese, Drea, and Chloe are always eager to share about what's going on in their lives. Drea and her new baby are moments from coming into the world. I can't wait to meet her! I haven't been around a baby before, but I know I will love baby M. She hasn't shared the name with us yet. She and Colton are gonna co-parent while she lives at her grandma's house.

More times than not, the guys come over, Ty excluded. He's been too busy for all of us, it seems. Me, especially. I don't know what I did but I can feel him pulling away. The farther he gets, the more I retreat. I can't stop the sadness creeping in on me. I just wish I knew what I did. Even with my friends–they've stopped asking me what's wrong. I wish I could tell them but I don't know what to say. What if they know what happened with Ty and are protecting me from the truth? It's better to not know.

I thought I had at least until the fall before he was gone. He dropped that bomb about going for the summer and I found out with everyone else. Why would he keep that from me? I don't understand. I thought that we would be together. I thought that he wanted to be with me. I know we're young but he said that he wanted a life with me.

Sitting on my roof is out of the question. The memories of Ty and me are too much to take. I feel like I've lost something every time I make my way up there. I scoop Wesson up and make myself comfortable on the little chair I found in a consignment shop the girls and I went to one weekend. Chloe has made it her mission to help me decorate my room and then all the other areas of the house that I am in. My dad didn't even notice as new things started popping up in the house—on the walls or outside. I don't think he sees any of it, maybe he does but doesn't care. As functional as a drunk could be. I get a little lost in my thoughts before Tyson clears his throat.

Wesson hops from my lap immediately to greet him. They reunite like old friends before I find my voice, "You don't want to sit?" I say gesturing to the other little chair next to me.

"I don't think I should." *So, this is it.*

"Okay..." It's barely evening, but somehow it's gotten darker out here. Wesson climbs up my legging to his previous spot. I'm thankful for something to do with my hands other than fidget.

He blows out a breath and crosses his arms tightly. "I never say goodbye right."

Goodbye. "I don't know if there is one," I whisper. The words barely escape me. I should have seen this coming. I thought maybe I had more time. I thought wrong.

"You know what I mean... With my mom, it was bad too."

My brows pinch, "What are you talking about, Ty?"

He shakes his head. "See? I'm doing this all wrong." Walking over to me, he squats in his shorts and I have to look down at him. "It shouldn't be like this. It's unfair for me to expect your life to change just because mine is."

"My life is already changed because of you." Everything has changed because of him. Because of him, I'm happier than I've ever been. I was... for a time there.

"I know." He grabs my hands to stop my fidgeting. I meet his eyes and it hurts just like I thought it would. My heart has learned to accept that loss is inevitable. I've lost everything that has ever meant anything to me. Mom. Dance. Dad. It shouldn't still hurt to lose another. I should be used to it.

I'm not.

I won't beg him to stay. I can't when he has so much in front of him. I'm just the dead weight he has to cut so he can fly. I'd never cost him that.

"If we're really meant to be together, then we will be again." I pull my hands from his grip. I hate those words more than the others. I don't want false hope when we both know he's meant for more than I can give. "When I'm a man who deserves to protect something as precious as your light and your love, Melody. I will be back." His eyes shine in the setting sun. The last we'll share together. I'm grateful that he didn't ruin our place. I'll still have somewhere to go and reminisce, untainted by his words here tonight. To imagine what our story could have been if he wasn't him and I wasn't me.

He caresses my cheek. "I'll miss you. We'll have our time again," he says, swiping a tear with his thumb. "I have to believe that."

"Believe what you want. Please just leave, if you're going." I stand from the chair and leave him on the porch by himself.

My limbs are heavy and aching when I flop onto my bed.

"I HEARD ABOUT MY asshole brother," Chloe says from my doorway. I didn't hear anyone come into the house. The three of them are here. But I guess it's hard to hear someone when your ears and nose are stopped up from crying for so long. I don't know how many days I've been here. For those last few weeks of school, I was thankful that everyone was so focused on final exams and their own end-of-school-year business. Ty is gone. He never even said goodbye before moving into his dorm on campus. Life is moving past me as I am stuck in the sad loop of thoughts containing my own inadequacy. I could hole up in my room unnoticed and unbothered. Now that school is over, my absence has definitely triggered my friends into action.

"We brought the essentials." Drea holds up several bags and plops them by the door to my room.

"You're way too cute to be wasting your tears on a high school boy." Reese scoffs, kicking her boots off and scooting into the bed with me.

"Too late for that," I murmur. God, I have to look and smell awful. I don't actually know when was the last time I did anything outside of this room.

"Okay... shower and then we'll talk. I don't care if he's my brother. You're my sister and he can fight me if he wants to say differently. Fucking idiot." She rolls her eyes pushing me into the hall and toward my bathroom.

I don't bother looking in the mirror. I already know what heartbreak looks like on my face. I never thought that it would be Tyson to put it there. I do my business, as rote as it is, and return to the room. Chloe loads up *Bring It On* to no one's surprise on her laptop and we all snuggle into my full-size bed to watch and eat the snack they brought over. We don't actually talk about what went down with Ty. It's pretty self-explanatory with how he had been pulling away.

When the movie ends, they order pizza and we sit on my roof eating it. I've never been more grateful for these girls. They came to pull me out of the longest depressive episode I've had since I moved to Alpenglow Ridge. I finally have another happy memory on my roof to make me feel like maybe the world isn't ending the way I suspected it was.

I can move on from Tyson. I can live life after him.

------◆◆◆◆------

A SMALL STACK OF lemon poppy seed cookies breaks my stare off into the distance. I startle before Mack steps in front of me. "I was gonna take these back to my house but I figured you could use them more."

I take the napkin with the cookies. "Thanks." I bite into one and there is no denying that Chandie deserves a blue ribbon for these.

"Don't mention it," he says. "So, no horse for you?"

"Nah," I respond, sitting on the patio swing. "I don't actually know how to ride." Reese, Chloe, Quincy, and a couple of the other hands rode off to the trails. I chose to stay back. I'm sure I could ride with someone but the sunset view from Reese's back porch is next level. The ambiance isn't too bad either.

"I thought you were from Texas."

"What does that have to do with anything?"

"You all have horses there, right?" he looks confused. "Isn't their football team named after cowboys?"

"Not everyone—" His face breaks into a grin and I shove at his arm. "You're teasing me." The giggle catches me off guard. It doesn't happen that often anymore.

"Maybe a little. I could teach you to ride, you know?" His cheeks pinken and he rubs a hand over his face, chuckling at the possible innuendo. A small smile raises my own cheeks at his nerves. He's usually much more smooth than this. When he's not drinking. "I mean... that's also what I do here. I train the horses... when I'm not mucking. I could show you how."

"Oh. I don't know... They're beautiful but like four times my size. That doesn't seem like a good idea."

"I started riding when I was way smaller than you. It's fun when you get the hang of it. I promise." He stands from the swing, holding out a hand. His smile is infectious. I give him my hand and we walk over to the stables.

"Tough break with you and Abrams. He's an idiot. You know that right?"

I stop right outside of the lard door of the barn. "I don't really want to talk about that." He turns and finds my eyes. "I don't want to think about him, okay?"

He nods. "We don't have to." I follow him into the stables and he pats a large tan horse that sniffs into his hair immediately. "Besides, Legend is kind of a handful. You'll need to be one hundred percent focused if you're gonna ride this hot head."

"You know? You aren't making it sound all that fun. Hot head? Is it safe?"

He chuckles, "I'm just messing. He's charming with the ladies. With me, he's a bit of a menace. I'll get him saddled up and we can just walk around the pasture. Nothing scary about it. I'll be holding the reins the whole time. Unless you're feeling brave."

I shake my head, "You holding the reins is just fine with me." And maybe I meant that for more than just with the horse. It's no secret that Mack still likes me. If I gave him a shot, he would take it. With Tyson long gone from Alpenglow, maybe I should.

I take a seat on the little stool he pulls aside for me. Watching him work, I reminisce on a time when I knew nothing about Mack. If I didn't know anything about him now, would I still put him strictly in the friend-zone? He's been sober since I've seen him outside of a joint here and there. He seems happier than he was after the party.

"Are you ready to go? I'll show you how to mount him." Mack takes his time showing me how to ride this horse. The sun almost kisses the mountains as we walk and he talks idly about all that he does on the Ranch. He's able to keep the conversation going though I don't offer many long responses. It's easier than the prying questions that the girls try every now and then since they found me holed up in my room.

Not for the first time I think about how easy it would be to be with Mack. He's not a bad guy... he's cute even. And those eyes... still deep, sparkling blue.

Easy is better than alone.

CHAPTER 49

Tyson

MORE UNANSWERED TEXT MESSAGES. I've texted Melody no less than ten times for the past three days that I've been here. I leave the studio and wait out front on the bench for an Uber to come pick me up.

The music has been easy. Simple even. My label is happy with how quickly I've been able to get everything recorded. Four new songs and I have just one left. Once that's done it'll just be the producers and engineers jobs to complete them for release.

Reese's wedding is this weekend. I think it's my last chance to do something about my failing relationship with Melody before it's too late. *I could actually lose her for good if I don't.*

My sister says that she's fine, but that could mean anything. I don't know if her loyalty lies more with me or Melody. I'm still worried with how I left things. I'm scrolling on my phone, when a big SUV pulls up right next to me in the parking lot. I turn to see Jordan getting out, brushing his shoulders off.

"What do you want?" I tuck my phone into my back pocket.

"I want to talk."

My chuckle is long and exasperated. "You want to talk? Where the fuck have you been Jordan? Finally dried out from your bender? Need some more good press?" I throw my arms up. "I'm a little busy at the moment."

His lips quirk at one side. Instead of looking charming, it's unhinged and sinister. A chill creeps down my spine but I stand my ground. "My press is your problem. I made you. You should hope that I intend to keep you in the spotlight. Everything you have is because of me and my press, good or bad. Don't be stupid. Get into the truck, Tyson."

"Me? Being stupid. What do you think this is?" I gesture between the two of us. The doors on the SUV open and now Jordan is surrounded by three men who stand behind him ready for... I don't know what.

I cannot believe this man hired goons to take me. There is no way that I'm getting out of here unscathed.

"I should have known you would try to replace me. It's not like I can be anyone other than who I am. You were nothing until I pulled you up," he sneers in my face.

"Man, what was I supposed to do? Just let the stage go empty and disappoint all those fans who came to see us? I had to fill that time. We had a contract." I explain.

"Ah! So, you do know there was an *us*. Funny how *us* only meant you on stage though. JT without the J."

"You're overreacting. It's not even that big of a deal."

"Oh, really?" He shrugs and puts his hands into his front pockets. I relax for a moment. "Maybe it wouldn't be a big deal but I have intel from Miles & Miles Records that they signed a solo contract with you for the unreleased music you debuted in Harmony Hill. Saying, 'There has to be more to the soulful songs that had the crowd in an uproar. It's unlike anything they have seen before.' Does that seem like overreacting to you?"

"Those songs were for us. I just made do with what I had, J."

He takes a step toward me that brings us face to face. "You could have just performed our old stuff. So what the fuck was that?" He throws his arms up. "I'm done talking. Grab him."

I should have expected that he would do this. *I should have known.*

I kick and dodge two of the large men's advances for a good bit, but when the third sends a hit to my temple—I'm out.

I WAKE UP IN my hotel. It's quiet in the suite and I take a few minutes to think about what I've gotten myself into.

My head is throbbing and all I can think about is how worried Melody must be right now. Or pissed. Maybe she feels no way at all and is just happy that I'm not texting her anymore.

There's nothing I can do. I wiggle my arm to realize he zip-tied my hands to this chair. *Fuck.* My fingers are numb and I have no idea how long I've been here.

"Jordan! What the fuck is this?" I'm met with silence. "Jordan," I call out again, but no one answers.

The clock on the wall says it's ten. Ten A.M. Friday. The next day. I'm already very late for my last recording spot. *Shit.* I sit here for hours before I hear someone coming into the room. The housekeeper takes one look at me and starts to back out of the doorway slowly. "No. Please help me!" I beg.

She gives me a once-over and leaves the room. "Please just untie me!" A few moments later, she's back with scissors. "Thank you, thank you!" My wrists are mangled from how I rubbed them trying to get free and not injure myself all at the same time.

Passing a mirror on the way out the door, I see my bruised face and it's not pretty. God, I look like shit. I need a shower but I need to get to the studio to at least show my face today. I don't want a reputation for being a diva. I'll have to figure out what I'm going to do about Jordan later. The music always comes first.

I search the room for my phone and it's nowhere to be found. I waste precious minutes looking for it before I decide to hell with it and get down to the front desk. The receptionist looks over my face but reluctantly calls a cab for me. My wallet was still in my back pocket to pay for my drive when I get back to the studio downtown.

I see the same black SUV from before parked out front. Though I could be wrong, I know I'm not. I recognize the big man standing outside of the door and know I'll need to get into the luxe building from a different entrance. Thankfully, I had already taken many breaks out of the other side. I locate the side door easily and navigate to where the producer and I had been working all along.

Jordan's eyebrows raise when he spots me walking into the lounge space. He starts to speak and I pay him the kindness he's shown me with a hit to his face using my elbow to protect my strumming hand. He doubles over holding his nose as the blood starts gushing. "What the fuck T? I think you broke my nose."

"What do you think you're doing here? Did you think you could just take my spot?"

"My nose... I can't breathe right." He holds his face and blood runs down his arm. I got a good hit in. Fucker deserved it. "I need to get to a hospital."

"Maybe you should get your henchmen to take you." I quip.

"Grow up. They aren't henchmen. They're private security. Maybe you should consider getting some." He huffs out

"I'm gonna just go..." The producer says when he sees the blood and tension between the two of us. My face in combination with Jordan's gripes is enough to signal trouble. He grabs his bag and backs out of the main room, closing the door behind him.

"Now that he's gone..." Jordan pulls a gun from the back of his pants.

I blink, sure that I'm seeing things all wrong. A gun? Why would he be strapped? "Goddamn, Jordan. Where the fuck did you get that from?"

"Don't worry about it. We're settling this here and now."

"What is there to settle?"

"You. You will be done using me to get what you want."

I scoff and internally curse myself because... This dude has a gun! *Shut the fuck up, Ty!* I still can't stop from saying what's on my mind. "I can't believe you man. You came to me. Asked me to work with you and now you want me to disappear?"

"I didn't expect you to stab me in the back!"

"Stab you in—that's rich! Look who is holding the gun!"

"Look who signed a solo deal—off my back! You used me to get ahead."

"Are you fucking stupid? It's not solo. Zeke and Robert are on the contract too. It's your fault they even came to me. You were too busy getting blown and wasting your money in the casino to show up to our show that night. *Nice*, by the way. If anything, you stabbed your own self in the back. I know why you needed me anyway. You ruined your reputation, your music was washed up and I saved you from being another has-been. I tried to anyway. You need help. Look at you. You need to talk to someone."

"Fuck you." He yells into the mixing room. He holds his shirt to his nose with one hand and it's soaked through. His arm shakes with the gun pointed at me. He's losing so much blood. I need to try and get that gun away from him. *This can't be how I go.*

"Step aside and go out with some grace." If I rile him up maybe he will be distracted enough for me to kick the gun away or something. "I'm not going to miss this opportunity when you couldn't take it."

"You were supposed to be on my side. On my team! Lacey left, man. She's fucking gone. I cleaned up for her. She believed in me, in us. Or so she said. But she's still gone. And you didn't do shit but take advantage of my pain. Just like everyone else has. They only like me when I'm sad."

I knew what losing the woman you loved was like. I hope I can turn things around with Melody and me. I have to make it out of this building alive. "That's not true. I don't know what happened with you and Lacey but there's more to life than just that. You can put all of this into the music. You don't need the alcohol or the drugs, J. You were doing so good for a while there."

"She's gone. Everything—everything is slipping through my fingers."

"It's not. We're still JT. We still have the band. It's not over." I plead.

He shakes his head, not hearing a word I've said. "You have two options right now. I'd suggest you choose the one where you get out alive." He blinks a little too slowly and I charge him into the couch he was sitting on before.

"I make my own choices!" I yell into his face as he tries to resist me.

The gun falls somewhere into the cushions. I try to look for it but he catches me by surprise, hitting me in the head with something I can't see. The blow connects in the same place that still throbs from his guard's earlier attack.

I stumble back and Jordan grabs my throat, trying to choke me. My legs kick out at anything I can make contact with. I hear the clunk of the gun to the floor but he doesn't let up from my throat. "I made you! You wouldn't have these choices without me!" Blood drips from his nose down onto my face and hands. I don't care about that or the petty words he's saying. I stop trying to pull his hands from my throat to reach for the gun. He notices just as my fingers make contact with the muzzle.

We struggle for control of the gun before I feel the agonizing sting of the first shot in my abdomen. I headbutt him with the last of my strength. The pain explodes through my head.

Everything goes black.

The last shot is loud and then the ringing is even louder in my ears.

The last happy memory I have of her filters in through the dark as I fall in and out of consciousness.

"*I love you, okay?*"

"*Only if it's okay that I love you back.*"

"*Never stop.*"

"*I never could.*"

If I'm gone, does that mean my love for her stops? I can't be the next thing Melody loses.

Chapter 50

Melody

I can't do this again. Even with me telling myself that I wouldn't get my heart involved a third time, I still did. So much for whatever that third thing was supposed to be. I can't be sad and depressed about losing Tyson again. Having him back in my life showed me just how much I need him, *want* him, to be in my life. Why does it still feel like only an option for him? I won't let him break me again. If I say it enough times, maybe it will stick.

Note to self: Stop giving Tyson your firsts... Even if it feels so damn good at the time!

Disco Cowgirl's Last Ride is the theme for the party that's wrapping up as Chloe corrals guests out of Cory's backyard. Reese and Chloe decided to have the party here instead of on the Ranch because they are working on the wedding day setup. Knowing Reese, it will be huge.

I am slowly sipping my third margarita from this large cowboy boot-shaped stein. I'm thankful that it is not jalapeño this time. Reese's bachelorette party looks exactly how you would expect from the most sexually empowered woman you know. There are a plethora of dick-themed decorations and trinkets as well as groovy text and cowboy hats. The bachelorette in question is wearing a lei with a mix of tiny penis-shaped charms, miniature pink cowboy hats, and sparkling disco balls—in groups of two—hanging between the flowers. Chloe and Drea are here with some women I recognize from the bar and some who now work on the Ranch with Reese's family. I watch everyone saying goodbyes and leaving from where I sit at the picnic table.

A hand presses softly to my shoulder. "How can someone be sad sipping from a dick-shaped straw? This seems criminal." Reese seems genuinely upset when I look up at her. I put my cup with the silly straw down on the picnic table. She sits on the bench next to me, rubbing her ankles.

"I'm not sad sipping. I'm just thinking." I murmur.

"Uh-huh. And I'm Dolly Parton." She props her feet up on the bench, sighing in relief. "I will pull the pregnant card if you don't tell me what's bothering you."

"It's not like that will help anything," I mutter under my breath.

"What does that mean? Melly, so help me God, you will talk to me about what has been going on."

"I will not!" I stand to try and make my exit, but it's wobbly at best. I need to stop drinking, effective immediately.

Drea comes over to my side and props me up. "Whoa there. Let's sit it back down."

"I wanna go," I whine, flailing my arms out toward the back fence everyone else exited from.

"Alright, I got everybody out. We're doing this." Chloe stands in front of me. I'm boxed in by my two friends with no easy way around what I know is coming.

"No, no, no. We aren't." I pout.

Chloe puts an arm around me, walking us over to the picnic table again. "Okay, I'll go first. Bon has been sad. I've noticed it and I let it go because of all the drama and being busy with the wedding planning. But, I've peeped it."

"I've just been tired."

"Bullshit. So what is it? Did my brother do something? Am I gonna have to whoop his ass?" Clo raises an eyebrow. I hate when she does. It means she knows something and I'm not gonna like it.

"No. Well, yes, but not really." I admit.

"Okay, I'm going next." Drea meets my gaze and I flinch under the intensity. "I noticed her disappear right after Reese's pregnancy announcement and come back from taking some phony call outside looking... different. Then, at the cake tasting, she ran out when we started talking about our babies."

"I did not."

"You did, Mel. Then you came out of my bathroom like nothing happened and Tyson picked you up."

"Okay, It's my turn!" Reese swings her legs off the bench to face me, as well. "What the hell is up, Melly? You have been so distant. I thought it was because you were enjoying some prime dicking... but, you are sad. You have the sad eyes. I haven't seen you Mel smile in way too long. Plus, I feel like we haven't talked in a while. Not really. I thought you would be my fairy godmother for the twins but I barely see you."

I wince at their observations, hiding into my hair, I look down at my hands.

"We're your girls. Melody. Please talk to us."

You should tell them, Melody.

Like some ironic angel, Tyson's voice comes into my liquid thoughts. I don't want to do that. Not yet. Hopefully never—like I planned.

"Tyson is gone." I announce instead.

"To Tennessee... so what?" Clo questions.

"So what? He's signed a contract with Miles & Miles. That is major! He's not under Jordan's wing anymore. He's leading the band as the voice of something wholly his own."

Clo's brows knit, "I looked it over with him and it looks—"

"No." I shake my head. "Forget the contract. I'm sure that it's sound or however that works. That's not the point." My thoughts are hazy and tequila-soaked but the sting of his actions rings clear for me to voice them. "He keeps leaving, thinking that he's doing what's best for me. He said some stupid shit about picking back up when he gets back."

"Picking back up?" Drea ask. "What the hell does that mean?"

Reese answers her, "Like taking a break while he's away." She looks to me for confirmation and I nod once.

"Take a break for what? What is that dumb shit?" Clo says pulling her phone out.

"Please don't, Chloe."

"I didn't know why he kept asking me about you. I knew you were upset about something. If I had known it was him, then I would have cussed him out already."

"Don't bother. I kicked him out before he got on the plane."

"That's my girl! Men are shit." Drea says holding her hand out for a high five.

"D, it's the worst." I don't high-five her and she slowly puts her hand down. "He's supposedly doing what's best for me. I don't get that. He is what's best for me. No one understands me or loves me like he does. It just makes me more confused. I can't deal with his fickleness when it comes to our relationship. How can I trust him or my feelings when I'm left holding my broken heart in my hands."

"God, I'm going to fight him... As soon as he is done playing perfectly for this wedding I've sold my soul to create magic for. He better be on that plane tomorrow."

"It's fine, Clo."

Reese takes a bottle of something from her purse and begins rubbing it on her ankles and feet. "No, it isn't, Melly. You love him. Why can't you two make it work?"

"I don't know." And I didn't. I could likely spend a lifetime trying to justify things for him. "He was at least texting me, though I wasn't responding but today... crickets. I'm probably overreacting but I can't stop thinking about it. Maybe he's sick of trying to work on us."

"Ugh. He sounds like such a fuck boy right now. I feel bad that we encouraged you to go for it." Drea rubs my arm.

"It's not your fault. I should have known better. Only a fool goes back to the guy who broke up with her twice before." Fool me twice, shame on me... *Fool me three times?*

"Are you the fool in this situation?" Drea asks.

"Unfortunately." I hang my head, blinking back tears.

"I don't think that's true," Chloe says. "I think you've just been through a lot. We're here for you. We can't help if we don't know what's going on." She lifts my face to hers. "We're your girls. We respect your boundaries as best we can but if you push us away we don't know how to help. Right girls?"

Drea and Reese agree. Both of them come to where Chloe stands in front of me. "I know," I say. The three of them hug me and I melt into their embrace. "I'm sorry."

"There's nothing to be sorry for. You're still our girl."

THE REHEARSAL DINNER COMES the next day and still no word from Tyson. The seat beside me is empty. Of course, I thought he would come here by some miracle and save me. Just like he always has before.

It's not Tyson who sits next to me. "This seat taken?" A voice breaks into my thoughts and I look up to familiar blue eyes.

"Be my guest," I say, though he is already sitting.

I take a sip of my water and focus back on the instructions being given by Chloe and Reese's mom at the front of the massive tent. The white monstrosity seats about two hundred people. Even in the middle of her land, there are a few people on horseback talking to each other as they continue moving around the property, making last-minute adjustments to the event.

"So where's your guy?" Mack asks after a while.

"You know? I really don't want to ta—"

"Talk about it? I know. But, I think it's funny how, once again, I'm here and he isn't. Why do you put your faith in a man who can never show up for you?"

"You don't know what you're talking about, Mack."

"Don't I? I would never stand you up. I never have. Even after years of coming in as the consolation prize — I'm here."

"Mack," I sigh. I don't know if I'm actually calm enough to have this conversation but he asked for it. There's no getting around what Mack wants. "Can you not see how fucked up that is? You're not a consolation prize. You should be someone's gold medal. I wished for so long that I could be that person, but I'm not. I can't do that to you. I don't want to keep doing that to you. I can't give you what you want. I'm not her."

His voice is a little too loud when he responds, cheeks going pink. "And I'm not him. But still, you're so blind as to think he will be the one when it's been me all along."

I stand from my chair and pull him up with me. We garner a few looks at Chandie is mid-speech and I apologize quietly. Holding tight to Mack's arm, I walk him over to the back side of the tent where no one is likely to hear us.

"Listen to me, Mack. Listen and process before you respond." I wait for him to nod his head. He looks into my eyes for a beat before crossing his arms and agreeing, reluctantly. "We cannot be together again. Not ever. When I needed you to be a support to me, your wife at the time, you could not do it. I was struggling. My depression was at an all-time high. I woke up and went to bed crying, in secret, because you wanted me to be happy when I wasn't. To walk it off like my mental health was taxing on you. You don't get it. You never have. I couldn't be... I couldn't be me. There is nothing wrong with not being happy all the time. I am a person with depression. Sometimes, I am able to fake it. I've learned to keep it to myself to hide from friends and dad, while he was alive. It's something I've been managing on my own without medication. My brain chemistry does not allow me to just walk it off." He shifts uncomfortable but I have to keep going now that I'm on a roll. I've been responsible for his false hope. I need to relinquish the guilt I carry and cut this off completely.

"Introducing all those new hormones and bodily changes with our pregnancy almost broke me. What I wanted most was for you to support me. And you couldn't—didn't know how. Even years of being married never prompted you to see past the facade. You saw what you wanted. You saw how you won me and that I was a trophy. Gold and shiny on the outside when I was rusty and falling apart inside. I thought that was what I wanted. To be treated 'normally'." I take a stabling breath. I force his eyes to mine with a hand on his face. "I'm not weak. I'm not broken. I'm just a person and I'm trying. I thought I wanted to be on this pedestal you put me on. That I deserved it after everything that went down with Ty. But I deserved to be human more. To feel like I could come to you when I was down and you be a comfort for me. I didn't."

"I don't know what to say." He sits in the grass looking defeated. I feel a little better that maybe this time what I'm saying is going to stick. "How come you never said this before?"

"I'm sorry." I fidget with my dress while I think of a response. All the steam was gone from my earlier confession. "I tried... I didn't know how."

"No, Mel. I'm sorry. I knew you were sad... I just—I never knew it was..."

"Depression."

"And he knew." He says, not asks.

It was never a secret to him. I feel even more sad that I haven't heard from him in two days. "Yes."

"I miss every goddamn thing. Fuck. I just thought it was your break up with him... and then when Phil died that made sense to me. But with Callan, I thought that was our fresh start. I thought we could move forward."

"I will always have love for you, Mack. You were the reason I survived for so long, but I couldn't be the woman you needed. We both needed more."

"Doesn't change the fact that he's still not here now."

"Doesn't mean that you need to be either. Maybe he and I are just never meant to be... That is something I will have to face on my own. I have to learn that." I didn't want to but if it came down to it, I would have to find a way to move on that did not involve hurting someone else.

CHAPTER 51

Melody

REESE RIDES INTO THE ceremony on horseback. Her long train blows in the wind behind her as she approaches the altar built specifically for this wedding on the Ranch. The matching bejeweled and pearled cowboy hat she wears has a sheer veil that billows elegantly around her.

Her dad comes to help her down from the horse carefully. In her second trimester now, her belly pokes through the tulle of her skirt and makes her look even more like a radiant goddess with her dark hair flowing in waves down her back. It's the sweetest moment her and her dad share before the music starts and she walks down the aisle. Even his cane is decorated to match the decor of the event. It's a beautiful moment that I'm so grateful to be a part of. Looking over to Cory, he wipes the corner of his eye as Reese nears. Reese beams, but her watery eyes make my own start to smart. When she reaches us at the large archway, the officiant begins the ceremony. She leans over to say something to Cory that makes him laugh. They laugh together and I smile at their happiness.

A real smile.

There is no facade here. I am genuinely so happy that the two of them found each other. They both deserve the love they share.

There have been times in the past few weeks that I felt like some wicked witch because I couldn't be there for my friends in the way that I thought I should. Everything that I thought I was carefully concealing but I truly wasn't. I haven't been myself. Avoiding my friends. And then keeping everything from them. There are still many things I haven't shared but it doesn't gnaw at me like it was before. I have Ty to thank for that.

This ceremony is picturesque and everyone here is here to celebrate—including me.

Held in the tent we had the rehearsal in, I sit patiently through the tearful speeches and a final toast to the newly married couple. Drea and Clo shared such sweet words for them. My dislike for public speaking of every kind was acknowledged and I was able to skip participating in that part of the event.

I'm on the far end of the table next to a woman I faintly recognize from the bachelorette party. My saving grace from having to admit that I was not paying attention to introductions the other day is the name cards that I know Clo painstakingly crafted for each one of us in her beautiful calligraphy. *Cameron "Cammie" Clyfford* is staring dreamily at someone at the table where all the ranch hands are currently conversing. I nudge her gently. "I think you might want to pick up your jaw before someone besides me sees you..." I tease.

Me? Teasing? I know I must be feeling better.

Cammie startles and then sips from her champagne glass. "Thanks," she says under her breath. I don't know how you all survive being surrounded by the cowboys all day. What is in the water here?"

I chuckle at her observation, "I remember thinking the same thing when I first moved here." Her hair is gelled back on one side with a beautiful arrangement of coordinated flowers in her bouncy curls. I recognize that it looks like the boutonnieres that the groomsmen all had for the wedding. "I love that you did this. It's so pretty."

She pats the flowers and smiles, "Thanks. You said you moved here? I just assumed everyone was from Alpenglow Ridge. You all seem so close."

"Oh, no. I moved here from Houston about ten years ago. Where are you from?"

She blows a raspberry, "Portland. My parents thought I was nuts for going into hippotherapy when I never rode a horse before but I cannot say that I'm upset I chose it. Reese's MHA program is the first to take me on without years and years of experience."

"She must have seen something in you. My friend doesn't trust easily. Masons' Horsing Around is her baby." She agreed, thoughtfully. We talk over our meals as my other friends mingle about with the other guests.

I haven't seen Tyson, Zeke, or Robert, but that can't be unusual for the band to only be there for the entertainment instead of the full ceremony. I wait for the band to be introduced or start setting up, but there is no one there. After eating, music begins to play over on the dance floor they've constructed but still no band. The first dance with Cory and Reese begins and still no band.

I start to worry now. I haven't heard anything from Tyson and now he's missing from the event entirely. I flit around the wedding guests looking for the woman in charge of it all.

"Where's the band?" I ask Clo when I find her talking with Jan and Sammie, Cory's aunts.

Clo excuses herself from the conversation after the two older women greet me and wander off to another chat. Her hostess's face drops into a scowl. "Your guess is as good as mine. No one is answering their phones. I had a playlist ready to go for after their set so I was able to recover quickly. I'm so gonna fight Ty the next time I see him."

"He's not answering your calls," I mumble to no one in particular. Clo has wandered off with one of the waiters to a different problem that is more pressing. I don't bother catching up. I return to my place setting and watch the revelry unfolding around me. This time I don't feel like an outsider. I find myself wishing that Ty was here, if not for the music but so we could be out there dancing together. I try calling him again but it goes straight to voicemail.

There could be any number of reasons as to why he's not answering his phone. Maybe he really has made it big and is too busy to do wedding ceremonies anymore. He's not just a local act. He's crossed state lines a long time ago. Like he said, Nashville is where serious Country musicians live. *Or he's finally given up on trying to make it work.* If that's what he wants, I will find a way to be okay with that.

I plop into my bed when I make it home from the busy day. A sigh of relief escapes me that quickly becomes a hollow feeling. I had been thinking about Ty all night but something just doesn't feel right. He doesn't break promises. And no phone call or text to at least apologize? Maybe not to me, but at least to his sister who he knew worked hard to pull this wedding off. It just doesn't sit right.

I hate admitting it. *I really do.*

But I am thoroughly regretting pushing him away. Protecting myself was the main objective. I didn't like what he was saying. I didn't like how closely his words sounded to the ones in my head.

He needs more.

He needed more than I could give him.

Tyson Abrams was too big to remain in Alpenglow Ridge with me.

He said we would make things work but he left. I couldn't hear anything past, he needed to leave me to get what he really wanted in life, the fame and recognition. He needed to grow. I couldn't stop him from that. I couldn't handle that truth and I didn't want to see him chip away at us slowly when I could just cut it off right away. Could that have been the wrong approach?

Yes.

I miss him and now every inch of this house has a little piece of him here. There is no room in this house where I don't have a positive memory of him.

Him cooking for and with me in the kitchen after a long day at work. Him holding me on the couch when I was too sad to move. Him making me moan in the shower, the living room, the dining room, and here in this bed.

Him kissing my tears away and helping me get out of my head when it was too dark to see on my own.

I can't believe we left everything the way we did. This time, it's all my doing.

I miss him and I don't know what I can do about it, again.

CHAPTER 52

Melody

WE ALL SIT AROUND Chloe's fireplace, minus Reese, watching movies and eating ice cream. Clo flips over to the news between movies because she needs to see if the anchor she follows online has a new hairstyle. "She normally puts Queen Latifah to shame with the silk presses but she came last week with some butterfly braids and the co-anchor was sick about it. He kept fumbling around his words. It was hilarious and live! Now that's entertainment," she says.

The anchor did have a new style but we don't get a chance to acknowledge it because what she's informing us about is much more harrowing. A mugshot of Jordan Hurst is on one side of the screen and the other side has a photo of Tyson from a photoshoot he was in. "We have been following this story for several days as more and more information comes in. Beloved country singer Jordan Hurst has been arrested on charges of aggravated kidnapping and assault with a deadly weapon after police apprehended him outside of Miles & Miles primary recording studio on Friday morning. Footage was released to support the claims of his former bandmate and Country's newest chart-topping lead singer, Tyson Abrams. He has since been admitted to a local hospital for treatment, the nature of which is unknown. This video may be alarming to some as we see Abrams being grabbed by two individuals, who were working for Hurst, and put into the black vehicle. Abrams was later found by a staff member at the hotel he was staying in. She freed him from the chair Hurst and his associates secured him to with zip ties. We will have more for you as the details of this case continue to unravel."

The silence in the room is absolutely deafening. It's too quiet.

My phone rings and though I don't recognize the number, I answer immediately. "Melody. " His croaky voice comes over the line. *Tyson.* He sounded like everything that was on the news is true. I look up to my friends whose faces all look me over.

"I'm gonna step outside for a bit." I don't bother with anything but my shoes when I rush out of Clo's house.

"I saw what happened on the news," I mumble into the phone, stock still. "Where are you? Are you okay?" I try to keep the panic from my voice but it's very present. He's very quiet and I don't know if that's good or bad. "Please, Ty. Tell me where you are." My voice is watery and it sounds as helpless as I feel.

"I can't lose you," his scratchy voice says. Each syllable grates against my heart.

The tears are already running from my eyes and down my face to my neck. I don't bother wiping them. I have to get to him. "You aren't losing me. Just tell me where you are. I need to see you."

"It hurts to talk," he manages, "Zeke's here."

There is a bit of rustling before Zeke's voice comes onto the line. "Mel? He lost his phone at some point last weekend..." Zeke recounts most of what went down at the studio between Tyson and Jordan. I get light headed as he rattles off the injuries that Tyson has sustained.

...bullet wound to the right flank...

...bruised windpipe and potential paralysis of his vocal chords...

...concussion...

...severe hearing loss in his right ear, potentially permanent...

He sounds choked up, himself. I don't know how I'm still standing when Zeke sends me the information for the hospital where I can find Ty.

Everything is a blur of tears and movement when I relay as much as I can to the girls inside before Clo and I board a plane to see him later that night.

———◆◆◆◆◆———

THE BANDAGE ON TY'S forehead is the first detail that I take in after being led to his room by the nurse on duty when we arrive. The thick white bandage circles around one ear with more gauze and such wrapped around it. When the nurse steps aside, his eyes water as he takes me in. I rush to the bedside table. It hasn't been that long since I've had him in my arms but I inhale as much of the scent of him as I can. It's mostly gone with the antiseptic hospital smell taking over most of my senses. I'm still grateful to have him here anyway. My arms can't wrap around him much because of all his bandages but any contact with him is good enough. "That was a lot more than a misunderstanding between you too," I huff out between sniffles. Anger at what Jordan did to him is thick in my voice.

"Damn straight," Clo says from behind me. I move to Ty's side so that he can see his sister fully. "He's lucky he's behind bars because he would have to deal with me." She squeezes his arm and he smiles back at her. "Mom and Dad are gonna be here tomorrow. I'll give you two some time but I'll be outside. I love you, big bro." She kisses his cheek before raising her eyebrows at me.

The whole flight here, we talked about how I needed to be clear and direct about what I want and stand up for myself. I didn't expect I would be the main one talking.

He points to the notepad beside him on the table. I grab it and the pen. He taps the page and there's already something written there. I read the words aloud. "I wanted to tell you before it hit the news. I have to rest my throat and I can only hear out of one ear for now."

Dragging the chair in the room close to where his bed, but also on the opposite side of the bandaged ear, I ask, "What did you want to tell me?"

He writes on the pad again and I read it aloud. "Do you remember my eighteenth?"

I grab a hold of his hand holding the pen. "About your mom?"

A sad smile lingers on his lips, but he shakes his head.

I suggest instead, "You asked me if I would still perform if no one came to see me."

He nods, writing, "Yes. Would you?" He looks up at me with an inscrutable expression. My heart cracks that little bit more as I think about the regret he must be feeling right now. None of this is his fault for pursuing what he loves, and getting caught up with someone so horrible.

"I don't know. I haven't given professional dance much thought in a long time. Life kinda got in the way," I answer, honestly. What Jordan did to him was disgusting. I am still in shock that he survived. Grateful as hell, but it's still a miracle. "I don't know if I've said this but I always considered you to be strong and good—through and through. I've admired how committed you were to your music. Even when I hated you, I envied your accomplishments. Not because I wanted them for myself, but because you made it look easy. You are so talented, Tyson Abrams. Don't let him take that from you." I wipe at the corner of my eye with a knuckle. "I never thought I would do you any justice on your arm after you left."

His thumb catches a stray tear. He clucks his tongue, "No" he mouths. Our eyes catch and he holds my gaze for a moment before writing, "Any strength I have now is for you, Melody. I might be strong, but not very smart it turns out. I wished I had done things differently."

"I wished things had been different too. Everything with Jordan was not your fault. And before... we were young, foolish, and scared and now we know better." I shake my head, "I know better and I'm going to work harder on us. I believe in us. Our happiness and our love. There is no way you can get rid of me now."

He tries to scoff, then winces. He shakes his head, vehemently. Extending his thumb and index fingers, he thrust his hand toward me, raising his pinky. "I love you," he signs.

"I love you too." I blubber. Doing my best not to hurt him, I hug him close to my body. I'm hit with happy memories of all our life together. It's a mix-mash of highs and lows that I wouldn't trade for the world.

I stay at his bedside through various family members, friends and staff. And when it's time for him to be released from the hospital, I help him move into my house in Alpenglow Ridge.

* * *

AFTER MANY YEARS WITHOUT it, I am talking to a therapist online. Tyson may or may not have been the influence on this since he also has a therapist he's seeing. We have both been through the works and it's nice to have someone who is only there to help recover from that.

While there is no magic bandaid for anxiety and depression. Sometimes therapy can work wonders. Sometimes medication, in combination, will help. Changing my relationship with those tender parts of me, giving them the space needed, and acknowledging their presence in my life is my biggest accomplishment. My fear of the worst, the sadness of the losses I've taken, and the defense mechanisms I developed to protect myself in the best way I knew how are a part of me. My therapist and I are working towards finding new ways to cope with my fluctuating emotions and fortifying the relationships in my life that I value.

My mental health is, at last, an uphill battle and no longer my most defining feature. Ty's support is such a big reason for that. I'm so happy to finally have him in my life again.

With him home, it had finally started to feel like luck was on our side again.

After three weeks, he was able to talk again without discomfort and his hearing had returned in his right ear. Miracles. So many miracles. It was such a relief to hear his voice again. He began seeing a physical therapist who worked specifically with trauma survivors. His voice is his instrument and it terrified him that he was in danger of losing that ability. With how we took everything so slowly, he has been able to sing and reach a similar range to where he was before, even able to sink into a slightly lower register that made my panties dampen when he practices at home. His rehearsal set-up had transitioned to a new place in my house since I never used the "office" the spare room that was once going to be a nursery. His guitars and other instruments hang on the wall with some soundproofing panels. Seeing him on the stool working on some new music lights my soul up in a way I couldn't imagine before.

After a month and a half, he felt more comfortable moving around and mostly healed from his gunshot wound. Thankfully there were no fragments as the bullet went clear through his side. The wound was low enough in his side that it didn't affect his breathing for singing, but it was more difficult to hold his guitar until recently. The smile he gave me when he could rest it comfortably against his body, spoke volumes. I was a blubbering mess, kissing his face before he got to the end of *His Home and Mine* with the lyrics he has changed for us. I'll never get over how much I love his version more. When he gets to my new favorite part, in his new deeper range, I'm simply melting for him, pressing and rubbing my thighs together until he finishes because I don't want to miss a single moment.

My life, our life, and my love, our love,
Grows stronger with every moment we spend in this home.
This home is mine.
Whatever miracle I've been granted, I never take it for granted.
This home is mine.

The best aspect of his recovery is getting to hold him without the fear that I'm hurting him. Even better with him being able to squeeze me tight and kiss my neck until I'm so wet and begging. Today is one of those days.

His movements are slow and deliberate as he sets his guitar on its stand. I hop from my seat over to him and loop my arms around his neck. I'm not shy about wrapping my leg around his body, rubbing my panty-covered center over his thigh. "Please tell me that I'll get to have you inside me today... Your doctor cleared you for physical activity. I want you bad. I promise to take it slow. Please..." I look up at him and pout.

Tyson kisses me fiercely, nipping my pouting lower lip. "You know I can not resist you when you beg me, Melody." His fingers gently shove my panties aside to glide through my lips, collecting all the arousal weeping from my core.

"But I need you. Would you like me to show you just how much?" I writhe on his fingers, hoping one will slip inside. We've been like teenagers with how close we have gotten to actually having sex to choose something non-penetrative instead. The man is still very good with his hands but I know he wants more.

"I can already feel how much," he says before I feel his erection press into my hip.

His sweatpants and boxers are off and I'm entranced watching him stroke his self. The dark head was swollen with need and glistening. I drop to my knees to lick up that little bead of precum. Shivers race down my spine at the first taste of him and my fingers continue to the job he started between my own legs.

"Let me see those," he says, eyes never leaving where my mouth stretches around his impressive length. He sucks on my fingers and I match the pace he sets, taking him further into my mouth with each dip of my head. He moans around my fingers and I think I might come just from the sounds that practically vibrates down my arm.

Tyson pulls me off of his dick to his mouth. We kiss and I crawl over his lap. I don't put my weight down fully. His erection weighs heavy on my ass with each pulse of his desire. I break our kiss only to murmur, "Please," against his lips.

I feel him smile against my mouth, moving my hips with both hands over his lap until his head is pressing at my clit. I cry out from the unexpected pleasure of his warmth rubbing against my own. Moving my own hips, I manage to get his notched right at the entrance of my pussy.

Our eyes lock. His browns on my own. "Take all of me, my Melody. Let me fill you up." His hand cups my face as a single tear escapes at the sheer delight of how good it feels to have him sliding deeper and deeper inside me. I kiss him again when he's fully sheathed and my ass is on his thighs.

Our tongues swirl around each other's mouths, both seeking to have more of the other's taste. I'm feral by the time he breaks the kiss to nip at my neck. I rock on his lap, finding a rhythm that brings that moan I love from his lips.

I ride him slow and steady, telling him how proud I am of his recovery. For believing in us. For being the sexiest man I've ever seen with the vocal cords to make me this wet for him. There is nothing sexier than hearing him moan in my ear and grip my hips while I bring us both to climax. Repeating the same movement until sweat beads up on his forehead, I'm rewarded with more of that delicious sound. His *voice* is my undoing.

I'm the first to let go and my eyes flutter close as my heart beats out of my chest to get closer to this beautiful man beneath me. He flips me onto the oversize lounge chair and pumps his cum into me, filling me just the way he likes.

My thighs are weak but I stand, feeling the mixture of our cum runs down my legs. Ty leans forward to rub the mixture into my legs. I give him a questioning look and he shrugs. "Did I ever tell you how much I love your thighs?" he asks.

"Yea..." I respond, still not knowing where this is going.

"I have some primal need to mark them as mine. Damn, I was dumb to not have you riding me this whole time." He looks into my eyes. "I need you to do that again." A big smile I can't resists tops off his request and I'm eager to do just what he asks of me.

CHAPTER 53

Melody

IT'S MY FAVORITE TIME of day—the gloaming—where the sky is a mixture of navy, purple, and smears of pink. Sitting on my little conversation set was different tonight.

"So this is the legendary tea that caught Melody a Country Legend?" Reese says holding her glass of tea out in front of her. Biting the lemon slice, she hums in appreciation before dropping the rest of it back into her glass. Her belly pokes noticeably in the dress she's wearing as she paces back and forth on the porch. Apparently, she can't be comfortable doing much of anything besides moving around. In her third trimester now—she could be days away from delivery.

"Ever heard that it's not the ingredients, it's the method?" Drea asks Reese with a wink in my direction.

I smile back at her, "Something like that." Tapping my nails on my own glass, I add, "I think it's a nostalgia thing for him."

Chloe leans her head on the siding of my house in her matching chair to mine. "You two were cute when we were young. It's nice to see you two together again."

Together as in: committed in a relationship. The fact still makes me want to pinch myself. In the months that he spent recovering from the damage

Jordan had inflicted upon him, three of the five singles he recorded in Nashville soared on the charts and are still sitting in the top one hundred of the Country genre. *The Melody I Lost* went platinum with a million copies sold. I guess all publicity really is good publicity. Jordan will never work in Country music again after multiple big names in the industry showed their support for Tyson. Tyson started a foundation that brought awareness to both gun safety and music literacy for young artists.

My life had become a cycle of kissing Tyson backstage or kissing him when he returned back home to me. Like now. He's coming home any minute now.

Drea pulls her hair out of the bun it was in and fishes a clip out of her purse. "Agreed. If there was a better choice for you Mel, I have no idea who it could be. I've seen you genuinely smile more since he came back to Alpenglow than I have since we've known you." She clips the hair into place and sighs. "Maybe I need a Country star too."

Reese waves Drea's statement away like its a pesky fly in her face. Her pacing halts in front of me. "I like that look on you." Her black curls blow in the evening breeze and I return her smile. The girls hum in agreement with her, adding their own smiles.

I'm grateful for these women. They are my tribe and my support. *My family.*

I take a deep breath to prepare myself for the conversation I have been putting off for as long as possible. It will never be the right time. No better time than the present. With advice from my therapist and so, so much encouragement from Tyson, I stop fidgeting and blurt out, "I had a miscarriage." There is no finesse or elegance to the statement. But the words are out and I can't take them back. I squeeze my eyes closed to stop admonishing myself for not finding a more tactful way to approach the subject.

It takes a few moments of deep breathing before I'm able to open my eyes. When I do, I'm met with shock and concern from these three.

The first to speak is Drea, she scoots her chair closer to mine. The sound grates, but her hand on mine feels as soothing as the gesture was meant to be. "When did this happen?"

My gaze falls to the wooden planks under my flats. "I was fifteen weeks when I lost him. It was the day I filed for divorce from Mack."

Three identical gasps follow.

"You didn't tell us, " Clo says. It's not a question because I obviously did not. I'm still struggling now that I've said something. There's pain in the lines of her face that I can't look at for more than a moment.

I fiddle with the aluminum straw in my glass, eyes downcast as the truth settles around us. "No. I didn't."

"But... why not? Is this why you never wanted to talk about your divorce?" Drea asks.

Responding simply, "It's impossible to talk about one without the other."

"What can we do? Does Ty know?" Reese questions.

"He and my therapist are the only ones who know, outside of my doctor and Mack. It wasn't legally in our papers but I asked Mack not to say anything since our pregnancy was a secret either way."

Reese is back to pacing. "I can't believe he kept this from me!" After a moment of stomping her feet, she amends, "Well I can if you asked him not to but sisters should get special privileges." She huffs a final time. "What can we do, Melly?" She asks again.

"I honestly don't know. I've been keeping this secret for so long it was eating away at me. His name was Callan. For just a moment I was a mom and now I'm a person who has slowly come to terms with the fact that I am not one any longer."

"Whether you lose your child or not, you are still a mother. God, my heart hurts for you so much, Bon. I can't believe you went through this alone. I wish we could have been there for you. Everything makes sense now about why you were so skittish about the divorce and then..."Clo cuts herself off. Fierce determination overtakes her previously gloomy expression. "Never mind that. Come here. This warrants a hug."

She stands, walking over to me. I stand too, overwhelmed with so many big emotions that I can't place a specific one. Her arms are the first around me. Then, Drea hugs me from behind. Finally, Reese comes over to wrap her arms as best as she can with her belly poking into me.

"I've never cared what Tyson says, you are my sister. I love you no matter what."

"Me too. I love you." Drea agrees.

"Me three, I love you most," Reese says and Clo rolls her eyes.

"Can you just be a little less right now?" Clo asks the pregnant woman who is back to wearing a hole in my porch with her back and forth.

"I'm literally three right now." She deadpans.

"You said you're talking to your therapist about it. How are you feeling now?"

"I'm feeling better. Had I been around Reese being this pregnant around the time of her wedding, I don't think I could have been present for it. That fact saddens me but I think things are better." I shake my head, "No, I know things are better. I made the best choice I could for myself by getting an IUD and my divorce was finalized. It's not permanent but I don't think babies are in the cards for me. I have to protect my mental health. The last time I miscarried destroyed me. It's been almost three years and I'm still deeply wounded by losing Callan. There's more to life than children." Thinking back to what Ty told me the first time I shared about him, I add, "He is an angel who received his wings sooner than I wanted. I'm thankful I can make the choice of whether to go through that process again. For now, I'm not. I am happy just seeing my healing progress and creating a life I love with Ty."

Reese swipe at a tear. "That's beautiful Melly. Looks like healing if I've ever seen it before."

The rumbling sound of Old Red comes down my driveway. Wesson stretches a paw out of the front door and waits by the step for the only man he's ever cared about. Ty's face breaks into a grin when he opens his truck door and hops down. The cat walks back and forth, impatient for his cuddles.

Ty scoops him up and comes to me immediately after. He kisses me deeply, tongue sweeping in my mouth, making my toes curl in my shoes. He breaks our kiss and I feel a little woozy. He then kisses the top of Wesson's head and the cat settles into the crook of his arm, content. His other arm snakes around my waist keeping me close to his body.

"Well, that's one way to dismiss your guests." Clo glares at him, "Hi and bye bro. I'll be by when the reunion isn't so filled with sexual tension." She puts the brush she was using away in her purse before saying to me, "Thank you for opening up to us. Please remember that you can tell me anything. Call me whenever. Especially if it's juicy."

"Okay," I chuckle at Clo as she hugs me goodbye, ignoring her brother's lack of easing up with his hold on me.

"I can read a room," Reese says, "And the room is getting very hot. I'm gonna get home to my herd." She hugs me, as well, but Ty allows her to hug me with none of the resistance he had with his sister. "Facetime me when you get a chance." I nod in response to her before she waddles back to her truck.

Drea squeezes my hand, "I'll see you at work tomorrow," she says before leaving just Ty and me on the porch.

Note to self: I love my girls.

"I'm proud of you," Ty says when we make our way inside to plop onto the couch.

"For what?"

He rubs soothing circles on my thigh, "For finally telling them."

"Oh... that." My lips quirk to the side. "How did you know?"

"I could tell. You look a lot lighter, " he responds.

I shove one of his shoulders, softly. "You can't tell that."

"I can..." He smirks. "Okay, fine. Chloe texted me on my way home." I laugh, a full-bodied sound that only makes his smirk grow to a full smile.

"Home, huh?" I'll never get tired of him calling this house his home.

"Wherever you are." He clarifies.

"Wherever we are." I confirm.

CHAPTER 54

Melody

"MEL?" HIS EYEBROWS PINCH when he sees my face. I am likely the last person that Mack expects on his doorstep. But it's about time I do this.

"Yea... Can I come in?"

"Sure." The door swings open behind him and I walk in.

Deep breaths, Melody. Deep. deep breaths.

"You want something? Water or, I don't know, a beer?"

"No, I just want to talk... If that's alright."

He looks a bit stunned but gathers his composure quickly. "Really?" I nod and he walks out to his back porch. He's living in one of the condos on the opposite side of town. It's very much what I would expect for a bachelor to live in. I asked Reese for his address the other day so that I could have this conversation with him. It's long overdue. I swallow down the pressing guilt and remember what my therapist said.

You can choose to accept guilt or question the source and make a resolution for yourself. Tackle the problem head-on and make a decision that you can stand behind.

"So, what's on your mind?"

"A lot, actually. There's a lot on my mind and I think it would be unfair to leave you out of the journey I've been going through."

He swallows and looks down at his work boots. I caught him right after his shift at the Ranch. "Is that right?" he asks and I nod again. He nods back and crosses his arms over his chest.

"First, I want to say thank you. You were my friend when I wasn't even a friend to myself. You were a companion and you held me up when no one else did. What we had saved me in so many ways and I'm sorry for how it ended–how I ended it. I wish I could have been honest with myself and with you so that you didn't end up as collateral in my self-destruction."

There's utter silence for a few moments. I twist my sweater in my lap and resist the urge to fill the uncomfortable silence. Mack bites his lips as he processes my words. He looks a lot better than I remember him looking. That's been an ongoing thing, the improvement. I wonder if he's happy. I hope he is.

"I appreciate you saying that, Mel. I thought about what you said at the reception. I thought about it long and hard. For all intents and purposes, I don't think there's anything to forgive. I really don't. We got married too young, made mistakes. Hell, I knew you weren't over Ty and I still thought that would just go away. Despite all that, I thought that maybe you could still move on and love me. If I loved you hard enough, you would forget."

"I couldn't. That's my problem, and I made it yours, too. It never should have been. I wasn't a good friend or partner to you." I take a slow, deep breath. "I likely don't deserve it, but I'd like to be a better friend to you moving forward."

Mack huffs out a laugh. "I don't think we were very good friends to each other. We could give it a try, in time. Gonna need more time to sit with this and figure it all out. You know?"

"Yea. I know." If he decides that he doesn't want anything to do with me again, then I'll have to make my peace with that. It's not uncommon for divorced people to be completely gone from each other's lives. That is probably the norm. We have nothing but time to figure it out. My next request is not going to go over as easily. "I know you and Ty have beef and that is likely my fault. I'm asking that you give him a chance to mend what I broke between you two. Before I came into the picture, you were good friends. It's been years but if you're willing to forgive me, maybe you can forgive him too."

"I don't think so." He scoffs, adding, "That's not fucking likely. There's too much between us just to be water under the bridge. If that's really why you're here then you can just leave."

"That's not why I'm here," I say, moving past his rough rejection and pushing forward. I didn't imagine that years of animosity would be resolved in one statement but I want to put the thought out there. Tyson will be pissed that I spoke for him but it at least makes me feel a little better to know that I tried. This will not be the last time I make the suggestion for both of them. If I can be the crack in the foundation, maybe I can be the olive branch as well. "My second point has nothing to do with Ty. I want to say that I'm sorry for not being there for you when we... lost Callan. I wasn't stable enough to be a support to you like you were for me, even when you didn't necessarily know how. You still tried in the best way you could. I didn't even do that for myself. I didn't realize it before, but I forced you to go through everything alone. It wasn't right. You respected my decision to keep our angel baby a secret. All that grief," I shake my head, wipe a stray tear and continue. "You deserve the right to process that loss however you need to. It's been years and I still can't think about Callan without crying. I just want to say that if you need anyone to talk to, I'm here for you. I will make time."

He seems less agitated than before, but I can see his jaw working. "It was hard. I almost lost my mind. I couldn't understand what you were going through but I knew if it was even a bit comparable to what I was... it had to be bad. I still get sad thinking about him. Sometimes, I'm grateful that people didn't know so I could have my own time to grieve. It's better they thought I was a drunk who lost his wife so they'd leave me alone to process. Then all that went down with Alex... I got dealt a shit hand. Not gonna lie. Like it probably is in all small towns that gossip got old and it's not so bad now." Mack looks off into the distance for a moment and I allow him to gather his thoughts. This is the most we've talked in years that hasn't become awkward or painful for me. Hearing him acknowledge these things aloud is what I needed. I've only guessed at what it was like for him and I could see some things, but I'm not responsible for all that happened to him—like he isn't responsible for all that happened to me. Talking about it together is what we should have been doing from the beginning but I wasn't ready.

I am now.

He taps on the table a few times. "I didn't handle everything in the best way. I know that now... I couldn't stop myself before anyway. Never have I ever stopped caring about you, Mel. Even when you picked him over me. I just wanted to be there for you when he wasn't here... I was the only one trying to bring any light to your life in the only ways I knew how. Fucking hell." He rubs a frustrated hand over his face. "You've got him back now. Hopefully, he's doing a better job than I ever did."

Biting my cheek to keep from waxing poetic about just how much, I give him a nod instead. "I am happy," I whisper.

He nods a few times, before standing and dusting his hands off on his thighs. "Well, I could sure use a beer after all that. QBs?"

"Sure."

✦•••✦

Tyson

I SEE ALL HEADS turn when my girl enters the double doors with her ex-husband. There's a little hush that comes over the bar. I stand immediately to meet her by the door. I give him a nod of acknowledgment without another word. When we reach the tall top with our other friends. Tony, Drea, Quincy, Clo, Taylor, Ashley, Zeke, and Robert share a few pitchers of beer. I don't know who had the foresight but Mack sits at the opposite side of the table as me and Mel. For once, there are actually enough seats for all of us here because Cory and Reese were at home with their twins, Kelsie and Kyra.

Conversation floats around us as our friends drink and share their stories of the week but I have just one person I want to talk to right now.

"So, how did it go?" I ask Mel, who sips a tea.

She shrugs, turning to face me fully. "It went well, I think." Her lips quirked to the side, "Better than I expected it to. I am an olive branch." Her little mischievous smile gives me pause.

"Melody... what does that mean?"

"Nothing right now, but it may in time." I wrap an arm around her waist to bring her closer to my body. She giggles and relents when I start kissing her on the spot at her neck that makes her squeal. Though she doesn't hate PDA anymore, she would never be okay with moaning my name in the bar if I keep this up. "Okay, okay!" She pinches my side when I let her go. "I may have suggested that you and Mack mend your relationship if he and I could mend ours."

My sweet girlfriend is always thinking about others before herself, much to my chagrin. "And why would you do that?" I whisper in her ear. She shivers and I trail my finger down her spine.

I've been home for a few days after having spent a month visiting some of the amazing facilities that are housing my foundations. It's amazing what adding music to a kid's life can do to improve so many other aspects of their lives. It's fulfilling to give someone the opportunities I had to make for myself. After making the decision to join JT with Jordan Hurst, charmed by his name and the prospect of what he could offer me, only to nearly die in the process is not something I want for anyone else. I can't promise them fame, but I can show them how to foster a love for music in more creative ways.

Fame is not all it's cracked up to be anyway. It'll be a while before I'm out touring. Writing and recording music when I can return home to my girl is pretty damn good for me right now. I love playing to a crowd, and I love when Melody can be there in the crowd or side stage with me. The next time I'm booking tour dates, she'll be the first one to sign off on when and where we go. I want to take her everywhere.

"You know why, baby. He said no, but I figured I'd try anyway." I reel back and she giggles.

"No?" She nods, still giggling. "He said no *to me*? Fucking jerkoff."

"I'm confident you two will get there." She pats my thigh.

"Don't say that like I want it." I've been keeping up appointments with my therapist to work on trust and surviving the traumatic experience of being kidnapped. It's been a journey, to say the least, but it's helped me to see that not every battle is worth fighting. Some are worth it more than others. I'm not sure if it's worth it to allow Mack back into my life like he was before. But I can see that it makes Melody happy to try healing her relationship with him, and that makes me happy. I'm still so proud of her for having the hard conversations with the people in her life besides me.

"Don't you?" She lifts a suspecting eyebrow at me. "Why are you so upset if you don't want it? Be nice." She boops my nose like she does to Wesson and I grumble, sipping from my beer.

"Don't worry, Mel. We'll keep him in line." Robert says from across the table, winking in her direction.

"I'd love to see you try, Rob. Stop winking at my girl." Melody giggles some more and the sound of her happiness spurs me on. I whisper, "That ass is mine when we get home," before nipping her ear. She covers another giggle by sipping her tea, moving my hand from her waist to her thigh. I will be between these later. I'm already counting down the minutes.

"Oh damn. Another 'down boy' from Ty. You really have been racking those up, huh?" Zeke says, clapping Robert on the back with a laugh.

"Excuse me," Sarah Jane says with a tray full of bright blue shots. We turn toward her standing there with an irritated expression on her face. "Eleven AMF shots for the table, courtesy of," she rolls her eyes, "The shot queen." Before passing the shots around to everyone gathered at the table.

Drea pops up to film the tray and everyone at the table. She raises her phone, on a Facetime call with Reese apparently. The shot queen, herself. "Bottoms up, bitches! Make bad choices in our honor! Or good ones..." She winks and everyone raises their glasses to the phone screen. "We can't be there right now, but since it's the first night where I can't make sure everyone is getting nice and inebriated, this rounds on me!"

I clink my glass to Melody's, then to everyone else's and we shoot them. Everyone winces at the liquor with a collective, "Oof" before returning to their other conversations. It's good to be home with friends again.

It's even better to be with my Melody.

CHAPTER 55

Melody, Nine Months Later

"Can I look now?"

"We're almost there. Just about." Tyson holds my hand and I follow him slowly. More awkward than I usually feel, so we have to be on unpaved ground wherever he's taken me. "Watch your feet."

"I hear the water... Is this the part where you chop me up and throw me into the river?"

He chuckles, "Will you just trust me?"

I pause, "I do trust you." He takes the bandana off my eyes. I blink a few times before I focus on his face.

His cheeks stretch to a wide grin. "Good. Do you want to take a look around?"

"Look around?" I lean around his big body and the gasp that escapes me can't be helped. "Tyson! You didn't." My eyes are glued to the building in front of me.

Massive Fir trees surround the two-story structure like I drew this up from my dreams. Most of the first floor is expansive windows that showcase a dance studio which makes me quicken my pace to get a better view inside.

His smug smirk is damn near audible as I jog up the path to the glass doors, trying to get a better view of the studio from the outside. "Do you think this will work?" He asks, unlocking and opening the door for me.

"Work?! This is amazing." I run my hands over the barre and touch the weight rack in the corner. "When did you..." My words catch over the emotion clogging my throat. It's not long before I feel those first tears start to blur my vision.

His arms come around me from behind as he watches us in the floor-to-ceiling mirrors. I wanted to show you after I purchased the land in September." He grimaces, "But then I was shot so we never made it back to the river. Gave me more time to actually expand on the idea."

"Is this—Tyson, is this our spot?" He nods his head, still smug as ever. "Show me, please."

He holds my hand again and leads me back out of the doors to the tree. Our initials are still carved there though it's a few feet higher than I remember. I trace over the initials and feel the rough texture under my fingertips.

"No one will ever have this place again. It's ours. My hope is that I can be a part of you thriving here with this little bit of my help."

"Little?" I jump on him. My arms circle his neck and he squeezes me tight to him. "This is incredible. Thank you, Tyson. this gift is so much more than I could have ever dreamed of." After all that went down and a lot of persuasion from Tyson, I got recertified to teach ballet. Finally, I left my job teaching at our old high school and waitressing. I have been between jobs since then.

"They'll be coming from all over to be trained by you, baby. Happy Birthday."

I flush under his praise. "Thank you... can you show me more?"

We walk through the studio to a small sitting area that leads to stairs. When he unlocks the door, I follow behind him. Squeezing his hand, my breath catches again. I might swallow my tongue next if he shocks me with one more thing.

"How did you get this?"

I walk over to the first massive frame. The lights shine down on it and reach out to touch the glass where the small signature is scrawled. Cressida Fletcher.

"When your dad passed, I figured he had to store them somewhere. I tracked down the storage cell and they were all there. Just had to find someone to restore and frame the ones that were in a little worse condition." My tears are coming in earnest now. I don't bother wiping them. "Was that okay?" he asks, a little unsure of himself.

"It's perfect, Ty." He shows me all the other paintings my mom poured over and I tell him about the ones I remember her painting. The memories come to me easily, but I don't feel the same immense sorrow I did when she passed. All those moments, that were lost in my mind from my own misery, are teased to the surface like a warm embrace from the woman who loved me more than anything. I welcome them all as he shows me more and more of them in the apartment.

I finally take a look at how it's decorated here, outside of just the art on the walls. Tyson sits on a sectional that faces the large window overlooking the river. "When you're ready we can replace all this furniture with your own or we can buy new ones. I don't care. I didn't know how you would like it."

"Oh, I love it all, Ty. This is an amazing, albeit very extravagant, birthday present." Hugging him around the waist, he holds me back. Amber and mahogany fill my senses and I sigh in relief.

"Here take a look at the kitchen, all new appliances." Pointing out details and special features of each one, I listen intently to his spiel.

It's kind of cute how he is geeking out over something so mundane and domestic. I look in the fridge which is already fully stocked with our favorites. When I close the door and turn around he's gone. "Tyson?"

"I'm in the bedroom," he calls from somewhere in the flat. I follow the sound of music that has started to play.

What could he be doing?

All of his old bedroom furniture is here. Complete with the headboard I loved. It's bright with a large bay style window that also faces the river.

There are a few more of my mom's smaller pieces on the walls. There's even a new cat tree for Wessie. "You know? This actually feels right. I liked the furniture from your apartment."

"You did?" I nod and he smiles his small smile. "I wish I would have known that." Walking over to it, I run my hand along the rustic dark wood. I turn again to see Tyson's kneeling there. My eyes zero in on his hands.

Is that?

"Melody." He looks up into my eyes and my heart squeezes tight in my chest. His hand shakes a little before he grabs mine in his. "We have so much history together and still so much ahead of us. I don't want there to be any questions as to where my intentions lie. I want you by my side. I want you as my partner. My best friend. To hold the most important place in my life no matter where our careers take us. Even if you end up with thirty cats."

I chuckle. "Why would I have so many cats?"

He smiles, eyes shining. "And yelling at stranger's kids to get off our lawn..."

"I don't care about the lawn. They better not get in our part of the river though." I huff, in mock annoyance.

"And especially when you get so invested in your choreo that you play the same repeating section of a song over and over until you figure out exactly what *your legs should be doing.*"

I laugh. "Okay, I am prone to doing that. Anything else?" My impatience showing in the way I bounce on the balls of my feet for him to continue.

"One last thing." He opens the box. "Will you marry me and make me the happiest guitar-strumming fool for the rest of our days?"

"Yes! Yes, forever." I yell, dropping to my knees in front of him. I hug him so hard that we fall over.

He kisses me softly for several moments and I forget all about everything else.

"I think I should put this on you now." He says from underneath me.

I straddle his waist and he reaches the box from where it's fallen beside us. "Right," my laugh is watery, brand-new happy tears already running.

The ring slide onto my finger with ease and I stare at the beautiful jewelry he picked for me. Two filagree bands twirl around each other in gold. The diamond on top is marquise cut with smaller oval diamonds like little leaves. It's beautiful and reminds me of something straight out of a fairytale. "I wish I had better words than—It's beautiful. But... it's beautiful, Tyson."

"Well, there are other words that I'd love to hear you say."

I quirk my head to the side, "Like what?"

"How about, "God, Yes. Tyson, I'm coming. Please, Tyson," in that order?" He smirks. I smack his chest playfully, pulling my dress over my head. He bites his lip. "Melody, where are your panties?"

"I don't know," I giggle, trying to get up from his lap. He grabs me around the waist before I'm able to get too far. I wrap my legs around him as we fall into bed.

He smacks my ass, "Hands and knees, baby."

Sneak Peek

DREA

"Mireya, I need you to get dressed. You have to get ready."

"But Mama, I'm watching a documentary on fast fashion. Did you know that more than eleven tons of clothes end up in our landfills every year? It's so sad. Just think, that tank top you made me throw away is now contributing to global warming. It's killing our planet."

I sigh, long and deep. "You will not use global warming as a way to guilt trip me," I swear last week, I was raising a five-year-old. Since when was I the mother of a teenage girl? I thought I had more time. "We'll talk about this later. I need you to get ready."

She stomps out of the room and the ever-present slam of her bedroom door lets me know she is at least in the vicinity of the things she needs to get dressed.

The doorbell rings and I rush to the front door to see who is there. "I'm here. What do you need?" Chloe enters my house with a clipboard.

"God, I am so glad you're here." I rush back over to the living room where there are boxes of flyers and promo materials like our mugs, napkins and biodegradable straws. The last thing is a specific request from my resident mother earth protector. I have to admit that I'm happy she is interested in something that has a soul to it. It could be much worse.

Like drugs... or boys.

"Umm... heavy lifting is not for me." She turns back toward the door yelling for Quincy. He comes up to the house from where I'm sure he was just sitting in their car. "Honey, please help Drea with her boxes to her truck." He looks over to where I have the boxes stacked up.

"Of course. Hey D." He throws a hand up, doing what his wife asks him. It's quick work for him as Drea looks me over.

"Come with me," she says. It's not long before she has blown out and curled my hair into a style. She tsks at the sweatpants and tank top I'm wearing. "We can do better than sweatpants. We can always do better than sweatpants."

I admire her work in the mirror. She picked a mocha brown mock neck sweater with a full pleated skirt that both accentuates my curves while still being low maintenance and fabulous. *Thank God for good friends.*

The last thing I need to do before we head over to the bakery is grab my moody and empowered teenager. "Mireya, please tell me that you're ready to go. If we don't leave now we will be running behind."

My daughter comes out of her room in the dress I bought for her last week. She looks so pretty. *Thank God for small miracles.*

It has been months of toiling over this new business. I have been working extra shifts at the bar and picking up any gigs I can find around Alpenglow Ridge and some of the neighboring towns to save up for this. Not to mention the years of working way too hard to make everything work despite Colton and his minions. It finally has paid off.

When Eric Walter decided that he was ready to retire, I was first in line to take his place. It is no longer Walter's Coffee Shop. It's my place now—Drip and Whip, a coffee shop and bakery. I can keep the clientele from his business happy because I managed to get the old man to share all his recipes with me. A fact that my friend, Melody, is ecstatic about. She is kind of a fiend for his lemon Danishes. I was also able to keep most of the employees so that I don't have to worry about who will be working the coffee rush with this being the only coffee shop in town.

The biggest bonus is that I also get to keep my own clientele. My van and I have been hauling around our custom cakes, desserts, and pies for the past three years. The daytime was for baking. The nighttime was for bartending. But now, It's round-the-clock coffee and sweets. A fact I could not be more happy about.

We arrive at the shop and check that everything is going smoothly. It is. *Thank God for disaster planning.*

"Where's Tony?" Melody asks while she helps put up balloons Chloe is unloading from her car.

"You know Ant. That man could not be on time if his life depended on it." A fact that I'm grateful has not been made a reality of his. I even told him the wrong time so that he could accidentally get here early. *Whoops! Ain't I a stinker?* He'll thank me later for that.

The bell on the front door dings several times in quick succession. A blur of curly hair blows past me to get to the glass display case. He looks lovingly at the desserts illuminated in neat rows behind the glass.

Bren. My friend's son is always moving at breakneck speed. "Ah, ah. No sweets until I get everything in place. I, at least, want to get pictures before the inevitable chaos ensues today." He gives me puppy dog eyes. "I know." I boop his cute little nose. "But I promise there will be plenty of sweetness for you later on, okay?"

"Okay, aunt D." Mireya and Reese's kids spend so much time together, we have just told them to think of each other as cousins. He hugs my leg and Reese, the diva herself, comes in with the rest of her family. Her twin girls are happily babbling to each other from the stroller that her oldest son pushes. Her husband and youngest son are right behind with more decor from Chloe.

Reese hugs me and takes one look around. "Where is Tony?"

"I have no idea, but I need to finish some last-minute details. Would you mind telling him to come find me when he gets here?" She says she will and I work on staying calm since our opening time isn't that far away.

My heart is aglow as friends, family, neighbors, and clients come to celebrate the grand opening. I mingle around and pop back and forth behind the counter to share treats I've recommended to guests. It's all a happy blur, really. *Life really can be sweet sometimes.* As a single mom, I'm often the only one doing everything at once. I have all the hats and sometimes I need to wear many of them at one time. I'm blown away by how my little community has come together to really make this night easy and special for me. Still, I can't ignore the absence of one friend in particular.

Where is Ant?

I'm behind one of the registers to keep the line moving when a woman comes up to me. "Hi! I'm Steph," she exclaims. She doesn't look familiar, but it's clear that she expects I should know who she is. I take my gloves off and reach across the counter to shake her hand.

"Andrea Montoya," I say, tentatively. I still struggle to place this woman. "I'm glad you could make it."

"I'm so happy to hear that. I was a little nervous to meet the famous Drea that Tony is always talking about." Her drawling southern accent is more noticeable now and I begin to search my memory for how exactly I know her even harder. "Maybe we could even be friends."

My brows pinch and I laugh awkwardly, the sound coming out a little too forced. "Of course, we can be friends." *Who is this woman?* I look around to see my friends are happily talking with other guests at the opening party. *Where the hell is Ant?* How is he still late?

Then, I see him. His broad shoulders and tall build take up all the space in the doorway. He ducks to miss hitting his head on the bell hanging there. I instantly feel more at ease when he spots me and walks over to the counter *my new friend* and I are standing at.

His long legs make it easy for him to get here quickly. "You are the latest man I have ever met. I'm glad you finally made it though. What took so long?" I chastise.

"There is nowhere to park with all these people here at once. I had to drop Steph off and then walk from the community park. That's no short hike." He shakes his head and I tilt mine to the side.

"Drop Steph off?" I ask.

"Yea..." He rubs a hand over his waves and then his mouth. No longer is he trying to grow his hair out. He keeps it cut short now and his face clean-shaven. I thought it might make him look young, but somehow he looks more mature. He's not that much older than me. My thoughts wander off to the first day I saw him without a beard. I snap out of it when I think he says something peculiar. "... my girlfriend."

I blink a few times, "I'm sorry, could you repeat that? I thought you said—"

"D. This is my girlfriend, Steph." His deep voice is firm and there is no wavering in his eyes as he delivers the news.

"G-girlfriend? I stutter.

"Hi... again..." Steph says awkwardly doing a little hand wave at me. I feel my face malfunctioning because she backs into Ant. Seeking comfort from my—*friend*.

"Oh," Is all I can manage as my gears start turning and all the ingredients come together. "You're dating someone?"

WE'RE GOING BACK TO Alpenglow Ridge for Drea and Tony's story: **Coming December 2024!!!**

PREORDER BOOK 3 HERE!

Potentially Sensitive Content

Explicit Sexual Content
Miscarriage (off page) /Infertility
Loss of a parent (off page)
Alcohol and Drug Usage
Profanity
Violence/Gun Violence
Kidnapping
Anxiety and Panic Attacks
Depression and Depressive Episodes

Consider Leaving a Review!

Thank you so much for reading Verse to Acclimate! I am so grateful to have you here in Alpenglow Ridge. It means so much that you joined me on this journey. By reading and reviewing this book, you are making my author dreams come true! ♥

If you enjoyed this book, please consider leaving a quick review on Amazon/your favorite site, and share on your socials!

Keep reading for an excerpt from Cory and Reese's story...

Saddled
with
Finesse

CH 1: Riesling Mason

> **Teddy**
> : It's been a while.

COLD SWEAT COLLECTS DOWN my back. Holding the phone with both hands, I lean onto the serving station. My elbows sting against the grooves of the rubber tray beneath them. This table's bar drinks are currently sweating and getting watery.

"You gonna run these or what?" My manager, Jamie, snaps me out of my state of panic.

A *while*.

Nine months is more than a while. And if I have any say in it—which I do—to say I never want to see Teddy again is an understatement.

"Relax, Jamie! I'm going." I slide the phone into the middle pocket of my standard Peak's Restaurant apron. Each drink gets placed strategically on my tray so that I can carry them all to my awaiting table. The last thing I need is to be doused with whiskey, coke and beer tonight.

Oh how the bougie have fallen.

In the time it takes to walk these drinks over, my mind has begun to wonder about the text. Why is he messaging me now? I've stayed out of his life. Asked for nothing. I've said nothing to anyone. I've been good.

Why now?

After I place the drinks on the table, I go into my spiel about the specials for dinner today. Twirling a bit of my blonde ponytail around my finger as I pop my gum. Peak's isn't known for its culinary prowess. Mostly men come to this place for the beautiful women in tiny, tight tops and shorts. I knew that and *they* know that. Given this information, it also does not shock me that I'll be carrying nearly one hundred and fifty fried chicken wings back to this table... accompanied by an equal amount of fries.

I read back the order to them, "Six Quarter baskets with extra crispy fries, extra ranch, coming up!" I look back to my notepad, "Scratch that, one with extra blue cheese." The man sitting in the far corner winks at me.

I'm used to how these guests treat us, at this point. They think that because I'm in this skimpy uniform I might give them a happy ending with their fried chicken.

This isn't a strip club and I'm no dancer.

Somehow talking about blue cheese has elicited this skeevy wink. *Gross.*

Tips are the reason I'm here though. I just smirk briefly before turning on a heel to enter the order in for the kitchen.

Better for them to think they have a chance... before the bill comes out.

The night drones on this way as the dinner rush picks up and I get into a rhythm of constant movement. Bouncing from table to bar, to putting in another order with the kitchen, to table to bar to putting...

You get it.

I'm thankful for the influx of guests. It means I can keep my thoughts off of the phone currently burning a hole in my apron. Every time I thought I had a second to check a notification, I would get a new table before I could even unlock the screen.

I couldn't check, but that didn't mean my mind wasn't going over every possible reason why *he* would send that message. The last time I saw him face to face, I was wiping blood from the corner of my mouth.

Never again.

My sidework to close out my shift flies by with my mind spinning over what sparked his message. Marie and Karla don't mind filling in my silence with talk about how their tables drove them crazy tonight. I nod at the appropriate times and walk out to my car with them after we lock up for the night.

Driving in the silence of my Mustang and trudging up the three flights of stairs all blur with how exhausted I am. I have no plans to move from my bed until the sun comes up.

Thanks to my infatuation with Teddy, a man who was never any good for me, I'm living in Denver. I like it here, but it's not home.

I toe off my work-mandated, slip-proof black sneakers at the door of my tiny studio apartment. Promptly flopping face-first onto my bed, drained from how busy the night was.

The stack of cash from the tables I served tonight goes into the jar I have under my nightstand. Thankfully, I can reach it from where I lay sprawled on the bed. Sliding the apron from under my body, it thunks to the carpet. I had completely forgotten my phone was in there. I'd been on autopilot the whole way home.

With a huff, I scooch my body close enough to the edge of my bed using as little energy as possible to retrieve my phone. I could use some mindless scrolling until I pass out.

My social media was once glitz and glamour. Pictures of me at this five-star restaurant. Pictures from this fancy trip wearing the shoes every-one was salivating over, but could never afford. Selfies of my flawless beat at the dinner party only six-figure men could afford to attend. Everyone in my hometown thought I was living a charmed life because I did my best to show it that way. Leaving out all the darkness behind the scenes.

Now, I barely post anything outside of the occasional thirst trap.

What?

I'm still fine as hell. Just broke.

Likes and comments from a post I shared earlier today line up neatly down my screen. It was an old picture of me at the ranch surrounded by the staff and my parents. The horses moseying about in the background of the photo twist my heart in knots. The last day I was in Alpenglow Ridge. Maybe the last day I was truly happy.

Teddy
: I want to see you. Are you home?

Home?

My tired brain finally makes the connection. I hardly ever post about my past. It's too painful and unattainable after everything I've done. But, I felt homesick this morning.

I missed my family.

I missed my friends.

All the people in this photo mean so much to me and I barely get to see them now. The last time I did was when my father was recovering in the hospital after a massive heart attack. With tearful eyes, I gave and received hugs from every one of them who came to visit.

This picture had been the last we'd all taken before my father's health took a plunge. Like the shitty daughter I am, I left before the lies I told could catch up to me.

That was six months ago.

I don't respond to his text. There is nothing to say. I clear the notifications with a flourish. Reaching blindly for my charging cable, I plug my phone up to charge and slide it onto the nightstand. Wrapping the comforter around my body like a burrito, I give into the drooping of my eyelids. I let my exhaustion overtake me.

MY RINGTONE BLARES INTO the small space, waking me with a start. Pawing the general area of the nightstand to find my phone is not as effective as I'd like it to be. I hear it thunk to the ground. *Great.* Fully awake and frustrated now, I kick with ferocity at the blanket to free myself.

At least, the sun is up.

I don't check to see who's calling before I answer the phone. "Good morning, honey! Did I wake you?"

"Mom, you know you did. I work nights." I try to keep the eyeroll I'm doing out of the tone of my voice, but she knows me better than that.

"Well, we're on ranch time here so I've been up for a couple of hours. You do remember what time we get started right?" The playful teasing in her tone makes my heart squeeze a little too tightly. I rub at my chest.

Sighing, I respond, "Yea, I remember." Looking at my phone to see if there were any texts I missed from her before I picked up the phone, I ask, "Is dad alright?"

"Oh yes! I didn't mean to alarm you. Or maybe I did... since this was a wake-up call." She chuckles at her own joke. "It's nothing that dreadful, thank God. Your daddy wants to talk."

"And you're sure it's to me?" My huff is long. I love my dad, but my refusal to work at the ranch is a major point of contention for us. When I left, I didn't give any reasoning or time for him to adjust to the abrupt decision I had made. The opportunity for more came to me and I did everything I could to take advantage of that as quickly as possible. I had always felt that the things that cost at least a comma and, or, have some sparkle were what my life should consist of. Ranch life though, doesn't come with the same razzle-dazzle I was after.

With his heart, I hate being the focus of his attention and causing him more stress. My choice is the same. It makes me feel twice as bad for letting him down.

"Yes, Riesling. Your dad is being cryptic with me and I can't stand it. I tried to use a little back rub to get him to give me any sort of details. I barely got this irritating task of trying to get my only daughter to come home for once."

I was there last month to get my hair done. There for the appointment and left shortly after, but I was there, technically. I just didn't see them.

"Okay... Please don't ever share about you and dad rubbing anything with me. It's... strange. Definitely too much information at—" I pull the phone from my ear to check the time. "—eight AM on a Tuesday."

"Honey, you know how you were made, right? It was not by immaculate conception, you know." The smile in my mom's voice makes me smile as well. I miss her. It's been so long since I've seen her happy.

I'd driven to Alpenglow Ridge in a blaze of tears and panic, thinking I only had a sliver of a chance to see my dad again. The drive is just over an hour away. Each second moved at a glacial pace. I had her on speakerphone in my car for the entire drive. Neither of us said anything. The sounds of the bustling hospital whirred over the sound of my tires ripping the highway up. The cold from that lobby waiting room followed me from the hospital for weeks after.

I couldn't shake that chill.

To hear her smile again, erases that guilt I had felt for coming back to Denver. They were more than surviving in my absence. There's no way I can be in Alpenglow Ridge for long stretches of time since I left. It's too risky.

But this smile. This small little bit of happiness in her voice is enough to make me smile too. Still, I can't picture myself even packing that suitcase I've laid out on my floor now without remembering the last fateful time that I tried to pack it up. Going back to Alpenglow Ridge is probably the dumbest thing I could imagine doing.

It's not smart. And in most things, I would consider myself to be smart. Except when I was younger and made the worst decision, over and over and over again.

"Mom, please." I start grabbing clothes from my laundry basket and throw them into the luggage. From the clean clothes basket, instead of my dirty clothes laundry basket, of course.

"I want to know why dad couldn't call me. Why can't he just call me like you're doing now and tell me what's up?" I walk into my small bathroom across the open studio space. "Toothbrush, toothpaste, face wash, face creams, toner..." The ones *he* preferred ran out a long time ago. I could likely repurchase the bottles I'm packing all for under fifty dollars. But, I don't have fifty dollars to spare.

I throw them into my smaller toiletry bag. My eyes snag on the gold wrappers sticking out from the bathroom drawer. It's not like I've needed them for months. I pick up the roll of condoms considering how necessary it would be to pack.

Why second guess? Better safe than sorry.

"Honey, I don't know what your dad wants. Only that he asked me to get you up here. I take it that you're packing so I can tell him you're on the way, right?"

I brush through my extensions. The tangled mess I woke up with is almost untamable since I went to sleep without my scarf on last night. *Scary.* A little hair oil couldn't hurt. I rub some argan oil in my hands before smoothing it over my blonde ends. It almost looks perfect.

Plugging in my straightener, I answer my mom, "Yea, I guess. I'm working a double on Friday. I'm not staying long." I press the straightener over my hair, flipping the ends just how I like them. "Tell him that because I don't want the guilt trip."

She chuckles. "Of course. Because that's going to do something. Your dad has his own plans. I'll have breakfast waiting for you, honey."

I hang up after we exchange I *love yous* and stare at my phone a little longer.

I'm going to Alpenglow Ridge. Fine. Just a few days. No big deal. He'll never know. I repeat it in my head as I carefully apply makeup and lashes.

Shoes are the last thing to get thrown into my suitcase. My tank top and skinny jeans are cute enough for the ranch. But my chucks? Oh no.

Definitely need my boots.

These wine-red cowboy boots were a present from mom. It's been a few years and I only wore them on the ranch a few times before they sat here useless in my closet.

They aren't who I am anymore.

I shrug to myself in the full-length mirror on my wall. Turning to get a view of my backside, I do a little twerk. Confirming, "It's still fat, baby!" I smack my ass and blow a kiss to myself. All the happy times with my friends and family are taped along the edges of this mirror. Including the photo I posted yesterday.

I focus on the one I took after Mel's twenty-first birthday party. We had spent the better part of that weekend miserably hungover, but it was the best night. It's been a while since we all hung out. Things aren't the same anymore. On the off chance I spend some time in town there, I've decided to throw in something other than tank tops... just in case.

Satisfied with what I've packed, I drag my small suitcase down all three flights of stairs. I'm Alpenglow Ridge bound.

CH 2: Cory Whitfield

"IT'S NOT FAIR FOR our teachers to stay here longer than they are expected to. The school year is almost over and they are tired, Mr. Whitfield." *I'm tired.*

"I know, it's my wi—their mother's day to pick them up and I guess she just forgot or something. I'm coming as quickly as I can. Give me fifteen minutes... tops! Please."

She sighs a heavy sound that presses down on my shoulders. I try my best to be safe, but also quick, making it through rush hour traffic in Denver. "Fifteen minutes, Mr. Whitlock."

I arrive at the school in fourteen minutes where Cory Jr. and Brendan are sitting on the curb in the pickup line. Their vice-principal, Alison Blackburn, waits behind them with her arms crossed. I park and get out of the car to open the back door of my truck for them. I'm fully prepared to give her the long speech. The one about how I'm trying to make things work with the custody agreement I have with their mom. I still haven't been able to get in touch with her and she didn't tell me that she couldn't make it to pick up the kids today.

My mouth opens to begin my story, but Alison holds up a hand. "It's fine, Mr. Whitfield. They're good kids and were no trouble at all, but you must find a way to prevent this from happening so often. I've made a note in your file about it, but with just three days left of school, I'm certain you can figure it out." She gives me a stern look with an eyebrow raised. Her teacher's tone makes me feel like a chastised student... instead of a thirty-year-old man who is drowning in his own life.

I nod. "Yes, of course." She nods back to me and heads over to her car, parked behind where I pulled up and drives off like a bat out of hell. When I turn back to my truck, CJ gives me a lopsided tilt of his lips. I scrub a hand over my neck. I have no idea what to tell them. None of this conversation should be happening in this after-school pickup line. I hustle back to the driver's side and check my rearview. "Everybody buckled?"

"Yep" they both respond. Bren from his booster and CJ from the other side of the car seat for my youngest.

"Alright. Let's hit it." The daycare that Gabriel, my two, almost three, year old is at stays open until six for pick up. It's five-thirty, so I should make it there well before they close. It's only around the corner from my two oldest's elementary school. "How was taekwondo?" I look at them in the rearview again.

"Today was the last day. We just had a party to celebrate," CJ responds.

"That sounds like fun. Was there cake?"

"No cake. But we got juice and snacks! They had my favorite rainbow Goldfish, dad!" Bren adds in with a bounce. He pulls, a now crumpled, piece of paper from his backpack. "And our certificates of completion! Can we hang it up in the living room?"

Before I can reply, CJ speaks up. "That means we will need to be picked up at three-thirty tomorrow... And Thursday and Friday." He reminds me, just a hint of bitterness in his tone. My heart squeezes at being judged by my oldest. He knows too much. Has felt the hurt of our separation the fiercest, as well.

"I know, son. I know." I consider throwing Vanessa under the bus like I very well deserve to do. That doesn't change the fact that my kids were the last ones to be picked up today. I keep my mouth closed.

We arrive at Sunshine Tots with time to spare and I get my toddler situated in his car seat.

Back at home, my phone vibrates on the dining table. I ordered something to be delivered for dinner when I acknowledged there was nothing in the fridge worth trying to combine for an actual meal. The screen shows a picture of my aunt Janet and me when I was eighteen. I smile with my whole face as she looks down at me. I pick up, saying, "Hey, auntie."

"Hey, Cory. How are you?"

Considering how to respond, I go with the truth. "I'm tired as hell. What about you?"

"I've been better. You know what today is?"

It takes me a second, but I realize that today is *that* day. The day that changed my life forever. "How can it be that twenty years have passed?"

"I don't know, but I miss her every day. Even your dad too." She pauses like she's choosing her next words with care. "You doing okay?"

I scoff, wiping a tear she can probably hear in my voice but I respond, "Yea. I'm good." I look in on the boys getting ready for bed. Bren and CJ are following their routines and Gabe sits happily in the room on the floor in his pajamas. He's rolling a truck on the carpeted rug that looks like a series of roads overlapping all in dizzying patterns. Stepping back into the kitchen, I start putting away to-go containers and wiping the table down.

"You sure?"

I sigh. "No. I'm not, but I'm too tired to think about something else that I need to be handling better. Van forgot to pick up the boys from school. I have to give away two of my properties this week because I can't chance that she will forget them again. I have no idea what I'm going to do with the boys when school is out. Somehow, I forgot to find some sort of activity or camp or something for them. I've been up since four this morning. I'm tired, Jan. I'm really fucking tired."

"You can always come home." *Home.* My aunt moved to Alpenglow Ridge about ten years ago after I graduated from high school. She's built a life there. Found the love of her life, Sammie, and seems happy. Hell, I'm happy for her. But... "I don't know if that's a good idea."

"And why not? You say that every time I suggest it. The boys will be out of school. I know you're paying that condo month to month. Denver is still the worst place to buy a home. Just give them the proper notice and come stay with me."

"I can't just leave, Jan. How am I supposed to feed my boys or myself with no job? We'll eat you out of your house and home. We would be too big of a burden on you there. You do remember I have three kids right?"

"And I have three guest rooms. How is that any different from your condo there? As far as work goes, you think Alpenglow doesn't have lawns and such. Let me ask around, I'm sure I could get you something started."

Could moving in with my aunt be a good idea? There are so many reasons why it could be. For one, I need a damn break. A full day of hauling soil bags, digging holes, sweating in the sun... trying to make everyone else look like they have the picture-perfect house. It's as much as I can take.

Vanessa still hasn't responded to any of my texts or calls. How do you... Just forget to pick up your own children? I mean really... What the hell? She doesn't want to be with me? Fine. Our marriage was not the best thing in my life, but it was ours. She wanted out, I let her go. But the boys? She can't decide to be in and out whenever she feels like it. I'm there for them in the good and bad times.

I'm not usually one to complain, but I'm reaching a breaking point.

"It'll give you a break and you can start somewhere fresh. I work from home, I can watch the boys for you. I miss my littles anyway. Christmas was so long ago and I came to you all." I start to respond and tell her all the reasons that I think this is a bad idea. But, she's right. A break sounds nice.

"I don't know, Jan."

"What about starting your own landscaping company? That used to be your dream, the goal. Is it not anymore?"

I had been working for Mark for the past five years. It's nice to have a little bit of direction in what and where I go day to day. I love not having to think about anything. I simply show up and do my job. It's easy.

What if I did have help though? Starting my own business could be...

"It is something I want. I want that very much so. But I don't know. Janet, that's a lot of work. And with the boys..."

"I said I've got them. Only until you figure it out."

"I'll think about it."

"I love you, nephew."

"I love you. Listen, I need to finish putting the boys to bed. I'll call you later okay?"

"Take me in there so I can say goodnight on speaker."

I do what she asks and let her go.

Laying in bed that night, I think over her proposal again. It's not that far-fetched of an idea.

Reaching into my nightstand, I pull out the old worn envelope and look it over. The edges have long been rubbed away. The small sticker that used to keep it closed is no longer sticky, but I've since used Cellatape to hold it in place.

> *To my son on his birthday,*
>
> *First, I love you. You are the best present that your father and I ever received. How lucky is it, that on my birthday, I gave birth to you? We are so blessed to have you in our lives. Everyday that we get to watch you grow has been the best day ever. Never forget that you are loved and will always have someone on your team as long as we are around. Our wish for you is to keep that love in your heart for your friends, your family and this earth. We know you will make us so proud this year! Your dad says that he still expects you to make the honor roll. I do not doubt that you will. The big 1-0! Enjoy your party tonight and make a splash!*
>
> *All our love,*
> *Mama and Daddy*

I stare at the ceiling for a few minutes. Wiping the tears from my eyes, I return the card back to its spot. The last handwritten thing I ever received from them. How many times have I read it? Vanessa never understood why I still held onto their memory so tightly. But how could she? She's never lost anyone.

It's only me who is always losing. My life—a series of losses. People don't seem to stick around as far as I'm concerned.

Seems like the best thing for me is to go where I can have even the smallest bit of support. To be closer to my remaining family. I've got a bit saved away. Not enough for long, but enough to make it work for a few months. I've made up my mind. Come Monday, I'm putting in my two weeks. Alpenglow Ridge, here we come.

* * *

CONTINUE READING SADDLED WITH FINESSE HERE

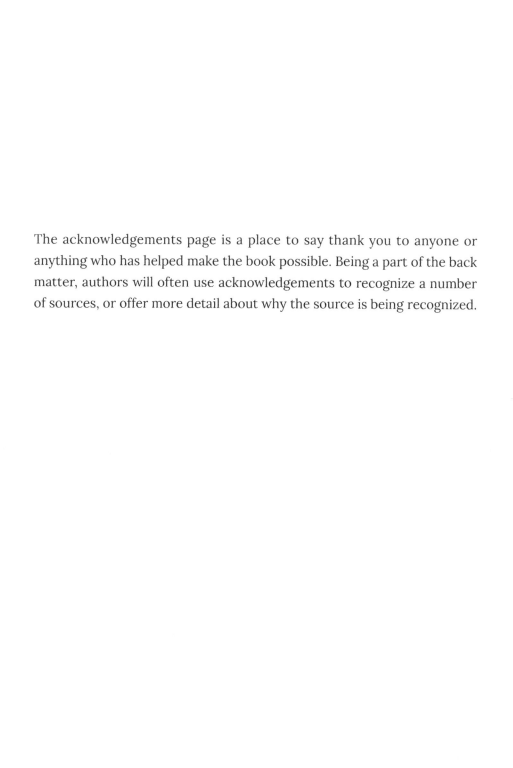

The acknowledgements page is a place to say thank you to anyone or anything who has helped make the book possible. Being a part of the back matter, authors will often use acknowledgements to recognize a number of sources, or offer more detail about why the source is being recognized.

About the Author

Zea Kayleigh is an author of small town romance. As a lifelong romance obsessed reader, she is finally putting her degree and years of anthropological research to use, creating a fictional world with men who fall hard for their heroines.

Zea lives in Colorado with her husband, daughter, and their very posh cat. When she is not cooking, designing clothes or hiking, she can be found curled up with a romance novel and eating sweets.

www.instagram.com/zeakayleigh
www.facebook.com/zeakayleigh
Signed Book Shop: https://www.etsy.com/shop/AuthorZeaKayleigh

Made in the USA
Monee, IL
22 September 2024

65664191R00225